**and His Thrille**

MW01600368

"A riveting entry in a ~~~~~~~~~~ ~~~~~ that continues to deliver strong characters and suspense."

*- Kirkus Reviews* on *Vatican Shadows*

"Exciting, tightly written action scenes comprise the final act, but there's humor sprinkled throughout the narrative, as well... A short but kinetic tale featuring a consistently entertaining hero."

*- Kirkus Reviews* on *The Traitor*

"...an addictively entertaining five-star read."

*- BookViral Reviews* on *Cathedral*

"My grade for this series went up... As of this writing, it is an A and let me tell you, it sometimes leans upwards towards the A+. It is really good! As spy books go, it has lots and lots of action. It has a whole lot more thinking than most genre books do. It definitely has more actual preaching (sermons) and prayers. Most importantly, it has a ton of humanity."

*- SpyGuysandGals.com*

"A fast-paced, exuberant outing for the virtuoso clergyman and his numerous comrades."

*- Kirkus Reviews* on *Deep Rough*

"... a page-turning and unpredictable ride, and a firm foundation for Keating's enticing new series."

*- Self-Publishing Review*, ★★★★, on *Cathedral*

"A first-rate mystery makes this a series standout..."

*- Kirkus Reviews* on *Wine Into Water*

"A hugely entertaining thriller... Typically underpinned by Keating's extensive religious and historical research, *Under the Golden Dome* is richly layered in a way that puts more conventional thrillers to shame... A highly enjoyable, intelligent and thought-provoking read, *Under the Golden Dome* is unreservedly recommended."

- BookViral Reviews, ★★★★★

"Mr. Keating knows how to tell an exciting story. And these books, like the James Bond novels, are ridiculously entertaining. As for larger themes, there is vocation, of course. I see these books as honoring the pastoral ministry. Because in real life, pastors are heroes engaged in saving the world."

- Gene Veith
"Cranach: The Blog of Veith"

"It was my great privilege that Ronald Reagan and I were good friends and political allies. This exciting political thriller may be a novel but it truly captures President Reagan's optimism and principles."

- Ambassador Fred J. Eckert on *Reagan Country*

"First-rate supporting characters complement the sprightly pastor, who remains impeccable in this thriller."

- *Kirkus Reviews* on *Lionhearts*

"Keating does an excellent job, as usual, integrating heady concepts and moving his recklessly intense plot forward, and the dialogue is snappy, believable, and purposeful. All told, this is another strong installment in a series that always delivers."

- *Self-Publishing Review* on *Under the Golden Dome*

"Tight action scenes complement the suspense ... The villains, meanwhile, are just as rich and engrossing as the good guys and gals. The familiar protagonist, along with sensational new and recurring characters, drives an energetic political tale."

- *Kirkus Reviews* on *Reagan Country*

"Grant is a selfless and fascinating protagonist. Keating pulls back the walls of the pastor's psyche and lets readers root around, providing a sense of intimacy and closeness with the central character from very early on in the novel. *Warrior Monk* is full of intentional, thoughtful writing that hits hard and carries the story to the end. After devouring this opening salvo, new fans will dive in eagerly to the future adventures of Pastor Stephen Grant."

*- Self-Publishing Review*, ★★★★½, on *Warrior Monk*

"Author Ray Keating delivers a timely, high-octane, and well-penned thriller with his latest novel, *The Traitor*. The inimitable Pastor Stephen Grant must unexpectedly navigate the shadowy waters of international espionage to keep his country safe and strong. With a gripping plot that feels torn from last week's headlines, Keating knows how to capture his readers immediately and never let go. Pastor Grant continues to surprise as a character and the dialogue hums with authenticity, making the newest Pastor Stephen Grant Novel another hit in this ever-growing series."

*- Self-Publishing Review*, ★★★★½, on *The Traitor*

"Often, a pitfall of Christian fiction is that it can become too preachy or detached from the storyline; however, Keating, as ever, has pitched this just right, ably balancing Christian values with the thrill of the chase whilst not sacrificing either style or narrative."

- BookViral Reviews, ★★★★★, on *For Better, For Worse*

"The author packs a lot into this frantically paced novel... a raft of action sequences and baseball games are thrown into the mix. The multiple villains and twists raise the stakes... Action fans will find plenty to love here, from gunfights and murder sprees to moral dilemmas."

*- Kirkus Reviews* on *Murderer's Row*

"Ray Keating is a great novelist."

- host of KFUO radio's "BookTalk"

"A gritty, action-stuffed, well-considered thriller with a gun-toting clergyman."

*- Kirkus Reviews* on *The River*

"I miss Tom Clancy. Keating fills that void for me."

*- Lutheran Book Review* on *Murderer's Row*

"The plot is vigorously paced, crammed with vividly depicted action and drama... the reader is never lost in this accessible tale of international intrigue."

*- Kirkus Reviews* on *Persecution*

"President Ronald Reagan's legacy will live on in the U.S., around the world and in the pages of history. And now, thanks to Ray Keating's *Reagan Country*, it will live on in the world of fiction. *Reagan Country* ranks as a page-turning thriller that pays homage to the greatest president of the twentieth century."

- Tom Edmonds, producer of
the official documentary on President Reagan,
*Ronald Reagan: An American President*

"Mr. Keating's storytelling is so lifelike that I almost thought I had worked with him when I was at Langley. Like the fictitious pastor, I actually spent 20 years working for the U.S. intelligence community, and once I started reading *The River*, I had to keep reading because it was so well-crafted and easy to follow and because it depicted a personal struggle that I knew all too well. I simply could not put it down."

- The Rev. Kenneth V. Blanchard
*The Washington Times* review of *The River*

"Keating's creativity and storytelling ability remain on point, for a fun and different take on Pastor Grant, and one that's just as satisfying as longer books in the series."

*- Self-Publishing Review* on *Heroes and Villains*

"Must read for any Reaganite."

"A first-class thriller and an uncompromising five-star read!"

"Pastor Grant continues to be one of the most entertaining heroes in the political thrillers and suspense genre. With occasional pop-ins from fan-favorite recurring characters, *Deep Rough* fits in perfectly with the rest of the series – quirky, tightly woven, and difficult to put down. Keating manages to keep his writing fresh and surprising with every new Pastor Grant book. This series satisfies yet again, finding unique ways to entertain and enlighten along the way."

"*Root of All Evil?* is an extraordinarily good read. Only Ray Keating could come up with a character like Pastor Stephen Grant."

"This gripping tale of deception, retribution, and redemption is filled with espionage, action, and a good deal of enticing mystery. Keating's original twists and singular protagonist result in another solid ride."

"This condensed mystery is enjoyably gripping, and marked by the author's characteristic style of suspense."

"Thriller and mystery writers have concocted all manner of main characters, from fly fishing lawyers to orchid aficionados and former ballplayers, but none has come up with anyone like Stephen Grant, the former Navy Seal and CIA assassin, and current Lutheran pastor. Grant mixes battling America's enemies and sparring with enemies of traditional Christian values, while ministering to his Long Island flock. The amazing thing is that the character works. The Stephen Grant novels are great reads beginning with *Warrior Monk*, which aptly describes Ray Keating's engaging hero."

- David Keene
*The Washington Times*

"*Warrior Monk* by Ray Keating has all of the adventure, intrigue, and believable improbability of mainstream political thrillers, but with a lead character, Pastor Stephen Grant, that resists temptation."

- *Lutheran Book Review* on
*Warrior Monk*

"This is a fantastic novel... If you are a comic book fan who is fed up with the political correctness that's going on, you have got to pick up *Heroes and Villains*... I highly recommend this book."

- Jacob Airey, host of *StudioJake*

# MENACE

## An Agent Dean Cold Novel

# RAY KEATING

For more information:
Keating Reports LLC
raykeating@keatingreports.com

ISBN-13: 9798291484685

Cover design by Jonathan Keating.

*For
Beth,
Jonathan
and
Mikayla, David, Phoebe & Lydia*

**Alliance of Saint Michael Novels Series...**

*Subversion: An Alliance of Saint Michael Novel* (2024)

*Cathedral: An Alliance of Saint Michael Novel* (2022)

**In the nonfiction arena...**

*10 Points from Walt Disney on Entrepreneurship* (2024)

*The Weekly Economist III:*
*Another 52 Quick Reads to Help You Think Like an Economist*
(2024)

*The Disney Planner: The TO DO List Solution* (2023)

*The Weekly Economist II:*
*52 More Quick Reads to Help You Think Like an Economist*
(2023)

*The Lutheran Planner: The TO DO List Solution* (2022)

*The Weekly Economist:*
*52 Quick Reads to Help You Think Like an Economist* (2022)

*The Disney Planner 2022: The TO DO List Solution* (2021)

*The Lutheran Planner 2022: The TO DO List Solution* (2021)

*Behind Enemy Lines:*
*Conservative Communiques from Left-Wing New York* (2020)

*The Lutheran Planner 2020: The TO DO List Solution* (2019)

*The Pastor Stephen Grant Novels Planner 2020:*
*The TO DO List Solution* (2019)

*The Disney Planner 2020: The TO DO List Solution* (2019)

*Free Trade Rocks! 10 Points on International Trade Everyone*
*Should Know* (2019)

*A Discussion Guide for Ray Keating's Warrior Monk*
(Second Edition, 2019)

*The Realistic Optimist TO DO List & Calendar 2019* (2018)

*Unleashing Small Business Through IP:*
*The Role of Intellectual Property in Driving Entrepreneurship,*
*Innovation and Investment* (Revised and Updated Edition, 2016)

*Unleashing Small Business Through IP:*
*Protecting Intellectual Property, Driving Entrepreneurship*
(2013)

*Discussion Guide for Warrior Monk:*
*A Pastor Stephen Grant Novel* (2011)

*"Chuck" vs. the Business World: Business Tips on TV* (2011)

*U.S. by the Numbers:*
*What's Left, Right, and Wrong with America State by State*
(2000)

*New York by the Numbers:*
*State and City in Perpetual Crisis* (1997)

*D.C. by the Numbers: A State of Failure* (1995)

"The Soviet government held a vastly different vision of the future. In the world of its design, security was to be found, not in mutual trust and mutual aid but in force: huge armies, subversion, rule of neighbor nations. The goal was power superiority at all cost. Security was to be sought by denying it to all others. The result has been tragic for the world and, for the Soviet Union, it has also been ironic. The amassing of Soviet power alerted free nations to a new danger of aggression."

- Dwight Eisenhower
April 16, 1953


"In space, all warriors are cold warriors."

- General Chang
*Star Trek VI: The Undiscovered Country*

# Chapter 1

*Doesn't feel right.*

Secret Service Special Agent Dean Cold couldn't put his finger on anything specific, but there just seemed to be something off about this evening's visitors to the Oval Office. For good measure, the lateness of the meeting was unusual.

Cold had begun his presidential protection assignment on November 5, 1952 – the day after Dwight D. Eisenhower won the election. Eisenhower quickly appeared at ease with Cold. As a result, among Ike's Secret Service detail for the past nearly four months, Cold and his partner, Special Agent Andrew "Stant" Stanton, had spent the most direct time with Eisenhower. Since both Cold and Stant were single, the agents didn't mind the extra time spent with the president. After all, as Cold, a veteran of the Office of Strategic Services during World War II, often reflected, *This is Ike!*

The meeting just starting to play out in front of Cold was a briefing by two aides to the secretary of state about the Korean conflict. Eisenhower – or "Providence," the code name given the president by the Secret Service – and Allen Dulles, director of the Central Intelligence Agency, were being briefed.

When the aides had first arrived, Cold wondered what could be reported that required this meeting, given that Dulles' brother, John Foster Dulles, was the secretary of state. That bit of self-indulgence was pushed into the recesses of Cold's mind. His narrow brown eyes closely inspected the visitors.

Eisenhower was behind the mahogany Theodore Roosevelt desk, with Dulles seated to his right. The two visitors – Arnold Kendall and Dennis Hart – sat across the desk from the president.

After general niceties, Dulles asked, "What's this about, gentlemen? The secretary mentioned nothing to me about this meeting."

Hart hesitated, glanced at Kendall, and then replied, "Yes, I'm sorry, Director Dulles, but as you know, the secretary is traveling."

*Why the hesitation? Nervous about briefing the president? Understandable, I guess. Seems odd, though, since they've both been here before, and Kendall worked under Ike during the war.*

Eisenhower threw a glance in Cold's direction.

*What was that for?*

Kendall and Hart opened their respective briefcases. There was a manila folder inside each. The cases were left open on their respective laps.

Eisenhower leaned back in his chair, looked directly at Kendall, and smiled. "Before we get started, Arnie, I have to ask about Cassandra."

Cold noted that the hesitation lasted longer this time. Kendall looked up, and his face was expressionless. "Sir?"

Eisenhower replied, "Dear God, Arnie, you were always trying to leave our meetings in London early so you could see her." His words were met with silence. Eisenhower added, "You know, during the war?"

Kendall stared back at the president. Hart turned his head slightly to the left to glance at Stanton, and then slowly rotated his gaze to the right, in Cold's direction.

The five-foot-eleven-inch Dean Cold tensed. He was no stranger to this feeling of alertness, such as when standing under center while quarterbacking the Harvard football team or when his OSS team was ready to strike during the war.

While Kendall's face was unmoving, Cold watched his left hand move inside the briefcase. Hart was similarly moving his hand.

Cold heard the faintest clicks.

*That's it.*

As Cold bolted forward, he started to pull out the M1911A1 handgun holstered inside his suit jacket.

From the back of the room, Stant followed Cold's lead.

Cold spotted the suppressor attached to the barrel of a handgun pointed in his direction from inside the briefcase. He dove left just as Hart squeezed off a shot. The projectile missed, and Cold landed behind one of the two couches in the middle of the Oval Office.

Stanton, however, wasn't so lucky. The shot fired by Kendall landed in the left side of his chest.

While this was happening, Eisenhower had started to rise from his chair, but Dulles tackled the president. For a man who looked more like a professor than a spy master, Dulles was unexpectedly strong and agile.

Cold chose another direction. He pushed his body along the carpet, gained a clear sightline, and fired off two shots at Hart's chest. Both hit home. Hart staggered, and then fell to the floor.

With Hart down, Cold now had a clear shot at Kendall, who was moving around the desk to get to Eisenhower.

Cold took no chances. He fired three shots at Kendall's head. The first missed. The second struck Kendall in the neck, and his head started to drop forward. The third slug entered the side of his head.

Cold jumped to his feet, and moved first to check Hart. The assailant's body was sprawled in front of the president's desk.

*Dead.*

He found the same situation with Kendall, who lay against the curtain hanging just beyond where Dulles had been seated originally.

Cold announced, "They're down, Mr. President."

Dulles rolled off Eisenhower, got to his feet, and then helped the president do the same.

Cold sprang to Stanton's side, and saw life drain from his eyes. "Stant, stay with me!" He hung his head and whispered, "Crap." Cold ran a hand through his thick brown hair.

*Stant, shit. Lord, be with him.*

The door to the Oval Office burst open, and one of Cold's fellow Secret Service officers entered, sporting his weapon, his eyes darting around the room.

The president declared, "Agent Stanton is down."

The officer looked at Cold, who was on one knee next to Stanton's body. Cold looked up and shook his head. The agent tried to stay focused.

At the same time, Dulles was looking at Kendall's body. His eyes settled on the neck wound. He crouched down for a closer look. Dulles then stood up, whirled and looked at the newly arrived Secret Service agent. "Get this entire building shut down. No one in and no one out. And don't let anyone into this office."

The man looked from Dulles to Eisenhower.

Eisenhower nodded. "I'm alright. Do as Director Dulles says."

"Yes, sir." The agent took a deep breath and withdrew.

When the door closed, Eisenhower said, "Thank you, Agent Cold." He moved quickly to Cold and Stanton. "Is he...?

Cold managed to report, "Didn't make it, sir."

Eisenhower put his hand on Cold's shoulder. Cold worked to keep his emotions in check while next to the body of a man who was his partner and one of the few real friends he had in Washington, D.C.

Eisenhower then turned to Dulles, who was now inspecting Hart's body. The president said, "I knew something was wrong the way Arnie was acting. He never would have forgotten Cassandra Lewis. Who the hell got to him? The Soviets? And why would he have gone over?"

Dulles' back was to Eisenhower, as he still stared down at Hart. "Somebody ... got to them. Yes. But I have no idea who or what this means."

"What is it, Allen?" Eisenhower walked over to Dulles, and looked down at Hart. Dulles pointed to a small scar and slight bulge in Hart's neck. Eisenhower crouched down to take a closer look. The president rubbed his chin. Ike asked, "What the hell?"

Dulles merely replied, "And over here, sir." As Dulles turned to go back to Kendall's body, Eisenhower followed. Looking down at a man he had known since he was Supreme Commander of the Allied Expeditionary Forces in Europe during the war, Ike said, "What … is that?"

Cold stood up and walked over next to Ike. The president crouched down, and reached out to the neck wound. All three men had seen too much death in their lives. There was still a hesitation by Ike. Cold understood why. But the president proceeded to push aside flesh and blood to reveal something metallic.

Cold watched the president's fingers explore the dead man's neck, and what was revealed. *What the hell is that?* Cold found himself asking, "Do either of you know what that is? Seen anything like it before?"

Eisenhower stood up straight, pulled out a handkerchief to wipe his hands. He turned, and looked back and forth at Dulles and Cold. He settled on Dulles, "Allen?"

"I have no idea, Mr. President." Dulles turned to Cold, and demanded, "Go to lockdown."

Cold looked at Ike, who nodded. Cold then went to the table behind the president's desk, and opened a drawer. He flipped two switches, and metal shades came down to cover the windows, and behind the walls, bolts could be heard locking each door in place.

Ike repeated the question at hand, "Who … or what … is this?"

That seemed to snap Dulles out of a bit of a haze. "I don't know, sir, but I don't think any of this…" He paused and looked at the two bodies of the attackers. "… should go beyond this room until we know more."

Cold added, "Yeah, until we know a hell of a lot more." Eisenhower raised an eyebrow at Cold. The Secret Service agent added, "Sir."

Eisenhower declared, "I agree. How do we do this?"

Dulles said, "I have a small team at the CIA for quietly cleaning up situations. They can move these two, along with

Agent Stanton, to a place where we can have matters evaluated. It's a very limited team, and they can be trusted."

"Fully?" asked Eisenhower.

"Absolutely, sir."

Eisenhower reflected for a moment, and then said, "Do it, Allen." He pointed at his desk, "Use that phone."

While Dulles made his call, Cold moved back to Kendall. He crouched down, rubbed his pointed chin, and decided to be bolder than the president. Cold pulled the small flashlight off his belt, flipped it on, and then held it in his mouth. With his hands, Cold opened the neck wound further. Thinking about Stant, he used more of his strength. He pulled, tore and dug.

*This goes against everything we're taught about handling a dead body and a crime scene.*

Pushing away flesh and blood, Cole shined the light into the wound.

Without objection, Eisenhower now leaned over Cold's shoulder. After nearly a half-minute in which the only noise in the Oval Office was Dulles quietly giving instructions on the telephone, Eisenhower asked, "What do you see?"

Cold didn't respond while he continued to investigate.

After another near-minute, Eisenhower said, "Dean?" There now was impatience in his voice.

"Yes, sir. I'm trying."

Dulles ended his call, and joined Cold and Eisenhower. He saw what was going on and whispered, "Dear God."

Cold looked up at two of the most powerful men on the planet. "That thing seems to be wrapped around ... the spinal column or base of the ... brain ... I guess."

Ike echoed Dulles, "Dear God."

*       *       *

Across the street from the White House, four well-armed men had been sitting in a black Cadillac Fleetwood. The driver looked at his watch. "Time's up. Whatever happened, they're not coming." He started the vehicle and drove away.

# Chapter 2

Death had been stalking Chairman Joseph Stalin, leader of the Soviet Union. His health had been deteriorating for some time. Of course, no one spoke openly of this to each other, never mind to Stalin, as jail or execution would likely follow.

Therefore, the transformation in Stalin during the last two weeks of February amazed all who had contact with him. At the suggestion of Stalin's closest aide, Arkadi Sokolov, head of the MGB, Oleg Abramov, a new doctor from Moscow, had arrived at Stalin's retreat, Kuntsevo Dacha. Sokolov promised that Abramov had the right treatment for the chairman. The suggestion, again, seemed either courageous or stupid on the part of Sokolov.

It only took a few days of regular injections to see a change begin in the 74-year-old. On March 1, 1953, the day after President Eisenhower had been attacked, Sokolov and Abramov had entered Stalin's massive bedroom for his morning injection.

As was the case each day, per Dr. Abramov's orders, the room was cleared. On this day, only one person needed to leave − a woman with short blond hair who finished buttoning a blouse as Sokolov and Abramov had arrived. Daria Popov was one of Stalin's secretaries. She didn't even glance at the two men as she left the room. Sokolov locked the door behind her. Stalin remained in bed. As Sokolov approached, the chairman smiled. He pointed his head toward the door, and said, "She is beautiful, no?"

Sokolov answered, "Yes, she most certainly is, Mr. Chairman."

"It had been too long, but I feel invigorated." Stalin turned to the doctor who was readying the injection, and said, "You have brought about a miraculous change in me, Dr. Abramov. I will award you with the Order of Lenin."

The doctor waited with the syringe in hand. He said, "I am deeply grateful, Mr. Chairman."

Stalin took off his shirt, and said, "Let's get on with it. I plan to get out and walk today. If not in the snow, then around the inside of the home."

"Excellent, sir," replied the doctor. He ran an alcohol swab over Stalin's left bicep, inserted the needle, and deposited the fluid. After placing a small bandage on the injection spot, Abramov proceeded to check the chairman's vitals.

When that was finished, Stalin asked, "All is well, Dr. Abramov?"

"You have improved dramatically." Abramov nodded at Sokolov, and said, "It's time."

Stalin turned his head toward the doctor. "Time? For what?"

Sokolov moved quickly. He jumped on the bed while pulling out a Makarov pistol from its holster inside his jacket. Sokolov turned Stalin's torso, and slammed the chairman's face down on the bed. "Shut up, or I will shoot you in the head." The barrel of the gun was now pressed against Stalin's temple.

Stalin spoke into the mattress, "Are you mad?" His five-foot-six-inch body struggled, but even with the renewed strength from recent days, it was to no avail.

The doctor pulled a device out of his bag. It was gray, and looked like an oversized gun – longer and bulkier. The barrel also had a wider opening than a typical handgun.

"You have him?" asked Abramov.

Sokolov shoved his knee further down into the chairman's back, and pushed the gun harder into Stalin's temple.

Stalin declared, "You will die for this."

Sokolov ignored what Stalin said, and replied to Abramov: "Yes, I have him secured."

Abramov maneuvered himself onto the bed next to Sokolov, and looked at a tiny indicator light. It flashed green. He placed the barrel of the device on the back of Stalin's neck.

Stalin started to say, "No, no, please..."

When Abramov pulled the device's trigger, a hissing noise was followed by a sudden jerking of Stalin. The chairman's body went still.

Abramov and Sokolov moved off Stalin's back. The doctor shifted so he could look at Stalin's eyes.

The two men waited in silence.

Stalin's eyes suddenly popped open, and the pupil in each expanded and contracted several times. The eyes blinked three times, and then focused on Abramov. Stalin's mouth broke into a broad smile.

Abramov smiled as well. He patted Stalin on the back, and asked, "Everything is normal?"

Stalin sat up in the bed. He looked at Sokolov and then back at the doctor. He continued to smile. "This is incredible. Everything seems to be working as it was described."

# Chapter 3

Before entering Stalin's bedroom, Arkadi Sokolov had dismissed the two guards posted outside the door.

As a result, after she left Stalin's bedroom, Daria Popov found herself alone. She quickly and quietly scouted the adjacent hallway and rooms.

Finding no one, she removed her shoes, which allowed her to run without sound to a spacious cloakroom. She entered, and closed the door.

Just as Popov hadn't been called to Stalin's bed in weeks, she hadn't been in this large closet for an even longer period. But she knew exactly where to go.

Popov moved a stepstool in place, and at five-feet-five-inches tall, had to climb to the top step. She slid a set of blankets aside, and stuck a fingernail in between the ceiling and wall panel. A small section of paneling – about six inches high and eight inches wide – popped off and revealed a shelf with a small black box. A wire was attached to it with a tiny earpiece on the other end. A four-inch-wide glass allowed a view into Stalin's bedroom.

Through the wall, a cord ran to a microphone attached just on the inside of a frame hanging in Stalin's bedroom. The large frame housed an assortment of items marking the day in March 1922 when Stalin took power in the Soviet Union, including the front page of an edition of *Pravda*, a sword, and assorted medals and ribbons. It was a shadow box that no one would dare move or touch without Stalin's permission. The miniature camera lens had rested safely inside the shadowbox for months, as Stalin ordered no one to touch it, other than to gently remove dust atop the frame.

Popov shoved the earpiece into her small left ear, and flipped a switch on the black box. A crackling came through the earpiece, followed by voices from the other room. Popov pressed one of her gray-blue eyes against the viewfinder. Her eyes seemed large given that her nose and mouth were rather tiny.

But her mouth grew as she smiled. The grin evaporated, though, as she heard and watched Sokolov move against Stalin.

Her mouth dropped open and her gaze was transfixed, as the doctor shoved a device against Stalin's neck.

She couldn't see Stalin's face, but could hear his protests. And then the silence, and eventually Stalin's voice once again.

Popov stared intensely at the smile on the chairman's face, and a look of fright crossed her own.

When Stalin moved to get up from the bed, she shut down everything, put the paneling back in place, and then the blankets. After climbing down off the stepstool, Popov reached out and grabbed a shelf to steady herself as her knees buckled.

After taking a deep breath, Popov went to the door, and opened it slightly.

At first, she listened. It was still quiet. She then stuck her head out and looked around. With no one present, Popov moved quickly, barefoot, and shoes in hand.

# Chapter 4

Despite being rather cramped, the important meetings were held in this room.

A metal table rested in the center of a space with gray walls. A persistent humming loomed in the background. The six metal chairs at the table were filled.

The discussion had been unusually lively, but the time had arrived to wrap things up.

Commander One declared, "The outcome wasn't exactly what we wanted, but Stalin was far more important. After all, these Americans have a more dispersed form of power."

"Yes, they call it 'separation of powers,' or 'checks and balances,'" volunteered Commander Three.

There was irritation in Commander One's response, "Yes, I'm aware. Thank you."

Commander Two interjected, "And there is no way to know that this Nixon would be any stronger or weaker."

Commander Five responded, "Oh, please. We decided to eliminate Eisenhower for a reason. Nixon lacks Eisenhower's abilities in nearly every way. Indeed, we can't ignore that Eisenhower remains a danger."

Commander One leaned back in his chair. "No doubt. We will have to figure out another way to take care of him."

A brief silence followed, and then Commander Four said, "I still don't know if the right choice was made here, in terms of what we need."

While Commander Three nodded in agreement, the response among three of the others wasn't just unsympathetic, but it was overtly hostile.

Commander One raised his voice, and declared, "Let there be no doubt about this choice. It was correct. The

Soviet Union shares our general outlook, and has made clear its willingness to do whatever is necessary."

"Didn't the Americans prove much the same when they dropped not one but two atomic devices to end their war?" asked Commander Three.

"Enough!" ordered Commander One. "The debate is over, and has been over for some time. Not only are the Soviets like-minded, but Stalin was the perfect choice – remote, volatile, unpredictable and willing to make the hard choices. All of this means that he is the ideal vehicle, and any small shortcomings we might still have in terms of the technology will go unnoticed." He glanced at Commander Five, and continued, "That definitely would not have been the case with Eisenhower or Nixon – never mind Churchill."

Commander Four asked, "But are we making the same mistakes?"

Commander Three shot a surprised look.

Meanwhile, Commander Six remained unperturbed, simply watching.

The others, however, reacted with vitriol, once again.

Commander Four retreated into silence, while Commander Three said defensively, "We have long treated these meetings as being open to questions and debate to make sure that we are carrying out the mission correctly."

As the temperature in the room began to cool, Commander Six soothingly said, "That is true."

Commander One added, "Yes, but the time for debate is now over. Do we all agree?"

Affirmations came from all at the table, with Commander Four being the last one to utter agreement.

"Good," said Commander One in a calmer voice. "Each of us understands that much time already has been spent, and more will be needed to complete the mission. But having Stalin was the primary requirement. Now, we just need to choose wisely at each stage moving forward, which" – he nodded at Commanders Three and Four – "is why we need to be able to discuss everything openly here, at the table."

Further agreement came from each chair.

Commander Two then asked, "What about the implants in Kendall and Hart?"

Commander Five answered, "There is no reason to think that they won't react as designed. Each unit will have shut down at death and wiped itself clean. When the Americans detach them, they'll melt down, again as designed. That will create questions for which they will have no answers."

Commander One nodded.

# Chapter 5

Though he was a Lutheran and actually hadn't been to church in a while, Dean Cold currently felt at home in the National Presbyterian Church at the southeast corner of Connecticut Avenue and N Street NW in Washington, D.C.

*What would Dad say?*

Secret Service leaders and colleagues, along with President Eisenhower; the First Lady, Mamie; assorted members of the administration, including CIA Director Allen Dulles; and others from official Washington, were crammed into the pews. They were all brought to this distinctive, Romanesque-Revival-style church, with its rounded arches, rough-cut stone facing, and massive 150-foot tower, for the funeral of Andrew Stanton.

The official story was that Stanton perished stopping a madman, wielding a gun, who managed to make his way into the White House. Dulles had provided the details that went to White House staff, the media and the public.

Cold's fingers and feet moved expertly over the keys and levers of the pipe organ, while the congregation sang *Amazing Grace.*

When the pastor of the church had called to ask if Cold would be willing to play the organ for his friend's funeral, he said, "I know that you and Andrew were partners at the Secret Service, and I thought that since you're an excellent organist, you might want to play for your friend's funeral."

Cold immediately thanked him and agreed. He thought that concentrating on playing during the funeral would provide enough distraction so that he would not break down in the church. He had done enough of that while alone in his apartment since the death of Stant.

Before hanging up the telephone, Cold had asked, "Pastor, how did you know that I played the organ?" At that moment, he had wondered if Stant had somehow mentioned it to his pastor.

The pastor answered, "It came from the very top, Mr. Cold. It was suggested to me directly by President Eisenhower."

Cold wasn't completely taken off guard given Ike's link to this church. Cold had been stationed outside the National Presbyterian Church as Ike became the only president to be baptized while in office, which occurred a month before the Oval Office attack. But Cold was surprised that the president took time to make the suggestion.

Tears moved down his cheeks as he played, and the congregation sang...

> Yes, when this flesh and heart shall fail,
> and mortal life shall cease:
> I shall possess, within the veil,
> a life of joy and peace.

*So much for not breaking down at the church.*

At the close of the service, Cold played "For All the Saints." He knew the hymn so well that he could play it without much thought. And while doing so, his mind wandered back to the last time that he and Stanton had a few beers together in a D.C. bar – two weeks before Stanton perished.

\*       \*       \*

"I'm telling you, I plan to retire one day, and my wife and I will head down to Florida each February to watch the Tigers at Spring Training. And then we'll visit the grandkids, wherever the hell they might be," announced Stanton. He then took a big swig of beer.

Cold laughed. "Yeah, sounds nice. Maybe we'll join you after we check out the Dodgers for a bit. Of course, we both have to find wives first, and have some kids."

"Details."

"True, but those details are kind of important."

Each man finished his beer, and the bartender refilled the mugs.

Stanton asked, "What about Max?"

"What? Do you think I'm still longing for a woman after we gave up a long time ago?"

Stanton eyed his friend. "I do."

"Screw you."

Stanton laughed.

Cold asked, "What about you? Did you ask out the woman you've been talking to at your church?"

"I'm easing into it. The timing has to be just right."

"Holy shit."

"What?"

"We're both kind of pathetic," observed Cold.

Stanton took a long drink, and replied, "You're not wrong, unfortunately. But don't worry, we'll get to those Tiger and Dodger games, along with the palm trees, one day."

They raised their glasses, clinked them together, and discussed their mutual dislike for the New York Yankees, who had beaten the Dodgers in the previous year's World Series.

\*　　\*　　\*

A little over an hour after the funeral ended, a far smaller group congregated at Arlington National Cemetery.

Cold was only half listening to the passages being read by the pastor. He stared at the coffin, and was thinking about his friend's killers. In particular, he was trying to work through what those devices in the attackers' necks might have been, especially given the president's surprise at Kendall's response when tested about his past.

The twenty-one gun salute jolted Cold out of his reflections, and back to a mix of sadness and anger, and a need to do … something.

In the small crowd, two of the mourners, a man and a woman dressed in Army uniforms, stood next to each other at the back of the assembled group. They weren't watching the pastor or the coffin. Nor did they have their eyes closed and heads lowered in prayer. Instead, they watched Cold throughout the graveside service.

# Chapter 6

Ten days after the death of Andrew Stanton, Dean Cold was back on night duty at the White House. He was paired with John Bartley. Cold knew Bartley on a professional level, but the two had not had many interactions beyond that. Bartley, though, happened to be the agent who had briefly entered the Oval Office on the night when the president was attacked.

The two were positioned outside the Oval Office when the door opened, and Allen Dulles stepped out. His eyes scanned the general area. It was quiet, as expected, since it was just after midnight.

Dulles looked at Cold, and said, "Agent Cold, could you please come into the office?"

"Yes, sir," responded Cold. He saw no discernable reaction from Bartley while moving toward the door into the Oval Office.

As Cold stepped in, Dulles closed the door, and the president moved from his desk to one of the couches in the middle of the room.

Eisenhower said, "Please, take a seat, Agent Cold."

Cold stopped, "Sir?" He looked from Ike to Dulles, and then back to the president.

Eisenhower smiled. "It's alright, Agent Cold. We have things to discuss."

It didn't feel right to Cold to be part of the events in the Oval Office, as opposed to simply observing and protecting. But the relevance of such a notion had evaporated ten days earlier. He replied, "Yes, sir," and took a seat on the other couch. Dulles sat next to Eisenhower.

Ike asked, "How are you holding up, Agent Cold?"

"Fine, sir." It wasn't a complete lie. He was doing better now than during the immediate aftermath of the attack and Stanton's death. In recent days, he was more frustrated at not being able to do more, and not getting answers to a host of questions. He also was annoyed by the reality that such questions likely would get answered higher up the chain of command, and that he might never know everything.

"You're quite the organist. You played wonderfully at the funeral," commented Eisenhower.

Cold felt a bit off balance. "Thank you, sir."

"You've played since you were a kid, starting at your father's church, right?"

*Where is this going?*

Cold glanced briefly at Dulles, whose expression said nothing, and back to Eisenhower. "Yes, sir. My father is a pastor in Brooklyn, and learning the organ was part of the deal growing up. I took to it."

"Yes. Bill Donovan mentioned that you took the opportunity to play in a church here and there during the war, and some of your fellow OSS agents called you 'Keys.'"

Cold wanted to ask what this was all about, but since this man across from him was the president, he merely responded, "Yes, Mr. President, a few did." But he decided to add, with a wry smile, "I wasn't quite sure if they were appreciating or mocking my abilities at the organ."

Eisenhower's wide smile appeared, and as he turned to Dulles, the CIA director smiled as well. Ike looked back at Cold. "After hearing you play, I have no doubt it was a compliment." Eisenhower paused. "And it wasn't just your organ playing, your work with the OSS also was highly regarded by Bill. He had nothing but positive things to say about you."

"Thank you, sir. I was privileged to serve as an aide to General Donovan, and be part of several missions during the war."

"Missions that you led."

"Yes, sir."

Dulles continued to watch as Eisenhower engaged Cold.

"Was it easy to go from public school in Brooklyn to studying philosophy at Harvard? That must have been quite a change?"

*Well, suddenly I'm on* This Is Your Life. *Strange. But that's Ike, not Ralph Edwards.*

"I've always done well in school, sir. So, it wasn't about the academics. There were some early adjustments until I figured out who people were, and then it was fairly smooth."

"You apparently adjusted alright – started as the Harvard quarterback for two seasons?"

"I've always enjoyed playing football, as well as baseball, sir. But I was much better at football."

Ike nodded. "And from what Allen tells me, you were planning on going to seminary after Harvard?"

Cold shifted in his seat. "Yes. The plan was to enter the family business, so to speak. My grandfather was a Lutheran pastor, as is my father. I was working for General Donovan, and after a year, the plan was to go to seminary. But then Pearl Harbor happened, and well, we all know the story from there." He looked back and forth at Eisenhower and Dulles.

"We do," affirmed the president. "No regrets about not getting back to the seminary after the war?"

Cold hesitated. This was something he still wrestled with, and wasn't sure how to answer the question. He decided to be forthright with the president.

Ike added, "If you don't mind me asking?"

"Of course not, sir." He paused once more. "I have few regrets in life, so far. And I wouldn't say that I regret not going to seminary, Mr. President, but it is something that crosses my mind now and then. As for my parents' regretting my decision, well, that is another matter."

"I can understand that, Agent Cold. A military career was, to say the least, unusual in a Mennonite family. My mother was not a woman who cried, but she did when I went to West Point."

It was Cold's turn to nod. "That sounds very familiar, sir."

Dulles interjected, "Your mother is deceased."

"Yes, sir."

Ike leaned forward. "I know this is highly unusual, Agent Cold, but will you bear with us for a bit longer?"

"Of course, sir. Whatever you need."

Eisenhower looked Cold in the eyes. "Are you serious about anyone, Agent Cold?"

*That's one of those questions when your commanding officer is about to send you on a mission that could end in death.*

Cold tried to answer dispassionately. "No, sir. I'm not currently seeing anyone."

"Dr. Marshall?"

That, again, surprised Cold. "Um, well, no, sir. Dr. Marshall and I haven't … dated … in some time."

"I see. Thank you, Agent Cold." The president sat back on the couch, and looked at Dulles.

Allen Dulles said, "Agent Cold, what I'm about to tell you stays between you, me, and the president of the United States." He stopped talking and waited for Cold's response.

"Yes, of course, sir."

"Good." Dulles went on, "The Agency had an operative positioned very close to Stalin. She left the Soviet Union in order to tell me, directly, something she had … experienced."

*Stalin? Where's this going?*

Dulles went on to tell the full details relayed by Daria Popov. He concluded, "This all happened, by the way, on the same day as Kendall and Hart took action here in the Oval Office."

Cold felt a chill go up his spine. He managed to whisper, "Jesus."

Dulles resumed his reporting. "The strangest thing is what happened when my team went to remove those devices or implants attached to the spinal cords of both Kendall and Hart." He looked at Eisenhower and then back to Cold. "Once detached, they … melted. These things, as relayed to me, just kind of melted into a mix of a kind of … goo. And now, they're trying to figure out what the hell that goo is."

Cold was trying to make sense of this, but was oddly distracted by Dulles' discomfort with using the word "goo."

After a few moments of silence, Eisenhower said, "Agent Cold, Allen wanted to put the full force of the CIA into action to get to the bottom of this. Is this all related to some kind of coup in the Soviet Union? Are the Chinese at work? Who the hell has this kind of technology?" Ike paused and took a deep breath. "But I have a strange feeling that this is different than a Soviet or Chinese op. Of course, I could be dead wrong."

Cold observed, "I agree, sir. This seems ... beyond the Russians or Chinese, at least as far as I'm aware."

Eisenhower reassured, "Feel free to weigh in as you see fit, Agent Cold."

The nerves that came from speaking to the president and CIA director in the Oval Office melted away. "To be honest, I don't know what to think. How do we put together an attempt to murder you, sir, with whatever it was that happened to Stalin on the same day? These neck devices...? This is mysterious technology that seems beyond reality." He looked at Dulles and then Ike. "This is just plain ... weird."

Ike observed, "We're immersed in weird, Agent Cold. Go ahead."

Cold started to summarize what had happened in an attempt to make sense of it all. "Are we looking at some kind of mind control with devices that, when discovered, and are about to be dissected, simply melt away into a goo?"

Cold took note of the expressions on each man's face across from him.

Cold added, "It appears that whoever is behind this, well, they were interested in assassinating you, while seeking to perhaps control Chairman Stalin."

Eisenhower and Dulles looked at each other.

*This is nuts.*

Cold decided to say it out loud. "You think I'm nuts, Mr. President. And you might be right because it sounded nuts as I was saying it."

Eisenhower replied, "Well, if you're a nut, Agent Cold, then so is Allen, and so am I. And I don't think anyone wants to talk about the president of the United States being nuts, do they?" Ike managed a smile.

Cold responded, "No, sir, no one does."

*What now?*

Eisenhower leaned forward once again. "Dean, this is the strangest set of circumstances I've ever come across in my life, and that's saying something. The potential explanations range from, as you put it, weird, to deeply troubling. But whatever is found, the danger to the United States and to the free world and perhaps to the entire globe, is serious, in my view. We need to figure out what this is about, and who is behind it. At the same time, we need to accomplish this in utmost secrecy. Nothing can go public, no matter what, at least until we can assess the dangers and threats properly." Ike stopped talking and looked directly into Cold's eyes.

"I agree, sir," responded Cold.

"Good, Dean."

*He just called me by my first name twice.*

Eisenhower continued, "I want you to head up this operation."

*What?*

"Excuse me, sir?"

"I know this is unexpected. But it's critical. It needs to be kept among very few people. This small group needs to be skilled and trustworthy, and the leader will report directly to me. This will be my team, and I need someone I can trust to lead it. You fit the bill, for me and for your country." President Eisenhower added, "I trust you, Dean. Can I count on you to do this?"

# Chapter 7

During the war, Dean Cold had learned how to sleep whenever the opportunity presented itself.

After a night shift guarding the president, he would arrive in his Q Street NW basement apartment a little after ten in the morning. Cold would fix himself a hearty breakfast. With water or juice substituting for a caffeine-rich cup of coffee, he'd eat while reading the morning newspapers. The breakfast and reading would make it easier to get a sound sleep.

But other than a breakfast of two sunny-side-up eggs, bacon, and toast, sleep wasn't on the agenda this time. After finishing his meal, Cold's mind kept grinding as he moved into the apartment's living room. He tuned the Crosley radio to a favorite station. Jazz now played with the volume low. Cold sank into an armchair. He had a small, leatherbound notebook and a pen on his lap. But he closed his eyes.

*What have I gotten myself into? I suddenly understand how Ike got men to follow orders during the war and why people voted for him.*

But Cold admitted that whomever up the chain of command had asked him – didn't order but asked, interestingly  to take on this mysterious threat, he would have agreed.

After the Oval Office attack and the death of Stanton, Cold had been wrestling with the details and possible implications of what had happened and what he saw. He acknowledged to himself that it was odd that what weighed on his mind least was his shooting and killing two men.

His mind wandered briefly to Kendall and Hart.

*Dulles said that their deaths would be reported as happening somewhere else with a very different explanation. How was that going to work?* He sighed. *Not your problem. You've got enough on your plate.*

His focus returned to what President Eisenhower and CIA Director Allen Dulles had told him.

*Who the hell are these people? They tried to kill Ike and did ... what .. to Stalin? Devices implanted into people, onto their spinal cords, to what end? Controlling them? Apparently. How? And what about the devices when removed melting down into a ... goo?*

As the day wore on, Cold's mind went through assorted possible answers. He ruled none of them out – from China to unaccounted for Nazis to some kind of international entity countering the United Nations. But in his mind, he was leaning on the idea that the Soviet MGB – Ministry of State Security – was behind this. What if that meant some kind of secret coup in Russia? But even that didn't seem to fully gel.

Something unusual started to gnaw at Cold. He felt a wave of being overwhelmed.

The ringing telephone provided a much-needed break. He turned off the radio, and when hearing the voice on the other end of the call, Cold felt better. "Hi, Dad, it's good to hear your voice. How are things?"

Cold quickly slipped into a comfort zone of discussing family and church matters. He also knew these conversations helped his father, who, though busy taking care of his congregation in Brooklyn, was feeling lonely since Cold's mother, Theresa, had died three years earlier. Dean's sister, Alice, and her family being close by on Long Island helped, but Dean and his father, Gary, had an easier relationship. They could talk freely about almost anything, except details of Dean's work.

As the conversation was coming to an end, Gary asked, "How are you doing? You're back to work, right?"

"I am. Stant's death is still ... raw. And there are ... issues at work that are on my mind."

"I know it sounds hollow coming from your father far away in Brooklyn, but if there's anything I can do…"

"It's never hollow, Dad. I appreciate it."

"I pray for you each morning and night, Dean."

"Thanks, Dad, I think I need those prayers."

"You know what your mother and I always told you and Alice, take it to the Lord. Prayer, the Divine Service, your playing, it all helps."

"You and Mom were right. Playing at Stant's funeral helped. It did." Dean paused. He hit that point of feeling a touch of guilt when talking with his father about church, not just because he hadn't regularly attended for some time – actually since his mother had died of a heart attack – but because of his choosing not to go to seminary. "And I know I need to get back to church more regularly."

"You will, son. You'll know when it's right, and it will make all the difference. But you already know that."

"You're far too understanding for a pastor, you know."

His father laughed at that. "That's doubtful, but I have learned that scolding people or yelling at them to go to church doesn't work all that well."

*A far wiser man than I'll ever be.*

"Thanks, Dad. Our talks always help. But I have to get back to an assignment."

"Our conversations help me, too. It's your turn now. Give me a call when you can."

"I will, Dad. I love you."

"I love you, too, Dean."

After he hung up the telephone, Dean Cold felt like he had gained some much-needed perspective, and his mind started to turn to what Ike ordered after Dean had accepted the task.

The president had said, "I need you to present me – and only me, along with Director Dulles, of course – with the people you would like to have on this small squad." He started, "I…" Then the president had glanced at Dulles, and said, "We need to know your thinking on each person's role, and your assurance that they can be trusted. And Dean, I say keep it small to limit the chances of this getting out. Once more, this has to stay top secret."

Cold had assured, "Yes, sir. I'll have my selections for you ASAP."

He recalled thinking at the time, *I have no idea whom I need or want.*

Now, it was time for Cold to dig into his mind's Rolodex to see who would make sense to unravel this bizarre mystery, and whom he could trust completely.

# Chapter 8

Whispers throughout the Kremlin called this moment "Stalin reborn." Though not spoken about openly, it hardly had been a well-kept secret that Joseph Stalin had been on the decline. This renewed Stalin was being treated as some kind of miracle – well, if miracles were permitted in the atheistic Soviet Union.

This Chairman Stalin took no chances. He moved quickly to consolidate power in a way that hadn't been seen in quite a few years. A re-energized and more determined Stalin wasn't good news for many who had risen within the Party as the Chairman had been in retreat.

Stalin and Arkadi Sokolov turned to Mikhail Ryumin. Ryumin was brutal, and enjoyed torturing anyone, but in particular, he reveled in torturing enemies of the State. In late 1952, after appointing him a year-and-a-half earlier, Stalin dismissed Ryumin from the number two position at the MGB for incompetence. But now, Ryumin's willingness to carry out this Stalin's wishes in swift, brutal fashion, and without much thought, was deemed a major strength.

In just over a week's time, the amount of pain inflicted and blood spilled was staggering. Assorted leaders, including those who might have succeeded Stalin, including Georgy Malenkov, Nikita Khrushchev, Georgy Zhukov, and Lavrentiy Beria, were grabbed by Ryumin's thugs, tortured and, finally, killed personally by Ryumin. There was no opportunity for the doomed to make some kind of public statement.

Stalin, Sokolov and Dr. Abramov expressed admiration for Ryumin's ruthless efficiency. Sokolov had identified 22 targets to Ryumin. All were now deceased.

As Ryumin made his report in Stalin's Kremlin office, the three men – Stalin, Sokolov and Abramov – listened with rapt attention. Ryumin said, "And when it came to the likes of Malenkov, Khrushchev, Zhukov, and that other one, Beria, after inflicting the pain they deserved, I made sure that their end came in your preferred way, Chairman Stalin."

Stalin replied, "Yes?"

"I personally smashed each one's skull in with an ax, and then had their bodies driven over with a truck."

Stalin said, "Excellent."

Ryumin continued, "The work, though, continues, as I believe Director Sokolov has additional names?" He glanced at Sokolov, who nodded in response.

Stalin then shook Ryumin's hand, further complimented his work, and dismissed the man. When the three were alone, Sokolov said, "We can find help for our mission – people willing to do brutal, but necessary work. It's surprising."

Stalin raised an eyebrow. "Surprising? Why? Look at what the Nazis were willing to do. Look at what has gone on here in the Soviet Union."

Abramov added, "Indeed. Yet, there's a reason why the genocide and other atrocities carried out by the Nazis were deemed to be crimes against humanity."

It was all discussed clinically.

Sokolov nodded. He then looked at Stalin, and noted, "Have you heard that they're calling your re-emergence 'Stalin reborn'?"

Stalin nodded, "I have. What's been the reaction?"

Sokolov casually answered, "Fear, terror and admiration."

"Good. Exactly what we were seeking," replied Stalin.

# Chapter 9

After several days of wrestling with whom he wanted on his team, Special Agent Dean Cold was back at the White House. Once more, Special Agent John Bartley watched Cold go into the Oval Office at the behest of Allen Dulles. Though this time, it was early in the morning, and Cold hadn't been on duty with Bartley.

Eisenhower was at his desk, and said, "Dean, come in. Grab a seat."

Dulles took one of the chairs across the desk from Ike, and Cold followed the CIA director's lead by taking the other.

Cold had come to know that Eisenhower was an optimist at heart, and he always seemed to put the best spin on most situations being discussed in the Oval Office. But right now, the president wore a frown.

Eisenhower looked at Cold, and said, "Before we get to your proposed team, there's news that you should be aware of."

"Sir?" responded Cold.

Ike looked at Dulles.

The CIA director said, "We've gotten disturbing news from the Soviet Union. Stalin is back at purges, and this time it seems to have been directed at nearly anyone who even might be considered a rival or successor."

Cold whispered, "Dear God."

"Yes," continued Dulles. "And we're talking top people – the ones who were positioning to succeed Stalin when apparently we all thought he was on his way to hell. That includes Khrushchev and Malenkov. And Stalin has handed the job over to Mikhail Ryumin, reinstating him as number two at the MGB."

Dulles said Ryumin's name in such a way that Cold knew he should have known who he was. But he didn't. Cold also understood that Ike had no taste for evasiveness. So, he declared, "I'm sorry, Director Dulles, but I don't know who Ryumin is."

At the same time that Dulles let out a little sigh, Eisenhower interjected, "No reason that you should. He falls in and out of favor with Stalin, apparently, and is a madman who, as Allen tells me, enjoys torturing prisoners – and it matters not whether they're foreigners or Russians."

"And he's now second in command of the MGB? We thought they were bad before." Cold continued, "If most or all of the top brass around Stalin have been murdered, who is he listening to now?"

Dulles answered, "One of our people inside had indicated that Arkadi Sokolov and Dr. Oleg Abramov spend the most time with Stalin."

"The two that Daria Popov told us attacked Stalin and injected ... something into his neck."

"Correct," answered Dulles. "We're worried that all of this – from the Stalin attack and rejuvenation to the attempt to murder the president to what we found inside Kendall and Hart – is about an MGB coup, especially given Sokolov's closeness."

Cold nodded. "I actually was thinking the same thing about the MGB being the lead candidate, and now hearing that Sokolov spends the most time with Stalin – a Stalin who could be under some kind of mind control just like Kendall and Hart seemed to be – well..."

Ike said, "You just took assorted leaps forward, Dean."

Cold didn't respond.

The president continued, "But Allen and I have done the same. It's hard to think of any other source for all of this."

The room went silent for a minute or so.

Cold debated whether he should say what was in his head, but he decided that the president needed to know his thinking. "Of course, I have to admit that in the back of my mind I'm even struggling with the MGB angle, sir. After all, what we've seen in terms of actions by individuals and mystifying technology, I'm not convinced that the Soviets are capable of this. But that begs the question: Who the hell could be?"

Cold watched Dulles and Ike exchange looks.

The president admitted, "I have similar questions, Dean. And given all of this, let's get to your team. Whom do you have in mind to get to the bottom of all of this?"

Cold answered, "I have four names, sir," and proceeded to make his case for each.

Not that he minded it, but Cold was surprised at how few questions Eisenhower and Dulles had about his choices. The two certainly asked pointed questions about each candidate, and why Cold wanted each. And they pressed on the two names that Cold expected would raise the most doubts. But in the end, it was all rather straightforward.

At the end of the meeting, Ike looked at Dulles and asked, "How long do you need?"

"Normally..."

The president cut him off, "This is anything but normal. How long?"

"Two days?"

"That'll work." Eisenhower turned to Cold. "Continue making preparations as if each of these people is going to be approved, and we'll meet in two days."

"Yes, sir. Thank you."

Eisenhower stood up, and extended his hand. Cold took it, and Ike said, "Thank you, Dean."

# Chapter 10

Mikhail Ryumin was finishing his report on the list of additional officials he had murdered according to the instructions of Arkadi Sokolov per Joseph Stalin. Ryumin seemed to take more delight in telling Stalin about the torture and murders this time.

Stalin watched Ryumin leave the office. After the door closed to the chairman's personal study, he turned to Sokolov and Oleg Abramov. "That man is interesting."

"In what way?" asked Abramov.

Stalin scratched his bushy mustache. "Look at him. He is so ... average looking. He has a round, sad face. His hair is thinning. And yet, look at what he has done in such a short time."

Sokolov added, "He clearly enjoys doing it. The reports that I received from elsewhere are that he particularly likes doling out the torture. Nothing seems to faze him."

Stalin nodded. "Yes, interesting. Ruthlessly efficient and lethal."

"And his commitment to you, apparently, is blind."

"Even better."

Abramov commented, "There is something admirable, and disturbing, about one man being able to oversee the murders of..."

Sokolov corrected, "Don't forget, he personally ended each life."

Abramov shifted in his chair. "Alright then. Something admirable and disturbing about one man overseeing the kidnapping of so many top brass, and then personally killing each man."

Stalin commented, "We know that you need individuals like that."

After a few seconds of silence, Sokolov said, "Demyan is next." He looked at Stalin. "You need to order him here."

Stalin nodded.

Abramov asked, "With so many killed, how can you make sure that he doesn't think he is going to be next? After all, he has made rumblings against Stalin, against you."

"I will reassure him," answered Stalin with a smile.

Sokolov added, "I'll have some people watching him to make sure that he follows the order, and doesn't try to do something unwise."

"And if he chooses something unwise before arriving at the dacha?" asked Abramov.

"Then we'll take care of him, and move on to another."

Abramov nodded. "Hopefully, that will not be necessary. I think, though, that if we let Ryumin loose, he would be ecstatic over torturing the man."

# Chapter 11

Dean Cold's telephone rang. He picked up the receiver. "Hello."

The person on the other end of the line simply said, "Dean, you have the go-ahead. Each person is approved."

Cold recognized his voice. "Thank you, Mr. President."

Glancing at his watch, Cold saw the military precision of Dwight Eisenhower. It was about an hour inside the two-day deadline that the president had set for Allen Dulles' review of the people Cold wanted on his team.

Cold thought he heard the president sigh.

Eisenhower added, "I know this will be out of the blue, but Allen has an additional person in mind."

*Dulles wants his man.*

The president continued, "Now, I agree with his reasoning, but if this person doesn't fit, just say so."

He said, "I understand, sir."

"Good. Allen will let you know."

"Yes, sir."

Ike went on, "I'm sure you understand all of this already, but we need to be clear. Make the offer without details first. Explain that it's a top-secret national security undertaking, and that it will require them to leave behind what they're doing. It also will require complete secrecy, to the point that if they walk away, now or in the future, and this effort or its findings remain secret, then uttering even the smallest detail will be considered treason." The president paused, and then added, "With full consequences."

Cold felt the hairs on his neck stand up. Any lingering doubt as to how serious this all was had just been erased by the president of the United States.

"I understand, sir."

He felt a brief pang of concern – or was it guilt – for what he was about to present to these five people.

*Well, they'll have a chance to walk away before getting started. Are you rationalizing, Dean?*

"Dean, one thing that you can mention to each of them is that the invitation comes from me as well. I hope that will weigh in our favor – unless they voted for Adlai."

"I do not doubt that it will help a great deal, sir."

Eisenhower declared, "It's time to get to work convincing them."

"Yes, sir."

"Good night."

"Good night, sir."

After the call ended, Cold walked over to his kitchen, and sat down at the table. He had four files spread out in front of him. He needed to get from Dulles who the fifth person was, whatever background the CIA director would provide, and then poke around himself.

*Okay, so who's going to be first?*

His eyes jumped from name to name. And his mind returned to one thing that Ike said.

*Break your silence in any way, and it's treason. That means execution, and no one will know the real story.*

Cold knew that this went for him as well.

He, once more, proceeded to review the files that he now knew by heart.

Across the street, the two people who had watched Cold at the funeral and burial of Andrew Stanton occupied a third-floor apartment. They couldn't peer into Cold's basement apartment, but they were able to see Cold come and go, along with any visitors he might have.

# Chapter 12

When Stalin was on the decline and increasingly in isolation, General Arseni Demyan had advanced quickly through the ranks of the Red Army and the Communist Party apparatus.

Demyan had signaled to key party officials that the Soviet Union wasn't meant to be a cult of personality – particularly a volatile, unpredictable, brutal personality. The general also communicated that while he wasn't interested in succeeding Stalin, if the right man stepped in, he would make sure that the military stood behind that leader.

Of course, many whispered that Demyan wasn't all that different from Stalin. The general had no one close to him. His friends were just those for whom he saw a use during certain periods of time. He was ruthless, but in more ambitious and political ways, as opposed to Stalin's paranoia and willingness to have seemingly endless numbers of enemies put to death. And like Stalin, he was unpredictable in order to keep people off balance and in line.

But now, everything had changed.

In his home in Moscow, he spoke forthrightly to his wife, Polina, probably for the first time since they were married nearly ten years before. The marriage was more a contract than anything else. Demyan made clear that he enjoyed having sex with her, and Polina apparently appreciated the financial and personal security of being married to the general. Indeed, they rarely spoke whether in bed or over meals, which covered most of their time together.

And even now, with Arseni summoned to Stalin's Kuntsevo Dacha, the two said nothing.

Arseni finished buttoning his uniform jacket, and downed a not-insignificant glass of vodka.

Polina watched from an armchair.

Arseni took another look at himself in the mirror. He was five feet, eight inches tall, but it was a fat five-eight. His black hair had retreated on his head, with thin traces left on the sides. And his eyes were sunk into his skull in contrast to a large, protruding nose.

Arseni picked up his hat, and slipped it under his right arm. He looked at his wife. "It is unlikely that I will return."

She stared at him. "You did what you thought was right, I assume?"

"I did."

"Then there is nothing more you could have done."

Arseni said, "Thank you." He added, "Unless the pig Stalin comes for you as well, you should be fine with what has been put aside."

She merely nodded.

He then walked across the room, opened the door, and left.

Polina said nothing. In fact, she never rose from the chair. However, she did sigh.

# Chapter 13

Dean Cold understood that approaching each person under consideration for his team required a different strategy. He knew one person professionally, two quite well, and the other two not at all.

Cold decided to start close to home.

John Bartley, fellow Secret Service special agent, had just rung the doorbell at Cold's apartment.

Cold opened the door, shook Bartley's hand and welcomed him inside. Bartley was tall. At six feet, two inches, he had three inches on Cold. Feeling short was unusual for Cold. Bartley also was thin and sported black hair cut short.

On the few occasions when Cold saw Bartley off duty, he had been a bit surprised by Bartley's easy smile and laugh. That stood in stark contrast to a strict seriousness while on duty. But Cold acknowledged that the same could be said about himself, and most others at the Secret Service. It was the nature of the occupation.

Cold's apartment had a living room separated by a half-wall from the kitchen with a Formica-topped table. The larger of the two bedrooms had the bathroom attached. Bartley commented, "Nice place."

"Thanks. Beer?"

"Yeah, sure. Mind if I look around?"

Cold replied, "Not much to take in, but please do."

While Bartley glanced around the rest of the apartment, Cold returned with two large mugs of beer.

After each took a drink, Bartley pointed at the piano. "I heard you played, and that they called you 'Keys' during the war."

"Guilty."

"Did you actually stop amidst the fighting to play some church organs?"

"Well, it was during downtime, if you want to call it that. It's not like it was during firefights."

Bartley chuckled. His focus settled on the four large bookcases in the living room. "Nice collection."

"Thanks."

Bartley took a swig of beer, but kept his eyes on the book titles. "Theology and philosophy. Makes sense. I heard that you studied philosophy at Harvard, and considered going into the seminary."

"Yeah, I was all lined up. The attack on Pearl Harbor changed that."

Bartley nodded. "Your father is a Lutheran pastor, right?"

*Who is doing the interviewing here?*

"He is. What about you – Catholic, right?"

Bartley looked at Cold with a raised eyebrow. "Yeah. I confess to not having been to Mass in some time, though." He looked back at the books.

Cold continued, "I heard you're a big reader. If there are any books you want to borrow, let me know."

"I appreciate that. Same on my end."

"Big library?"

"About double what you have here." Bartley smiled.

"What's so funny?"

"How many agents are comparing the sizes of their libraries?"

"Now that you mention it, probably not too many. What do you prefer reading?"

"Open to almost anything," answered Bartley, "but I read a lot of classics."

"Who?"

"Shakespeare and Dante are my favorites."

"Impressive," said Cold half mockingly. He took a slug of beer.

Bartley drank from his glass as well. "It sounds a hell of a lot more impressive than it is. I also confess to liking science fiction."

"A little break from the Bard?"

Bartley nodded. "You might say that. I studied Literature at Villanova on the GI bill after the war, but even with all that study, you wind up barely scratching the surface."

"I get that. And you know German and Russian?"

"Yeah, I studied those before the war."

"You were studying German and Russian when you were a cop in Philly? Okay, you're starting to impress me."

"I knew we – I mean the United States – would eventually get off our asses and enter the war, and that Nazi-Soviet agreement in 1939 scared the shit out of me. So, I thought German and Russian might come in handy."

"And?"

"The German did during the war. Who knows with the Russian now?"

Cold asked, "No interest in going back to the police work after the war?"

"In a sense, I have gone back to the work. What about you? Still reading theology, apparently. Any regrets about the Secret Service over the pulpit?"

It was always the same. Cold didn't like asking himself that question, never mind when someone else did. When Ike asked this question, Cold was about as forthcoming as he ever had been. This time, he reverted to his usual evasion. "I try not to look back."

"I get that. As I'm sure you know, I was supposed to get married, but that didn't exactly work out."

"Sorry," commented Cold.

"Getting left at the altar, literally, has an effect. The job and reading have been my ... salvation in a way. Your question about going back, I had lots of reasons not to. College, the Secret Service, moving to D.C. – it's a new life." He added, "Though, you never completely leave parts of your life behind."

Cold decided to shift the conversation both in terms of focus and location. "I hope you're good with a salad and lasagna for dinner."

"Lasagna? Is that what I smell? Sure. You a good cook?"

"I've gotten better out of necessity, but not this. There's an Italian place around the block, and they sell trays of all sorts of dishes. I just put it in the oven, and it's like I accomplished something."

"Nice."

As they ate, Cold guided the conversation between lighter and heavier topics. But as the last of the lasagna was eaten, Bartley said, "Don't get me wrong. This was a great meal, and I've enjoyed the conversation. But I get the feeling that there was more to this invitation than getting to know your partner better."

During the evening, Cold's decision to offer Bartley a spot on the team was confirmed. Now he was considering how to broach the subject.

Before Cold said anything, Bartley commented, "I know we were ordered not to talk about the Oval Office incident, but does tonight have anything to do with that?"

*Okay, here it goes.*

"It does," replied Cold. "John, I have an offer for you."

"Offer? Like a job offer?"

Cold actually chuckled. "Well, yes." His mind returned to his telephone conversation with Ike, which served as the basis for the pitch he was about to make. "This is a top-secret undertaking, and it has significant national security implications. I can't give you any more details unless you decide to sign up. But you'd have to leave behind your current position with the Service, and it would require the utmost secrecy. If you mentioned anything about it, the smallest detail, even afterwards if you decided to leave the job, it would be considered treason with the most severe consequences."

Cold stopped talking, and Bartley stared back amidst the now-thick silence.

Bartley actually smiled, and declared, "That's the shittiest job offer I've ever heard. Here's a position that I can't tell you anything about unless you accept it, and by the way, if you ever mention anything about it, to anyone, ever, you're a dead man."

"That's about it. Oh, wait, there is one more thing. This offer doesn't just come from me. It's from the president of the United States as well."

"You might have led with that." Bartley smiled. He returned to staring and silence. He finally admitted, "I'm intrigued."

Cold now smiled. "I can tell you that you'd probably get a raise ... a small one."

"Oh, that's different." Bartley actually laughed.

The two men fell silent, once more.

Bartley finally said, "I'm not completely sure why I'm saying this. Well, maybe it's because of Ike. Yeah, count me in."

Cold was surprised. "Are you sure you don't want to take more time to consider this?"

Bartley merely replied, "No."

"Okay, then you're in."

Cold extended his right hand across the table.

Bartley took it, and they shook hands.

"So, what did I just get myself into, Dean?"

After cleaning up the kitchen table, Cold spread out his files, and proceeded to explain everything to and answer the questions from a shocked and bewildered John Bartley.

Bartley whispered, "I guess my Russian will come in handy, after all."

Nearly four hours after dinner had ended, a person in the third-floor apartment across the street, who had written down when Bartley had arrived, now registered on a legal pad the time when Dean Cold's guest departed.

# Chapter 14

Stalin's Kuntsevo Dacha rested amidst a birch forest, along with a wide assortment of security measures and personnel. General Arseni Demyan had no trouble being allowed to drive on the thin road cutting through the trees.

Contrary to the concerns he had voiced to his wife, Demyan strode into Stalin's personal study as a model of Soviet military confidence. When Stalin rose from his large desk and greeted the general with a broad smile and an actual hug, Demyan was clearly perplexed. He stiffened as the chairman patted him on the back robustly.

Two others were in the office – Arkadi Sokolov, head of the MGB, and Dr. Oleg Abramov, who had gained secret renown for reportedly bringing Stalin back from the brink of death. As Stalin showed Demyan to a seat, the other two merely nodded at the general.

Demyan sat in a chair facing Stalin, just a few feet from the Soviet leader. The general again seemed uncomfortable with Sokolov and Abramov now behind him. As Stalin started to make small talk, Demyan's eyes went from the chairman to trying to see what was going on behind his back.

Stalin finally said, "Rest easy, Arseni. You are among friends here."

"Yes, well, thank you, Mr. Chairman," Demyan managed weakly.

"Of course," replied Stalin. "By the way, how is your wife? Her name is Polina, correct?"

Demyan was working to regain his footing. "Yes. Well, she is... Might I be direct, sir?"

Sokolov raised an eyebrow at Abramov.

Stalin answered, "Of course. I need you to be direct and honest, Arseni. After all, I will need this from the new Minister of War." The chairman smiled.

"Pardon me, the new... I do not understand." He paused and then said, "You asked about my wife. To be honest, sir, she is worried that I won't be returning home ... ever."

Stalin briefly moved his eyes from Demyan to Sokolov, and then back to the general. He said, "Ridiculous. You are going to be the Minister of War."

As Stalin spoke, Sokolov quietly rose from his seat and moved toward Demyan. Abramov followed Sokolov's lead. As Sokolov withdrew his Makarov pistol, Abramov pulled the bulky injector gun from his bag.

General Demyan, however, had spotted the movement of Stalin's eyes. He jumped up and whirled his weighty five-foot-eight-inches more quickly than anyone likely expected. Demyan grabbed Sokolov's wrist which was holding the weapon. The head of the MGB added his other hand to the joint clench. The two briefly stared at each other with their faces just inches apart. As Demyan struggled to save his life, his eyes widened when seeing the dark sneer worn by Sokolov.

Sokolov maneuvered his left foot behind Demyan's right leg. Once in position, resignation seemed to dawn on the general's face – although he continued the fight. But Sokolov merely needed to shift his weight, and Demyan fell backwards. He crashed to the floor, with Sokolov on top of him.

The general was dazed, with the air knocked out of him.

Sokolov quickly rolled the general over onto his stomach, and waved in Abramov.

Stalin watched without getting up from his chair. He said, "You won't know it, General Demyan, but you will be the Minister of War."

The general tried to say something, but the loss of air silenced him.

Abramov put the injector gun in position, checked the light, and pulled the trigger.

# Chapter 15

Agent Dean Cold was in what was referred to as the second basement of the Pentagon. He found the room he was looking for, and knocked on the door.

A voice from inside called out, "Yes, yes, it's open. Come in."

Cold entered the room, which was smaller than he had expected. It was rather dark. The overhead lights were off, and the three lamps that were on had limited lumens.

Dr. Michael Strickland remained seated at a desk overflowing with paper. Indeed, paper seemed to be everywhere in the room, spread across an eight-foot-long table in the middle of the space, and atop the filing cabinets that lined much of the walls. Cold assumed that the filing cabinets were near capacity as well.

The only space in the room free of paper was a set of drums in one corner. Cold could barely pull his eyes away from the incongruity of the drum set not only being in this office, but also in the Pentagon.

Cold said, "Hello, Dr. Strickland?"

Strickland leaned back in his chair, which squeaked. He was a round man marked by disheveled blond hair and eyebrows, a rumpled gray suit, and a black tie pulled down slightly with the top button of his shirt open. His thick, square-framed glasses rested on his nose lightly askew.

Strickland replied, "That's me." He smiled, which made his appearance more endearing. "Are you General Donovan's man? Agent Cold?"

"I am."

Strickland stood up, reached across the desk, and the two men shook hands.

"Pull over a chair. Well, that chair." Strickland pointed at the only chair without papers stacked on it. He chuckled. "Sorry about the mess. But this is pretty much how it is all of the time in my office."

As he positioned the chair across the desk from Strickland, Cold said, "I have to ask…"

As the two men sat, Strickland interjected, "About the drums?"

"Yeah."

"I started playing before the war. It helps me clear my head. You know, think more creatively. It's the Big Band stuff that works for me."

Cold nodded. "I certainly understand that."

"Yeah, Wild Bill told me that you play the organ and piano. Stopped in and played at a few churches in Europe during the war."

*Word gets around.*

Strickland continued, "Earned the nickname 'Keys'?"

"I did. And what do they call a man who has two PhDs – one in physics and one in chemistry – who worked on the Manhattan Project, and who plays the drums?"

"Dr. Strickland," he answered, expressionless. And then he broke into a laugh.

Cold laughed as well.

Strickland added, "But you should call me Mike."

*In his file, Donovan did say that he was brilliant and odd. But I like this kind of odd. I think.*

Cold nodded, adding, "Okay, and it's Dean."

Strickland asked, "So, what's this all about, Dean?"

Cold reset to the basic script of how he broached this with John Bartley. "I have an offer for you."

Strickland stared back, waiting for more.

Cold went on, "This is top secret, and has, or could have, major national security implications. And unfortunately, I can't give you any more details unless you decide to sign up. You would have to leave behind your current position." He paused and looked around the room. "And it would require such a high degree of secrecy that if you mentioned anything about it, the smallest detail, even afterwards if you decided to leave the job, it would be considered treason with the most severe consequences."

Cold stopped talking, and was taken a bit off-guard by Strickland's subsequent smile.

"Dean, I worked on the Manhattan Project, and the work I'm doing right now isn't exactly for public consumption. I get the 'if you talk, you're either dead or tossed in a dark cell for the rest of your life' scenario. Hell, I've been living it for over a decade now."

Cold merely responded, "Alright, I also should mention that this job offer doesn't just come from me, but from the president."

Strickland wryly observed, "Now I've received personal invites from FDR and Ike. I might get an inflated ego."

Cold actually chuckled.

Strickland got up from his chair, and started walking around the room, rubbing his chin. He then sat down at the drums, picked up his sticks, and started to play.

Cold watched in a bit of amazement.

*Okay. This is new.*

After nearly five minutes of beating the drums, Strickland stopped. And while twirling the sticks in his hands, he said, "You came highly recommended by Wild Bill."

"As did you."

"Would I be able to bring my drums?"

"What?"

"My drums – would I be able to play wherever you set up shop?"

Cold smiled. "I see no reason why not. Hell, I just might set up a piano as well, so we could jam if you wanted to."

Strickland declared, "I like you, Keys. I'm in. Now, how about the details?"

Cold proceeded to lay out everything to Strickland. And while John Bartley had been shocked by what he heard, Strickland appeared intrigued.

When Cold was finished, Strickland, who had continued twirling his drumsticks, said, "Holy crap. This is going to be fascinating." He then stopped twirling the sticks, and asked, "By the way, do you mind the 'Keys' nickname?"

"I can't exactly say that I mind it, but..."

"Good."

"But you know that Donovan dislikes the 'Wild Bill' nickname."

Strickland smiled. "I do, indeed."

*Well, I've got a drum-playing scientist on board. Why has this been easier than I expected, at least so far? Maybe it's because, like me, John and Mike are in government jobs that deal with secrets and security. Or maybe they just respect Ike. Let's see how it goes with the others.*

# Chapter 16

The drive from Washington, D.C., to New York City was quick on this Thursday morning. Dean Cold had left his apartment just after 4 am, and pulled into the airport parking lot just before 11 am.

With his Secret Service credentials, Cold had no trouble finding his way to a National Airlines hangar. In fact, a New York City police officer drove him to the building.

When the car stopped, Cold said, "Thanks, Officer."

"Yeah, sure. Not gonna need a ride back to the terminal?"

"No, thanks, I'm good."

Cold opened the passenger door, and stepped out of the vehicle into a biting wind whipping across Idlewild Airport in Queens.

He shut the car door, and pulled his brown fedora further down on his head so it wouldn't blow away. He then shoved his hands into his overcoat's pockets, and strode with alacrity to a door, which opened into the large hangar.

When he stepped inside, Cold was surprised to find no planes. A group of three men across the open space seated around a desk turned their heads. Each wore blue mechanic jumpsuits.

Cold moved in their direction, and one of the men casually walked toward him. As they met in the middle of the empty building, the mechanic asked, "Can I help you, buddy?"

"I hope so." Cold pulled out his Secret Service ID and added, "I'm looking for Cameron Jefferson."

The man squinted at Cold's badge. "Secret Service. I hope he's not in any trouble," he commented with a wry smile.

"Absolutely not. I served with him. We're old friends."

The man shrugged in response. "The boss is in his office." He pointed to a room at the back of the hangar.

"Thanks," said Cold. He turned, walked in that direction, and knocked on the door.

A voice from inside called out, "Come in."

Cold opened the door, and there was his fellow OSS officer from the war, sitting at a desk. The man's head was down, and he was writing.

Cold said, "Hey, are you still writing in those journals?"

Cameron Jefferson's head popped up. He smiled and said, "Dean, what the hell are you doing here?"

The six-foot, slim black man stood up, and moved around his desk.

"Cam, it's good to see you."

"You, too, Keys."

The two embraced and slapped each other on the back.

"Throw your coat and hat over there, and grab a seat," instructed Jefferson, as he returned to his office chair. "What's going on?"

Cold did as his friend requested. He pulled a chair up and said, "You first. You're the boss here?"

Jefferson nodded and said, "Damn right, and a black man, too." He winked.

"Well, you can build and fix anything, and I'm well aware of your ability to organize things. Talent wins over bigotry?"

"Sometimes."

"And what's with the facial hair? A goatee?"

Jefferson laughed. "Yeah, I've been playing some Friday and Saturday night gigs, so it helps to look the part." He spun his chair around, reached into a bag and pulled out a pair of dark sunglasses. He slipped them on, and declared, "This completes the look."

"Glad that you're still playing."

Jefferson was a trumpet player. He and Cold shared a background of both playing in their churches as kids.

As he took the glasses off, Jefferson said, "By the way, I've stopped in at your dad's church on an occasional Sunday."

"He mentioned that." The pang of guilt hit, so Cold moved on. "I'm sorry we haven't talked in a while."

"I would imagine that protecting the president can be pretty time consuming." He added, "Your father mentioned that you lost a partner, a friend. I'm sorry."

"Thanks. I appreciate it." Cold cleared his throat. "And what else is happening in your life?"

Jefferson leaned back in the chair and eyed his old friend. "There's a lady, sort of."

"Sort of?"

"Millie Foster. She sings with the band."

"And?"

Jefferson ran his hand over the goatee. "She says she loves me, but keeps warning me that marriage isn't on her agenda, at least for now."

"Worth waiting for?"

"Yeah. What about you?"

"No time."

Jefferson raised a knowing eyebrow.

Cold replied, "Actually, there's something about her, but I'll get into that later."

"Interesting."

"More than you know."

"Okay," said Jefferson, "what I know is my superior officer in the OSS has shown up at my job unannounced. And he's with the Secret Service. And he's being cagey. It's great to see you, Keys, but why are you here? If it's to catch up and have a few beers tonight, that's great. But I don't think that's the reason. Am I wrong?"

*You're not wrong.*

"I need your help."

"You got it. You know that. What's up?"

"No, this goes deep, real deep. I have a job offer."

"Really? Let's hear it."

Cold paused.

Jefferson added, "This is top secret shit, isn't it?"

Cold reverted to what he now thought of as his script. "It is. National security and all, plus I can't give you any more details unless you decide to sign up. You'd have to leave this work behind."

"And?"

Cold nodded. "And it's so top secret that if you mentioned anything about it, even the smallest detail, and even if you left the job later on, it would be considered treason."

Jefferson whistled. "A mystery job and if I say anything about it, Uncle Sam will end me. Is that what you're offering?"

Cold answered, "That's about it."

"You have a set coming in here with this. Why in the world would I say 'yes.'?"

Cold smiled. "The pay will be pretty good, especially for government work."

"Oh, well then," mocked Jefferson.

"Also, this offer isn't just from me. It's from Ike as well."

"Are you kidding me? As my father would have said, you buried the lead." Jefferson's father was an editor at *The New York Amsterdam News*, New York's oldest black-owned newspaper.

Cold replied, "Guess I did."

Cold took a deep breath, and looked his friend directly in the eyes. "During the war, I could count on you, and you could count on me. And we saved each other's ass more than a few times. This is important, and the more I've been thinking about it, the more I have come to realize that it could have implications not just for this country but perhaps the world. I need someone with your abilities, sure, but more important I need someone whom I can trust without question."

"You suck. You pulled the saved-each-other's-life card, the friend card, *and* the trust card."

"I meant it all."

Jefferson looked down for nearly a minute. "I assume it's more adventurous than keeping planes flying?"

"I can answer that: Definitely."

"I do get a bit bored here now and then."

"I'm pretty sure boredom would be kept to a minimum," declared Cold.

*He's on board.*

Jefferson looked up, and finally said, "Shit, fine. I'll do it for Ike. What the hell is this all about?"

Cold said, "Thanks."

"Yeah, yeah, I know. Again, what am I quitting this sweet job over?"

Cold went on to explain it all.

While Jefferson listened, he said nothing, but offered one of his whistles here and there. When Cold finished, Jefferson quietly said, "Again, I'm sorry about your friend."

Cold nodded.

"This is bizarre shit," commented Jefferson. "They almost offed Ike, and what's with the goo?"

"We're tasked with finding out everything."

Cold went on to answer Jefferson's questions. And at one point, he said, "I asked when I first came in if you were still writing in your journals."

"I am, but I get it. None of that during this mission."

Cold said, "No. Just the opposite. In addition to you being our expert on all things mechanical and technological, I'll need you to keep a record of what we're doing and what we find."

"You sure?"

"It's essential."

"You got it." Jefferson added, "Please tell me that you've got others lined up for this effort, and this isn't going to be some kind of Batman and Robin thing."

Cold chuckled. "No, it's not just you and me. We've got a fellow Secret Service agent, John Bartley, and an interesting scientist, Michael Strickland. He's a chemist and a physicist. He worked on the Manhattan Project. Oh, yeah, and he's a drummer and kind of quirky."

"A drummer?"

Cold nodded. "A drummer."

"All drummers are 'quirky.' But I've never met one with two PhDs." He shook his head. "Shit, are you putting together a team to investigate whatever this is, or a jazz band?"

"Now that you say it, it seems like it might be both. The jazz thing wasn't planned."

Jefferson smiled. "Jazz rarely is. Okay. And what was your comment about earlier, when you said there was something about … 'her'?" He leaned forward at his desk. "You're going to ask Max to join this team?"

Cold paused before answering. "I can trust her, and she's brilliant. I checked it out, and she just finished her residency in Boston. After you and I are done, that's my next stop."

"And the fact that the relationship is over? That's not an issue?"

Cold stiffened his back. "I don't see why it would be."

Jefferson laughed. "Oh, you don't? Please. Who ended it?"

Cold ignored the question. "It'll be awkward at first."

Jefferson rolled his eyes.

"Besides, she'll probably say 'no.'"

"Or she'll say 'yes.'"

Cold said, "And that would be ideal."

Jefferson shook his head, and looked at his watch. "How much longer are you around for?"

"I'm only going to be able to stop in for a few minutes to say a quick hello to my dad, and then I have to head up to Boston."

"How about a quick lunch? The food is crap in the terminal."

"That's enticing. Sure. By the way, if you can do whatever's necessary to wrap things up here over the next few days, I'll call you over the weekend with the logistics."

# Chapter 17

Dean Cold pulled his red 1951 Studebaker Champion into the small parking lot at St. Mark's Lutheran Church on Monroe Street in Brooklyn's Bedford-Stuyvesant neighborhood.

*Home.*

His father had been the pastor at the church for the past 35 years, and the family's brick home – the church's parsonage – was right across the street.

Cold hadn't called ahead. He knew, though, that on a Thursday afternoon, barring a unique situation that might call him away for a parishioner, his father would be in his church office putting final touches on the Sunday sermon.

As he got out of the car and walked around to the front of the building, he gazed up at the stone church with its arched, stained glass windows along the side, and above the main doors, a large, round window featuring a winged lion symbolizing St. Mark. A tower reached into the sky topped by a cross. He turned and looked across the road at the modest three-bedroom house where he had grown up.

Until he had his own family, Cold reflected that this place would be home.

*Probably always home to some degree.*

Since leaving for college, he had lived in the dorms and an apartment at Harvard, then came to Washington, D.C., where, since just before the war, he had lived in three different apartments. Each felt like he was a guest. Indeed, that was Washington itself. Cold often reflected that unless you had grown up in that city, or planned to make government your career, it otherwise was a transient place.

People came for a time, and then left – often disillusioned by the experience of government and politics.

There was none of that with this home and St. Mark's. Cold considered this his foundation. Even when his mother passed away, he was comforted by what he had been immersed in, everything he had learned and loved.

*A joyful hope. A joyful certainty.*

His mind suddenly felt uneasy with that word "certainty." He pushed it aside, and thoughts went to missing his mother. Even during this absence from church, Cold found solace in knowing that they would be reunited. Again, uneasiness pushed back. But that strangely was mixed with the question that had nagged at his conscience since the end of the war.

*Did I make the right choice?* He looked up at the cross in the sky.

He ascended the front steps of St. Mark's, took his hat off, and entered. He felt warm, not just getting out of the March wind but, once more, because of a feeling of familiarity and comfort.

His father's office was just to the right. The door was closed. Cold decided to enter the nave before visiting his father.

He walked down the center aisle of the neo-Gothic interior. The dark, heavy pews and altar rail contrasted with the sunshine allowed in through the stained glass windows, as well as lights shining on the altar. His eyes went from a carving of the Last Supper at the base of the altar up to a crucifix on the wall just above the altar. His gaze rose still higher to a massive statue of a risen Jesus holding his hands in the air in a blessing. To the right of the altar were stairs leading up to a pulpit with a winged lion, once more, symbolizing St. Mark, staring out at the congregation. And to the left was a lectern for the readings of the day and announcements.

Cold knew it all intimately, from running around as a small child to serving as a reader and an acolyte. And up in the choir loft at the rear of the space, under the large round stained glass window, was the pipe organ, which he had played countless times. Looking up, he simply felt the urge to play what he had come to think of as his organ.

He quietly ascended the stairs to the loft, and sat down at the Wicks organ.

Cold didn't think about it. He simply started playing what came naturally – "Crown Him with Many Crowns." It was his mother's favorite hymn.

After the first stanza, tears rolled down his cheeks.

That was the case for Pastor Gary Cold as well, who, at the sound of the organ, emerged from his office and climbed the choir loft stairs. He stopped at seeing his son at the organ. The tears had quickly formed in his eyes.

When Dean finished, he didn't turn around, but he knew his father was behind him. "I hope you didn't mind, Dad."

His father wiped away tears. "Mind? How could I possibly mind that you're here, seated at your organ, and playing the hymn that your mother never tired of hearing you play?"

Dean turned, and when his father saw the tears in his son's eyes, he resumed crying as well. "Welcome home, Dean. It's so good to see you."

"You, too, Dad."

They embraced.

Gary stepped back and observed, "You know, your mother would be rolling her eyes if she saw the two of us bawling like this."

"I don't know about that, Dad."

He nodded. "You're right, of course. She'd be crying with us." Gary took a deep breath and said, "Come on down to the office."

The two sat down at a small table in Gary's office. His desk and jam-packed bookcases also populated the office.

Gary asked, "So, why are you in town, and are you able to stay for a few days?"

"It's work, and unfortunately, I can't. I actually have to get back on the road in a few minutes. I'm heading up to Boston."

"That's too bad. I'm glad that you were able to carve out a little time to stop in."

"I know we cover a lot on the telephone, but you look good. Everything alright here at church and at the house?"

Dean appreciated being updated on parishioners he had known growing up, as well as some new people who had joined the church. He was glad to see that his father hadn't lost a step – or at least not many – in his work at St. Mark's and in the local community.

"If I never said it before, Dad, you amaze me with all you've done and continue to do." He could see that the compliment made his father feel a bit awkward.

Gary waved his hand, and said, "All by and through Him." He paused, and added, "You know, Dean, I'm proud of the man you are and the work you're doing for your country. Whatever each of us is doing, it's our calling, our vocation."

Dean knew that this was his father's attempt to say it was okay that he went the Secret Service path rather than becoming a pastor. "Thanks."

They talked more about his sister and her family, the Dodgers' upcoming season, and some details on the house.

Cold reluctantly looked at his watch, and said, "Unfortunately, I have to get on the road."

"I understand."

They stood up and hugged.

Gary added, "I'm so glad you were able to stop in."

"Me, too."

"If you need anything."

"I know, Dad, I'll let you know. Thanks."

As Dean left the church and looked across at his house, the slight pull not to leave lurked. That was something from the past, but no doubt a wonderful statement about that past – with his family, in his home, and in this church.

# Chapter 18

"Is everything secure?" asked Joseph Stalin.

He was in his personal study at Kuntsevo Dacha with Arkadi Sokolov, head of the MGB, Minister of War Arseni Demyan, and Dr. Oleg Abramov.

Stalin was at his desk, while the other three were seated at a table.

Sokolov declared, "Everyone has been removed from the building, and my men guard each way in and out."

Stalin nodded. To the right of his desk on the wall was his portrait. Stalin clicked a latch behind the bottom left of the frame. With the latch detached, the picture swung like a door revealing a wall safe. Stalin sped through the combination, and opened the safe door. He reached in and pulled out a case and placed it on the table. He entered another combination, and the case opened to reveal a rectangular device, along with a speaker, microphone, and a small square box. Stalin proceeded to set up the device and then sat at the table as well.

The four men waited, and then a gentle beep sounded over and over again. Stalin reached out and tapped a key on the device's keyboard, and a voice came over the speaker. "Are all four present?"

This was a scheduled contact, and with their group now expanded to four individuals.

"Yes, Commander," replied Stalin. "The situation is secure."

Commander One declared, "First, your execution has been excellent so far. I don't think any of the command team dreamed that we would be able to effectively seize control of the Soviet Union with such efficiency. But you have served flawlessly as Defenders."

Each man at the table said, "Thank you, Commander."

Sokolov added, "Of course, it was the planning and strategy that made this possible, sir. We simply serve the mission as trained."

Each man at the table then offered reports on the part of the plan that they were responsible for overseeing.

When completed, Commander One said, "This all confirms that we are ready to take the next step. You have everything needed to do so?"

Stalin responded, "Now that we have Demyan at the head of the military, yes, we are ready."

Sokolov added, "The work is nearing completion."

Commander One demanded, "It is. And there are no leaks or problems. Do you foresee any?"

Demyan replied, "I cannot imagine any, sir. The combination of this being a project under control of Sokolov's MGB, the military now being brought in, and the clear advantage this will provide over the West, the challenge will be controlling the joy that stems from our success."

That drew smiles from the others at the table.

Stalin added, "For good measure, once the transformations are complete, then any nonessential personnel will be dealt with."

Additional aspects of the plan were discussed. Commander One's voice softened ever so slightly. "Rest assured, each of your former bodies is being monitored, and everything is functioning perfectly normal. You stand ready to lead for a long period."

Each man at the table smiled once more, and expressed his thanks.

The normal sternness in Commander One's voice quickly returned. "Of course, that is as long as you continue to execute our plans and deal appropriately with challenges that inevitably will emerge."

Smiles faded, with each man responding, "Yes, sir."

Stalin added, "We are fully committed, Commander One, to all of the Command officers and the mission. Have no doubts about that, sir."

"I don't. The next time we speak, I trust you will have more good news, and I should have some reports for you from the Defenders in the United States."

# Chapter 19

The drive from New York City to Boston turned into an extended period of debate in Dean Cold's mind.

A kind of defeatism would first take hold.

*Why in the world would Max go along with this? I'm going to need a Plan B for a medical doctor after this trip is over. But who could you trust and who would have her...* - he struggled for the right word – *... openness?*

But hope would push back.

*She always told me, "This is the way that I can best help people." Maybe she'll see I'm sincere in telling her that this work will make a difference in countless lives.*

The end of their relationship would interject.

*Would she trust you? Does she have a reason to trust you? After all, you let the relationship die. You couldn't see how it would work, so you let it go. Then again, so did she.*

And then came the berating for the doubt and for self-indulgence.

*What the hell is wrong with you? Why would you doubt her compassion and professionalism? She's stronger than you in many ways, and she's a patriot as much as you are.*

And then more doubts and questions.

*Not being able to tell her would mean that she would have to have faith, to have trust, in you.*

The point-counterpoint raged on until he parked in front of a small pub around the block from her brownstone on Beacon Hill. He turned off the Studebaker, and looked at his watch. It was just about 9:30 pm.

*Long drive. Long day.*

He fought off the lurking exhaustion.

*Probably too late, but give her a call. If she can't meet tonight, then hopefully some time tomorrow – if she agrees to see you at all.*

He regretted that last thought. Cold knew that Wanda Maxine Marshall would see him. She was too gracious, and they had too much history not to do so. He took a deep breath, and got out of the car. Cold entered the pub, and asked the bartender, who was reading a book, where the telephone booth was. The man pointed toward the back of the establishment – just beyond the end of the bar.

He pushed the door of the booth open, stepped inside, and closed the door as he sat down. Since he had thought of Max for the team, he had memorized her address and telephone number. A nervous anticipation grew as the telephone rang on the other end.

"Hello."

Cold actually smiled slightly at the sound of her voice.

"Hi, Max. It's Dean."

After a pause of a couple of seconds, Marshall replied, "Dean. This is a surprise." She quickly added, "But a nice one. How are you? Is everything alright?"

*"Nice one"?*

"Everything is fine with me. Thanks. How about you?"

"Good. I finished my residency," Marshall announced.

He recognized the excitement in her voice. "Congratulations. That's great. I always knew you'd get it done."

"Thanks."

"Listen, I'm in town…"

"Really? Where are you?"

"Well, I'm actually at a payphone in a pub around the block from your brownstone."

"What? At Murphy's?"

"Yeah, that's the name of the place."

Marshall went silent for a couple of seconds, and then asked, "Dean, what's going on?"

"Max, I want to tell you everything. That's why I'm here. Or, one of the reasons I'm here, to be honest. Can we meet?"

"Tonight?"

"Tonight or early tomorrow, perhaps? Whichever works for you?"

Cold wondered about the additional silence.

Marshall finally said, "I'll meet you there. Give me 20 minutes."

"Great."

After the call ended, Cold looked at the bartender and said, "Someone's meeting me in a few minutes. Mind if I wait until she gets here before ordering?"

The bartender looked up from his book. "Yeah, sure, buddy. Grab a seat wherever you want. Not exactly busy tonight."

There was one other person in the pub. He was sitting at the bar, a few steps from the front door. Cold grabbed the booth at the other end of the narrow establishment. He sat and felt his nervousness growing. Cold wasn't used to this feeling.

Nearly 20 minutes to the second from when their call ended, the door opened and in walked Dr. Wanda Maxine Marshall.

Cold swallowed. She appeared even more beautiful than he had remembered. Marshall's blonde hair was now cut shoulder-length, shorter than the last time they had seen each other. Her head turned as her large blue eyes, behind horn-rimmed glasses, scanned the room. Her gaze stopped when she spotted Cold at the back of the room.

As he got up from the bench, the bartender said to Marshall, "Hey, Doc. How are ya?"

"I'm doing well, Tommy."

"What can I get ya?"

"Two usuals – one for me and one for my friend."

Tommy smiled. "Sure. He's with ya, huh?"

As Cold approached, Marshall smiled warmly. While looking at Cold, she answered, "He is."

Cold said, "It's good to see you, Max."

"You too, Dean." She surprised Cold by adding, "The round is on me. I'll bring the drinks over."

"Uh, okay, thanks." Cold went back to the booth. As he walked, a familiar feeling had returned. Maxine Marshall was one of the very few people who could put him just a tad off balance. Cold had forgotten how much he appreciated that.

*Is this a good idea?*

The bartender apparently was listening to the instruction given by Marshall to Cold, and wore a broad grin as he finished pouring two beers from the tap.

Cold stood by the booth. Marshall deposited two mugs on the table. She was an athletic five feet, nine inches. She sat down, and Cold took the other bench across the table.

He said, "Thanks."

"You're welcome. You look good."

"So do you. Are you still playing tennis?"

She shrugged. "A little. I haven't had much time for it, unfortunately."

They each took a sip from their respective mugs.

Cold asked, "What are we drinking? Still insist on whatever's local?"

She nodded. "Haffenreffer Lager."

Cold sat back, looked her directly in the eyes and declared, "You're a doctor."

"I know," she replied with a grin.

"Like I said earlier, that's great.. I never doubted that you'd do it."

"And you're a Secret Service agent doing who knows what."

"I am."

*Will you know what I'm doing shortly or not?*

They drank, again.

Marshall said, "I'm glad you called. You know, I owe you a big 'thank you' and an apology."

Cold was surprised. "How so?"

"When we were ... together, you kept me grounded. I was on my way to leaving the Church, but your faith affected me."

Guilt hit Cold again, but this time it was harder.

Marshall continued, "Thanks for that."

Cold managed a nod, adding, "The Holy Spirit."

"And like I said, I owe you an apology."

Cold could see how uncomfortable Marshall suddenly was. He was about to say something, but she persisted, "I was selfish. I so wanted to become a doctor that I assumed that doing that meant a relationship, our relationship, just wasn't possible."

Cold had a lump in his throat. "I didn't try to convince you otherwise, and I never reached out. I'm sorry for that. I regret it."

They both took a drink of their Haffenreffers.

Marshall said, "Regrets to go around, I suppose."

Cold was conflicted as to what to say next. Part of him wanted to see if she was interested in starting up the relationship once more. He now admitted to himself something that he had been pushing to the back of his head. He acknowledged that some part of his reason for approaching Marshall to become a part of this effort was the possibility that they might get back together.

*And what do I do with this?*

The other part of his brain reflected that going down that path, or even broaching it with her, would be unwise given the work at hand.

Marshall declared, "Look at the two of us now, though. A Secret Service agent and a doctor. Not bad, I suppose, but it does sound like the start of a joke."

"Not bad." He resigned himself to the mission, but comforted himself that if she agreed, then they might have a chance somewhere down the road. Cold looked at the bartender and customer.

*They're far enough away.*

He lowered his voice and leaned in closer. "That combination – my work with the Secret Service and you being a doctor now – is the reason why I contacted you."

Marshall stared at him, and Cold couldn't read her look.

He pressed on, believing that he would revert to his script – at least as much as he could with her. "I need you. Your country needs you."

She interrupted and matched his whispering. "Which is it – you or America?"

*Okay. That question and my full, honest answer run deep.*

He acknowledged, "Both."

Her expression softened. "How can I help?" She now leaned in as well.

"Unfortunately, it's not that easy. I have a job offer."

"A what?"

Cold took a deep breath. "I'm offering you a position that not only has national security implications for Americans, but this could be something that affects the entire world. It's top secret, and if you were to take the position, you would have to leave your current work behind."

He paused, while Marshall looked at him.

*Tell her the rest.*

"Max, you need to understand what I mean when I say, 'top secret.' You not only can't say anything about what you would be doing now, but effectively for the rest of your life. And if you were to say anything at all, the consequences would be severe and grave."

Marshall still said nothing, but while listening, she had straightened her back and lowered her hands into her lap.

*And now for the kicker.* He felt oddly guilty thinking that.

Cold added, "By the way, it's not just me extending this offer. It also comes from the president of the United States." He paused, and then went on, "This work is important, and we need, I need, a doctor with intelligence, imagination and compassion. And I know that I can trust you, and I hope you know that you can trust me."

He stopped talking and drank from his beer.

Marshall finally said, "You and President Eisenhower. Well..." She took a sip of her beer. "I do trust you, Dean. But I also have a lot of questions."

"I know, but I can't answer most of them unless you commit to this. It's not fair, but it has to be that way."

"You want me to upend everything I've worked for – for what? For you? For the president? For the country?" Her tone wasn't accusatory. It reflected a struggle to comprehend what was being presented.

Cold answered simply, "Yes."

"You know how bizarre this all is, right?"

"I do."

Marshall didn't say anything in response. She picked up the mug and finished her beer. "I'm considering this for two reasons. First, it's coming from the president. Second, it's from you."

"Thanks."

"And you can't tell me the details, but you need to know quickly." It was a statement, not a question.

"Unfortunately, yes. I have to head back to D.C. at some point tomorrow."

"Tomorrow?" Marshall stood up suddenly.

Cold was surprised, and got to his feet quickly.

She looked at Cold with what he perceived as pleading eyes.

While she slipped on her coat, Marshall asked, "You have a place to stay tonight?"

"Yes, I'm staying at the Bellevue."

"That's good," she said in a voice tinged by bewilderment. "I'll call you there in the morning."

"Sure, that will be fine. Are you alright?"

Marshall smiled faintly at him. "I'm not sure, Dean." She paused and took in a breath. "No, of course, I'm not. You've thrown me for a loop. I have to go."

"I'm sorry, Max. But when I realized that it made sense to have a doctor on board, you were the person I thought of. Plus..." He hesitated. "Plus, I needed to see you. It was too long."

"I'm glad to see you as well, even though you're intent on upending up my life."

"Max, please don't say that. That isn't why I've come to you."

Marshall softened. "I know, Dean." She reached out and touched his arm, and then added, "Good night."

Marshall turned and started to walk away.

Cold said, "Good night, Max."

As she walked past the bar, the bartender said, "Night, Doctor Marshall."

"Good night, Tommy."

# Chapter 20

The hotel telephone rang just before 7 am.

Cold was already awake, staring at the ceiling. His mind had picked up where it left off the night before. He thought about this mission, from the death of Stant to Ike and Dulles to the unexplained. He was still struggling to wrap his mind around mechanisms attached to the base of brains that turn into goo. And then there was the group he now was assembling to figure this all out.

Cold deeply appreciated that Bartley, Strickland and Jefferson had signed up. He trusted each man. Well, he knew that he trusted Bartley and Jefferson, and felt like he could trust Strickland. In turn, their willingness to sign up, based in part on his word that this was a gravely important undertaking, was a sign of reciprocal trust.

*Well, yeah, there's Eisenhower, too. And what about Max?*

As he went over their history and discussion last night, the telephone's ringing almost made him jump.

He rose from the bed, walked across the small room and picked up the receiver. "Hello."

"Are you up?" asked Maxine Marshall.

"I am. And you?"

"I'm downstairs in the lobby."

"Well, alright..."

"We need to talk, but I was called into the hospital. I have less than an hour."

Cold replied, "Give me ten minutes to shower and dress, and come up to my room." He told her the number. "Does that work okay?"

"Sure. Ten minutes."

Cold hung up, showered, and partially put on his suit –
gray pants, black wingtips, and a white button-down shirt.
With the knock at the door, the tie and jacket would have to
wait.

Cold opened the door, and was reminded that seeing her
at the start of any day gave him pause. She was dressed
smartly, befitting a doctor, with a blue-and-white checked
jacket over a red vest and a matching red skirt. But the
formality of the look certainly didn't diminish her beauty,
Cold reflected. "Good morning."

"Morning." With a sly smile, Marshall asked, "Are you
going to invite me into your hotel room, Mr. Cold?"

"Oh, yes, sorry. Please come in."

Cold took the wool coat that Marshall carried, and invited
her to sit down in the armchair in the corner of the room. He
sat in the chair that accompanied the small desk, looked at
her and said, "What questions do you have?"

"Correct me if I'm wrong, but I don't think you'll be able
to answer the long list of questions that I have until I give
you an answer."

Cold nodded. "That's true, unfortunately."

"Your call came at an opportune time for me to consider
this. I've just finished my residency, and been thinking more
deeply about the direction I want my life as a doctor to take.
Not just in terms of where and exactly what I would be
practicing, but also my full life. This pursuit has been far
lonelier than I had anticipated."

Cold responded, "I imagine that it's been hard, especially
for a woman. I also understand the feeling of being on your
own."

They stared at each other for a few seconds, and then
Marshall said, "I do appreciate that you still think highly
enough of me to ask me to do this. I also know that you don't
overstate things. And Dean, I do trust you. And of course, I
can't ignore the fact that President Eisenhower is behind
this invitation." She paused. "But there's also the unknown
of this, and the potential danger. Other than trying to figure
out difficult medical cases and doing research that hopefully
would help people, I've never actually thought of getting into

the kind of unknowns that you might be more familiar with. And the idea of, as you put it last night, 'grave consequences,' definitely never entered into my thinking."

*She's saying "no"?*

Cold started, "Max, I know..."

She interrupted, "Please, let me finish."

"Yes, of course."

Marshall declared, "In the end, though, your ... efforts apparently need a medical person to be involved. And as I wrestled with this throughout the night, I came to realize that this might be the way that I can best help people. But it's kind of a leap of faith."

"It is."

"You know about that. Again, you were the one who kept reminding me of my faith, and given your family and the fact that you almost followed in your father's footsteps, I'm willing to take this leap with you, Dean."

"That's fantastic, Max."

He felt a surge of joy and stood up. She tentatively followed his lead. They shared a hug, as Cold said, "Thank you."

The embrace was short-lived, and each stepped back awkwardly.

Marshall looked at the thin watch on her wrist. "I'm guessing that what you're now ready to tell me is going to take a heck of a lot more time than what I have."

Cold admitted, "I'm not sure that you'll want an outline to only head off to the hospital. You're bound to have lots of questions."

"Okay, I understand. Before I leave, at least tell me how many of us are there?"

"Now, there are five, and I have one more person to contact. By the way, Cameron Jefferson is on board."

Marshall smiled. "Cam, that's good news." She eyed him closer, "And it makes sense that you'd invite him. Alright, let me go on that happy note." She slipped past him and walked to the door. She turned and said, "You'll apparently have to stay in town until tonight."

Cold agreed, "Apparently."

"As long as things don't go awry at work, come by my place at nine. I'll whip up a late dinner, and we can talk. Does that work for you?"

"It does. Thanks, Max."

"I hope I don't regret this, Dean." She opened the door and left.

*No more regrets? Hopefully.*

# Chapter 21

When Dean Cold arrived at the Beacon Hill brownstone of Maxine Marshall, an awkwardness lingered between the two – or at least that's what Cold felt.

After initial pleasantries, Marshall invited Cold into the kitchen, where she already had started preparing dinner.

"I poured myself a glass of Chablis, would you like a glass, or something else?" she asked.

As Marshall checked on dinner, Cold replied, "Wine would be good. You're busy, I'll pour it."

"Thanks. I don't want the cod to go too long, or it'll be ruined."

Cold knew that Marshall enjoyed cooking, and that she had picked up real culinary expertise while doing some international travel with her parents. Cold had gotten into Harvard on his smarts and a scholarship. Marshall had done so on her intelligence as well, along with her family's ample wealth.

While Marshall finished pulling together the baked cod, the two had a chance to catch up on more details about their lives, families, and mutual friends.

Cold also commented, "This is a beautiful home, by the way."

"Thanks. Mom and Dad helped out with part of the down payment. But I really have grown to like Boston, so I took the plunge and bought it about a year ago." She paused, turned from the stove to look at him. "It gives me some sense of roots, of home."

Cold thought she was going to say more, but she turned back to preparing dinner.

A few moments later, the two were seated across from each other at the dining room table with plates of baked cod topped by crushed Ritz crackers, accompanied by roasted potatoes and broccoli. The glasses of Chablis were refilled.

She asked, "Dean, would you like to say grace?"

For some reason, he was surprised, but said, "Yes, of course." He quickly reflected on and chastised himself for the length of time since he had engaged in daily prayer.

They blessed themselves, bowed their heads and folded their hands.

"Dear Lord, thank you for this meal and all that you have provided, and for dear friends who have not seen each other in too long. Bless the work that lies ahead of us. Give us the strength and clarity to do what's right, and most of all, keep us strong in our faith in you. In Jesus' name we pray, Amen."

Marshall echoed the "Amen."

Cold said, "Thanks for making dinner, Max."

She smiled, and replied, "Try it, first, before you thank me."

They both took a forkful, chewed and swallowed.

"As always," Cold commented, "you've outdone yourself. The cod is perfect, and I love when it's topped with the crackers. My mom made it this way."

"So did mine. Well, the 'Mom' seal of approval. Thank you."

"And it's very Boston."

After a couple of more mouthfuls and sips of wine, Marshall said, "Alright, let's hear it. What have I agreed to join?"

Cold again thought about how odd it was to hear four people now ask him to reveal the details behind a decision they had made based on nothing more than an invitation from Ike and himself.

*Don't get carried away with yourself.*

He started with the death of Andrew Stanton in the Oval Office, and proceeded to go through the details of everything since, including the backgrounds on John Bartley, Michael Strickland and Cameron Jefferson.

Throughout, Marshall listened and ate. Even when Cold paused to take bites of food, she simply waited to hear more.

When Cold thought that he had exhausted all of the information, he declared, "That's all of it." He moved to finish what remained on his plate, waiting for her to finally respond.

"I have no idea what to do with this." She looked directly at Cold. "What I mean is, at this point, what you just told me defies logical explanation."

"Yeah, I know. And hearing the initial reactions from you and Dr. Strickland, ramps up my ... concerns .. regarding what this is all about."

The conversation continued while the two cleaned the table, washed the dishes, made coffee, and then sat in the large living room. Marshall focused her inquiries on the neck devices attached to the two White House assailants, and the details of what the CIA spy had seen regarding Stalin.

As the questions came to an end, Marshall asked, "What's next?"

Cold answered, "Right now, I could use one more cup of coffee, and then I have to get on the road back to D.C."

"At this time of night?"

Cold nodded. "I'll drive through the night."

Marshall swallowed. "That's crazy. You can stay here for the night, and then get on the road fresh in the morning."

"Thanks for the offer, Max. I appreciate it. But I need to get back to Washington, and finish setting things up for your arrival, as well as for Cam and Mike."

"Oh, right." She smiled faintly and looked around the room. "I'm going to see if someone at work wants to lease this place while I'm gone." She looked back at Cold, "I'd ask how long you think this will take, but I know you don't have an answer."

"Unfortunately," Cold acknowledged.

She straightened up in her chair, and added, "Not to worry. I know at least three doctors who would take the place."

Cold wasn't sure exactly how to react. "That's good. Again, I can't tell you how much I appreciate that you're doing this."

"As you said, figuring this out is vital. I won't get into the crazy possibilities that have been running through my mind. This group you're putting together will get to the bottom of this."

Cold responded, "We will. And by the way, when you come down to D.C., I'm going to explain to all that we need to share everything on this, and that includes ideas that might seem crazy. What I've seen and heard so far means that nothing can be ruled out."

Cold rose from his chair, and Marshall did the same.

She observed, "From where we are now, we're bound to be surprised by the answers. The question is: Just how surprised?"

Cold agreed, and as they walked to the door, he asked her to move as quickly as possible on getting down to D.C.

Stopping at the front door, Marshall stood straighter, gave him a mock salute, and said, "Yes, sir."

Marshall handed him his coat and hat. After he put them on, Cold paused and then said, "Thanks, Max. This is all strange and troubling, but the bright spot is seeing you again and being able to work together."

Marshall replied, "I feel the same way, Dean."

They exchanged a quick hug, and Dean stepped into the cold night air.

Before getting on the road to D.C., he stopped at a gas station, filled up the tank in his Studebaker, and stepped into a telephone booth.

# Chapter 22

After the long drive from Boston to Washington, D.C., Dean Cold was in his apartment for just about a minute when the telephone rang. It was the White House. President Eisenhower was requesting his presence in two hours.

Cold took a cold shower, and slipped on a clean shirt and suit. He ate some buttered toast, downed two cups of hot coffee, scanned the newspaper, and then was back in his Studebaker, heading to 1600 Pennsylvania Avenue NW.

When the president's secretary indicated that it was time for him to enter, Cold opened the door to the Oval Office himself this time. The president was the only person in the room, with his head down reading and signing documents. "Thanks for coming in so quickly, Dean."

"Of course, Mr. President."

"Grab a seat." Eisenhower indicated that Cold should claim a chair across the desk from him. "Just give me a minute."

Cold sat down and waited.

When Ike finished signing his name, he closed the folder in front of him, and leaned back in his chair. "So, how have your invitations been received?"

"So far, each person I've talked to is on board – John Bartley, Cameron Jefferson, Dr. Strickland, and Dr. Marshall."

"Four for four. Stan Musial would be jealous."

Cold smiled, and replied, "Or Duke Snider."

Ike nodded. "Right, you're a Dodgers fan."

Cold took the opportunity to ask a question that had been knocking around his head since he started on Eisenhower's Secret Service detail. "Mr. President, I know this is way off topic, but I have to at least ask. Did you play minor league ball?"

Eisenhower eyed Cold closely. "I said I trusted you, Dean. And if I can trust you with this investigation, then I know you'll not spread this. Yes, in 1911, I played centerfield for the Junction City Soldiers. I needed some cash before heading off to West Point, so, for three months, I played under an assumed name. Mr. Wilson hit .355."

The pride Eisenhower took in that last statement was evident to Cold. "Mr. Wilson's secret is safe with me, sir."

"I called you in to give you these." He pulled open a desk drawer, and grabbed two sets of keys. Ike extended them to Cold.

With a look of bewilderment, Cold took them and asked, "What are these for, sir?"

"Director Dulles made two acquisitions. One of the CIA's fronts purchased your townhouse and the one next door. These can serve as a base of operations, as well as apartments for your people."

"That's ideal, sir. Thank you."

Ike merely said, "Thank Allen."

"I will." He added, "When can we take control over the two buildings?"

"Allen tells me right now. The transactions are completed, and everyone has moved out – been moved out. Outside of your apartment, of course."

"The timing on this is perfect. I've asked each person to move quickly in wrapping up their current positions." He paused and then added, "By the way, sir, there's no doubt that mentioning that you were the one extending these invitations made the difference."

Eisenhower declared, "It made *a* difference, Dean. I'm not so sure it made *the* difference. I appreciate your generosity, but I've found that trust in the person doing the asking, who will stand next to someone through the challenges and risks, makes *the* difference in the end."

Cold wasn't sure how to respond to that. He finally asked, "Is there anything else, sir?"

Eisenhower took a deep breath, and said, "I just want to make sure that you're not limiting this investigation in any way?"

"Sir?"

"I try not to let my imagination run away with possibilities here. But I also learned in the military, as well as in politics, to be ready for anything, including, as best you can, the unexpected. As you said before, Dean, this could get weird."

Cold admitted, "I've been thinking the same thing, Mr. President. I'm open to wherever the facts lead us, and I've made sure that each person who is part of this effort understands that they must be as well. And I'll make that point clear with the final person being considered for the team."

# Chapter 23

Each man had arrived on Capitol Hill at the end of the war. And since then, barring personal or political interruptions, every other Monday night was a time for three friends – to the extent that each was capable of friendship – to gather over drinks. The time was spent gossiping about the exploits of assorted politicians, and perhaps kicking around a few ideas.

These gatherings also turned out to be the only real constants in each man's life.

Clay Walsh was a lone wolf. Unlike his boss, the new junior senator from Massachusetts, John F. Kennedy, who could charm and engage all kinds of people, Walsh barely hid his lack of patience for those he deemed wrong, beneath him, or usually both. His look – tall, gaunt, early baldness and round glasses with thick frames and lenses, along with tweed, three-piece suits and a pipe – reinforced an air of aloofness.

Meanwhile, Jerome "Jerry" Debrowski had a quick political mind, much quicker than his boss – Senator Joseph McCarthy from Wisconsin. After all, Debrowski knew when to stop drinking, and preferred hard numbers over wild speculation. He also had the look of a political fighter, more often than not with tie askew, suit jacket off, and shirt sleeves rolled up. His red hair also tended to be a bit out of control.

Finally, Ken Roberts often dominated any room that he was in, not due to his personality or intellect necessarily. Instead, he was large – an obese man with thinning brown hair, a wide nose, and squinting eyes. He also possessed an oddly high voice.

Roberts was the only one of the three who married, though he was now divorced. Debrowski never had time for a wife and family, while Walsh decided that no woman could measure up to him.

Behind the closed door of Walsh's office in the Senate Office Building, he and Debrowski sat quietly at a table opposite a desk. With a knock at the door, each man picked up the glass of whisky resting in front of him. Walsh called out, "Yes."

The door opened, and in stepped Roberts.

Debrowski declared, "You're late, Ken."

Roberts closed the door and zeroed in on the drink waiting for him on the table. He dropped his substantial girth in a chair, and downed the brown liquid.

"My, my, Ken," said Walsh. As he unscrewed the bottle, he asked, "Another?"

"Yes, definitely."

Walsh asked, "Something interesting at the CIA, perhaps?"

"Yeah, you could say that."

Walsh smiled wryly. "Do tell."

"Yeah, let's hear it," added Debrowski.

Roberts sat back, with the chair creaking from the stress. When it came to these Monday night meetings, Roberts long ago put aside his oath of secrecy. But he hesitated, looking back and forth at the two men staring at him. He finally said, "Alright, I'd like to hear your takes."

Walsh and Debrowski shared a passing glance.

Roberts asked Walsh, "Are you sure no one's around, that they've all left?"

"This is government, Ken. No one's staying late unless forced to do so. And that's not the case today."

Roberts took a drink. "Okay then..." He went on to explain that he had just heard from CIA Director Allen Dulles that a team had been put together to figure out who a couple of assailants were who got into the White House.

"Into?" asked Debrowski.

Roberts again hesitated before answering. "This goes nowhere beyond us."

"Always the rule, you know that," Debrowski assured with a note of irritation.

"Right, I know," said Roberts. "It was two guys from State. They're dead, but there were some kind of strange implants – Dulles wouldn't say more – in their necks. Dulles is focused on the MGB."

"Shit," said Walsh.

Debrowski asked, "Who's handling this?"

"Unusual group. I've been running background checks." He left it there for the moment.

The conversation dragged on, filled with what seemed to be baseless speculation.

Walsh got up, and walked over to his desk chair. He opened a drawer and withdrew a pipe. He filled it with tobacco, tamped it down and lit a match. After puffing on the pipe a couple of times, he took it out of his mouth and pointed it at Debrowski. "Do us a favor, Jerry, don't mention this to your boss, otherwise he'll be adding to his tally of Reds in the State Department." He chuckled at his own joke.

"Funny, Clay," replied Debrowski.

They kicked things around further. Beginning to feel more comfortable with the conversation and saying that he wanted to know if Walsh or Debrowski had any information, Roberts offered up what he knew about each member of the Dulles team.

# Chapter 24

Dean Cold had been in the CIA's headquarters at 2430 E St. NW in Washington, D.C., many times, but that was when it housed the Office of Strategic Services during the war. Indeed, he considered the building to be his home base during the war for the short stints when he wasn't in Europe.

It was early on a Tuesday morning when he drove into the complex, parked his car, and walked through the front doors of the columned building. He was headed to Director Allen Dulles' office. It was the same office used by William Donovan when he had led the OSS.

Dulles was waiting with a top aide, Ken Roberts. Dulles and Roberts rose from their respective seats – Dulles with far greater ease than Roberts – and exchanged perfunctory greetings with Cold. These were followed by Dulles nodding to Roberts, who waddled over to a second door at the back of the office. Cold knew that the backrooms beyond the door were used to shuttle people in and out who weren't supposed to be there – at least that was the case under Donovan. He now knew that it served the same purpose with Dulles, as Roberts opened the door, and in came the person he was there to see.

Cold thought that Daria Popov was beautiful. While she was petite, there was something else about her. Her freckles, short blonde hair, and round gray-blue eyes gave her a girl-next-door quality. But her body language, and a tight-fitting, brown sweater, matched by tan pants and shoes, made her seem formidable. Cold thought that there was something both innocent and vaguely dangerous about her.

Dulles said, "Agent Dean Cold, this is Daria Popov."

Cold extended his hand, and said, "It's nice to meet you, Miss Popov." He noted, as no doubt did Dulles and Roberts, that she didn't immediately reach out and clasp his hand.

*Apparently, she's evaluating me as well.*

She replied, "It is nice to meet you as well, Agent Cold." Her voice carried just the trace of a Russian accent. The two shook hands.

Cold turned and looked at Dulles.

Dulles sat down at his desk, and said, "Everyone understands what this is about, so I thought we could all work together."

Cold didn't like the presumption, the setup, nor the fact that Roberts apparently had been read in by Dulles. His mind worked quickly on how to proceed. "Director Dulles, no offense, but the conversation I am going to have with Miss Popov requires privacy."

Dulles smiled and nodded. "Of course, it does, Agent Cold. Forgive me." He turned to Roberts, and said, "Come on, Ken, let's leave them to it."

Roberts briefly seemed confused, but acquiesced. He followed Dulles out the back door of the office.

After the door closed, Cold looked around, and pointed to the rectangular table off to the side. "Shall we?"

Popov replied, "Yes." After taking seats, she reached inside her small handbag, and pulled out a silver cigarette case. "Do you mind if I smoke?"

"I do."

She raised an eyebrow. "Pardon me?"

"I don't like the smell of tobacco. Do you mind if I ask you to wait until after our meeting?"

Popov smiled briefly. "Not at all." She returned the case to her bag.

Cold said, "I'm not sure how much Director Dulles told you..."

She interrupted, "The director has told me nothing except that you wished to talk with me."

*I doubt that. Apparently, though, some of this has been a test from Dulles. Don't like that.*

"I see. This is about a position."

"What do you mean?"

"I'm here to offer you a job, Miss Popov."

"A job? What kind of job?"

Cold answered, "This actually wouldn't be all that different from what you've been doing for the CIA…"

She cut him off. "Do you mean that I will have to sleep with people I hate?"

Cold was taken aback, sat up straighter, and stared at her for several seconds.

*She's testing me.*

He replied, "No, who you sleep with is none of my business. I mean that this work demands the greatest secrecy; and it's about the national security of the United States, but also could carry significance for the West and perhaps the world."

She sat back in the chair, crossed her legs, and declared, "That's quite a pitch, Agent Cold." Popov smiled.

"I understand that."

"I also assume that this is an offer not just from you?"

That caught Cold off guard. "Meaning?"

"This comes from Director Dulles, and perhaps even President Eisenhower?"

Cold nodded slightly.

"What else can you tell me?"

*Tested or toyed with.*

"Not much, other than a warning that if you in any way violate the secrecy of this work, during our efforts or afterward, the consequences will be grave."

She stared back for a moment, and said, "I understand what you are saying."

"Miss Popov, we don't know each other, so you have no reason to trust me."

She didn't reply.

He continued, "However, I know what you've done when faced with incredible danger, and you didn't waver. You managed to thrive, from what I could tell from your file, in very different situations. Plus, you come highly recommended from Director Dulles. I'm willing to take a leap of faith, and trust you. That's why we're having this conversation."

As she looked at him in silence, Cold now felt like she could penetrate his thinking.

Popov finally said, "We would not be having this conversation if not for the director. He not only recommended you as well, but also declared complete faith in you."

*Thank you, Mr. Dulles.*

"He also said that the work you had been assigned to do was vital to America, the West and the world." She rose from her chair, and started pacing back and forth. "You apparently have been informed about my background, Agent Cold, so you know that I have a rather lengthy list of reasons for despising the communist regime in my country."

Cold had read that her parents had been murdered by the government for so-called subversive ideas, and her siblings sent off to the gulag. Indeed, she, too, had been imprisoned, but had set out on a path to eventually get her moving amidst the Soviet leaders, and gaining their secrets. Popov maneuvered her way out of the gulag, and into Moscow. She landed a waitress job at a club frequented by some midlevel communist officials, and rather quickly found herself singing in front of a band. When he came across that information for the first time, Cold wondered what the hell a Russian jazz band might sound like. Popov parlayed that position into entertaining at high-level functions, where she caught the eye of Stalin. She wound up in his employment. And while moving from waitress to singer, Popov tapped into a dark network that she had heard would lead to contacts with the Americans. Cold admired how Popov methodically and skillfully pursued her objectives to undermine the communist government, including a willingness to make terrible personal sacrifices to do so.

Cold merely commented, "I do. And I'm impressed with what you've accomplished."

She took a deep breath, returned to her chair, and smiled, once again. "Thank you, and how could I turn down the president of the United States? Tell me more about my new position, Agent Cold."

# Chapter 25

It was early the next morning, and Maxine Marshall walked across the hospital parking lot to her blue Pontiac Chieftan.

She started the engine, nudged her glasses up on her nose, and set out on the short drive to her Beacon Hill brownstone.

Marshall had no idea that a car was following her at a discreet distance.

Almost 20 minutes later, she pulled into her usual parking spot in front of her home. The dark Chevy DeLuxe that had been tailing her, pulled into a spot about 30 yards up the street. The driver, Roy O'Keefe, a man of average build with black hair and blue eyes, was dressed in a dark overcoat and fedora. He cut the engine, and watched as Marshall exited the car, climbed the steps of the home, unlocked the front door, and disappeared inside.

It was still dark at 5:30 am.

O'Keefe scanned the area, and spotted two heads moving in a sedan parked across the street and just ten yards ahead of him. He reached inside his suit jacket and felt the handle of a Colt Commander with a suppressor attached. Staying low, he then slid across the front bench, quietly opened the passenger side door, and slipped out of the vehicle. O'Keefe silently closed the door, and squatted along the side of the car, with just his hat and eyes appearing above the hood. He remained still.

About 10 minutes later, the front doors of the sedan opened, and the driver, in a brown trench coat, and the passenger, wearing a gray overcoat, got out. They looked around, and started to move toward Marshall's brownstone.

O'Keefe watched.

Each of the two men reached inside his coat, and pulled out a handgun, also with a suppressor attached. That was the signal to move. O'Keefe pulled out his weapon, and silently moved at the others who had their backs to him.

"Hold it right there, gentlemen."

In the middle of the street, the two whirled around. Seeing the Colt pointed at them, the man in the brown trench coat froze, but the other didn't. He began to raise his weapon in response.

O'Keefe didn't hesitate. He fired off a shot, which landed in the chest of the gray-coated figure, who toppled backwards to the street.

The man in the brown coat snapped his head to his partner's now lifeless body, and then back toward the man who fired the shot.

O'Keefe ordered, "Drop the gun."

The man hesitated, but then finally tossed the weapon aside.

"Don't move a muscle," demanded O'Keefe as he went to retrieve the two guns on the pavement. He then looked around at the buildings. The suppressor apparently had muffled the shot enough that no one seemed to take notice, yet. He added, "Okay, drag your buddy over to the Chevy."

The other man didn't move.

"Now!"

The man acquiesced and dragged the body down the street. O'Keefe popped open the spacious trunk of his car. He ordered, "Get him in there."

Once more, the order was executed, as the man in the brown trench coat hoisted his dead partner into the trunk. He then looked at the man who held his fate.

"Now, you, too."

The other man started to protest, "Is this really...?"

He was cut off, as O'Keefe pointed the barrel of his gun between the other man's eyes.

"Okay, okay," came the reply, while raising his hands in a sign of submission.

"On your stomach."

The other man muttered, "Shit."

After maneuvering himself next to the dead body with his face down, he asked, "What now?"

O'Keefe didn't answer. Instead, he reached down, and proceeded to grab the collars of each prisoner's trench coat, suit jacket and shirt. He pulled down hard.

O'Keefe commented, "Nothing."

"What the hell are you talking about?" asked the prisoner who turned and looked up.

"Never mind."

Before O'Keefe could straighten up, the prisoner swung his leg up and his shoe landed hard on the CIA officer's cheek. As O'Keefe was thrown off balance, the man in the brown coat scrambled out of the trunk while withdrawing a knife strapped above one of his ankles. Leading with the blade, he lunged forward. But O'Keefe had regained his balance, and managed to grab the assailant's wrist. O'Keefe also never dropped the gun in his other hand. While deflecting the thrusting knife, O'Keefe drew the spy closer. And with their faces inches apart, O'Keefe fired three shots into the attacker. The man dropped the knife and as life drained away, O'Keefe supported him enough to push him back into the trunk. The assailant's eyes went lifeless.

O'Keefe picked up the knife, tossed it into the trunk, and closed it.

He got behind the wheel and pulled the car away from the curb. As O'Keefe turned the Chevy DeLuxe around the corner at the end of the street, no one on Beacon Hill was aware of what had happened, including Dr. Maxine Marshall. It would be a long drive to CIA headquarters in Washington, D.C.

# Chapter 26

While Roy O'Keefe was dealing with matters in Boston, Cameron Jefferson was finishing breakfast in his small, brick house in Brooklyn.

He ate the last bit of oatmeal, and drank the final slug from his cup of coffee. After washing out the bowl and cup, and placing them on the drying rack, he started walking back to his bedroom. Jefferson always ate and had coffee first in the morning, then followed by brushing his teeth, a shower, and slipping on his standard work clothes.

As he completed the brushing, rinsing and spitting, he paused and looked at himself in the mirror. He said, "Well, last day for this."

He had told his manager that this would be his last day. The man was not happy to hear this.

Jefferson reached up to undo the top button of his flannel pajamas when he froze due to a sudden noise outside. Someone or something knocked over an item on his backyard patio.

When with the OSS, Jefferson always made sure that he and others in his unit were safe during the night. Depending on where they were at the time, what he used varied. But it often meant setting up something that would make noise if anyone approached – the sound served as a signal. For some reason, Jefferson never stopped doing the same thing after returning from the war. And whether consciously or subconsciously, he set up what amounted to little obstacle courses on his back patio and front porch. If you weren't aware and moving in the dark, odds were high that something would be kicked or knocked over. The sound would be a signal.

A second signal now came from the front porch.

Jefferson whispered, "What the hell?"

He moved quickly into the bedroom, reached under the bed and slid out a box. Inside was an M1911A1 pistol. He slipped a cartridge in, and stayed on one knee bedside. With a bedroom wall at his back and the open door across the room, he steadied his gun on the bed.

He slowed his breathing, as the back door crashed open, followed by the same happening at the front.

Two men in dark hats and coats moved into the house, with guns extended in front of them.

As one stepped into the bedroom doorway, Jefferson fired off two shots and the intruder fell.

The other stopped outside the door.

Jefferson fired two more shots in the doorway, as he leaped over the bed, landed softly on the carpeted floor, and moved silently behind the door.

The second intruder fired wildly into the room as he jumped by the doorway.

Jefferson waited in silence.

Neither man moved.

The hallway floor creaked as the assailant finally took another step into the doorway.

Staying behind the door, Jefferson reached around and fired two quick shots.

The assailant grunted and fell back against the wall.

Jefferson moved around the door to see his attacker using his right hand, which held the gun, to push against the bullet wound in his left upper arm.

Their eyes met.

Jefferson's gun was trained on the man.

In futility, the assailant tried to point his weapon at Jefferson.

Jefferson pulled the trigger, and his opponent slid to the floor with a hole in the forehead.

After checking the bodies of each intruder, Jefferson went into the kitchen, put his gun down on the table, sat down and took deep breaths. He rubbed his head.

He finally rose, and picked up the receiver on the telephone. Jefferson dialed a Washington, D.C., number. When the call was answered, he relayed to Dean Cold what had happened. After making sure his friend was alright, Cold eventually asked him to do something. Jefferson replied, "Shit. Right. Hold on." He put the receiver down.

After checking each of his assailants' bodies, he picked the receiver up once more. "Neither one has a mark on his neck."

Cold told him not to call anyone else, and that he would call back shortly to let him know who was on the way.

Before hanging up, Cold declared, "I'm glad you're okay, Cam."

"Yeah, me, too."

# Chapter 27

When Cold hung up the telephone, John Bartley asked, "What the hell happened?"

Bartley had arrived about a half-hour earlier. The two were about to go through the rest of the two townhouses and further organize the operation.

Cold quickly filled in Bartley, and then dialed a special number for CIA Director Allen Dulles.

Dulles answered, "Yes?"

Cold cut to chase. "Cameron Jefferson was just attacked in his home. He's alright, but had to kill two intruders. No scars or bumps. I told him to hold tight, and that I'd get back to him with who would be arriving."

Dulles muttered, "Shit." He paused, and then proceeded to tell Cold what had occurred outside Maxine Marshall's home.

Cold asked, "She's okay?"

"She is, and has no idea what happened."

*As far as you know.*

Dulles proceeded to tell him that he had decided to give Marshall protective surveillance, and then gave the names of the two officers who would be going to Jefferson's home.

After that call ended, Cold again relayed to Bartley what had occurred outside Marshall's brownstone as he called Jefferson. Bartley also asked, "Are they sure she's okay?"

Cold started to answer, "I'm not..."

He was interrupted by the sound of shattered glass and a projectile flying into his basement apartment. He instinctively yelled "Grenade!"

As each man fell to the floor, a grenade did, in fact, explode in his living room.

Cold was temporarily stunned. The apartment was shrouded in smoke and debris thrown into the air.

*Where the hell is my gun?*

Bartley called out, "You okay, Dean?"

He managed to reply, "I think so."

The half-wall separating the living room from the kitchen had saved them from worse injuries. Each had hit the floor just before the grenade had gone off.

The front door managed to remain closed and locked. So, the assailants were slowed briefly. By the time the door flew open, Bartley was able to fire in that direction, and Cold was able to spot his M1911A1, which had slid just under the refrigerator.

Bullets flew in their direction from the four figures that were moving into the apartment.

The half-wall was still partially intact, and gave the Secret Service agents some cover.

Bartley managed to hit one of the intruders with a shot, but he took a slug in the shoulder and fell back against the kitchen cabinets.

At the same time, Cold grabbed his weapon, and landed a bullet in the chest of a second invader.

The two trailing, though, were in position to finish off both Cold and Bartley.

Two shots then rang out from behind the assailants, and each man fell to the floor with a hole in the back of his head.

Emerging from the still lingering smoke were a man and a woman in Army uniforms with guns in hand.

The man, a colonel according to the silver eagle on his uniform, asked, "Are you two alright?"

Cold's mouth was open, but he didn't respond.

The woman proceeded to start checking the four bodies.

Cold managed to ask, "No one else?"

The colonel responded, "No. We didn't see anyone else."

Bartley groaned.

Cold looked over at him, and spotted the blood. He moved quickly, placing his gun on top of the half wall and looking at the wound. The colonel watched.

Bartley said, "I'm okay. It just clipped me."

Cold looked closer. "Looks like you're right. I'll get something to clean this up and bandage it." As he stood up and moved toward the bathroom, Cold glanced at the colonel. "Thanks for saving our lives. Both of you."

Cold caught the nod from the colonel.

While Cold grabbed what he needed from the bathroom, the woman was kneeling next to the last of the four people strewn about the apartment. She looked up at the colonel, and shook her head. She said, "All four."

Bartley was watching them, and asked, "I'm not sure what I should ask first. I'll start with two questions. Who are you? And who were they? I'll throw in a third. Why are you here, not that I'm not grateful for the save?"

Cold heard the questions as he came back into the kitchen with first-aid equipment.

The woman stood up and smoothed out her shirt and pants. She then looked at the colonel.

Cold proceeded to address Bartley's wound.

He said, "I'm ... Colonel Robert Weathers, and this is my assistant, Corporal Grace Armstrong."

Cold responded, "Somehow, I think you know that I'm Secret Service Agent Dean Cold, and this is Agent John Bartley."

They all heard voices outside the building.

Weathers turned to Armstrong. "I think you'd better go out there, and keep people away. Try to do the same when the police arrive."

On cue, sirens were heard in the distance.

"Of course," replied Armstrong, who stepped around bodies and debris, and out the front door.

As Cold dealt with Bartley's arm, the three could hear Armstrong informing the group outside that they needed to disperse. "This is a military matter."

Bartley said, "She's not going to be able to hold off the police long." He looked at Cold, adding, "Your Secret Service creds are probably needed."

Cold nodded. He stood up a chair, and went to help Bartley into it, but was waved off. Bartley climbed into the chair by himself.

Cold then checked his telephone, and heard a dial tone. He moved the telephone into Bartley's lap, and said, "Let me check."

"Right," answered Bartley.

Weathers watched as Cold proceeded to check the backs of the necks of the dead assailants. At the last one, Cold looked at Bartley and shook his head.

Cold went over to Bartley, and grabbed the telephone. As he dialed, he told Bartley, "You talk to him, while I take Colonel Weathers outside to deal with neighbors and police."

Bartley accepted the telephone back. Cold turned, and while walking toward the front door, he said, "Colonel, you're with me."

Weathers didn't hesitate and followed.

Outside, after stepping on pieces of shattered glass, Cold spoke with the newly arrived police. He brandished his Secret Service credentials, introduced Weathers and Armstrong, and told the police that this was a national security matter – which it was – and that he needed the officers to leave the scene untouched. He added, "But it would be greatly appreciated, including by the president, if you gentlemen could keep people either in their houses, or well down the street."

Cold's tone, and no doubt his status as a Secret Service agent and the mentioning of President Eisenhower, worked, and the police became a help rather than another potential risk.

Armstrong remained outside, making sure that a curious neighbor or cop didn't get close. Once Cold and Weathers were back in the apartment, Bartley reported, "He's sending a small team over."

"Thanks," said Cold. He then turned to Weathers. "You didn't have a chance to answer Agent Bartley's questions."

Weathers rubbed his chin, and walked back and forth. "Yes, how to begin?"

Cold and Bartley waited.

Weathers looked at the two men, and then had an expression of resolve on his face. "It's time. And there's no going back now."

Cold folded his arms and asked, "Would you like to clarify what you're talking about?"

Weathers looked around at the bodies on the floor. He then turned back to Cold. "You checked each of their necks."

Cold nodded, while his body tensed.

Weathers loosened his tie, and undid the top two buttons on his shirt.

Cold held his breath.

Weathers then reached a hand around, pulled down on his shirt collar, and turned his body.

When he saw the scar, Cold quickly grabbed the M1911A1 handgun lying in front of him, and pointed it at Weathers. Bartley was only a second behind in reaching down to the floor for his gun, and also training it on Weathers.

# Chapter 28

Colonel Robert Weathers raised his hands in the air, and slowly turned. He was staring at the guns pointed at him by Dean Cold and John Bartley.

"Who the hell are you?" demanded Cold.

"I can..."

"Right now."

Weathers' hands remained in the air. "I'll give answers. However, I'm guessing that you" – he looked directly at Cold – "might want to consider who is on the way, and whether or not you wish to share these answers, initially, with them."

*This guy saved our lives, yet there's that mark. And yeah, he's probably right.*

Cold ordered, "Call your aide back in here, carefully."

When Armstrong entered, she paused in apparent surprise.

Bartley declared, "Close the door and then raise your hands."

Armstrong did so, and Cold collected each of their sidearms.

Cold asked Bartley, "Are you okay to take them upstairs?"

"Sure. Besides, they did save our lives." He nodded slightly at the two, who nodded back.

Five minutes later, Dulles' men arrived – driving two ambulances and dressed in suitable attire. They bagged the bodies, and cleaned up the aftermath of the explosion, including putting plywood up over the broken front window. Cold was assured that a team would show up tomorrow morning to replace the window and proceed with final repairs inside.

No one asked about anyone else, including Bartley, and Cold volunteered nothing.

The CIA clean-up team finished within an hour. They explained to the police whom their superiors should contact, and pulled away. The last of the spectators then left. A few police officers lingered, and eventually drove off in squad cars. The street was quiet as Cold climbed the stairs to the former main apartment of the townhouse.

The previous residents left some furniture behind.

Cold found the three in the living room. Bartley was in an armchair with his gun resting on his lap, while Weathers and Armstrong sat on a couch. Each had a cup of coffee in front of them.

Bartley asked, "All go smoothly?"

"Smoothly? I guess it did."

"There's a pot of coffee in the kitchen."

Cold poured himself a cup, returned to the living room, and grabbed another chair. He took a sip of coffee, placed the cup down on a table, sat back, and asked, "So, where do we begin?"

Weathers and Armstrong stared back, and then glanced at each other.

Weathers looked at Cold and finally said, "To start with, we've been watching you, from a third-floor apartment across the street."

Cold shifted in his seat. *I don't like that.* "Why?"

Weathers dropped his head and sighed. He rubbed his forehead, and then looked up. "You need to know all of this. It's going to be very difficult not to interrupt with questions and, no doubt, accusations. But I think this will work best if you let me get through the essentials, and then we can answer the many, many questions you'll both have."

Now Cold and Bartley glanced at each other, and Cold answered, "Get to it."

Weathers leaned forward in his seat. "We are — well, were, I suppose — part of a mission to infiltrate the governments of both the United States and the Soviet Union..."

Bartley started, "Who the...?"

Weathers interrupted with a raised eyebrow.

Bartley responded, "Okay, go on."

"The goal of this third party, if you will, is global control." While Cold and Bartley again looked at each other, Weathers continued, "I know what that sounds like, but things will become clearer shortly." He paused briefly, and then continued. "This is a plan that has been formulated over the past two or three decades, and began to be executed roughly eight years ago. And the technological power is there to make it happen. You've already seen the key to much of this." He turned in his seat, reached around and pointed at the scar at the base of his neck. He looked at Armstrong, and said, "Grace."

Armstrong stared back, and then turned to look at Cold and Bartley.

Cold watched her closely.

*She's not sure about this.*

Armstrong relented, undoing the top two buttons of her uniform. She slowly turned, and pulled down the back of her collar.

Bizarrely, Cold was getting used to seeing the scar and slight bulge. But his thoughts then went to what he knew was inside, and his discomfort returned.

Weathers went on, "Agents have been placed in key places in each government and elsewhere – in the U.S. and in the Soviet Union – and are set up as independent cells. Unless told by our superiors, each cell of two to four agents, or as we call them, 'Defenders,' has no idea what the other cells are doing. Again, unless we're updated from above." He paused and took a drink of coffee. After swallowing, Weathers continued, "The mission quickly came to be an infiltration of control in the Soviet Union, while in the U.S., it's more about spying, getting information, and when needed, taking more limited actions. The mission is to control and strengthen the Soviet Union, while at a minimum, undermining the West."

*Undermining, at a minimum?* Cold could no longer stay silent. "So, you people tried to murder President

Eisenhower, and control Stalin." It wasn't a question. It was a statement made with a hefty degree of anger.

Weathers replied, "Stalin and Eisenhower?" He and Armstrong exchanged concerned looks. Weathers continued, "As I said..."

"Yes, I know," retorted Cold. "But that's the case, isn't it? Those devices in your neck amount to some kind of ... of ... mind control, which makes me wonder who the hell is talking to me right now."

Weathers and Cold stared at each other.

The colonel finally said, "Our ... people ... understand the Soviet Union, and how control works. The United States, meanwhile, is far more troubling. Americans and your system don't lend themselves easily to central control." Bartley started to say something, but Weathers pleaded, "We honestly don't know most of the details of what other Defenders are doing – until it's deemed necessary. How do you know about what happened to Stalin?"

Cold decided to report the basics of Popov's experience.

"What your spy saw regarding Stalin was the key moment," declared Weathers. "We were briefed that the top echelons of the Soviet Union were now under our control."

*How does he know that? "Our"?*

Cold's eyes narrowed. "Stop screwing around. You need to put everything on the table, now. Are you Colonel Weathers?" He looked at his aide. "And for that matter, are you Grace Armstrong?"

Weathers asked, "Might I be able to note a couple of additional points before we...?"

Cold sternly responded, "No."

Weathers sighed. "No, I'm not Colonel Weathers, and she isn't Grace Armstrong. And we are terribly sorry."

Bartley wore an incredulous look. "What the hell does that possibly mean?"

"It means..." Weathers was struggling.

Armstrong interjected. "It means that, unfortunately, the individuals who were Grace Armstrong and Robert Weathers are no longer. But their bodies persist, and our essence, our thoughts, now reside in their minds. I'm now

Grace Armstrong." She pointed at herself. "And he is now Robert Weathers." She turned her finger at Weathers.

"You realize how … fantastic … this sounds?" asked Cold.

Bartley added, "Yeah, it sounds strangely like the science fiction that I've read and watched."

"And how would it even be possible? No one has such technical know-how," Cold pointed out. "Not the Soviets, as you apparently acknowledge."

Weathers replied, "Not yet."

Cold's head was swimming in wild speculation.

In a low voice, Bartley added, "And if what you say, somehow, is true, that would mean that Colonel Weathers and Corporal Armstrong were murdered."

Weathers replied glumly. "They were."

Bartley pressed, "By you?"

"No. And we – the two of us, at least – have been fortunate in not having to kill anyone."

Cold asked, "How many people have been killed? And who?" His mind was starting to accept, for some reason, what he was hearing.

Weathers responded, "Like I said, we operate as independent cells, reporting to our Commanders. Like you, we know of Stalin…"

Cold interrupted, "Stalin. Dear God. And others in the Soviet leadership. You said that your people have control in Russia." He already knew all of this, but it was the stated confirmation that shook him.

Cold and Bartley looked at each other in dread.

Weathers seemed to allow it all to truly sink in, as he nodded. He finally continued, "I would assume that in addition to Stalin, they have someone at the top of the military and the MGB, at the very least. And then there were the two killed in President Eisenhower's office. That's all we have direct knowledge of, but I can tell you that this mission started with more than 300 Defenders."

*Hundreds of spies infiltrating the Russians and us? And who else?*

Cold pushed, "That's twice you've called yourselves 'Defenders.' What is a Defender, and who exactly are you defending?" He feared the answer to the next question. "And where are you from?"

Bartley smirked and, his voice dripping with sarcasm, queried, "Yeah, are you time travelers or space travelers?"

Weathers and Armstrong glanced at each other, with Weathers finally declaring, "Space travelers."

# Chapter 29

While Agent Dean Cold struggled to wrap his mind around what he had just heard, General Arseni Demyan, the Minister of War, wrapped his hands tightly on the arms of his seat. The airplane that he and Arkadi Sokolov were in began its descent to a secret base in Khabarovsk Krai in the eastern Soviet Union. However, a storm was tossing the plane around like a child shaking a toy.

Demyan had been fully briefed by Joseph Stalin and his top spy, Sokolov, about the remote base and its operations. It was now time not only for Demyan to visit for the first time, but for Sokolov to evaluate the status of integrating aircraft technology shared with the leading Soviet aeronautical engineers.

During the flight, the two men had said little. They couldn't talk freely as their top aides filled the other ten seats in the cabin.

Sokolov glanced across the narrow aisle at Demyan's knuckles growing whiter as the plane was slammed around. Sokolov smirked.

Similarly, a row back, one of Demyan's aides, Major Denis Nusinev, seemed to be calmly observing all, including looking out the window as their plane descended.

The pilots managed a landing with the aircraft bouncing and sliding. When the plane came to a stop, Demyan released his death grip on the chair. The pilots then turned the plane and slowly rolled toward one of the smaller buildings on the base.

When the plane came to a stop, the passengers unstrapped and the door was opened. Sokolov was first out the door and down the short staircase that had been pushed over to the plane by the two-man ground crew.

As Demyan stepped into the snow being whipped about by the wind, he paused at the top of the stairs and looked around. He squinted at three massive buildings that loomed about 100 yards beyond the two smaller buildings. To the right in the distance was a five-story apartment building, which served as the living quarters for everyone on base. Behind Demyan on the other side of the aircraft were two more runways. He clasped the top button on his olive-colored military overcoat, and proceeded down the stairs. Sokolov, taking long strides, was well ahead of Demyan, but the general didn't rush to catch up.

Nusinev did much the same as his boss, stopping at the top of the stairs to look around. His eyes tracked a barbed wire fence that surrounded the entire facility, and a guard shack at the front gate. Along the fence, Nusinev's eyes also counted two tanks and a half-track with a mounted machine gun.

Upon reaching one of the small buildings, Sokolov waited for Demyan, and then opened the door for the general. When Demyan and Sokolov stepped inside, the two security guards seated at the desk bolted to their feet and stood at attention. They saluted, and one of the guards was suddenly breathing heavily.

Sokolov dismissively said, "At ease." Looking at the man struggling with his breathing, he added, "Calm down, Lieutenant ."

The stream of aides and guards for the two leaders waited in a line outside the door.

Sokolov said, "Please, come, General." He went out the back door, followed by Demyan. The line of MGB and military officers passed through the building in pursuit of their superiors.

Sokolov, Demyan and company stepped into a room that was the security checkpoint in the first large building. The other two edifices were lined up to the east of this building.

Again, the guards knew who these two men were, and saluted.

Sokolov said, "Give us the room." The security guards left. Sokolov glanced at Demyan, who nodded. The head of the MGB turned to his and the general's aides. There were five of each. He said, "Comrades, you are about to walk into the most advanced weapons facility not only in the Soviet Union, but in the entire world. That's right, this is something that the Americans can only dream of having."

Smiles of pride broke out in the small group, but for one of Sokolov's aides, Sofia Belov, who remained expressionless.

Sokolov continued, "This also is the most top-secret facility in the world. Outside of Chairman Stalin, General Demyan, me, and the scientists, pilots, soldiers, and workmen who contribute here for the good of the State, no one else in the Soviet Union, or anywhere else, knows about this place. You now know its location, and will see what is happening." He paused, adding, "And let me make this perfectly clear, comrades, if any of you speak of this to anyone, even your wives or girlfriends" – glancing at Belov – "we will know, and you will be terminated. Do you understand?"

They signaled their understanding, as each had heard such threats before. They also had firsthand knowledge that the warning was very real. After all, most of them had carried out the terminations of others.

Sokolov looked into each face, and then said, "Alright, comrades, follow me into the future." He opened the door into a massive manufacturing facility. As they stepped into the hangar-like space, the expressions worn by Sokolov and Demyan didn't change. After all, Sokolov oversaw the construction of the entire base – achieved in record time for any known project within the Soviet Union. Meanwhile, Demyan came in knowing what kind of operation this was.

However, the two sets of aides stood dumbfounded. They had no idea what to expect, and had never seen anything like this in their lives.

Two endeavors were happening in the one-hundred-yard-long building. Across the far side of the facility from end to end, the basics of a steel smelting plant had been upgraded with technology that Sokolov introduced to the top MGB scientists and engineers who manned the facility. They were producing a light metal that, at less than an inch thick, was stronger than steel.

The work going on closer to the visitors focused on the production of miniaturized electronic systems for various purposes in aircraft and missile controls.

A short man came forward sporting a balding scalp, a robust black-and-gray beard, thick square-rimmed glasses, and a white lab-style coat. He was smiling, extended his hand, and said, "Director, it is good to see you."

"And you, Dr. Golikova." As they shook hands, Sokolov introduced General Demyan.

Demyan said, "Yes, Dr. Golikova and I have met before. It was some time ago, like it was another time and place."

The briefest look of acknowledgement passed over Maksut Golikova's gaze. "Yes, of course. I apologize, General."

"Not necessary, Doctor."

Sokolov and Demyan proceeded to introduce the doctor to their respective aides.

Sokolov announced, "Dr. Golikova will take us through the entire facility, explaining, to the degree necessary, what is going on in each part of this operation." The aides nodded in response. Sokolov then turned to Golikova. "And while Dr. Golikova is doing that, General Demyan and I will be doing a close inspection as to how matters are proceeding."

Golikova smiled and replied, "I think you'll be quite pleased, Director. We are ahead of schedule."

Sokolov responded, "That would be welcome news – exactly what Chairman Stalin wants to hear."

Over the next three hours, the aides were led through the current building – simply named Building A – as Golikova gave a rudimentary explanation of what was occurring along both production lines. He summed up, "So, these tiny but powerful computers will push Soviet aeronautics far beyond anything that we or the West have achieved in terms of speed, maneuverability and power, and the same case holds for the alloys that have been developed to make Soviet aircraft and missiles not only strong enough to withstand high-speed maneuvers, but also render our planes and missiles basically invisible to radar."

One of the aides finally spoke up. "Doctor, did you say 'invisible'?"

"I most certainly did."

That stirred chatter among the aides.

Golikova smiled with satisfaction, and instructed everyone to follow him into Building B.

This second production building was four times the size of Building A, and housed what amounted to three assembly lines.

One line assembled missiles that were dramatically smaller and lighter than what the world thought possible.

Those missiles were meant to be attached to what was being produced on the second line. That production line – the widest in the building – actually was a refurbishing undertaking. Two MiG-17 fighter jets were being worked on at the moment. The jets essentially were being gutted and reskinned. The inside workings were being largely replaced or upgraded with the computers and electronics made in Building A, as well as the parts of the bodies being applied with the new alloy.

The third line clearly drew the closest attention from the aides of both Demyan and Sokolov. What was moving along the line was a mystery to these visitors.

Golikova smiled at their perplexed looks. But first, he explained what was going on with the MiG-17s and the missiles. He concluded, "So, these aircraft now will fly at three times the speed of any other plane in the air, be fantastically maneuverable, and as noted, be undetectable by radar. The missiles that are fired will be guided by the plane's systems to their targets, and those targets can be far out of visual range."

While their aides listened in amazement, Sokolov and Demyan moved about the facility, watching and inspecting, just as they had in Building A.

Golikova said, "Finally, you no doubt are wondering about that." He pointed to what looked like a massive metal tube – 30 feet long, 12 feet wide and 8 feet tall. There also were assorted doors along the craft. Golikova explained to his audience that those doors slid open for a mix of cameras, and propulsion systems that allowed for rapid acceleration and deceleration, and maneuverability in virtually all directions.

One Demyan aide asked, "How can the pilots possibly handle those types of movements?"

Golikova smiled ruefully. "Who said anything about pilots? These are drones." He went on to answer the quizzical looks. "They are unmanned crafts that fly by robotics and are meant for surveillance and reconnaissance."

Golikova answered several more questions, and when Sokolov and Demyan returned to the group, they proceeded to Building C.

This structure was just as large as Building B, but upon entering, visitors were first greeted by a surprising silence. And then it was the fact that this was where 11 upgraded MiG-17s and their missiles, and 6 drones waited for their first mission.

After brief explanations to the visitors, Sokolov and Demyan pulled Golikova off to the side.

Sokolov asked, "Everything appears to be on schedule?"

"It is actually a bit ahead ... comrade," answered Golikova with a smile. "And with the general on board, we will have additional resources to stay on track."

Demyan nodded, and then asked, "And the tests?"

"There have been no problems in terms of the upgrades to the MiGs, the new missiles or the drones. They are performing as designed. We lost two MiGs due to pilot error." He looked around and then leaned in closer to the other two men. Barely above a whisper, Golikova continued, "None of our pilots, of course. Each was Russian. Our pilots have no problems, and the last group will be brought in over the coming days for the actual mission. They will be ready, and there will be no errors due to human failings."

"Excellent," said Sokolov.

# Chapter 30

Agent Dean Cold instinctively reacted by laughing, and declaring, "Oh, please." But his voice betrayed a nervousness. The unthinkable, which had been lurking in the shadows of his mind, was coming into the light.

*He's telling the truth. Isn't he? Don't be ridiculous.*

Agent John Bartley's head was on a swivel. He looked back and forth from Colonel Robert Weathers and Corporal Grace Armstrong to Cold. "This is insane." His gaze stopped on Cold, who was now silent and staring at Weathers.

*That Sherlock Holmes' quote never made sense to me. "When you have eliminated the impossible, whatever remains, however improbable, must be the truth." You don't eliminate the impossible. Instead, you test the possible, and then if all of the possibilities have been eliminated – if that's even possible – then you're left to consider the previously assumed impossibility.*

Cold's thoughts then turned in an unexpected direction. It was the Bible verse carved in the stone above the front door to his church back home.

*Mark 10:27. "And Jesus looking upon them saith, With men it is impossible, but not with God: for with God all things are possible." Dear Lord, help.*

After Bartley's declaration, the room fell silent.

Cold slowly turned his gaze to Armstrong. He then looked back at Weathers. "If I play along ... for a moment ... and assume that you're not two of the nuts who claim to have seen flying saucers..."

Weathers interrupted, "I wouldn't believe the flying saucer crowd, necessarily. Our ships are in high orbit and undetectable. But as for those claiming to see high-speed, highly maneuverable cigar-shaped UFOs, well, some of those folks might be right. That's especially the case around various U.S. military bases."

Cold wasn't sure what to say or think, other than the fact that he didn't like that comment. He looked over at Bartley, who was now rubbing his chin rather than checking his gunshot wound.

*And he's no longer saying this is insane.*

Cold simply demanded, "Proof."

Armstrong reached inside her uniform jacket, and began to pull something out. Bartley raised his gun and aimed it at her.

She stopped her movements, and waited.

Bartley commanded, "Slowly."

Armstrong pulled out what to Cold looked like an oversized gun – longer, fatter, and with a wider barrel opening. The corporal flipped the weapon around – the barrel now pointed at herself. She offered the handle to Cold. He accepted it carefully.

Weathers explained, "This is the device that allows people to be ... replaced."

"Jesus," Cold whispered, as he slowly turned the weapon around in his hand. He suddenly stopped and looked at Weathers.

As if he could read Cold's mind, Weathers shook his head. "It's alright. It won't suddenly go off."

Bartley was looking over at the device and asked, "How does it work?"

Armstrong answered, "When the safety, if you will, is turned off, the barrel is pushed against the base of the ... victim's ... neck, and if this light is green, then the trigger is pulled."

Bartley looked at her. "Okay. But what happens, exactly?"

"It's not easy to explain," commented Weathers.

"Try," demanded Cold.

"Before I do, this is the best proof we can give you at this point as to who we are, or who we aren't. Namely, that the Earth isn't our home, or wasn't until recently."

Cold watched as Weathers and Armstrong exchanged glances.

Weathers continued, "This injector has never been fired. The controllers, since they haven't been used, will not melt, as you no doubt saw with the two individuals who tried to kill President Eisenhower."

Cold interrupted, "Injector? Controllers?"

"The injector is the device itself, and the controller is what wraps around the base of the brain." Weathers continued, "The scientists that Director Dulles has in his employ should be able to confirm that no aspect of the device is made of materials on Earth."

Cold found it hard to argue with what Weathers was putting forth, in part because he lacked information. "Get back to what happens when the controller grabs onto the brain."

"Briefly, the device does two things almost at once. In terms of Colonel Weathers, it killed him by shorting out his brain, and then it transferred the essence of my mind into his brain and body."

Cold and Bartley were silent.

*Dear Lord.*

Among the questions in his head, Cold wanted to ask what the essence of their minds was and how it could be transferred, but decided on the more practical first.

*Practical?* He mocked himself.

"And what happens to the two of you? Your bodies? Where are they?"

Armstrong responded, "Our bodies are in a suspended state on one of our ... ships. They are kept alive there." She paused and took a deep breath. This was the first time that Cold saw some vulnerability in her expression. A certain sternness returned to her look, and she said, "As long as our original bodies, where our physical brains obviously reside, are alive, then we remain alive. And vice versa. That is, as long as these bodies live, that these physical brains" – she tapped her finger on her forehead – "continue functioning, then our bodies on the ship are kept alive."

Bartley pressed, "And if not?"

Armstrong looked at him for a few seconds, and then replied, "If our bodies on the ship are shut down then we die, and if these bodies perish, our Commanders will order that our bodies back on the ship be shut down."

Bartley persisted, "And how do you return, if that's the right word, to your original bodies?"

Weathers answered this one. "We don't. This is a one-way assignment."

Cold was getting fully drawn into believing what he was hearing. He went on, "And how do your superiors communicate with you and you with them?"

"That's more practical."

Cold found himself briefly amused. *Okay, practical, again.*

Weathers continued, "The bodies on the ship cannot give or receive information after the original transference and outside the life-death link. So, communications are more worldly, I guess you'd say. We have set times to check in via a kind of radio communications."

"And do they know where you are?"

Armstrong replied, "They know where our communications set up is when a line of communication is opened, and therefore, where we are when we're reporting in."

Bartley broke in, "Dean, do you mind?" He indicated that he wanted to ask a question. Cold nodded, and Bartley turned to Weathers and Armstrong. "Why are you telling us this? Why did you intervene tonight and help us? Why are you turning against your own people? After all, if your Commanders decide to unplug your bodies on your ships, then you're dead here as well. Right?"

Armstrong said, "Yes, that's correct."

"So, why?"

Weathers leaned forward in his seat. "That requires some background about our society, the mission we are part of, and what we – Corporal Armstrong and I – have come to learn while living among you for these past five years."

Cold asked, "Did you say five years?"

"Yes, the two of us have been here for just about five years."

Cold wanted to hear the answer to Bartley's questions as well. After all, their answers would play a big part in where this was all headed. Nonetheless, he asked, "Why were the two of you – well, Colonel Weathers and Corporate Armstrong – selected?"

It was Armstrong's turn, and she spoke in almost clinical fashion. "Weathers and Armstrong were having an affair. Our Commanders saw their positions in the military being of value, and the affair, once revealed to their respective families, would end their marriages. As Defenders here on Earth, they could work together, and not have to worry about being tripped up by people close to them. That's a key criteria for which bodies are taken over – who is less likely to be seen as experiencing a bizarre change. Each Defender studies up on the background of the person targeted, but there are things in life that those outside a family, for example, simply don't know."

*True enough.*

Armstrong said, "Two Defenders kept watch on Weathers and Armstrong, and the two conveniently would rendezvous at a remote hotel. While they were intimately engaged, the two Defenders moved in."

Cold felt queasy.

Bartley declared, "That's horrible."

Cold again saw a change in Armstrong's expression and heard a softening in her voice. She said, "It certainly is. It's murder."

Bartley put a hand over his mouth. And after taking it away, he repeated, "My question: Why are you here?"

Weathers finished the coffee in his cup. "Okay." He took a breath and sat back. "Unlike Earth, our planet has one government. That government is very much like what you would call totalitarian, like Germany was under the Nazis, and what the Soviet Union and China are today. But our government has been in place for more than two of your centuries. All aspects of life are controlled to serve, again as you would call it, the State. That includes who has children.

In just a few short years, the government decides what that child will become, and one's life, from daily activities to education, are planned out accordingly. No one knows anything else, and those who question even the smallest aspects of how this all works are terminated..."

Cold could hear the depths of despair and anger in Weathers' voice.

Weathers continued, "Armstrong and I have known nothing else but being Defenders. We are the best that our military has to offer, and we were honored when selected for this mission."

That led to more questions for Cold, but he'd have to wait. *Patience.*

"So, we were selected to infiltrate your world," reported Weathers. "We studied all we were given about Earth and its people. It was decided that since the Soviet Union was so much like our own world's government and society, that we would work to seize power there. The United States, while its power was evident to us, would not serve as a viable means of control. In the view of our leaders, Americans were too unruly and independent, and their government structure would not lend itself to being controlled. The U.S. then was marked for infiltration and surveillance, and eventually being wiped out, if necessary, by the power we would amass in the Soviet Union, especially with the advanced technology we would introduce."

Cold's stomach knotted up at those last remarks. He would pounce for more information based on what came next. He looked over at Bartley, who was about to say something, but Cold's look kept him at bay for the moment.

Armstrong took over. "I know that the two of you want to know about what Colonel Weathers just said regarding technology being handed over to the Soviets. At the same time, you need to know the 'why' to trust what we're saying."

*She's right.*

She paused, but neither Cold nor Bartley said anything. "As time passed, Robert and I came to learn foundational principles that eventually overturned all that we were told and taught. The idea that each individual has intrinsic worth and value, not based on whatever our rulers dictate or what they decide we should be used for, but simply inherent in what and who we are. That was a revelation to us. It went on. Individuals are not raw material to be formed as those in power see fit. And individuals need freedom to pursue the truth, and to flourish. It's the opposite of everything our society rests upon."

Weathers added, "We know that humans are not perfect – in fact, far from it."

Cold nodded slightly.

The colonel continued, "But we came to understand the ideas and ideals that you strive for. And that these can be traced to your belief systems, such as Christianity, and in the American Declaration of Independence and Constitution. These ideas don't exist on our world, or if they ever did, the government wiped away any trace of them." He paused and seemed to be debating his next words. "Perhaps that's not completely accurate. At the very least, to the degree that such ideas are even considered, the government stomps them down, including by terminating people who are called 'Carriers.'"

"Carriers?" asked Cold.

"Yes, these individuals are deemed to threaten our society, our culture, either as physical threats or by pushing, as it is said, 'lies that threaten our way of life.'"

Armstrong volunteered, "We live here now, and no doubt in the view of our Rulers, learned things too well. Rather than fighting the disease, as trained, we would be deemed to be infected by Carriers. In fact, we would now be Carriers. But I guess we've kind of become Americans. After all, can't anyone become an American; it's about a set of ideas?"

Cold was taken off guard, but reflexively answered, "Yes." The last thing he expected in the midst of this bizarre situation was an ode to the American experiment. He also didn't expect what came next.

Armstrong's eyes suddenly moistened, and her voice became just more than a whisper. She again looked at Weathers.

He said, "Yes."

She said, "And the two of us now have another person to consider." Her hand moved to rest on her stomach.

*What the...?*

Cold had no idea how to respond. He decided to ignore, for now, the idea that two aliens somehow housed in human bodies were going to have a child. Instead, he asked, "If you have superior technology – and obviously, the fact that you're here speaks to that fact – why do all of this clandestinely?"

"Our leaders understood that humanity could not know about this invasion," answered Armstrong. "If they did, the planet would unite against us. And while we have much technology that is far ahead of what humans have, the distance isn't that great that a full-scale invasion would be a guaranteed success."

"So, this is why you have these?" He pointed at the injector resting on a table between him and Bartley.

"The injector's original purpose was something else entirely. But it became the ideal weapon for this mission."

"What was that first purpose?" inquired Bartley.

Weathers replied, "When our leaders reach a certain age, they have an option to use injectors, and transfer their minds into Hosts, and extend their lifespans – nearly doubling how long we normally live."

Bartley asked, "Hosts?"

"Yes," said Armstrong. "Hosts exist to be receptacles of the minds of others."

"There are people on your planet who exist to be murdered, and their bodies used for others?"

Weathers shifted a bit on the couch. "It's horrific. Grace and I have come to realize this during our time here."

Cold prayed silently.

Armstrong eventually spoke up. "Regarding a full attack on Earth, an overt invasion resulting in a war, even if we prevailed, would work against the reason for this in the first place."

Cold leaned forward, as this was another critical point. "And that would be?"

She answered, "Our planet has been devastated. We've been taught that it was a series of natural matters out of anyone's control. But Robert and I..."

Cold noted that this was the first time either one referred to the other by first name.

"... have come to realize, after observing what's happened on Earth and the debates over ideas and among your people, that the truth is that our leaders, our government, our system resulted in these planetary ills. And no one either sees this or is willing to acknowledge it. They do other things to distract the people, and perhaps themselves."

Weathers interjected, "I believe you might call it 'bread and circuses.'"

Bartley commented, "To the extreme."

"Yes," Weathers acknowledged.

Armstrong said, "And suddenly, we were told that we had the means for traveling great distances in space. Our leaders presented this discovery to the people as something we had created to be able to search the stars for places where we could live well. Amazingly, this further fed faith in and blind commitment to our government. The mission to find another planet or planets became the new reason for complete control."

Hours had passed, and it was now in the darkest time of the early morning. But no one noticed. Cold briefly worried that something would be forgotten when he and Bartley took this to the president. But he knew that neither he nor Bartley would forget any of this.

Cold queried, "You said 'discovery' but not 'created' in terms of space travel?"

*Yes, I just asked that question in all seriousness.*

"We had a limited space program then, but the first mission to one of our moons revealed a phenomenon that was never seen from the surface of our world. It eventually was called a 'space pad.' And it was discovered that there are pads spread across the galaxy, linked by what amounts to tunnels through space. It didn't take long after several tests for our government to announce this as something we had built, and are spreading throughout the galaxy seeking new, better worlds."

Bartley responded, "So, who actually built and runs these pads?"

Weathers answered, "'Built' doesn't fit as the right word. They just seem to exist. Once a ship comes within a certain distance, the pad appears, and then once a ship moves in closer, it gets pulled in and launched to another pad vast distances away."

"How many of these things are out there?" persisted Bartley.

"Once again, we don't know. But our scout ships went through 11, and then arrived in Earth's solar system. Our readings showed that this planet was rich in all that we needed. Elation followed on our planet, and the mission was formulated."

Cold asked, "Given what you've said about your government, how do you know all of this?"

Armstrong answered, "As Defenders selected for this mission, we were told. It was deemed necessary. But Robert and I have filled in aspects that our leaders would not express directly."

Cold and Bartley once again said nothing. Cold assumed that Bartley was trying to process this like he was.

Bartley finally commented with frustration in his voice. "Okay. What does that mean? What are we supposed to do with any of this?"

Weathers said, "I understand your frustration. But while you wrestle with those questions, you need to know that even without the attack on you this evening, we were going to make contact. Our most recent communication with our Commander was last night, and it was one of the few instances when we got information, rather than us just reporting to them. On occasion, we get vague or specific information about what other cells are doing. These are meant not only to give us orders, but to tell us that strides have been made to advance the mission, and by doing so, maintain our commitment." He paused. "That's not quite right. Commitment is never doubted. Given how each of us was trained and selected, complete dedication is a given – or assumed to be a given. These communications really are meant to encourage us and boost our morale. Anyway, we were told that something big is developing in the Soviet Union, and we should keep our ears and eyes open to anything out of the ordinary that the Americans might pick up from the Soviet Union."

Bartley declared, "That's pretty vague."

Weathers agreed, "It is, but it's also out of the ordinary."

Cold got up from his seat, and picked up the injector. But another question needed answering. "Why watch me? Why step in to save us?"

Weathers said, "We were told about the attempt on Eisenhower and that it failed. We were ordered to keep eyes and ears open for any information related to it. We also found out about Agent Stanton dying, and knew that you, Agent Cold, were his partner. To Grace and me, it seemed likely that you were involved in killing the White House intruders, and that you might have some knowledge about the controllers."

Armstrong added, "We did research on you, and decided that you might be the person – the human – that we eventually might be able to reach out to. Obviously, this attack has sped up our plans."

Cold nodded and said, "Okay. Thanks again for stepping in. Now, I need you to remain here while I…"

Without hesitation, Weathers finished the statement, "So you can report this to President Eisenhower."

*I don't like that.*

Cold didn't respond, and instead turned to Bartley. "Are you okay with keeping an eye on these two, again?"

"Sure."

As Cold readied to leave, he stopped, and looked at Weathers and Armstrong. "Here's a basic question: What do you call yourselves?"

Armstrong answered, "We're from a planet called – roughly translated – Nykar."

Bartley raised an eyebrow. "So, you're what – Nykarians?"

Weathers said, "Yes, again, roughly translated."

Five minutes later, Cold was behind the wheel of his Studebaker Champion, with the injector in a case on the seat next to him. He was heading to the White House.

# Chapter 31

The clock approached 5:30 am, and Dean Cold was finally about to wrap up a report lasting nearly an hour. He had an audience of one – President Dwight Eisenhower.

While relaying what Weathers and Armstrong had said, Cold was struck by Ike not interrupting or saying anything. In fact, the president listened with little expression on his face. For good measure, part of Cold's mind was working to convince himself to stop.

*He thinks you're off your rocker. Maybe he's right. Why do you believe them? Because it adds up – bizarrely enough.*

Cold finished and waited.

Ike finally said, "Thank you, Dean." He got up from the seat at this desk, and began to walk around the Oval Office.

Cold said, "Yes, sir," and had nothing to add.

Eisenhower finally asked, "You believe this?"

Cold had to make a final decision. "The best that I can give you, Mr. President, is that I'm leaning heavily toward believing what I would have rolled my eyes at yesterday, and wondered if the person was crazy. If the CIA's scientists, or whomever you hand that off to" – he indicated the injector now resting on the Roosevelt desk – "verify what Colonel Weathers and Corporal Armstrong told us, well, then..." His voice trailed off. With no response from Ike other than him continuing to pace the room, while rubbing his chin, Cold added, "Right now, I'm wondering if you think I'm nuts, sir."

Eisenhower actually looked at Cold and smiled. "No, Dean, I don't think you're crazy. I'm guessing that given what you and I have seen and heard, that this was an unmentioned possibility tucked away in the back of your mind. It was in mine." He now paused his talking and pacing. "Now, I'm questioning my sanity."

Cold smiled in response to a chuckle from Eisenhower.

Eisenhower sat back down at his desk and carefully picked up the injector and examined it. He put it back down on the desk, and said, "Good work, Dean. Now, when does Dr. Strickland join you?"

"Tomorrow."

"Then this falls under his purview, correct?"

"It does, but..."

Eisenhower interrupted, "I've arranged for him to have a lab with, what I hope, is the latest equipment. If he needs anything else, come to me."

*He's tightening the circle, with our team at the center. Smart. We better be up to it. I better be.*

The president continued, "It's a nondescript, small building not far from Griffith Stadium. He'll need a couple of assistants. When you decide on who, before he approaches them, let me know and we'll run a full check. Keep in mind what we said earlier, we have to keep this small."

"Yes, sir. I can see that you're tightening the circle where it can be."

"Damn right. While we wait for the findings, or lack of findings, you or someone on your team needs to stay with this Weathers and Armstrong."

"Of course, sir."

"I'm sorry, Dean. I know you know that."

"Sir, no need for an apology. Please keep reminding me when you feel like you should. I can't guarantee that I won't miss something, and when your reminders line up with what we're doing, well, that's a positive."

"Fair enough." Ike asked, "Is Bartley okay? Is he still up to this?"

Without hesitation, Cold answered, "He is, sir. I have no doubts."

"Good. And the rest of your team?"

"In addition to Dr. Strickland, everyone else is scheduled to arrive tomorrow afternoon as well."

Eisenhower nodded his approval.

Cold added, "I'll bring them fully up to speed."

"Of course."

"And they need to talk to Weathers and Armstrong as well."

Eisenhower nodded his approval, once more, adding, "It's your team, Dean."

"Thank you, sir."

Eisenhower commented, "You know, their story jibes. This is how a planetary or space-faring Soviet Union would go about this, especially if their leaders were both evil and smart."

"I agree, sir."

Eisenhower shook his head. "Think about how close we came to that happening here with Hitler. And we've been focused on Stalin and the Soviets, and now they might be getting assistance from a power from beyond bent on global domination. How would people react to this threat?" He paused. Cold thought he was allowing his own thoughts to sink in fully. The president added, "If this turns out to be true, these invaders are right to worry about humanity fighting back. At the same time, though, if word were to get out, the potential for grim reactions cannot be ignored, including, I fear, widespread panic. Think about what happened with that radio broadcast by Orson Welles before the war."

"The *War of the Worlds* broadcast."

"Yes. While much of that has been overblown, there's a disturbing amount of truth in terms of the panic that hit many people. Think about the real thing. Panic and worse? Man turning against man, and what would happen to our societal foundations?"

*That possibility is on my mind as well.*

"As we've seen in recent times, we humans are capable of great good and great evil. The Nazi concentration camps..." Eisenhower shook his head slowly, and then looked directly at Cold. "But you know that better than I. Your father is a pastor, and you almost became one."

Cold merely replied, "Yes, sir."

Ike went on, "When I was at West Point, we were still training on horseback. Mechanization leaped forward in World War I, and then the Second World War and Truman's decision to drop the bombs on Hiroshima and Nagasaki." He sighed. "After living through such incredible changes and horrors, along with the vast improvements in people's daily lives, mind you, I guess I shouldn't be completely shocked by what you just told me." He placed his hands on the desk and leaned forward. "Dean, after being the supreme allied commander in Europe, I thought that was the end of world wars. But just being president for about two months, I've come to realize how easy it would be for another world war to break out. Just look at Korea. And we might be there now, in a war that no one could have imagined. I don't want to be in a spot like Truman. I didn't agree with his decision to drop the bomb, and I don't want to be put in the position of having to be involved in an even worse decision regarding the Soviet Union, or men from … Mars? Where the hell do these people say they're from?"

"A planet called Nykar, and they are Nykarians – roughly translated."

Ike shook his head. "There's a voice in my head saying, 'That sounds ridiculous.'"

"I understand that, Mr. President."

"I suppose 'Americans' sounds silly to them." He paused. "If this turns out to be true, then we need to fight this war in the shadows, and we need to win. On top of everything that you're dealing with, Dean, I'm going to add another important item."

"Sir?"

"I need you to assume the worst and think about what we need to fight this shadow war, including military requirements in case … when this periodically breaks into the light. And I know this is a hell of a lot that I'm putting on you, but rest assured that I'll be mulling over the same things. And given the communication that these two supposedly received from their superiors, time is of the essence."

Eisenhower stood up, indicating that the meeting was over. Cold rose to his feet as well.

# Chapter 32

The aides with both Director Arkadi Sokolov and General Arseni Demyan gathered in a spartan briefing room. After seeing what was being created in this secret facility, their excitement could barely be contained. A triumphalism permeated their conversations.

Leading the way in his enthusiasm was Demyan's aide, Major Denis Nusinev. He slapped backs, exchanged hugs, and spoke of the end of the "Western capitalists."

In contrast, Sofia Belov, one of Sokolov's top people, persisted in an aloofness for which she was known. Belov merely watched the others from the corner of the room, calmly sipping a cup of coffee. With her stark look – nearly six feet tall, black hair arranged in a pageboy cut, catlike eyes, pale skin, a pointed nose and always dressed in black – Belov could never really blend into the background.

When Sokolov and Demyan came into the room, all went quiet and the ten individuals took metal chairs that surrounded a long, gray table.

Demyan smiled and declared, "This is a great moment for the Soviet Union."

The response around the table was fervent, with hands banging on the table.

Still restrained, Belov smiled thinly at Sokolov.

Demyan encouraged the reaction, saying, "Yes, comrades, yes!"

The Minister of War finally raised a hand, and all fell quiet. "The ten of you will play central roles in what is about to unfold. You were chosen for your absolute dedication to the Party and the State." He looked around the table at intense faces. "When the work here on these MiGs, missiles and drones is complete, we will unleash an attack on America and its allies that will shake them to their very core. We are still finalizing the exact date, but the director and I can tell you that these upgraded MiGs – we are calling them MiG-Xs – will fly, undetected, to a base in North Korea. And from there, an attack will be unleashed first on America's naval forces, and then on Seoul. Atomic bombs will not be needed, as the speed, precision and invisibility to radar will leave enemy forces incapable of fighting back – although, they no doubt will try." He actually laughed, and once again, the reaction was robust, with further banging on the table.

The loudest reactions came from Major Nusinev.

Demyan turned to Sokolov and sat down. Quiet returned.

Sokolov rose and said, "Your roles in this will be taking over the operations of this facility. Dr. Golikova will remain in charge, and you will report to him. But you will each command various operations and sectors, and that includes security. Let me make this clear: No one working in this facility is permitted to leave, no matter the reason offered." There, of course, were no questions raised. He added, "And at some point, some or all of you – for security reasons – could be called upon to terminate personnel here. We need to know if any of you might have a problem with this. If so, let us know now, and there will be no repercussions."

No one admitted to any doubts, as each had served long enough to know that there would, in fact, be the gravest of repercussions if any reservations were ever acknowledged.

Assignments were doled out, and additional points made, again, without any questions raised.

When the meeting ended, one person did have an inquiry.

Belov slid next to Sokolov, and whispered, "Director, I assume that I, too, will be staying here, yet I received no assignment."

"You are coming back to Moscow with me."

"I am more than capable, Director, to handle myself among these men."

"Yes, Officer Belov, I'm well aware. Nonetheless, you will be returning with me."

Belov said, "That is a mistake."

"Pardon me?"

Belov leaned in even closer and whispered, "I can see that you trust Dr. Golikova. But this is a sprawling and vital undertaking. Who else are you absolutely sure about ... other than me? And you know that I will watch everything, and act when necessary to protect this operation – no matter what is necessary."

Sokolov stared at Belov, whose eyes were unflinching. "You would be ... missed in Moscow."

The thinnest of smiles made a brief appearance on her face. "Yes, and I would miss Moscow. But it wouldn't be very long, and we all must make sacrifices. Am I correct?"

Sokolov straightened his back. "As usual, Agent Belov, you have provided wise counsel. You will stay here as head of security."

"As you wish."

Across the room, a similar question was being asked by Major Denis Nusinev of General Demyan, though with a distinctly different undertone.

Nusinev stood upright, and said, "Excuse me, General."

Demyan replied, "Yes, Major?"

"Does the lack of an assignment here mean that I will be returning to Moscow with you?"

"It does, Major. I need your insights and advice. I trust you don't have a problem with this?"

"Of course not, sir. I appreciate your confidence in me ... in my efforts for the Chairman and Soviet Union."

Demyan dismissed him with a salute.

As the last two aides went to leave, Nusinev opened the door for Belov. He wore a smile, and in a low voice, said, "Apparently, Officer Belov, you and I are both heading back to Moscow."

She barely glanced at him, and responded, "No, Major, I will be staying."

# Chapter 33

When Cold returned to the Q Street townhouses, no one was in the living room he had left a few hours earlier. John Bartley was sitting at the table in the kitchen.

Cold asked, "Where are our two guests?"

"Grabbing some shut-eye." Cold waited, and Bartley explained, "One of the bedrooms has a full bathroom and no windows."

"They're both in there?"

Bartley smirked. "Yeah, well, they're adults, I think, and she's pregnant, so…"

Cold chuckled, and poured himself a mug of coffee. He offered some to Bartley, who indicated that his cup was near full.

Bartley commented, "Well, you returned, so Ike didn't think you were nuts and lock you up. And since no one else is with you, I assume we still have jobs? How'd he take it?"

Cold explained what happened in the Oval Office.

Looking at the injector that came back with Cold and now was resting on the kitchen table, Bartley asked, "And why is that back here?"

Cold relayed the setup for Dr. Strickland, and took a sip of coffee.

Bartley stared at his mug, as he ran a finger around the brim. Without looking up, he concluded, "So, Eisenhower, you and I are in the same boat of leaning heavily toward believing our guests?"

Cold nodded and declared, "To quote you from earlier, 'this is insane.'" He took another drink of coffee. "If the results on that gun" – pointing at the injector – "turn out how the three of us think they will, the president mentioned fighting a shadow war."

"Neither side wants this to get out, for different reasons."

"Right. Ike mentioned what happened with the Orson Welles' *War of the Worlds* broadcast."

Bartley actually laughed.

Cold asked, "What is it?"

"I thought about that, too, as well as the new motion picture."

"What picture?"

"There's a motion picture version of *War of the Worlds* coming out this year. There was a Hollywood premiere last month, and my sister and brother-in-law are writers in the motion picture business." He paused. "You know that from my file, right?"

Cold nodded.

Bartley continued, "They invited me out to the premiere, knowing that I like this science fiction stuff, and they still worry about me being jilted at the altar. So, I took some vacation time, and went to California. Anyway, the picture is interesting for a lot of different reasons, including some impressive visual effects. But how people reacted to the Martian invasion ran the gamut, and I was thinking about that while sitting here."

"How did the movie portray it?"

"Panic. Fear. Fleeing. Some were hurting others. Others trying to help."

"Sounds about right."

"The picture really emphasized God and faith in the story, at least at the end."

"Questions have popped into my head," Cold volunteered. "Would this news" – he had to add – "if true, shake the faith?"

Bartley explained, "You'll be happy to note that people seemed to hold tight to their beliefs, seeking refuge and prayer in churches. At least, that was the case in the picture."

Cold finished his coffee. He looked at his watch. 9:15 am. "John, one more thing. The president asked us to think about what we might need if this war were to periodically break out of the shadows, meaning, what would we need militarily. He's thinking about that, and we need to as well."

Bartley said, "Yeah, makes sense."

"Get some shut-eye. I'll keep watch with our guests, and prepare for the arrival of everyone else later today."

"You sure?"

"Yeah. There's no way that I could sleep now."

As Bartley got up, he winced slightly.

"You sure that wound is alright?"

Bartley nodded.

Cold added, "We do have a doctor arriving today."

"Good point. One more thing."

"Shoot."

"I wasn't planning on staying here with the others, given that I live nearby. But I think, given what we're doing, it makes sense for me to move in as well."

"I agree."

"Great. Besides, it'll save me the rent. Is Dr. Strickland moving in as well?"

"That's the plan."

"And I assume, it's the men in this place, and the ladies next door."

"That would make sense, but I don't know if Miss Popov is moving in or living elsewhere."

"Okay, well, I like the idea of grabbing the top floor, so if you don't mind?"

"First come, first served. The third floor is yours. I'm staying in my basement apartment. We'll leave it to Cam and Mike to work out who gets the first and second floors."

They previously had started setting up the first and second floors next door as the group's main working spaces.

"Right. And Colonel Weathers and Corporal Armstrong?"

"If everything checks out, they'll have to stay at their apartment across the street, given what's expected from their" – he paused searching for the right word – "Commanders."

# Chapter 34

It was just before noon when Cameron Jefferson parked his dark blue Chrysler Saratoga directly across the street from the townhouse that he would now be calling home.

Jefferson had a black case in his hand as he checked the house number – 1732 Q Street NW. But the front door of the neighboring townhouse – 1734 Q Street – was opened, and out stepped Dean Cold. "Hey, Cam, we're over here."

Jefferson said, "Dean, you've got two places?" He started climbing the front steps.

Cold said, "As a matter of fact, yes." They shook hands, and Cold led him inside. He then introduced Jefferson to John Bartley.

Bartley said, "Welcome to the adventure."

Jefferson smiled, and asked, "What's the latest on the adventure?"

Cold answered, "I think John and I should bring everyone up to speed at once." He looked at his watch. "Max, Dr. Strickland and Miss Popov should be arriving over the next few hours. I thought everyone could start settling in, and then we'd get rolling over dinner."

"Good with me."

Recognizing the black case, Cold asked, "Papa?"

"You know it."

Bartley looked down, puzzled. "Papa?"

Jefferson placed the case down on a table. He snapped it open to reveal a shiny trumpet. Jefferson waved his hand over the instrument and smiled proudly.

"Right. You play the trumpet."

"I try."

Cold broke in, "Knock it off." He looked at Bartley, and declared, "I can personally attest to the fact that Cam is a great trumpet player."

Jefferson interrupted, "And you're not too bad either, Keys."

Bartley commented, "I think we should all start calling you 'Keys.'"

"Why not? This guy knows how to play anything with a keyboard – from church organs to Steinways to cheap pianos in smoky bars. And I can attest to that."

"I've only heard him play the organ," added Bartley.

Cold smirked. "Not sure if this is going to be a nicknames undertaking."

Jefferson reminded, "If the war can be a nickname deal, then why not this? You haven't become a stickler for rank, have you? Because if you have, that would make you more of a pain in the ass than you already are."

Bartley interjected, "I like you, Cam."

Cold deflected. "No, I haven't. But the Secret Service is different." He thought that this really wasn't an official Secret Service mission. In fact, beyond reporting directly to Eisenhower, it's clear that the president was letting him run things as he saw best. "We'll see." He looked at Bartley. "Anyway, Cam received Papa from a beautiful French lady who was impressed with Cam's playing, as well as some of his other attributes. She said that he played as beautifully as her late Papa, and eventually gave him that trumpet."

A touch of melancholy then crossed the faces of Jefferson and Cold.

Jefferson said, "Yeah, she was French Underground, and died in the war. After that, this was Papa."

Bartley nodded. "I understand."

A few seconds of silence were broken by Jefferson shutting the case, and asking, "Alright then, could you guys give me a hand bringing some of my stuff in from the car, and show me where I'll be sleeping?"

Cold said, "I'll help. John needs to stay here." He turned to Bartley. "In fact, why don't you take our guests over to their place for now? Let them get ready."

"Sure,"

Jefferson looked at Cold quizzically.

"It's part of what we'll cover later."

After Cold and Jefferson emptied the Chrysler and deposited the last of Jefferson's things in the second floor apartment, Bartley escorted Colonel Weathers and Corporal Armstrong across the street to their third floor apartment at 1737 Q Street NW.

\*      \*      \*

Roughly an hour later, Mike Strickland arrived. By the time he reached the top step on the front stoop, Cold thought the scientist looked out of breath. After sucking in air and shaking hands, Strickland looked at ease – though as disheveled as the first time they met.

*Thankfully, Cam took the second floor apartment. I think Mike needs the main floor.*

Cold brought Strickland into the first floor apartment that would be his and introduced him to Jefferson.

Strickland commented, "I'm the physicist, chemist and drummer."

Jefferson replied, "Great. I guess I'm the mechanic, technician, pilot and trumpet player." He tilted his head at Cold to more or less see if that was correct.

Cold nodded, adding, "Along with other skills."

"I like it, especially the trumpet part. I had mentioned to Keys here that perhaps we could play together."

Jefferson said, "Yeah, sure, I'd like that. And please call me Cam."

"And I'm Mike."

Jefferson glanced mischievously at Cold, and then looked back to Strickland. "If you insist. But I sat in on a few sessions going back with a group that had a bassist they just called 'Scientist.' And you're actually a scientist."

"You want to call me 'Scientist'?"

"Certainly not, unless you like the idea."

Strickland actually rubbed his chin in apparent consideration. "Alright, I'm okay with Mike or Scientist."

Jefferson smiled. He looked at Cold and said, "Nicknames."

Cold commented, "I feel like I'm starting to lose control." He looked at Strickland. "Let's get your stuff out of the car."

"Thanks, but I'll have to make a second trip. I only brought the drum set now."

Jefferson said, "We're definitely going to jam."

As Strickland led the way back down the front steps, he asked, "So, Cam, do you have a nickname?"

"Just Cam. But I play Papa."

"Your trumpet?"

"Yeah."

"Good enough."

Walking behind the other two, Cold just shook his head. Even with everything swirling around his mind, he liked each of these people, and they appeared to be a good fit. Cold also knew that Maxine Marshall would fit in. *Everyone likes Max.* The only question looming was Popov.

Strickland opened the back doors of a black Chevrolet Suburban station wagon, and there were the aforementioned drums.

Cold commented, "As for where you want to put the drums, the main floor of 1734 will likely wind up where we'll congregate the most – for work and otherwise."

Strickland replied, "So, you're saying that's the best place for the drums?"

"Seems so."

"Good for me."

After making his second trip with the Suburban, Strickland wound up staying in the apartment, unpacking and moving some things around, while Cold and Jefferson moved luggage and a few other items from the car, up the steps, and into the apartment.

Cold decided to take the moment to inform Strickland of his other digs – the lab that Eisenhower had set up for him – and his first assignment. Cold asked Jefferson, "Cam, can you handle the rest of Mike's stuff, while I talk to him in my apartment?"

"I got it," replied Jefferson.

Just a few minutes later, as they sat at his new kitchen table in a cleaned up and repaired apartment, Cold relayed the fundamentals of what was revealed by Colonel Weathers and Corporal Armstrong.

Strickland gasped, "Holy shit."

"There's more," declared Cold. He went into his bedroom, and returned with a carrying case. He spun the combination, opened the attaché, pulled out the injector, and placed it on the table.

Cold went on to explain the assignment, and the fact that the president had set up a full lab for him to use just a few blocks from the townhouses.

Cold was struck by the fact that Strickland just seemed to absorb everything. There were no protests or questions about this being rather preposterous. *Not yet.*

Instead, Strickland said, "I need to take this over to this lab, and examine it fully, or at least as best I can."

"Now?"

"Why not?"

Cold put the injector back into the case, and told Strickland the combination.

"Right," replied the scientist. "And where is this lab?"

Cold gave him the address, and the keys to the place.

Strickland adjusted his glasses, and pushed himself up from the chair. "Okay. Once I know anything, I'll call. I assume there's a telephone there?"

"I assume so. President Eisenhower tends to be thorough."

Strickland hesitated and said, "On second thought, maybe this is a conversation not meant for the telephone. I'm off and will return with some initial findings."

Cold watched as Strickland suddenly moved quickly. He said, "Okay."

Out the door and up the few stairs to the sidewalk, Strickland saw Jefferson taking a box up the front steps.

Jefferson reported, "This is the last of it, Mike."

"Thanks, Cam." He continued walking like he was on a mission, got in the car, and drove off.

As Cold stepped onto the sidewalk, he and Jefferson watched the Suburban move down the street.

Jefferson asked, "Where's he headed?"

"I'll explain. Let's go inside."

*Apparently bringing everyone up to speed at once wasn't realistic. Just a dumb idea.*

\*     \*     \*

After explaining most of what was happening to Jefferson – who, like Strickland, also declared, "Holy shit" – the two men heard a car pull up. Cold rose from his seat, leaving Jefferson to absorb what he had just heard. After opening the front door, Cold saw that a Pontiac had been parked in a curbside spot just a few feet from the front steps. Maxine Marshall stepped out of the car.

*She's here.*

When she spotted Cold, Marshall smiled and gave him a small wave.

Cold bounced down the steps, and said, "Glad you made it."

"I did quit my job, so…"

They stopped a few feet from each other on the sidewalk. A moment of awkwardness evaporated when she said, "Oh, please."

They briefly hugged.

Cold said, "I can help and then show you the place."

Jefferson slowly emerged, and came down the steps.

Marshall said, "Oh, my, Cam, it's so good to see you."

"You, too, Max. It's been way too long." He sounded slightly distracted. The two briefly hugged.

"It has." She eyed Cold quizzically.

Jefferson repeated, "Yeah, way too long."

Cold said, "Alright then. Let's see." He turned and pointed to the townhouse on the left. "1732 Q is housing for the men." He pointed to the right. "And 1734 is housing for the women, and our offices." He paused, and then went on, "Later on, you'll meet Dr. Strickland."

Jefferson recovered his voice. "Also known as Mike and Scientist."

"Scientist?"

Cold interjected, "Cam took the 'Keys' thing, and is pushing nicknames, with the help of John."

"Agent Bartley? When do I meet him?"

*Time to tell her, I guess.*

Cold said, "I'll help with your things and explain what's happening."

She merely replied, "Okay."

"Do you want the basement apartment or the third floor? You arrived before Daria Popov, and I'm not sure if she is actually staying here or not. So, you should pick."

"Thanks."

As they moved up the steps, Marshall asked, "With this nickname thing, Cam, does that mean I'm destined to be called 'Doc'?"

Jefferson responded, "Do you want to be called 'Doc'?"

Marshall smiled but made a noise. "Hmmm."

"'Max' it is," responded Jefferson.

After taking a quick look at each apartment, Marshall chose the basement.

Once Cold and Jefferson helped Marshall move her things into the apartment, Cold said, "Let's sit down, and I'll..." – he looked at Jefferson – "we'll bring you up to speed on what's, um, developed."

As the three sat at the kitchen table, Marshall asked Cold, "Has this all actually gotten even more interesting since we spoke in Boston?"

Jefferson interjected, "You have no idea."

Cold proceeded to take Marshall through it all. And when he was finished, he and Jefferson watched Marshall, waiting for a reaction. Her eyes had been focused on Cold as he spoke, and her stare continued, while she sat unmoving.

Cold finally requested, "Please, say something."

"I feel like we're back at Harvard, and I'm listening to Larry instead of you." She was referring to Cold's old roommate, who had crossed Cold's mind a couple of times over the last few hours. He pushed that aside for now.

Cold declared, "This is real."

Marshall looked over at Jefferson. "You're on board with this idea, Cam?"

Jefferson chuckled. "On board? I'm still working this out in my head."

"That's the case for each of us," commented Cold.

"But while I'm struggling now not to embrace this as the answer," said Jefferson, "I don't take the views of Dean and Ike lightly." He paused and then added, "I guess I'm waiting now – as we all are – on what Mike finds."

Marshall sighed. "I don't want to believe this, quite frankly. But as a doctor, I don't get to ignore evidence and facts, and just wish them away." She looked Cold in the eyes, and said, "And I also value what you say, Dean – not to mention the president's take."

"Are there other questions I can answer?" asked Cold.

She smiled. "I have countless, but I don't think you have the answers yet." Marshall leaned back in her chair. "Don't take this the wrong way, but I need some time to think this through more – maybe while I unpack."

Cold nodded. "Right. We'll leave you to it."

\*　　\*　　\*

The last person to arrive was Daria Popov. She walked up the street, climbed the steps to 1734 Q, and rang the bell.

Cold opened the door, and said, "Welcome, Miss Popov."

He noted that she was carrying a medium-sized grip.

"Thank you, Agent Cold."

"Where did you park your car?"

"I don't have a car. I walked."

Cold took her coat, and said, "I didn't hear from you. Will you be staying with us, or somewhere else?"

"I don't really have anywhere else, so I guess I'll be taking you up on the offer. Besides, it seems to make sense for the work, correct?"

"It does. That's good news." Cold got the impression that Popov was somewhat pensive compared to the confidence she had exhibited at CIA headquarters. "Let's go into the kitchen. You can meet some of your new colleagues, and then we can take you to your apartment. I hope you don't mind the top floor?"

"Top floor?"

He stopped walking. "Yes, the top floor of this townhouse." He quickly explained the living and working arrangements.

"That's more than adequate." She paused. "It's very kind. Thank you."

"Of course. But there's nothing to thank me for."

Jefferson greeted her and replayed much of the banter that already had taken place. As she listened, Popov seemed content to take in the situation and not say too much. She hesitated when told that first names, or even nicknames, would be the rule with the group, but finally said, "Well, then, please call me Daria."

Jefferson interjected, "You'll get used to the informality. It's very American."

Popov smiled and replied, "Yes, of course. You might be surprised to know that there are some Russians who, in the right place and time, like such informality."

"Like in the clubs you worked in?" asked Jefferson.

Popov responded, "That's right."

Marshall came into the room and gave Cold a look that he knew meant "I'm okay" based on their time together. Cold introduced Popov and Marshall, and the doctor offered to show Popov her apartment.

Cold added, "I'll join you, if it's okay?"

Several minutes later, after all three took a brief tour of Popov's new apartment, Cold said, "Daria, we've got more information, and it's, well, bizarre."

Cold noticed a shift in demeanor, closer to what he experienced at the CIA.

"Yes?" replied Popov.

As each took a seat in the small living room area, Marshall watched as Cold shared information, and Popov took it all in rather coolly.

When Cold finished, Popov declared, "So, we're waiting for Dr. Strickland's verdict at this point."

"That's the next step of many to come."

Popov observed, "My people could be enslaved by two invaders now – communists and visitors from ... space?"

Marshall broke her silence. "Daria, if you don't mind me saying, you seem very matter-of-fact about this?"

Popov said, "I'm not comfortable with any of this. It's strange. Nothing I've ever imagined, to say the least. And I hope this turns out to be something more grounded – here on Earth. But I have learned to deal with whatever gets thrown at me. I suppose it's part Russian fatalism, and part losing everything dear to me."

# Chapter 35

Dr. Michael Strickland found that the laboratory on U Street NW provided by the president of the United States was housed in a small two-story brick building. It had a parking lot with enough spaces for four vehicles.

The entire property had a shabby look about it.

After Strickland exited the Suburban holding the case with the injector, he looked at the faded sign above the building's front door. "National Munitions."

As he pulled the keys that Cold had given him out of his pocket, Strickland looked around. Finding the right key, the lock opened smoothly, and he stepped inside. Strickland found himself in a small room, with a desk and chair at one end, and in front of him, a four-foot-high and eight-foot-long counter. He flipped on a light switch, and closed the door.

Strickland moved around the counter to another door. Again, after slipping in the correct key, the lock opened easily.

Strickland spotted the light switch panel and as he hit each switch, the ceiling lights turned on, with each row of lights flickering on farther from him.

A scientist's dream lab was revealed.

"Oh, my," he said to himself.

He placed the case on a nearby desk, took off his coat and jacket, and tossed them on a chair. Strickland then circulated around the main floor, taking in the latest equipment and tools that could be used by a physicist, a chemist, and a few other areas of study.

The rooms off the back of the main space amounted to a tiny hospital. "For Dr. Marshall, I assume," he said aloud.

The second floor featured a walkway wrapping around the building and looking down on the main floor. He climbed the stairs, and looked in the various rooms, including additional lab space and an expansive library.

Strickland began to step into the library, but stopped. "Not now. Get to work."

He descended the stairs, and as he moved across the main room, he took off his tie and rolled up his sleeves.

Strickland grabbed the case, and dialed in the combination. He stared at the injector.

"Alright, let's see what you're about."

# Chapter 36

Returning from the neighborhood Italian restaurant with trays of meatballs, spaghetti and salad, along with two loaves of bread, Dean Cold parked his Studebaker.

Cam Jefferson came out to help him bring the food into the townhouse. But just as Cold was getting out of the car and Jefferson was descending the steps, Mike Strickland pulled up in his Suburban. He jumped out of the car without his tie, suit jacket or overcoat, and ran as best as he could toward Cold with the injector case in hand.

*This can't be good.*

Strickland had been sweating, judging by the stains on his shirt, but the cold air had put an end to that. Cold and Jefferson waited as he arrived in front of them and gasped to regain control of his breathing. He finally said, "I've never seen anything like this, and that includes the material it's made out of, as well as the internal technology."

Cold didn't like what he was hearing, but it didn't surprise him, either.

Jefferson looked around. The street was empty, and there were no open windows in this weather. Nonetheless, he kept his voice very low. "Are you saying that this device is ... other worldly?"

Cold didn't expect a quick answer, but the look on Strickland's face revealed frustration.

The scientist responded carefully, "I have no clue as to where this came from, and I need a heck of a lot more study. But at this point, I can confidently say that little about this device conforms with known materials or technologies."

Jefferson pressed, "On Earth."

"Well, yes, by definition."

Cold asked, "What's frustrating or annoying you, Mike?"

"Before we accept the aliens-from-another-planet idea, a lot of questions remain. One in particular."

Cold replied, "And that would be?"

"Given the impossibility of traveling vast distances in space, how the hell did they get here?"

The three stood on the sidewalk staring at each other in silence.

Cam declared, "I believe they called them 'space pads.'"

Strickland replied with annoyance. "Yes, yes, but what does that mean? How do these things work? Does this ... make sense?"

*The scientist, of course, needs to know the details. Good.*

Cold finally said, "Let's take the food inside, and we can ask."

Jefferson observed, "Spaghetti, meatballs and flying saucers."

"Thanks, Cam," retorted Cold.

As they crossed the street, Cold thought about one word that Strickland uttered.

*Our scientist said "impossibility." Back to Sherlock Holmes? Let's see the reactions of Mike and the others, and also hear their questions, as to Armstrong's explanation for being able to journey across space.*

# Chapter 37

Maxine Marshall stood ready in the kitchen with a preheated oven. The dining table was set for eight.

Cold looked at his watch.

*6:40.*

He was counting on Bartley to arrive with Weathers and Armstrong just at 7:00.

Strickland was introduced to Marshall and Popov. Cold noted how at ease the scientist appeared, as he engaged in similar banter as earlier.

"I'm the physicist and chemist, as well as the group's drummer." But then Strickland quickly added, "And please call me Mike or Scientist."

Marshall smiled, and said, "I'm Max, and I think I'll stick with Mike." Marshall paused. "But if I ever wind up calling him 'Keys'" – she tilted her head toward Cold – "then I just might call you 'Scientist,' especially if the three of you are playing some music."

"Do you play an instrument, Max?" asked Strickland.

"No, I'm afraid I don't. Cooking is my hobby, I guess. I picked it up while traveling with my parents."

Cold knew from hearing her in the choir on occasion when they were dating that Marshall had a nice singing voice. But she wouldn't want him to volunteer that.

Jefferson advised, "Don't bring that up again, Max, or you'll wind up fixing too many of the meals with this group."

"If that helps, I'd be glad to do it. I do love creating and trying new dishes." She focused on the three men in front of her. "However, I would stipulate that others do the shopping and the clean-ups."

Cold chimed in, "We'll do our parts."

Jefferson saluted and said, "Yes, sir."

Strickland turned to Popov. "And what about you, Daria? We might wind up jamming if situations present themselves, and I understand that you sing?"

She replied, "I do, but I have mixed thoughts on my singing. My mother used to tell me that I had the voice of an angel. However, we were only able to sing when visiting family members in the country. Then there was no one nearby who could inform on you for singing hymns."

Cold said, "I'm sorry, Daria."

Popov nodded. She continued, "And as for my recent singing, it was a tool to get close to communist officials, and eventually, to my surprise, to Stalin himself."

Silence draped the room.

Marshall finally observed, "If you wish to sing among friends, I for one would like to hear that angelic voice."

Strickland added, "Me, too," and both Jefferson and Cold indicated agreement.

Popov offered a warm look in response that again surprised Cold.

*A multifaceted woman, to say the least.*

Popov said, "I don't know about that. After all, I think my mother might have been a bit biased."

*This all matters, but we need to refocus.*

Cold glanced at his watch once more. "I think Mike should tell you two" – he indicated Marshall and Popov – "what he just told Cam and me outside."

When Strickland finished, no one said anything for several seconds. Marshall finally moved, opening the oven and slipping the tray of spaghetti inside, followed by the meatballs. When she closed the door, Marshall looked at Strickland, and started, "Are you...?"

She was cut off by the front door opening.

Agent John Bartley entered the kitchen, followed by Colonel Robert Weathers and Corporal Grace Armstrong.

*A few minutes early.*

Cold took in the scene of Marshall, Popov and Jefferson meeting Weathers and Armstrong face to face. Awkward wariness flooded the room.

*Keep it straightforward to start.*

Cold first introduced Bartley to Jefferson, Marshall, Strickland and Popov.

Bartley said, "We'll have the chance to talk more, but right now, I'm going to clean up before dinner."

Marshall offered, "Can I take a look at your wound?"

"No, thanks." He glanced at Weathers and Armstrong. "Maybe later?"

Marshall replied, "Of course."

As for Weathers and Armstrong, who were in civilian clothes, Cold decided to provide surface introductions, for now. Each shook hands formally with Jefferson, Strickland, Marshall and Popov.

Silence followed.

Weathers finally commented, "The food smells good."

Cold took the opportunity to say what they would be having and where it came from. He then asked if anyone would like a drink with dinner, offering non-alcoholic options.

Bartley returned just as everyone took seats at the table.

When eating by himself, with family or with friends, Cold usually said grace, or someone would. He looked around the table, and wondered if this was the right situation to do so. While doubts still lingered about his decision not to go to seminary, and guilt regularly grabbed him for neglecting his church attendance, this was a different kind of questioning. He also knew that it didn't have to do with this being a kind of work setting. Instead, it was about the two visitors. Cold decided, and said, "Before a meal, I usually say a prayer of thanks. Does anyone mind?"

No one replied.

Cold folded his hands, and he noted that nearly everyone at the table followed his lead, including Weathers and Armstrong. Only Strickland didn't do so.

Cold said, "Lord God, heavenly Father, bless us and these Thy gifts which we receive from Thy bountiful goodness; through Jesus Christ, our Lord. Amen."

Cold had a sense of relief at saying grace.

The food was then plated in silence.

After swallowing a forkful of spaghetti, Strickland declared, "That's quite good."

Cold nodded and swallowed. "The food from Mario's is always delicious."

Strickland took another bite, as the others partook of spaghetti or a meatball. He picked up the napkin from his lap, dabbed the corners of his mouth, and took a sip of water. He looked at Cold with an expression that seemed to ask, "Shall I?"

Cold gave the slightest of nods.

Strickland said, "There's no reason why we can't talk shop over a nice meal."

Everyone, but Cold, stopped chewing, and sat unmoving.

Strickland continued, "After doing an initial examination of the injector that Colonel Weathers and Corporal Armstrong provided, and their explanation of who they are, the major question I have is: Given the vast distances in space and, as far as I know, the impossibility of traveling such distances, where did you come from and how the hell did you get here? I suppose that's really two questions." He took another mouthful of spaghetti and looked across the table at Weathers and Armstrong, who renewed their chewing and swallowing.

Jefferson, Marshall, Bartley and Popov resumed chewing very slowly, as each looked at the two visitors.

Weathers swallowed and used his napkin. "The question of a scientist. I trust you found that the injector possessed materials and technologies foreign to Earth."

Strickland responded, "Unknown."

Weathers smiled. "A true scientist. Your initial findings will be confirmed, I assure you, especially when taken alongside what happens to the controller when disconnected from the base of the brain." He looked at Cold, and asked, "Shall Grace and I relay what we told you?"

"Please," replied Cold.

And for the next hour-and-a-half, Weathers and Armstrong told the story of their society, how they arrived, why they were here, and their various tools, including the background and use on Earth of the injectors and controllers. The group – especially Strickland and Marshall – peppered Weathers and Armstrong with questions throughout.

Cold took note that Weathers and Armstrong could offer significant details on how the space pads functioned, but the two couldn't add much as to how they actually created tunnels – or as Cold started thinking of them, shortcuts – across space.

Strickland pressed, "Do these pads create the tunnels or do they just provide access to tunnels that simply exist?"

Armstrong answered, "As far as we know – and given our roles, that would be limited – our people don't have answers to that."

Strickland clearly wasn't pleased with the explanations, or lack thereof. He persisted, "What is the experience like? I mean, after you … launch … off the pads, what happens? What do you see or even feel?"

Weathers responded, "Since we're Defenders, we didn't have access to the command decks of our ships. Instead, we were either strapped into our chairs or given certain assignments on our decks. Other than the strains that could be heard to the ships, and vague feelings of queasiness, there's not much we could tell you, well, other than the journey through each tunnel lasted about two weeks."

Eventually, Strickland's inquiries gave way to Marshall's. She asked, "How different is Nykarian biology from human biology?"

Armstrong said, "That's a big question. But in terms of the basics – you know, male, female, five fingers and toes, basic anatomy – we're not all that different. In general, we're a bit smaller, but have proportionally larger eyes, noses and ears. Our internal organs accomplish much the same, but in different ways, I suppose. Nykarians, though, have much thinner skin. The differences seem to reflect the differences between our planets, which amazingly aren't all that different, at least foundationally. Hence, why Nykarians chose Earth."

Bartley deadpanned, "Lucky us."

Armstrong nodded, and went on, "We, Nykarians, do have better healing abilities, from what we've seen."

Weathers added, "It also seems that we have a slightly longer lifespan than humans, but that would be on our planet. And like our technology in space travel, our medical abilities are ahead of yours."

"Yes," said Marshall, "as exhibited by what was done for, and then to Stalin."

Weathers nodded.

Armstrong then made a declaration that Cold had been thinking about not long after Weathers and Armstrong revealed their rebellion. She said, "Of course, whatever we can help provide America, we will."

Given the knowing glances tossed his way by Bartley, Jefferson and Marshall, Cold knew that he wasn't the only one thinking about this. Cold also understood that Ike and Dulles were pondering the same thing.

"Good. Thank you," replied Cold.

It also registered with Cold that the reasons for rebellion served up by Weathers and Armstrong seemed to hit home with the others as it had with him and Bartley.

After Armstrong spoke of their child, Marshall asked, "Have you had a doctor examine you yet?"

"How could we?" She tossed a worried look at Weathers and then looked back at Marshall.

"Of course," said Marshall sympathetically. "Now you have a full-time doctor. Perhaps tomorrow I can take a look at you and check on the baby."

Both Armstrong and Weathers smiled. Armstrong replied, "We would appreciate that. Thank you, Doctor."

Marshall insisted, "Max."

Armstrong responded, "Alright, and it's Grace and Robert."

Strickland interjected, "Max, you're going to like the setup at the lab."

She replied, "I'm looking forward to seeing it."

Cold was transfixed on how Marshall had just single-handedly changed the tone of the conversation.

At the close of the dinner, with plates, dishes and utensils cleared away, the eight were back at the dining table.

Cold declared, "I think we all have a great deal to think about tonight." He looked at Weathers and Armstrong. "And what are we to do with the two of you now?"

"Meaning?" asked Armstrong.

Weathers answered for Cold. "Agent Cold wonders if he can trust us to return to the apartment across the street by ourselves."

"Right," agreed Cold.

Jefferson added, "Can we trust you?"

Armstrong responded, "Trust us? We are putting our lives on the line here, and the life of our child. Plus, I think we helped in some way saving the lives of Agent Cold and Agent Bartley."

Cold spotted a slight smile from Marshall.

Bartley declared, "That is definitely true."

Cold decided to go with his gut. Since he was a kid, it rarely steered him wrong. His mind rushed back to his home, and how it bothered his father and mother when he would pronounce a kind of judgment, in privacy to them and his sister, on the character of various congregation members. While telling him that wasn't how Christians thought and that we were all sinners, they also would acknowledge that he usually turned out to be right. Cold wound up writing off this ability as a game that he'd play. That is, until he joined the OSS and went on to serve in the Secret Service. In each case, it turned out to be a valuable skill.

Cold said, "Fair enough. We'll reconvene here at seven thirty in the morning."

Everyone agreed.

Jefferson watched through the curtains as Weathers and Armstrong crossed the street, and entered the house. "They're in." He turned around to find everyone looking at him. "Yeah, okay, trust. But let's not be too hasty about this. We're talking an alien invasion … I think."

Cold smiled as did the others, except for Popov.

*My gut rarely fails, but I've never been reading space aliens before.*

Part of him laughed at his own thought.

# Chapter 38

As everyone dispersed to their apartments, Cold asked, "Max, can you stay to talk about something for a few minutes?"

"Of course."

They took seats in the living room area.

Cold sighed and said, "Okay, hear me out."

"Uh-oh. Whenever you used to say that, it was something that we would disagree about."

"But then I would convince you."

"Often. But at other times, I would talk you out of some kind of foolishness."

"I know. And that's why you're the only one I can bring this up to because you're the only one who knows, or knew him."

"Him? Silver?" she asked incredulously.

Cold nodded.

"You want to bring Larry into this?"

"I'm thinking about it. You have to admit, his ... background ... would lend itself to this."

"What? That he was an early UFO nut before there were UFO nuts?"

Cold kept silent, waiting to let Marshall fully reflect upon what she had just said.

She glared at him. "Yes, I know. We're all UFO nuts now."

Again, he said nothing.

Marshall continued, "Apparently, not nuts, I hope." She folded her arms and looked at the ceiling. Cold knew that this meant she was moving beyond the initial reaction and was thinking about what he threw at her more seriously.

He finally said, "I know you never liked him as my roommate at Harvard."

She continued looking at the ceiling, and admitted, "He was just so ... odd. I could never feel comfortable around him. And then the two of you would go off on some philosophical debate, and, well..." She sighed. "And then he heard the Welles' *War of the Worlds* broadcast, and became really strange."

*There's* War of the Worlds *again.*

Cold had forgotten that the broadcast was the trigger point for Silver to dive into an obsession with life elsewhere in the universe. At the time, Cold found his friend's path an annoying, pointless distraction.

*But now.*

"Is he still dabbling in this stuff?" asked Marshall.

"I can't say for sure, but quite frankly, I'd be surprised if he isn't."

"He's teaching at Harvard, right?"

"He is." Cold sensed she was moving in his direction.

She finally admitted, "There's a certain logic to this, maybe. I'm not sure what he'd contribute."

"I'm wondering about that, but you can't deny the guy is brilliant..."

"And eccentric."

"Granted, but his kind of eccentricity might work well with our group and the mission."

Marshall lowered her head, and looked at Cold. "You haven't approached him yet, obviously."

"I've been thinking about it, but just decided tonight."

"What's next then?"

"I'm going to contact the president and make a case for Larry, and if he is open to it, see how quickly he can have Director Dulles, or whomever, run a check on him. And then visit Larry, like I did with you."

She asked, "And when would this happen?"

"I'm going to call the president tonight. Hopefully, he'll pick up at this hour." Cold knew he would. "I'll grab a flight up to Boston tomorrow, so I'll be ready to move."

"What if the president says no?"

"Well, I also want to stop at home and talk to my father about some things that are on my mind with this. I'll either drive back with Larry…"

"If he has a car."

Cold nodded. "If not, I'll train it, and stop to talk with my father in New York."

Marshall said, "You were surprised that Colonel Weathers and Corporal Armstrong folded their hands and bowed their heads during grace."

*She still knows me pretty well.*

Cold nodded.

"Okay." She stood up, and Cold got to his feet as well. "I'll come along to offer another take on Larry. Besides, I'd love to see your dad, once again. If you don't mind?"

"I was hoping you'd say that."

Marshall smiled, and said, "Good night, Dean. See you in the morning."

"Night, Max."

\*       \*       \*

Cold returned to his apartment and picked up the telephone.

While speaking in sparing terms with President Eisenhower, Cold was surprised by the reaction regarding Larry Silver.

Ike replied, "The director had mentioned that you might be looking to add him to the team. That's your call, but he's deemed okay to invite."

"Thank you, sir."

"Is there anything else?"

"There is, but it requires meeting in person."

"Come by after you've settled the Silver thing."

"Yes, sir."

"Good night, Dean."

"Good night, Mr. President."

After hanging up, Cold shook his head.

*Director Dulles is thorough.*

# Chapter 39

Armstrong slipped into bed next to Weathers, and she rested her cheek on his chest. "Do you think they'll ever fully accept what we're doing?"

He kissed her on top of the head. "At some point, yes, I do. How long that actually takes, though? I have no idea."

Armstrong rubbed the hair on his chest, while Weathers gently scratched a spot on her back.

Weathers said, "It's strange."

"What is?

"Because of our training, we don't use our real names."

"It's just become natural for me to call you Robert."

"I know. I feel the same way."

They went silent for more than a minute until Weathers added, "It's who we are now. I know where we came from, obviously, but this is our home now, and..."

After he paused, Armstrong finished, "And our child will be fully human, and his or her parents are Robert Weathers and Grace Armstrong."

"Right."

Silence returned.

Armstrong asked, "Are we doing wrong by the baby? I mean, should we have just kept on doing what we were doing? Should we have continued being good Defenders? After all, if we're found out, then we come to an end. We die."

Weathers sighed. "I know. But we discussed this, and agreed. How could we do otherwise?"

She turned and rested her chin on his chest, looking into his eyes.

He continued, "That would mean giving our child a grim future. We know what happens if our people win this."

"Our people?"

"It's amazing how I say that, but it's foreign to who I am – who we are – now."

She kissed him, and returned her cheek to his chest. "You know what?"

"What?"

"I think you might be wrong. At the very least, I get the feeling that most, if not all, of this group has come to accept what we're doing. They understand the impulse for a better life for their children."

"I hope you're right."

Armstrong said, "No matter what, there's going to be unease with the idea of people coming from a faraway world. How could there not? Imagine if our people knew the truth behind the space pads."

Weathers replied, "True. It's going to be on us to earn their trust, while still operating so that the Commanders don't discover what we're doing. Independent cells help us to, well, stay alive."

Armstrong squeezed his arm.

Weathers changed the subject. "How are you feeling?"

"Fine. None of the queasiness I've read about, at least not yet. I like Dr. Marshall, and we're fortunate to have her with the baby."

"We are, indeed."

# Chapter 40

Ken Roberts, Clay Walsh and Jerry Debrowski had decided to step up their evening meetings from once every couple of weeks to once a week, or more often, if needed.

But Walsh and Debrowski were meeting first – before Roberts was scheduled to arrive. Debrowski just finished delivering his grim news.

Walsh flashed unusual anger. "Not one did what they were supposed to do? They all failed? They're all incompetents."

Debrowski had his eyes closed while massaging his forehead. "Nothing," he commented. He looked up and asked, "How will they react when we report this?"

Walsh declared, "We're not reporting any of this."

"What? How can we not tell them? They'll want to know the outcome."

"They don't know."

"What the hell are you...?" He paused. "You never reported the assignment."

Walsh shook his head. "Think about it. If it had succeeded, which it should have, then we would have been praised and recognized by each Commander. And I think you know what the reaction would be with failure, especially a failure as complete as this one." He shook his head. "Even if half the targets were taken out, we could have reported those, been commended, and they wouldn't have been the wiser for any failure. Now, we have a complete failure." He looked Debrowski in the eyes, and declared, "You should thank me."

Debrowski swallowed. "You should have told me. It wasn't your decision."

"What would you have said – honestly?"

Debrowski didn't respond.

"I knew and you know. And if we did what you would have urged, the plug would be pulled. We'd be dead."

At the knock on the door, each man took a deep breath and picked up a glass of whiskey that already had been poured. Walsh called out, "Yes, come in."

The door opened, but rather than the expected Ken Roberts, it was a slim, handsome man with a wide smile and blue eyes. "What are you boys up to in here?"

Walsh and Debrowski clearly were surprised. Each man jumped to his feet, declaring in near unison, "Senator."

As Senator John F. Kennedy casually strolled deeper into the office, Walsh said, "We're just going over some issues."

Kennedy mocked, "Yes, I can see that, Clay." He turned to Debrowski, extended a handshake, and said, "How's your boss, Jerry? I haven't had the chance to talk with him in a while, but my father appreciates Joe appointing Bobby to the Investigations Subcommittee. I do as well."

"Yes, Senator. Your brother is a pit bull."

Kennedy smiled at that and said, "That he is." His smile evaporated for a moment, and he added, "You know, you might want to advise Joe to be a bit more careful about what he's saying. I get what he's doing, but I have to say, that when he goes too far..." His voice trailed off.

"I understand," said Debrowski. "You're obviously not the first fellow senator to offer such advice."

Kennedy laughed, "Well, that's for damn sure. It was, what, three years ago, but Margaret's 'Declaration of Conscience' still stings, I bet, and Ike wasn't exactly chomping at the bit to be seen with Joe." Kennedy was referring to Senator Margaret Chase Smith.

"It's a balancing act, Senator."

"You're being generous. Joe has been pretty vicious with Margaret. He has problems with balance in assorted ways." And then Kennedy waved his hand. "You've heard it all before, I'm sure. Try to help him as best you can." He turned to leave when Ken Roberts filled the doorway.

Kennedy said, "Ah, another man to discuss the issues." He extended a hand again, and said, "I'm Senator Kennedy."

Roberts was taken off guard. "Yes, yes, of course, I know, Senator. It's nice to meet you. I'm Ken Roberts."

As they shook hands, Kennedy asked, "And where do you work, Ken?"

Roberts hesitated. "I work for Allen Dulles."

Kennedy kept his grip on Roberts' hand, and he looked back at Walsh. "A spook. Well, Clay, what kind of meeting is this?"

Walsh replied, "Ken used to work in the Senate. We've all known each other for several years."

Kennedy offered a good-natured grin, and said, "Then carry on, boys. Enjoy the whiskey, and by all means, see how many of the world's problems you can solve. By the way, Clay, it's good to see that you're loosening up a bit."

"Good night, Senator," said Walsh as Kennedy strode away.

Once the outer door of the office was closed, Walsh said to Roberts, "Close the door and lock it."

The three men sat down, with Roberts immediately grabbing his glass of whiskey. "What the hell was he doing here?"

Walsh answered, "Well, this is his Senate office, Ken."

"Yeah, I understand that, but..."

Walsh interjected, "He was just hanging around until his next conquest tonight. Don't give it a thought."

Roberts took a swig of his drink. "I suppose..."

"Listen," started Walsh, "I've been thinking about everything you unloaded on us the other night..."

"Yeah, well, there's more," interrupted Roberts.

"Meaning?" asked Walsh.

Roberts went on to provide details on the failed attempts to kill Agent Dean Cold and his team.

# Chapter 41

After briefing everyone in the morning, Dean Cold and Maxine Marshall drove to Washington National Airport, and were on a plane just before 10:30 am.

By mid-afternoon, a taxi dropped them off on the Harvard campus. It was a short distance to the building housing the philosophy department.

As they walked, Marshall commented, "This brings back some memories."

Cold replied, "It does. I haven't been back here since graduation. I assume you have?"

"Various times. But I was talking about walking with you here."

They continued in silence, and climbed the few steps to the front door of the brick Emerson Hall. Cold opened the door for Marshall, and she said, "Thanks."

A student directed them to the second-floor office of Professor Lawrence Silver.

Cold knocked on the door, and a voice from inside called out, "Come."

They entered an office lined with bookcases on two walls, and a window behind a chair and desk. The man at the desk had his head down, reading a student's essay on Aristotle's *Metaphysics*. He said, "How can I help you?" and then looked up.

The man had a long head, with thin-rimmed, round glasses. That fit the Larry Silver that Dean Cold had roomed with years ago. But that seemed to be about it. This professor was muscular; sported slicked back brown hair; and wore a neat, three-piece, dark blue suit, a crisp white shirt, and a paisley tie with a matching pocket square.

It took each man a couple of seconds, with Cold finally asking, "Larry?"

Silver smiled revealing teeth that were whiter and straighter than when they had attended classes together. "Dean! Welcome. It's wonderful to see you." He rose from the chair and started moving around the desk.

Cold stood with his mouth slightly ajar.

As Silver shook Cold's hand vigorously, he focused on Marshall. "Oh, my, Maxine Marshall. I mean Dr. Marshall."

He extended his hand, and she did the same. But rather than shaking it, Silver leaned down and kissed it.

Marshall shot Cold a confused look. She responded, "It's nice to see you, Dr. Silver."

"We're old friends, please, Lawrence."

*Lawrence? What's happening?*

Cold finally spoke. "Larry, I mean, Lawrence, you look great."

"Thank you. As do the two of you. Wait, did you two get married?"

Cold and Marshall looked uncomfortable at the same time.

Silver continued, "No? Alas, that's too bad."

*Alas?*

"So, to what do I owe the pleasure of this surprise visit?"

Cold said, "I ... we ... have something to speak to you about, and it has to do with national security."

"You're not here looking for commies on campus, are you?" He smiled wryly. "Please take those two seats, and let's talk."

While Cold and Marshall sat down in two chairs facing the desk, Silver closed the office door and returned to his chair. He slipped the paper he had been grading into a file, clasped his hands on the desk, and said, "I had heard that you were with the Secret Service, Dean, so you have piqued my curiosity. My old friends, you have my full attention."

Cold felt like this had become a waste of a trip.

*How do I get a read on where he is now regarding his former UFO fascination? I'm guessing he tossed it aside when he threw out his old look, clothes, and well, personality.*

Cold said, "Before I get to that, you've..."

"Changed?" Silver completed Cold's thought. "Yes and no. I needed to get serious about my work, and make a better impression on people." He now sat back casually and said, "When I was a child, I spake as a child, I understood as a child, I thought as a child: but when I became a man, I put away childish things."

"St. Paul?"

"Yes, but don't get any ideas almost-Pastor Cold, I'm still an atheist."

"I'm sorry to hear that, Lar... Lawrence. You know, 'Lawrence' is going to be hard to get used to."

Silver shrugged slightly. "However, my areas of interest largely remain."

Marshall chimed in, "Is that true?"

Silver smiled sideways at Marshall. "I know you thought I was Dean's crazy roommate, Maxine. But I've been seriously researching assorted topics from those days, and am working to bring them into the mainstream."

Cold replied, "Such as?"

Now, Silver flashed his smile at Cold. He turned his chair, opened the drawer of a small filing cabinet behind his desk, and pulled out a thick folder. He turned back and set the file in front of Cold. "Please. Take a look. Well, at the title. It is a work in progress."

Cold opened the folder, and looked at the underlined title on the page: <u>A History of Philosophical Reflections on Intelligent Life Elsewhere in the Universe</u>.

*That answers my question.*

Marshall leaned over and read the title. She looked up at Silver and observed, "That's quite a mouthful."

Cold smiled slightly for the briefest of moments.

Silver looked at her graciously. "I know, I know, the two of you always tolerated my musings on the subject, but when this book comes out, you'll see that a very long history of such speculations among philosophers, and even theologians, exists about life elsewhere." He looked at Cold.

"I look forward to reading it," assured Cold.

"Thank you, Dean." He reached across, took the file and returned it to the filing cabinet. "Now, why have you come to see me?"

Cold returned to his script. "We've come to offer you a position." He waited for a reply, but without one, went on, "This would be a top secret undertaking, with significant national security implications. Unfortunately, I can't give you the details unless you decide to come on board." Silver continued to listen and kept his brown eyes trained on Cold. "You would have to leave behind your current position."

That struck a chord. "Leave Harvard?"

"Yes, and it would require the highest degree of secrecy that if you mentioned this, even the smallest detail, while involved or even afterwards, that would be considered treason with the most severe consequences."

*How is it that I'm getting used to saying these things?*

Cold added, "To better understand at least the importance of this, the invitation doesn't come only from your old roommate; it comes from the president as well."

Silver straightened up and his eyes widened. "President Eisenhower?"

"That's right."

Silver looked back and forth at Cold and Marshall. "President Eisenhower," he repeated. And then while smiling, Silver added, "You know, I voted for Adlai Stevenson." He chuckled. "Is there anything else?"

Cold answered, "Of course, if you agreed to take the position, then you'd be read in fully."

Silver grabbed one of the pencils from a cup, and began tapping the eraser end on the desk. He asked Marshall, "This is how he pitched you as well?"

"It was."

Silver smirked. "And this secret undertaking requires a PhD. in philosophy who focuses on the unknown, with a Master's degree in astronomy?"

Cold asked, "A Master's in astronomy as well?" He was unaware of that, and it only boosted Cold's interest in his former roommate.

"That's right." Silver put down the pencil, and placed his hands flat on the desk. "I'm going to admit something to both of you. I am tempted by this."

Cold did reply to that. "Did I ever steer you wrong while your roommate?" He smiled.

Silver replied, "There was that girl. And there was your introducing me to bourbon. And what about...?"

"Okay, okay."

The two men chuckled.

*This is what I remember.*

"The reason that I am so tempted is that the chairman of the department is rather closed-minded. He's not fond of many of my ideas, such as that manuscript I showed you. I think my days as a professor at Harvard might be numbered." He smiled weakly. "Tenure certainly isn't in the cards."

Cold caught a glimpse of the insecure university student he knew. "I can probably offer greater job security." He half-shrugged.

Silver nodded. "And of course, I'm dying to know what this is all about." He picked the pencil back up and resumed drumming with the eraser. "And the president."

While Silver thought, Cold and Marshall waited.

"You don't have to decide right this minute," said Cold, "but I will need an answer in..."

Silver interrupted, "I guess I have to put off finishing that book. I will join the two of you, and President Eisenhower."

*That was quick.*

Cold said, "That's wonderful, Lawrence."

As they shook hands, Marshall agreed, "It is. Welcome, Lawrence."

"Do you mean that, Maxine?"

"I do," she assured.

Cold commented, "And you won't have to stop working on that book."

Silver raised an eyebrow. "Why might that be?"

Over the next two hours, Cold and Marshall explained everything, and Cold watched Silver have the most unique reaction among those he had told so far. His former roommate was giddy with excitement at first. And then upon hearing that this was a clandestine invasion, Professor Lawrence Silver looked stunned. "What? No, that can't be. Are you positive?"

Cold explained further.

Silver persisted, "Why would beings come so far to wage war? How could they even manage such technological feats in that kind of society? Perhaps we've misunderstood them, or failed to communicate properly. This really makes no sense."

Cold and Marshall exchanged quizzical glances.

Cold responded, "I think it's hard to make that case or assumption. After all, they haven't reached out to communicate at all. Instead, they've launched a secret invasion."

It seemed to Cold that Silver was only half listening. With greater authority in his voice, Cold declared, "I'm not being glib, Lawrence, but have you seen what terrible regimes have been capable of over the past twenty years?"

Silver commented, "I suppose."

In fact, Cold and Marshall had to do more convincing of Silver about these beings from another planet being hostile, rather than persuading him on anything else about these visitors, from their existence to their taking over the minds of humans to how they journeyed across vast distances in space. Cold wasn't fully confident that Silver was convinced about the intentions of the alien visitors, but it occurred to him that someone with a degree of skepticism might be helpful.

Silver did latch onto and celebrated the fact that Colonel Weathers and Corporal Armstrong were helping, as he put it, "we Earthlings."

When Silver's questions were seemingly exhausted, at least for now, he told Cold and Marshall that he would need two days to get his affairs in order, and then he could leave for D.C. After another reminder about the grave secrecy of all of this, Cold and Marshall were ready to leave.

The three got to their feet, and Silver took Cold off guard by hugging him. Tears formed in Silver's eyes. He said,

"Thank you, Dean. You've changed my life in a couple of hours."

Cold wasn't sure how to respond to this, especially given the threat they were all confronting. "Ah, you're welcome, Larry."

Silver corrected, "It's still Lawrence." But then he managed a smile. Silver then hugged Marshall, who seemed equally surprised. "Thank you, Maxine. You won't be disappointed in me. I'll do whatever is needed to get things right."

While being embraced, she offered Cold another bewildered look over Silver's shoulder. "I have no doubt, Lawrence."

Silver then stepped back, took a deep breath, and straightened his suit jacket. "To say the least, I am looking forward to working with the two of you, and others in the group. This is central to my life's work."

Before stepping out of the office, Cold shook hands with Silver, and declared, "Thank you for trusting me, trusting us, Lawrence."

Silver breathed a little uneasily, and nodded. "Now, go. I'll be in D.C. in a couple of days."

As they exited the building and started walking, Cold said, "That was like riding the Cyclone on Coney Island."

"To say the least," agreed Marshall.

"I suppose that I'm glad that Larry's worldview – I mean Lawrence's worldview – has been affirmed, well, to a certain degree."

Marshall asked, "Did his saying that he needed 'to get things right' strike you as peculiar?"

"His entire reaction was strange ... well, this whole thing is strange, but you understand what I'm saying." He paused and then continued, "He's not skeptical about aliens, but he doesn't buy that they're hostile."

"What do we do with that?"

"I hope he serves as a kind of check if the rest of us go too far in the other direction."

Marshall replied, "I wouldn't have thought of that, but I can see it."

They strolled for a few yards, and Marshall said, "Let's go visit your father."

# Chapter 42

As usual, Clay Walsh and Jerry Debrowski were in Walsh's office awaiting the arrival of Ken Roberts. They sat in silence. Three glasses of whiskey rested on the table.

When Roberts' knock came, Walsh and Debrowski picked up their glasses. Walsh said in a monotone voice, "The door's open."

Roberts slowly opened the door, entered the office, and locked the door behind him. He moved his girth more slowly than normal. His shoulders slumped and his head hung. Roberts fell into a chair.

Walsh asked, "What the hell is wrong now?"

Roberts looked up. Fear was written on his face.

Walsh placed his glass back down on the table without taking a sip, with Debrowski doing the same.

"You're never going to believe this. I still don't fully," declared Roberts. His normally high-toned voice was replaced by a weak rasp. "If this didn't come from Dulles, I would call it mad. Everything has changed."

"What?" demanded Debrowski.

Roberts finally reached for his glass, and downed the amber liquid in one large gulp. His eyes darted back and forth between the others. "This will sound insane." He went on to relay everything that Allen Dulles had told him about an alien invasion. Over two hours, Walsh and Debrowski seemed to take the bizarre journey from incredulity to dubious belief.

Eventually, Debrowski scratched his cheek, and said, "We have a new reality, so that means we need a new agenda, a new strategy. Before we agreed that America and the world need saving from communists, now we have communists working with visitors from space with powers that we can't even imagine."

Roberts' normally squinting eyes were now large ovals. "And? What's this new strategy?"

Debrowski answered, "Damned if I know at this point, but we're going to have to figure it out and fast. One thing that, unfortunately, seems clear to me is that America is suddenly at risk in a way that we weren't even during the war."

Roberts was the first to leave the meeting.

Debrowski looked at Walsh. "We need to report this."

"Of course," assured Walsh. "But let's do it when it will have maximum impact for us."

# Chapter 43

The return flight from Khabarovsk Krai to Moscow was far smoother than the flight to the remote facility. And it was much less crowded.

General Arseni Demyan sat about halfway back in the cabin, with Major Denis Nusinev behind him.

Across the aisle was MGB Director Arkadi Sokolov.

Sokolov turned in his seat so he could see the other two easily. Looking at Nusinev, he said, "The general and I need you to keep your eyes and ears open within your circles and beyond. If you detect even a hint of knowledge about this project, you're authorized to move against any individual or individuals."

Nusinev inquired, "Meaning?"

"Quietly grab that person and get him to either one of us, that would be the first option. If not, eliminate him."

Demyan added, "Is that clear?"

Nusinev declared with enthusiasm, "It could not be any clearer."

"Your role in this is magnified, Major, since it was decided at the last minute" – he glanced at Sokolov – "that Agent Belov would stay at the facility to head up security."

Nusinev asked, "Are there any details that I should know about that were not told to the rest of our people?"

Demyan answered, "We did not offer the others a timeline, but given where matters are in terms of refits and manufacturing, Chairman Stalin is looking at roughly a month from now to launch this attack."

Sokolov said, "While we have no exact date yet, this timeframe will work well as our group at the facility will not only absorb the operations, but will also be able to identify any possible weaknesses among the workers. Something that Agent Belov excels at." It was Sokolov's turn to throw a quick look at Demyan. "However, as you know, the longer something like this goes on, the greater the chance for word to get out."

Nusinev declared, "Such talk can be very damaging. Just consider the ridiculous rumors that spread about Chairman Stalin, and yet, he is as vigorous as ever."

"He is, indeed," assured Sokolov.

Demyan cut in, "Again, this is one of the reasons why we need you to be on high alert."

Nusinev declared, "I always am, General."

Sokolov exchanged a glance with Demyan, and then looked at Nusinev. "I do not have to tell you, Major, that we all must make sacrifices for the greater good, for the Soviet Union."

"I understand, sir. My life is to serve."

"Good. You might have noticed a different emphasis in terms of the security at the facility. Given the remoteness and secrecy of the operation, the main concerns are focused on internal rather than external threats. Of course, we have weapons and personnel who can stop anyone who attempts to intrude or spy." He waved his hand. "But security is mainly about internal threats, and stopping anyone who wishes to cause trouble, communicate with others on the outside, or even flee. No one can know about what is happening there."

Nusinev nodded. "Yes, naturally."

Sokolov continued, "Good. The general and I expect you to be an integral part of this project going far into the future."

The major sat up a bit straighter, and replied, "Thank you, sir. I will do my best."

Demyan responded, "I know you will, Major."

Sokolov then said, "You need to understand that when everything is completed at the base, it will be destroyed, and the next stage of weapons development will be set up elsewhere."

Nusinev replied, "It makes sense, sir. Staying in one place, even as ideal as that base is, would risk being found out, word getting out."

"Exactly," replied Sokolov. "But there's more..." He hesitated.

Nusinev interjected, "I would think, Director, that not only would the facility be destroyed, but, unfortunately, the personnel would have to be eliminated as well. There is no way that all of them could be counted on to keep quiet."

Sokolov said, "That is the unfortunate reality."

"Yes, the sacrifice we all agree to make if needed," observed Nusinev.

With the trace of an actual smile, Sokolov added, "The facility was built with a network of explosives for this eventual reality, or in case the workers somehow were led astray and tried to revolt. But with Officer Belov and my team there, that will not happen. In the end, Dr. Golikova will decide as to when to destroy the facility, while Officer Belov will make sure that no one leaves who isn't authorized to do so."

"You have thought of everything, Director," commented Nusinev.

"Thank you, Major, I'm so glad that you approve."

Nusinev stiffened. "Sir, I meant nothing by..."

Sokolov smirked and waved his hand. "Relax, Major."

Demyan and Sokolov laughed, with Nusinev joining in nervously.

# Chapter 44

Dean Cold called from a telephone booth in Boston's South Station letting his father know that he and "a guest" would be arriving late that night.

Cold and Maxine Marshall stopped at a newsstand. He grabbed *The Boston Globe*, and Marshall picked up a copy of *Time*. They found their way to the train heading to New York City's Pennsylvania Station, and sat next to each other.

As the train pulled out of the station, Marshall said, "It'll be nice to see your father. How is he?"

"He's doing well. It took him some time after my mom died to get back to something a little closer to normal. But that was the same for me as well."

"I was so sad to hear that. I should have called you... I... I'm sorry."

Cold said, "I know. It's okay. Thanks." He wanted to tell her more, how the hurt still periodically snuck up on him, and how he still hadn't found his way back to church.

*That's not where we are. Right now?*

He added, "Dad always thought you were great, and I have no doubt he still thinks so."

Marshall offered a small smile.

Cold turned to the *Globe*, and Marshall to *Time*.

For much of the four-plus hours on the train, however, Cold couldn't concentrate on the newspaper, nor could he gain any sleep even with his eyes closed. Instead, his mind kept going back to the joy that Lawrence Silver had experienced upon hearing the story about aliens.

*My reaction to space aliens? Anger. Fear. Doubt. Doubt about what? The story? My view of God? Assuming this is all true, should this make any difference to my faith – such as it is these days?*

Cold decided at that moment he was going to tell his father everything. He needed to hear what and how his father felt about this.

*Well, if he believes me.*

\*      \*      \*

The yellow taxi pulled up to the house. Cold paid the driver, and he and Marshall got out. The two stood in the cold night air for a moment looking across the street at St. Mark's.

Marshall commented, "Wow, more memories." She looked over at Cold. "Good ones."

"I'm glad you feel that way," replied Cold. "Come on, like I said earlier, Dad will be happy to see you."

And in fact, Pastor Gary Cold welcomed Maxine Marshall as warmly as he did his son.

During a brief hug, Marshall said, "It's good to see you again, Pastor Cold."

"You, too, Dr. Marshall." He emphasized the doctor, and added, "Congratulations on achieving your dream of becoming a doctor."

"Thank you."

Dean was amazed at how easily his father dealt with people, including when the situation could be awkward – like seeing his son's former girlfriend again, and having her stay at your house.

Dean and Marshall offered some pleasantries about their journey to Boston and the train ride back to New York. Dean knew that his father understood that if no details were offered, there was a reason.

Marshall eventually said, "I'm quite tired, and I think you two should have time alone. Do you mind if I turn in for the night?"

"Of course not, let me show you to the guest bedroom," replied Gary.

When his father came back downstairs, Dean was sitting in the kitchen. He looked up at his father, and said, "I need to talk to you."

"I knew there was something on your mind. Do you want something to eat or drink?"

Dean stood up. "Would you mind if we went across the street to talk?"

"We can do that. Just let me change." Gary had a robe on over his pajamas.

"I'll meet you over there. It's open, right?"

"You know it is."

After Dean walked in, he had planned on walking into the nave and sitting in a pew. But he stopped, and instead ascended the stairs to the choir loft. He sat down at the organ, and placed his fingers gently on the keys and then withdrew them. He was unsure what to play. And then he decided on "The Church's One Foundation."

As he was coming to the end of the hymn, he knew his father was behind him.

After playing the last note, Dean hesitated. His eyes went up to the large, round stained glass window. It was hard to make out the images in the darkness of the night, but he knew every detail by heart. While looking at the winged lion, he took a deep breath, and then turned around in his seat.

Standing just a few steps from the stairs, Gary commented, "That was beautiful, Dean."

"Thanks, Dad. Is it okay to talk here?"

His father nodded, and took a seat on the choir bench closest to Dean. "What's on your mind?"

*How do I even start this?*

Dean chuckled and said, "This is so ... unbelievable ... that I'm not sure where or how to begin. But I have to say this first, and please don't take it the wrong way."

"It's okay. Go ahead."

"What I'm going to tell you can never be uttered in any way to another person. If it was spoken of or even hinted at to someone else, the consequences would be grave ... for you and for me."

Gary raised an eyebrow and responded, "You mean like the seal of private confession?"

Dean smiled and nodded. "I know, Dad. Thanks. I had to say it."

His father nodded and said, "Go on."

Dean was still struggling with how to begin, and thought about Colonel Weathers' tactic. He finally said, "I'm going to tell you everything. I need to have you help me think this through. I need your perspective. So, you're going to want to raise questions and make comments. But I want you to let me get through this ... story first before we get into questions – yours and mine."

Gary, once more, agreed, and Dean proceeded to tell his father the essential details of what had occurred – from the attack in the Oval Office to the discussion with Lawrence Silver. When Dean was finished, his father stared at him in silence with his mouth seemingly frozen in a slightly open position. Gary finally licked his lips and leaned forward, resting his elbows on his thighs with hands clasped together. After a couple of minutes, Gary rose from his chair, turned and looked across at the crucifix and the risen Jesus above it. His eyes remained fixed in that direction for more than a minute. He blessed himself, and turned back to his son, who was watching him intently. Gary then returned to his seat across from Dean. "I'm not sure how to respond. It's incredible, Dean, but just like you had to ask me a question earlier that you knew the answer to, I still have to ask: Are you sure about this?"

"That's a more legitimate question than mine, Dad. But the answer is yes, based on the evidence we have so far, my read of both Colonel Weathers and Corporal Armstrong, and well, my gut."

Gary commented, "You could always read people. That's for sure."

"Right, but people." Dean looked perplexed. "Humans."

"I see your point." His father again leaned forward, but looked down at the floor. "I can only think of one reason why you would tell me this." He paused, and Dean said nothing. Gary continued, "It's raised questions in your mind about..."

He sat up straight, looked at his son, and raised and stretched out his arms. "...this."

Dean swallowed hard. *I can count on Dad to cut to the chase.* "Yes, well, I don't know. I'm not sure. I don't know what to do with this."

Gary nodded. "I understand. This changes a great many things. But it doesn't change God. It doesn't change..." He turned in his seat, and pointed to the opposite side of the space. "It doesn't change that." He turned back around. "But it does change, in certain ways, our limited view of God in the sense that it expands our witness of the vastness of His love, creativity, greatness and power."

Dean was amazed at how serene and confident his father appeared after hearing, no doubt, what he considered ridiculous less than an hour earlier. He couldn't find the words to say anything in response, whether from fear or ignorance.

Gary said, "This isn't the first time I've thought about this."

"Really?"

His father actually smiled. "Have you ever met Father Ed Duffy?"

Dean shook his head. "You've mentioned him. The priest at St. Peter's?"

Gary nodded. "He's been there several years now, but he kind of kept to himself, you know, to his church. But he reached out a few months ago. I was surprised, quite frankly, but pleased. We've developed a friendship, and try to have lunch about once a week now."

"So, he's a good guy?"

"He is, and he has this fascination with the unexplained. We sometimes wind up talking about a variety of mysterious phenomena. He keeps things in perspective, but seems to enjoy the speculation about assorted things, including the ideas of UFOs and visitors from other planets. He's read these tales and watched the news of various reported sightings and so on. But on a couple of occasions, he and I delve into the theology of such possibilities."

"You never mentioned this before."

Gary chuckled. "Why would I? How exactly would that come up in conversation?"

"Fair enough. But now, here it is."

"Apparently, and I have the occasion to tap into those conversations." He shook his head. "Definitely not something I ever expected to be doing, to say the least."

"And?"

Gary answered, "Ed and I have discussed assorted matters. First and foremost is the Incarnation. If visitors from another world ever came here, how might that affect God taking on human form in order to save mankind? And we didn't see how that would change, or how our view of it should change. We agreed that the only thing that could ever undermine our faith would be if the bones of Jesus were discovered. As Paul wrote in First Corinthians, 'Now if Christ be preached that he rose from the dead, how say some among you that there is no resurrection of the dead? But if there be no resurrection of the dead, then is Christ not risen: And if Christ be not risen, then is our preaching vain, and your faith is also vain.'"

*Dad is slipping into teacher mode.* Dean took comfort in that.

Gary went on. "I think that a discovery of other life in the universe *magnifies*, if that's even possible, the love of God for us." He then shook his head slightly. "It also magnifies the fallenness of human beings, and our need for the birth, life, death and resurrection of Christ, and through that His love, forgiveness, redemption and salvation."

"How so?" asked Dean.

"If we are not alone in this universe, the fact that the Incarnation took place speaks to how special mankind is, and not necessarily in a good way. It speaks even more to our sinfulness and depravity."

Dean quietly commented, "The depth of our sin and the heights of His love." He began to feel a calm returning, starting to push aside the uneasiness that had nagged in the back of his mind since he came to accept this revelation of a secret alien invasion.

"That's right." Gary continued, "And then there is the matter of whether or not these beings were fallen. Did they fall into sin like man did? Were ... are ... they sinners in need of saving?"

Dean responded, "Given all that I've learned, there is no doubt that they, too, are sinners."

Gary nodded. "That would bring up the third big issue that Ed and I have speculated on, that is, how would God go about saving these other people that He no doubt loves? Are they covered, if you will, by what Jesus did for humans? Were they offered salvation by another means? Did they possibly reject it?"

"Reject?"

"I know this is out there" – he paused as father and son exchanged a bemused smile – "but think about what would have happened to the Church and the faithful if the Nazis had prevailed? And think about what we know has happened in the Soviet Union? You mentioned what your visitors said about their society. That sounds very Soviet-style totalitarianism, and we know that, at least here on Earth, that's an atheistic monolith. One of the goals of Stalin and his ilk is the complete eradication of Christianity, and all other religions."

"I hadn't considered that an entire planet might reject what God offered." Dean also asked about something else that his father noted. "And what if what Jesus did for humanity on Earth applies to others?"

"Again, we're speculating, but when considering various possibilities from a wild scenario of visitors from another world, well...," his father replied.

"That's my life now."

Gary nodded. "So, it might mean that God began with us, and He will work through humans to spread the Good News. If so, humanity would have to pray for great humility and wisdom. Once more, God starting with us, if you will, doesn't mean that we're deemed the best or most favored, but instead that perhaps we were the worst of the lot and most in need of rescuing. Missionary work to beings from other worlds?" He shook his head. "Of course, we simply don't know what we don't know. Holy Scripture reveals what we need to know about our salvation. It all points to the death and resurrection of Jesus. That's the purpose, the point. Yes, it says much about other things, such as morals. I think Christians often get into trouble, opening ourselves to ridicule, when we try to make Scripture speak on something specific that it doesn't actually address. Indeed, the Bible doesn't speak about a great many things. Discoveries via science, for example, don't undermine our faith, but speak to the glory of God. What you're dealing with and have brought to me is the same. In the end, the existence of life on other worlds is a matter left to human inquiry – science, experiences, and so on – but if such life turns out to exist..." He stopped, looked directly at his son, and continued, "This is going to take some getting used to."

"I know."

Dean watched his father trying to find the right words. Gary finally said, "Now that we're pretty sure that such life does exist, countless questions arise, including what we've been talking about – their relationship to the Lord, and what God might call upon humanity to do."

"So much to consider. But you've helped to put me back in the right frame of mind to do so. Thanks, Dad. I needed this."

Gary smiled. "I have to say that the chats that Ed and I have had about this were more enjoyable as mere fantasy, like the intellectual exercises you might have in college over a few beers. It's, quite frankly, far less enjoyable now."

"It certainly is."

Gary paused. Dean could see that his father was reflecting further. He finally said, "I have to correct myself. I actually can't say that what Ed and I discussed was purely a fantastical, intellectual exercise."

"Why?"

"Ed told me that there were people involved in what he called the 'UFO crowd' who took this all very seriously, and he found that their being convinced that intelligent life existed elsewhere in the universe seemed to undermine their faith, at least for many of them." Gary fell silent, once more, and then added, "Ed enjoys science fiction and fantasy tales, as well as UFO talk and speculation about life elsewhere, but he's concerned that the mere idea of visitors from another planet could be a cause for some people rejecting God."

Dean contributed, "Or they've turned away from God, and are looking for something else to fill the void."

Gary said, "True. Thinking about our discussions now, I wonder if Ed has thought about being a kind of chaplain, for lack of a better word, to this UFO crowd."

"If word ever gets out on this, then Father Duffy might become a very busy priest."

Dean managed a chuckle, and his father smiled.

Gary added, "At some point, you might want to talk with Ed. He'll be able to give you a lot more, including that thoughts of other worlds aren't new in the Church. He's noted that assorted theologians over the centuries have at least noted or debated the possibility. He mentioned Chrysostom, Origen, Clement, Athanasius, Augustine, Aquinas, Melanchthon, and a sixteenth-century monk whose name escapes me, and others."

"Funny, Lawrence Silver also mentioned that this idea has been kicked around over the centuries by philosophers and theologians."

"If it makes sense at some point, I can invite Ed over for dinner and you can explore all of this more deeply with him."

"I just might take you up on that, Dad. Thanks."

Gary said, "I noticed that you're calling your old roommate 'Lawrence' now rather than 'Larry.'"

"Yes, he's gone through something of a transformation in terms of how he presents himself."

Gary smiled. "Well, he is a professor now."

Dean thought of another consequence of all of this. "You know, the order of things in our outlook on the world likely will need to be updated, I suppose."

"Meaning?" his father asked.

"We can see how our perspective on our fellow man can get lost – twisted – during a time of war, especially when working against vast evil out of necessity. As Christians, we're called to put God first, and then care for our fellow human beings from family to enemies, while recognizing when a just war is necessary and supporting our country when it's in the right. Now, God remains as the ultimate good, but are we called to love friends and enemies not just among humans but among these visitors as well?"

Gary replied, "You know the answer to that. Would you treat Colonel Weathers or Corporal Armstrong differently than any of the others you're now working with?"

"No. I wouldn't."

"Right."

They continued talking and speculating about ideas, challenges, and even opportunities. Looking at his watch, Dean was surprised by how much time had passed. "Dad, thanks for this. I'll come back with more thoughts and questions, and perhaps we can tap into Father Duffy's wisdom. But right now, I need to get at least some sleep before heading back to D.C."

The two men rose to their feet, and as they descended the stairs from the choir loft, Gary asked, "Would you like to say a prayer together before we go back across the street?"

"Definitely."

# Chapter 45

Major Denis Nusinev stepped into his Moscow apartment, and locked the door behind him. The dwelling was almost lavish by Soviet standards, but such were some of the rewards for those who served the State and the Party well, especially those in the highest ranks of the military.

He sighed. It had been a long journey, and Nusinev was tired. He checked his watch. It was almost 11 pm. He didn't go to bed. Instead, he tossed his coat and jacket aside, followed by his necktie. As he rolled up his shirt sleeves, Nusinev walked to one of the windows in the sitting room. He raised the shade, closed the thin curtains and turned on the lamp resting on top of a table at the window. The same style table and lamp stood at the second window, but Nusinev left that shade down and lamp off.

He grabbed a writing tablet and pencil, and dropped them on the kitchen table.

Nusinev then brewed some coffee. After pouring a cup, he placed it next to the tablet, and sat down at the table. He shook his head and picked up the pencil. Over the next two hours, Nusinev wrote down, in spartan, direct military style, everything relevant that he had seen and heard during his time at the facility in Khabarovsk Krai. He described the layout of the facility, the details of the new weapons being produced, including how they were being made, and the fact that the MiG-Xs were being readied for an attack on U.S. naval forces involved in the Korean conflict. He also detailed that security at the facility was mainly focused inward, and that when the operations were completed there, the facility would be destroyed. He relayed all he knew about that process. And he added that most of the personnel at the facility would be killed. The next stage of their weapons development would proceed at another facility, which he knew nothing about at this point. After providing all of the details he could, Nusinev concluded, "Given what I saw and heard, I do not doubt the veracity of the declaration that the forces opposing the communist North Korea will suffer significant defeats. Indeed, without some kind of intervention, North Korea will prevail, and the South will fall."

Several more times, he read and re-read his notes, making assorted edits. Nusinev finally rewrote a clean copy of the six pages describing the situation.

With his notes complete, Nusinev finished his third cup of coffee. He got up and went into the bedroom. He walked over to a large armoire, and dropped down on his back on the floor next to the heavy piece of furniture that dominated the room. His right arm just slipped underneath the armoire, and his hand began searching the bottom of the standalone closet. Nusinev's hand stopped on the item taped to the bottom of the armoire. He found the edge of the tape and pulled it off. Nusinev withdrew a small envelope. He sat up and opened the envelope. Inside were three small Minox cameras. Each was just over three inches long, about an inch wide, and only three-fifths of an inch high. Each weighed four-and-a-half ounces. The Minox was a tiny, reliable camera that, while available commercially, spies on both sides of the Cold War had come to love.

Nusinev took one of the cameras out, and returned the envelope with the other two back to their hiding place under the armoire.

When returning to the table, he carefully proceeded to take multiple pictures of each sheet of his notes with the Minox.

By the time he was finished, it was just after four in the morning.

Nusinev showered and dressed. He shut off the lamp by the window and pulled down the shade. Before leaving his apartment, he burned the pages he wrote, and slipped the camera into his pants pocket.

It was not unusual for Nusinev to rise early and set out on a walk to his office in the Kremlin. When doing so, he would stop at a small restaurant for breakfast along the way.

As he approached the restaurant, it was still dark. Nusinev went down the alley next to the building housing the eating establishment. In a dark corner, he spotted what he was looking for. The major looked around to make sure he was alone. He went into the corner, squatted down and looked at the dead rat. Nusinev reached inside his pocket, and pulled out the camera. He then reached for the rat. It had been cut open and gutted as expected. He picked it up, raised it to his nose and sniffed. The smell of pepper sauce was strong.

He slipped the camera through the incision in the rat carcass, and pushed the opening back together. The slit was unnoticeable if anyone for some reason decided to inspect a dead rat. Nusinev slipped the small carcass back into the corner, but this time pushed it behind some pieces of wood leaning against the brick wall. The pepper aroma would make sure the dead rat and its contents would be left alone by any scavengers.

Nusinev stood up. Again, he was still alone. He walked back down the alley, turned and opened the front door of the restaurant.

He was recognized by the waitress, who welcomed him with a smile.

Before eating, he went into the bathroom and washed his hands.

\*     \*     \*

An hour after Nusinev finished his meal and strolled off to the Kremlin, a garbage truck backed down the alley next to the restaurant. The driver hopped out, and emptied several cans of refuse into the back of the truck. And as he placed the last can down, the garbage man bent down and picked up the rat carcass. He slipped his hand inside the rat, withdrew the tiny camera and deposited it into his pocket, and then tossed the rat into the back of the truck with the rest of the garbage.

# Chapter 46

How would humanity react if it knew what loomed high above them beyond what they could see in the sky?

Unbeknownst to anyone, three disc-shaped ships had been orbiting the Earth for the past eight years. One was a control ship, the second a troop ship and the third was a supply freighter. The control and troop ships were each 70 yards in diameter and a height of 33 yards. Each had ten decks. The supply freighter was larger at 100 yards across, and a height of 54 yards, with 17 decks.

A fourth ship – same shape but about half the size of the control and troop ships – was orbiting Mars, not far from the space pad that had taken all four ships to this solar system.

Inside the control ship, six Commanders were seated at the metal table in the room with gray walls and the regular humming of engines and systems in the background.

Commander One, who not only was the leader of the control ship but also of the entire mission, was speaking to the group about the report they had received from the Defenders who were now in control of the Soviet Union. "What they have passed on aligns with the information we have been given by the facility's lead Defender as well."

"Excellent," replied Commander Two, who managed all of the resources on the mission.

Commander One said, "The Defenders who have been sent have performed remarkably." Looking at Commander Three, he added, "That's much to your credit."

"Thank you, sir," responded Commander Three. She led the Defenders program.

One asked, "So, do we accept the recommendations from the Soviet group?"

Three shifted in her seat. "They're on the ground and trained for this. Still, though, I would like more time to make sure we are fully prepared."

One stared back at her.

Commander Four, leader of the troop ship, said, "I have to agree with Commander Three. The Defenders are the best, and fully prepared. But they tend to be a bit more aggressive than perhaps is needed."

Commander Six was the leader of the supply ship and spoke rarely at these meetings. But when speaking, he provided a sound perspective. "While they might be overstating things, I think that Commanders Three and Four are right. However, given where things are, I think that no more than another two Earth weeks would be needed to provide some added confidence."

Commander Five, who led the technical division, shrugged his shoulders. "I see no downside to adding two weeks to the schedule. It's not like anyone at the facility in Khabarovsk is going to be in contact with anyone to leak what's happening."

"True," agreed Commander One. "Let's add those two weeks, and have the attack mission begin in six weeks. Agreed?"

Everyone at the table acquiesced.

Nearly an hour later, Commanders Six and Two were on a shuttle heading back to the supply freighter, and Commanders Four and Three were on another shuttle moving back to the troop ship.

On that second shuttle, Commander Three was helming the small transport. Commander Four was next to her, ready to take the controls if needed. But he was simply staring out the wide front window as they moved closer to the troop ship's landing bay.

Four observed, "I don't see any way that this can be stopped."

Three replied, "Neither do I."

They journeyed on in silence, until they spoke to the bay sergeant for confirmation on their approach and landing. As

Three guided the hexagon-shaped shuttle into the bay, Four said, "There's got to be something we can do."

After gently landing the shuttle and then shutting down systems, all Three could manage in response was, "Please let me know if you come up with something. But it's not like there is a movement on this mission for some kind of rebellion."

That remark went unanswered.

# Chapter 47

Along with Maxine Marshall, Dean Cold welcomed Lawrence Silver into 1734 Q Street. Silver, a now-former Harvard professor, was then introduced to the others who had been sprinkled around the first floor of the townhouse.

After exchanging niceties with John Bartley and Daria Popov, Silver turned to Mike Strickland. As the two shook hands, Cold said, "I hope it will work for each of you if Lawrence takes the other bedroom on the first floor next door? I believe there's more than enough space that you'll have privacy."

"I'm sure that will be just fine," replied Silver.

"Before you say that, Lawrence, I think you need to know that I'm a drummer."

"Pardon me?"

"In addition to being a physicist and chemist, I play the drums," declared Strickland.

Jefferson added, "Also, I have the apartment upstairs, and I play the trumpet. And of course, as Dean's old roommate, you know that he masters anything with a keyboard."

Silver chuckled. "I recall. Well, I enjoy music as much as the next man, and am sure it will all work out fine, as long as we arrive at a reasonable schedule."

Cold interjected, "I think that they're trying to be funny, Lawrence. Mike's drums are over here." He pointed to the drum set at the side of the room.

"I see," said Silver.

Strickland smiled. "Sorry, just kidding."

Cold said, "And I haven't officially introduced you to Cameron Jefferson."

As they shook hands, Jefferson said, "It's Cam." He smiled and added, "I understand, Lawrence, that you're the only one in the room not surprised by what's happening?"

"I wouldn't say that, Cam. I'm surprised, but in a different way."

"Right, Dean and Max said that you expected visitors to be friendly."

"I do, indeed. And I understand that at least two of these arrivals are friendly."

"That's true," interjected Bartley.

"Hopefully, many more are," added Silver.

Before anyone could respond, as if on cue, the front door opened, and in stepped Colonel Robert Weathers and Corporal Grace Armstrong. Each stopped at seeing an unfamiliar face. Likewise, Silver froze, looking at the two arrivals.

Cold made basic introductions. Weathers stepped forward, extended his hand, and said, "It's nice to meet you, Professor."

But Silver seemed to be cemented in place, and opened his mouth slightly without any sounds coming out. Cold noted that all of the smoothness of the new Lawrence had evaporated.

*Starstruck? Amazed that what he had dreamed of stood before him in reality. And ... perhaps a touch of fear as well?*

As Weathers' hand remained extended for an awkward length of time, Silver seemed to partially snap out of his stupor. He slowly reached out and shook Weathers' hand. "Welcome, Colonel."

Armstrong moved toward Silver as well, and extended her hand. Silver turned and shook her hand. "Ah, yes. You, too. Welcome, Corporal."

Silver took a deep breath.

*He's trying to regain his balance.*

Silver said, "I... I have a million questions."

Weathers smiled. "I'm sure you do, but first" – he turned to Cold – "I must speak with Agent Cold."

"Yes?" responded Cold.

"Two things. First, Grace and I need to get back to our jobs, or we're going to have some things to explain."

Cold shook his head. "You're both on your new assignments. You're already at work."

Armstrong said, "What does that mean?"

"President Eisenhower made your superiors aware that you're on a new assignment. No further explanations were necessary."

"I see," said Armstrong. She and Weathers looked at each other.

Cold asked, "And the other matter?"

Weathers said, "Yes, it's a reminder. Our next scheduled conversation with our Commander is coming up."

"Right. When?"

"Four days. Friday night."

"Is it possible for us to listen in? To be in the room at the time?"

Weathers answered, "Yes, that would make sense – as long as no one makes a sound."

"But what about language?" inquired Cold.

Weathers replied, "Meaning?"

This was an issue that had crossed Cold's mind previously, but he hadn't gotten around to mentioning it. "You have your own language. How would we understand if we sat in on the communication?"

Weathers nodded. "Ah, yes, I see. You would find the way that Nykarians speak very strange, but we actually do use English, or whatever is the language of the nation where a cell exists."

"Why?" interjected Silver.

Armstrong answered, "Each cell is immersed in the customs and culture, including the language, of their assigned country even before we ... arrive. It limits the possibility of any mistakes."

Weathers added, "Also, some argue that it's an additional safeguard if anyone somehow overheard our communications. Overhearing us in English, for example, obviously would raise questions, but hearing us speaking

Nykarian would draw immediate inquiries." He half-shrugged. "Depends on what's being said, I suppose."

"I see." Cold looked at Bartley. "John?"

Bartley nodded. "Count me in."

Cold looked at Weathers. "It'll be John and me, then."

"Good," responded Weathers.

With wide eyes, Silver asked, "Where are your superiors, if I might ask?"

Cold said, "Lawrence, you need to be brought up to date on a host of details that we didn't get to at Harvard." He looked around. "I think it makes sense to do so now."

Everyone took seats in the main living room, which was now a meeting space.

Cold said, "Grace, why don't you start by answering Lawrence's first question?"

Armstrong looked at Silver. "Our people arrived in your solar system on four ships, and three are now in high orbit around Earth."

The conversation went on for another hour, and Cold noted that Silver, rather than being worried as the rest of the group was when hearing about these visitors, seemed giddy.

When that discussion had run its course, for now, Cold shifted gears. "Let's take a half hour or so, and then get back together. John and I have been putting together a report requested by the president regarding our thoughts on what we – meaning this group – and the nation might need from a military standpoint, given what we're confronting." Cold saw that Silver wanted to say something, but stopped himself. Cold continued, "I know that's wide-ranging, but John and I have hammered out assorted things. I would like to get everyone's feedback before we take it to President Eisenhower."

All agreed to reconvene shortly.

Cold pulled Weathers and Armstrong to the side, and said, "You two obviously have knowledge of what your people, the Nykarians, have, and what the U.S. has, so your input will be critical."

"Of course," responded Weathers.

Cold added, "And that includes what you can help with in terms of bringing Nykarian improvements to what we're doing."

Armstrong declared, "Absolutely."

When the group reconvened, Cold walked them through the draft request that he and Bartley had put together for the president. It reflected their respective experiences in the war – Cold leading special operations missions in the OSS, and Bartley as an Army Ranger. It was about commandos having the ability to wage unconventional warfare, including infiltration and sabotage.

After finishing the presentation, the four individuals at the table whom Cold wanted to hear from most agreed that they had hit the essential requirements. That included, of course, the man whom Cold had worked with during the war, Cam Jefferson, and Daria Popov, who had lived the life of a spy for some time now.

Jefferson declared, "You know how Wild Bill described to FDR the types needed for the OSS? 'Men calculatingly reckless with disciplined daring, who are trained for aggressive action.' I always took pride in being recognized as one of those men."

Cold smiled, "Yeah, me, too."

Popov chimed in, "I like that – 'calculatingly reckless with disciplined daring.' But the combination is not so easy to find, based on my experiences."

"True," agreed Jefferson.

Cold turned to Weathers and Armstrong.

Jefferson offered additional thoughts with his main point stressing the need to have other assets available when needed, such as the ability to gain quick access to planes, boats and even submarines, while also tapping into the kind of manpower ready to do whatever was asked of them.

Colonel Weathers said, "You have zeroed in on the only way to fight, to disrupt, what my people are doing with the Soviet Union. You don't have the firepower to take them on in a conventional way..."

"Yet," commented Bartley. "We don't have the firepower yet."

"Yes, yet. But since that is the case, the ability to clandestinely move in, inflict damage and get out will prove vital and effective."

# Chapter 48

Pastor Gary Cold took a sip of his coffee. He knew the diner well. Over time and a great deal of caffeine, Cold was getting to know the man seated across from him in the booth.

Father Edward Duffy was in his mid-forties, slightly overweight, and gray was invading his light brown hair around the sides. His eyes were a bright blue, and his complexion ruddy.

The two had exchanged pleasantries while waiting for their food. The waitress arrived with a Reuben sandwich for Duffy, and a cheeseburger for Cold.

Only three other people were being served lunch in the small Brooklyn diner – one sat on a stool at a long counter, and an older couple sat in another booth.

After a bite of food, Cold said, "My son, Dean, came by the other day, and you'll never guess what we wound up discussing."

Duffy swallowed and replied, "The Dodgers."

Cold chuckled. "For a change, no. We talked about one of our topics, about visitors from other worlds and how, if they existed, they might affect what people think about God."

Duffy finished chewing his bite of pastrami, Swiss cheese, mustard and rye bread. "Your son, with the Secret Service, came from D.C. to chat about the possibilities of intelligent alien life?" asked Duffy in a joking tone.

Cold looked uncomfortable for a brief moment. He took another swig of coffee, and replied, "Our conversation went that way after I mentioned that you and I had become friends and met for lunch."

Duffy nodded. "I know you mentioned that he had considered entering the seminary before the war. So, I assume that he thought I was a mad priest."

Cold protested, "Not at all. He actually found what I relayed to be interesting."

"He's as generous as you are, then. Perhaps it's a Cold family trait?"

Cold chuckled. "Hardly. But he did seem to appreciate what we've discussed if such a ... fantasy were to ever become reality." He chewed more of his cheeseburger.

"Did your son, the almost seminarian, offer any insights for our discussions?"

Cold swallowed. "I can't say that he did. But he was intrigued by the idea that a rather long history exists of various theologians and philosophers at least considering intelligent life elsewhere in the universe."

Duffy nodded, and the two ate in silence for a couple of minutes.

Cold pressed on, "After our recent talks about this, I always find my mind wandering back to the Incarnation."

Duffy swallowed. "You're not alone. Did Christ's humiliation in becoming man, dying for our sins, and conquering death thanks to his resurrection cover only mankind, or is it something universal, encompassing other intelligent life? That issue naturally came up among the Christian theologians who entertained the possibility of other worlds over the centuries."

Cold commented, "Yes, assuming that these aliens were rational and spiritual beings, and fallen – as we've discussed."

"Right." Duffy took another bite of his Reuben, and wiped the sides of his mouth with a napkin while chewing.

"Who jumps out at you in terms of their thinking on this?" asked Cold.

"First, I'll never forget when reading Saint John Chrysostom, especially given that he was a Father and Doctor of the Church in the fourth century. It's burned into my memory. He wrote, "For with God, nothing is difficult, but as the painter who has made one likeness will make ten thousand with ease, so also with God it is easy to make worlds without number and end. Rather..." Duffy held up a finger, tilted his head in thought, and continued, "Rather, as it is easy for you to conceive a city and worlds without bound, unto God it is easy to make them; or rather again, it is far easier." Duffy was smiling.

The priest took another sip of coffee, and continued, "While related speculations and assertions were offered in subsequent centuries, no doubt more than we know about, it was in the fifteenth century that the French theologian William of Vorilong pushed the discussion forward in a way that no one, again as far as we can know, had done before. He hit directly on the matters of original sin, the Incarnation, and redemption in and through Christ."

Cold watched as Duffy reached inside his jacket pocket, and pulled out a small leather notebook. Duffy flipped through some pages, and said, "Give me a second."

Cold asked, "You have notes?"

As he continued paging through the book thick with notes, Duffy nodded. "I do." He found what he was looking for, and said, "Here's what Vorilong wrote...

> 'If it be inquired whether men exist on that world, and whether they have sinned as Adam sinned, I answer no, for they would not exist in sin and did not spring from Adam. But it is shown that they would exist from the virtue of God, transported into that world, as Enoch and Elijah in the earthly paradise. As to the question whether Christ by dying on this earth could redeem the inhabitants of another world, I answer that he is able to do this even if the worlds were infinite, but it would not be fitting for him to go unto another world that he must die again.'"

Cold finished his cheeseburger while watching Duffy start to flip more pages in his notebook.

Duffy looked up and said, "And then there was another Frenchman, a Catholic philosopher, Comte Joseph de Maistre. He argued..." He looked back down at his notebook:

> "'...that the blood shed on Calvary had been useful not only to men, but to the angels, the stars, and all created beings; an opinion which will not seem surprising if we call to mind what St. Paul says: "Because it hath pleased God to reconcile all things unto himself, through him who is the beginning, the first born from the dead, making peace through the blood of his cross, both as to things that are in heaven, and the things that are on earth," And if every creature groaneth, according to the profound doctrine of the same apostle, why should not also every creature be consoled?'"

"Interesting," commented Cold, as he seemed mesmerized by the passion of his friend.

Duffy added, "So, as we've talked about before, there are those who have spoken about extraterrestrials not having fallen into sin, or if they did, that the atonement of Jesus would or could apply to them. There also have been arguments that God could have chosen multiple Incarnations to save beings on other planets. And can that be fully doubted given God's infinite power and His love for all He has created?"

Cold didn't respond, and it didn't appear that Duffy expected a response. The priest continued, "I don't think so. But at the same time, there seems to be something discomforting about the idea that it might take away the depth, breadth and reach of Jesus, His death upon a cross, and His rising from the dead. It would feel like – and perhaps more than just feeling given much in Holy Scripture – limiting God's love and grace." He paused, and looked out the large window next to their table and up into the sky. "So, what would we do with the idea of a fallen race of aliens where Christ didn't come into their world to save them?

Through no merit of our own, the possibility would exist that humans have been given a mission to spread the Good News." Duffy looked back at Cold. "Is it hard to imagine not just on Earth, but into the heavens? Matthew 28: 'Go ye therefore, and teach all nations, baptizing them in the name of the Father, and of the Son, and of the Holy Ghost: Teaching them to observe all things whatsoever I have commanded you: and, lo, I am with you always, even unto the end of the world. Amen."

"The Great Commission – whether here on Earth or elsewhere?" asked Cold.

"Everywhere, right? Sign me up for such missionary work to the stars."

Cold ate the last French fry on his plate, and said, "If visitors from other planets were real."

Duffy took a deep breath. "Yes, if they were." He finished his Reuben.

"It's my turn to pick up the tab," declared Cold.

"Thanks, Gary, and I appreciate you putting up with my rantings. I'm attending a meeting with some of the UFO folks soon, and this helped get my thinking clear."

"I get the feeling, Ed, that you see yourself as a missionary or chaplain to that movement."

Duffy smiled. "You picked up on that." He nodded. "I do feel a kind of responsibility, you might say. Whenever the topic comes up, nearly all of them seem ready to give up on the Lord because they believe that there are other worlds with intelligent life."

Cold replied, "Chicken or the egg? Do they turn to the existence of alien life because they turned away from God first? Or did the idea of intelligent life elsewhere undermine a belief in God?"

"It's probably different for each person."

Cold smiled amiably and commented, "Perhaps your first step is to be a missionary to those who believe in UFOs, and that will prepare you if alien life ever actually shows up?"

Duffy didn't return the lighthearted look. Instead, he simply said, "Maybe, Gary."

Cold raised his eyebrow ever so slightly, and said, "Well, I'll keep you and those efforts in my prayers."

"Thanks."

# Chapter 49

An air of defeatism and fear hung over this gathering of Ken Roberts, Clay Walsh and Jerry Debrowski.

None of the three had words of hope. When it appeared that their pessimism couldn't have descended any further, Debrowski reflected, "These beings, for lack of a better word, have journeyed through space to come here to take over. They already control the Soviet Union, from what you said." He looked at Roberts. "We were struggling to keep the Soviets in place, but now they have unfathomable weapons and power. These space travelers are a hell of a lot smarter than Stalin and his goons ever were."

Roberts responded, "I'm aware. Believe me. I don't see a way out. What is your point?"

Walsh interjected, "It's your point, Ken. What's the way out? I don't see it."

"Neither do I," added Debrowski.

"It pains me to say this," said Walsh, "and I hope you two have thought of something that I haven't. But I don't see how these invaders can be fought with any hope of success."

The room was silent.

Roberts finally said, "You're saying it's futile to fight?"

"Please, Ken, Jerry, give me some kind of real hope. Show me the way where we can fight and save not just America, but the world. Please."

Debrowski sat back. "I've been racking my brain, and to be honest, I haven't been able to think of anything."

Roberts started sweating. "What the hell? Are you telling me that we go from working to stop the Soviets to working with them? To work with these alien invaders?"

"Shit," commented Debrowski. "I hope that's not what I'm saying."

The coming hour or so was filled by intermittent ideas to fight the communists and their alien allies, by questions and doubts as to how those efforts would possibly succeed, and by uncomfortable moments of silence.

A tear formed in the corner of Roberts' left eye as he said, "I don't see a way. I can't ... find another way."

Walsh and Debrowski eyed each other.

Debrowski asked, "What are you thinking, Ken?"

The large man's face turned red. "What the hell do you think I'm thinking, Jerry? We've essentially said it already. There's no way that I can see that we're able to fight alien invaders who have who-knows-what technology, weapons and powers, and are in control of the Soviet Union."

The three sat in silence for another two minutes.

Roberts resumed, "Maybe someday we'll be able to get rid of them, but for now, we have to ... compromise ... to save us all."

Walsh carefully asked, "Now you're saying that we should reach out to these visitors?"

"What else can we do? Unless I'm missing something big, how else do we stop countless deaths and – what? – slavery? Quite frankly, I don't want to die, and I don't want to be some kind of slave."

"I understand," declared Walsh.

Roberts seemed both surprised and relieved to hear Walsh's words.

Debrowski added, "It's the only real choice."

"Thank God," said Roberts. "I thought you'd think I was a traitor, a coward."

"Not at all," said Walsh. "We need to work together."

Debrowski noted, "No one wants death or war. When we all have the same purpose, it will be beneficial to each of us."

Roberts turned his head back and forth between Walsh and Debrowski. "Um, 'each of us'? 'We'? What the hell?"

Walsh said, "We knew that you would be someone who understood the reality of the situation, and what was necessary. You're a realist."

Ken Roberts sat unmoving, with his mouth open and seemingly frozen in place.

Walsh added, "Living together in peace and security is paramount to us, and it should be for America, too."

# Chapter 50

The four just finished their communication with Commander One, and glasses were filled.

"Gentlemen, this is a moment to savor." Joseph Stalin raised a glass of vodka. General Arseni Demyan, Dr. Oleg Abramov and MGB Director Arkadi Sokolov did the same, and each man took a drink.

Demyan cringed, and said, "I haven't figured out their fascination with vodka."

Stalin shrugged. "I like it, within limits."

Sokolov added, "Do not judge vodka too harshly, Arseni, at least until you have had something better than this swill."

Abramov said, "Yes. These Russians don't seem to make anything of quality – beyond some key weapons."

"Not all that different from home, perhaps," commented Stalin.

The other three stared at him.

Stalin put down his glass and raised his hands in innocence. "You know my meaning. After all, there are many reasons why we are on Earth."

Sokolov replied, "That might be true, but let's limit such glibness."

"You're right."

After a few seconds of silence, they all laughed, with Demyan declaring, "This *is* swill, and not much worse than our slop." He drank down the clear liquid. As he refilled his glass and topped off the others', Demyan continued, "It does not do justice for what has been accomplished, especially by you, Arkadi."

Demyan, Stalin and Abramov raised their glasses to Sokolov, who said, "Thank you." Sokolov took a drink, and went on, "But each of us has played our parts and will continue to do so. And the fact that we just received such positive feedback from Commander One speaks to all of us, along with the fact that our plan was accepted basically in its entirety except for adding a precautionary two weeks to the timeline."

Demyan added, "We were trained – indeed, bred and raised – for this, and yet, it was clear to me that Commander One was surprised at how smoothly this has gone, so far."

"I agree," declared Abramov with a shrug. "They are pleased."

Sokolov declared, "And they should be. Yes, the mission and plan were well thought out, but we have executed them. We have taken control of Earth's mightiest, or at least second mightiest, nation, and eliminated those who might challenge our Stalin. And now, we are close to overturning the order of things on this planet, as our technology and weapons put the West back on its heels."

Stalin added, "After this first strike, they will be frightened and with good cause."

# Chapter 51

Roy O'Keefe sped by a protesting secretary perched outside the office of CIA Director Allen Dulles. He knocked and already began opening the door as Dulles just started to say, "Yes, come in."

Dulles was at his desk, with his top aide, Ken Roberts, spreading his girth on a small couch to the right of the desk.

Dulles said, "Roy, you've got something?"

O'Keefe said, "I do."

"Pull up a chair."

O'Keefe ignored that and remained standing. He glanced at Roberts.

Dulles assured, "It's okay. Ken can hear."

Roberts gave a quizzical look.

O'Keefe said, "Sir, grave information from Nusinev." He handed over an envelope.

As Dulles pulled photographs out of the manila envelope, Roberts asked, "Nusinev? Major Denis Nusinev? Aide to General Arseni Demyan?"

Dulles raised an eyebrow at Roberts. "Yes, Ken. Now, shall we let Roy report?"

Roberts' expression turned sheepish.

O'Keefe continued, "The Soviets have a highly advanced weapons manufacturing facility in Khabarovsk Krai, and it's unlike anything that Nusinev has ever seen, or as he put it, anything he could even fathom. They're producing fighters, rockets and unmanned surveillance aircraft that, well, if Nusinev is right, will leave us completely vulnerable. And they plan on unleashing these new weapons on U.S. naval forces in Korea and on Seoul."

Dulles looked up from the photos now on his desk. "Shit." He then added, "When?"

"According to this, in about a month. No specific date is indicated." O'Keefe glanced at Roberts, who was now leaning forward and sweating.

Dulles took off his eyeglasses and rubbed his eyes. He put the spectacles back on and said, "Gentlemen, give me some time to read and evaluate what's been sent from Nusinev."

O'Keefe interjected, "He's been highly reliable, sir."

"I'm aware."

Roberts maneuvered himself to his feet. "But that doesn't mean that he's not compromised."

"What?" replied O'Keefe. He didn't hide a look of astonishment.

The still-sweating Roberts continued, "He's a top aide to their top military man. We have to at least consider the possibility."

Dulles had his head down reading Nusinev's report. "Yes. We always need to consider that, Ken. You two should return in an hour. Now, please..."

Roberts exited the back door of Dulles' office, and O'Keefe followed him.

Roberts looked over his shoulder at O'Keefe, and continued to lumber toward his office. When at the door, he turned and said, "Do you mind, Roy? I need to go over a few things ... in private."

"This will only take a minute," replied O'Keefe stoically.

"Oh, alright."

O'Keefe watched as Roberts' hands shook pulling out the key and unlocking the door.

After the two entered the office, O'Keefe not only closed the door behind them, but also locked it.

Roberts arrived at the desk and lowered himself into his chair. It creaked under the man's weight. "Grab a seat."

As O'Keefe was sitting, Roberts unlocked one of his desk drawers, and pulled it out an inch or so. He looked up and said, "I hope this is quick. I need to get to a few things before we return to the director's office."

O'Keefe sighed and looked Roberts in the eyes. "How did you get this job?"

"Pardon me?"

"You don't have any background in intelligence work."

"I'll have you know that I served on two Senate committees on the Hill that had direct responsibility regarding the OSS and then the CIA."

"Right," O'Keefe replied disapprovingly. "You certainly have gained the director's trust."

"And for good reason. I'm committed to the security of the United States of America."

O'Keefe stared back in silence, while Roberts returned to sweating rather profusely.

O'Keefe calmly observed, "You know, I've been in on several conversations with you and the director over some grave situations. Yet, I've never seen you perspire before. But now, you can't seem to stop sweating. Are you alright?"

"I'm fine," protested Roberts.

"Are you sure?"

"I've had enough of this."

"I haven't. I never liked you, Ken. I know you came from the Hill, and that's probably part of the reason I don't like you. You're too political. I've always felt like you'd do the politically expedient thing. Come to think of it, maybe that's why the director keeps you around. You know, to get the political take on things."

"He's a smart man."

"He is. But we all have our blind spots."

"What the hell does that mean?"

O'Keefe calmly watched as sweat stains spread on Roberts' shirt, and his face grew red. "Here's the thing. Not only do I not like you, but I don't trust you."

Roberts stared at O'Keefe with anger in his eyes. "Well, I'm not crazy about you, either, Roy."

O'Keefe nodded. "Fine. But my dislike and distrust of you go beyond the personal. You mentioned Nusinev being close to Demyan. You're close to Dulles."

Roberts moved his right hand, and began to pull the unlocked drawer open farther. "You think I'm spying against the United States."

"I didn't say that."

Roberts grabbed the Colt Commander with a suppressor attached. As he wrapped his hand around it, O'Keefe sprang from his seat. The gun started to come out of the drawer, but Roberts simply wasn't fast enough.

O'Keefe launched himself across the desk, and crashed his head and right shoulder into Roberts.

The fat man rolled backwards. The gun flew from his hand. The chair and Roberts crashed to the floor, with O'Keefe on top of him.

O'Keefe pushed himself up and began to move toward the gun that had slid away from the two men. But Roberts managed to swing his arm, and clipped O'Keefe's right leg. He tripped, and his head slammed against the desk as he fell to the floor. O'Keefe was dazed.

Roberts rolled his body on top of O'Keefe's, and wrapped his hands around his opponent's neck.

As Roberts squeezed, O'Keefe focused, and began to crash his fists against Roberts' chest. The blows did not affect the voluminous man.

Roberts said through gritted teeth, "I love America, Roy. But we can't fight this. They're too advanced. We can only cooperate if we want to survive."

O'Keefe tried to move Roberts with his legs, but again without success.

Roberts declared, "You won't have to worry about any of this. I'm sorry."

O'Keefe, in a final grab at survival, thrust his hips and legs upward, while grabbing and pulling down on Roberts' shirt. The effort moved Roberts just enough. O'Keefe reached up, shoved his thumb inside Roberts' mouth, and jabbed two fingers into Roberts' left eye. With all of his strength, O'Keefe drove his fingers deeper into Roberts' eye.

Roberts yelled, and his grip around O'Keefe's throat loosened.

O'Keefe moved his fingers around the eye socket. Blood streamed forth.

Roberts released O'Keefe's neck, and fell back, reaching up to his eye.

As O'Keefe struggled for air, he managed to roll over and began crawling toward the gun waiting across the floor.

Roberts was in a panic. But anger apparently helped him push aside the pain from his eye, and he struggled to his feet.

O'Keefe still gasped for air, but he closed in on the gun.

Roberts rose to his feet, and with blood flowing from the eye and rolling down his cheek, he said, "You bastard." He moved more quickly than he had in years. His working eye focused on O'Keefe.

O'Keefe reached the weapon, and rolled over.

Roberts was about to crash down on him, but O'Keefe managed to fire off two shots into the obese man's chest. Just after the second shot went off, Roberts smashed down onto O'Keefe.

Once more, O'Keefe struggled for air. With his face resting on O'Keefe's, Roberts whispered, "You're an idiot." Roberts' breathing then ceased.

O'Keefe tried to push Roberts' body off of him, but failed to summon enough strength while still working to take in air. Blood continued flowing from Roberts' eye, now streaming onto O'Keefe's face.

Banging started on the office door. Shouts could be heard from the other side.

O'Keefe tried to respond a couple of times, but couldn't raise his voice. On the third try, he managed to suck in more air and yelled, "Kick down the door!"

# Chapter 52

Allen Dulles stepped into the office, and walked slowly over to the desk. He looked down at the dead body of Ken Roberts.

Dulles sighed and asked, "O'Keefe?"

There were three others in the office. One person replied, "He's basically okay, getting patched up by the doc."

"Alright. Have him report back here when he can."

"Yes, sir."

Dulles looked back down at Roberts. "In the meantime, everybody out." But he jerked his head up at the three men staring at him. "Wait. Shut this down. No word gets out until this is investigated. And I mean no one. That is imperative."

"Understood" and "Yes, sir" came the replies.

Dulles ordered, "Get out and make sure this is kept quiet. Close the door."

There was brief hesitation, but then orders were followed.

After the door was shut, Dulles said to the dead man, "You piece of shit. How the hell did I miss this?"

He took off his suit jacket and tie, tossing them on a chair distant from the blood and body. Dulles rolled up his sleeves, and carefully moved directly over the body. He bent down, grabbed Roberts, and rolled the large man onto his side.

Dulles pulled down his shirt collar. "Nothing," he whispered to himself. He stood up, and started rolling his sleeves back down. A knock came on the door. "Yes."

The door cracked open. "Sir?" It was Roy O'Keefe.

"Come in, Roy, and shut the door." O'Keefe did so, and Dulles asked, "Are you alright?"

His voice was weaker than usual. "I am."

"The officer notifying me simply said that you had to kill Roberts, and you said he was a spy. Give me the details."

O'Keefe gave Dulles the details of the conversation and altercation he had with Roberts. "I had no choice but to shoot him."

Dulles commented, "Apparently. Thank God, you're okay." He moved a few steps closer to Roberts' body. "I must be slipping. How the hell did I miss this?" He shook his head. "You were right. I did want the political end of things on the Hill." He was referencing the details that O'Keefe relayed about the conversation with Roberts. "And he provided sound insights. Or at least I thought he did."

Dulles walked back to his discarded tie and jacket. "Roy, you're going to have to take this over. We need to know who he was passing information to, who was his handler." He started putting his tie back on. "He doesn't have a neck mark."

"Sir, of course, I can handle this, but to do so, I need to be read in fully. I know about these neck … things … but I don't know what they are about."

"I realize that, Roy." He finished straightening his tie, and slipped his jacket on. Dulles pointed to a chair. "You're going to want to sit down."

O'Keefe sat down, and Dulles pulled over another chair. With their knees nearly touching, Dulles completely read in O'Keefe on a secret invasion by beings from another planet, as well as the work of Agent Cold's group.

O'Keefe listened in stunned silence. When Dulles was finished, O'Keefe simply said, "Holy shit."

"Yeah, I know."

"And we're sure about all of this?"

Dulles didn't offer any qualifiers. "Yes. And obviously none of this is discussed with anyone other than me, the president and the Cold group."

"Yes, sir, I understand." After a few more questions, O'Keefe turned and looked in the direction of Roberts' body. "While I disagree, I can at least understand why Roberts said what he did to me about cooperating."

"Such defeatism would be fatal to the United States, to everyone on our planet."

"Yes, it would," responded O'Keefe with a slight sigh.

Dulles stood up. "I ordered that word doesn't get out about this. I understand the reality of that, but let the conflicting rumors swirl, while you get to the truth and we eventually release … something on him."

O'Keefe nodded.

Dulles continued, "Get what you need off the body. You'll need to pull this place apart, and then his home. Roberts lived alone, so the house is next. He got divorced several years ago. I'll get a few officers over to his house now to keep an eye on it."

O'Keefe again nodded.

"Roy, I've relied on you a great deal, and with this turn of events, I'll be leaning on you even more. Can you handle it?"

"Whatever you need, sir."

"Good. I have to tell the president what has happened. Ike's a reasonable man, but this will stir his anger, and justifiably so. I hope I'll still be your boss by the end of the night."

"I do, too, sir."

"Thanks." Dulles left the room, and O'Keefe locked the door behind him.

# Chapter 53

It was early Thursday morning, and Dean Cold was immediately welcomed into the Oval Office. As was the case on previous visits, Allen Dulles opened the door, and the president was waiting. But another individual was present as well.

Cold took note of the grim look on Eisenhower's face.

Ike simply said, "Dean."

"Mr. President."

Dulles said, "Agent Dean Cold, this is Officer Roy O'Keefe. He's my top aide."

*Top aide. I thought that was Roberts.*

Cold didn't allow the question to show as he shook hands with O'Keefe. "Officer O'Keefe, it's good to meet you."

"You, too, Agent Cold."

Eisenhower got up and walked around his desk. He set his hands on a chair in the center of the room. "Gentlemen, take a seat."

Dulles and O'Keefe sat on the couch to the left of Ike, and Cold sat on the other to the right. Cold placed the briefcase housing the finalized proposal for military support on the carpet next to his right leg.

Eisenhower looked down at Cold. "Dean, we've had two deeply troubling developments."

"Sir?"

Ike glanced at Dulles, and then turned to look Cold in the eyes. "The Soviets have an advanced weapons facility in Khabarovsk Krai that clearly is linked to our visitors. We have an on-the-ground report that MIGs are being upgraded, rockets are being added to these jets, and unmanned craft are being created. They plan on unleashing these new weapons on U.S. naval forces in Korea and on Seoul."

"Dear God," whispered Cold.

"And Dean, based on this report, we have nothing that could counter this, at least not in any serious way. If it's all true." He again looked over at Dulles and then back at Cold. "But there's no real reason to doubt this."

Cold fought off a reeling sensation. "When, sir?"

"The attack? Nothing exact, but our man says in roughly a month."

Cold asked more about the weapons, what was being done, and the facility. Dulles answered most of those questions as he was able.

When Cold had exhausted his line of questioning about what was happening in Khabarovsk Krai, Ike interjected, "There's more, Dean."

"Sir?"

Eisenhower looked at Dulles.

The CIA director said, "My former aide, Ken Roberts, is dead, and he apparently was spying for either the Soviets or the Nykarians, or both."

"Shit," reacted Cold, who looked at Ike and added, "Excuse me, sir."

Eisenhower smirked at Cold and waved his hand.

Dulles continued, "It was Officer O'Keefe who confronted Roberts, and in self-defense, had to kill him."

Cold commented, "I see," and gave a slight nod to O'Keefe.

Dulles went on, "Officer O'Keefe stopped Roberts before he could reach out to whomever he was working for to let them know that we now have this information about the facility in Khabarovsk and their plan."

"That's something, I suppose," said Cold.

Dulles raised an eyebrow.

Cold caught the look, and began, "I mean..."

Eisenhower cut in, "Yes, we all know what you mean, Dean, and we all agree."

There was a discomfort between the president and his CIA director that Cold hadn't previously detected.

*Dulles got his ass chewed out.*

The president continued, "Everyone was surprised by Roberts' actions. But based on what he said to Officer O'Keefe during their struggle, he seemed to think that America had no choice but to work with these invaders."

"That's a load of crap," commented Cold.

And before he could again apologize for his language, Ike declared, "I agree." He looked at the others. "We all do." Turning back to Cold, Ike added, "As should your team."

"They most certainly do."

"I know," said Eisenhower.

Cold reported, "And, sir, Colonel Weathers and Corporal Armstrong have their scheduled communication with their superiors tomorrow night. Agent Bartley and I will be able to sit in and listen. We could get more information on their plans for attack then, although, as we know, they're very selective about what gets shared among their various cells." Cold went on to explain the language issue.

"Well, that question is answered. Good," commented Ike.

Cold said, "Also, Weathers and Armstrong made it clear to us that whatever knowledge they have on all fronts, including technology and weapons, is fully at our disposal. I sense no hanging back, sir. These two are fully committed to us. That is, they have embraced America, and by extension, humanity."

Dulles declared, "Well, that's another something."

Eisenhower added, "It's more than 'something,' Allen. It's essential."

A silence fell on the Oval Office.

Cold eventually said while scanning each face, "I think the plans and requests that my group came up with fit in with how we stop this." He reached for the briefcase, withdrew a folder, and handed it to the president.

Eisenhower took the folder, and sat down in the chair he had been gripping. As he opened the folder, Ike said to Dulles, "Allen."

"Yes, sir." Dulles leaned forward. "We obviously can't launch an overt attack – like an air raid – that would spur World War III with the Soviets and their alien allies. This calls for covert action, along the lines of what you, Agent Cold, did during the war with the OSS."

At the end of Dulles' presentation, Eisenhower looked up from the report that Cold had handed him. He smiled at Cold and then at Dulles. The president stated, "You two are on the same page. I'll have to thank Bill Donovan for training each of you."

# Chapter 54

Dean Cold looked into the eyes of each person gathered around the room at 1734 Q Street NW in Washington, D.C.

Eight hours had passed since Cold had returned from the Oval Office meeting with President Eisenhower, CIA Director Dulles and Roy O'Keefe. And over those hours, Cold's entire team discussed and debated the plan that turned into a merger between what Dulles had put forth, and what Cold and Bartley, with the input from the others, had assembled previously.

*I think this will work. I pray that it works.* Cold then acknowledged to himself. *It's the best we can do given the situation.*

To the group, Cold summarized, "Think of the raid as the first battle in what I, unfortunately, believe promises to be a long war. And the D.C. effort is the start of building a stronger foundation upon which we can do whatever might be needed in this war."

Cameron Jefferson corrected, "What we think might be needed."

John Bartley responded, "That's part of what the D.C. team will be doing, figuring out how to respond as best we can to the unexpected."

Colonel Robert Weathers said, "Hopefully, Grace and I will be able to limit the unexpected."

Cold nodded. "We're all on board, then?"

Weathers replied, "We're with you," with Grace Armstrong agreeing.

"As am I," answered Max Marshall.

Bartley said, "Yeah, of course."

Jefferson added, "Me, too."

Lawrence Silver quietly offered, "Yes, I am as well."

Daria Popov merely replied, "No other choice exists."

And Mike Strickland said, "As Daria says, there are no other options. This is the best plan, and both teams need to succeed. But the raiders are putting it all on the line, and thank you for that."

It had been agreed that Cold, Bartley, Jefferson and Popov would lead the "raid," while Strickland, Silver, and Marshall, along with Weathers and Armstrong, would be doing more foundational planning – the "D.C. effort."

The others staying in D.C. echoed Strickland's thanks, with Marshall staring into Cold's eyes.

Cold said, "Cam, Daria, John and I will set out on Saturday afternoon, after we hear what's communicated to Robert and Grace tomorrow night."

The journey for the raiders, commanded by Cold, would be a multi-step trip, with help picked up along the way. Their ultimate destination would be the manufacturing facility in the Soviet Union's Khabarovsk Krai region.

# Chapter 55

Eight men and one woman stood in a line. All had their hands tied behind their backs. The wind, cold and snow tore at their faces. Tears emerged from the eyes of three of the individuals, and froze just a couple of inches down their cheeks.

Lights cut into the darkness, shining down from above.

Most of the personnel at the facility in Khabarovsk Krai were herded outside to watch what was unfolding. From the audience to the armed guards, all were dressed in massive coats. All had their heads engulfed by fur-lined hoods. Well, everyone, that is, except for the accused and one other person.

Sofia Belov walked back and forth in front of the accused, wearing black boots, pants and a waist-length jacket. The whipping wind and snow seemed to have little effect on her. Even her short black hair moved little, while her catlike stare didn't wander from her prisoners. Her movements were smooth and coupled with a slight grin. A holstered Makarov hung on her right hip. It was clear that Belov not only struck fear in the accused, but also created discomfort among her own newly acquired security personnel.

She shouted to be heard beyond those who were facing her sentence. "Each of you has broken the pledge you took… Ah, pardon me, each of you has attempted to break that pledge you took to Chairman Stalin, the State and the Party. You pledged not to communicate with anyone outside of this camp, and not to leave this facility. And yet here you are. As director of security in this place where vital, secret work proceeds, I must distribute justice."

With tears now streaming down her face, the lone woman in line cried out, "I am so sorry. I am loyal to our Soviet Union, but my mother is sick. I only needed to make sure that she is alright."

Belov walked toward the woman, and pulled out her Makarov.

The woman started to plead. "Please, please, no…"

Belov pointed the weapon at the woman's head and pulled the trigger.

The woman's body fell back into the snow. Belov took another step forward, and fired two more shots into the woman's head.

Belov looked around at the audience, and said, "Did you hear her? When it comes to our nation and its security, when it comes to advancing the revolution, there is no room for saying 'but,' or 'I only needed.' That is the gross selfishness that we must eradicate. The rest of these criminals will use much the same language, but in the end, in each case, such selfishness amounts to disloyalty and being an enemy of the State."

She walked over to the prisoner standing at the far end of the line. And over the next 15 minutes, Sofia Belov methodically shot each person in the head, followed by two more bullets to the head as the bodies bled out in the snow. She casually stopped twice during the process to slip a new cartridge into her Makarov.

When through executing these nine people, Belov re-holstered her gun, and walked into Building A. After the door closed behind Belov, her audience moved quickly out of the cold. The security personnel proceeded to move and dispose of the bodies until the only trace left of what had happened was the red blood that stained the snow.

Dr. Maksut Golikova stood watching, just out of the light.

# Chapter 56

Agents Dean Cold and John Bartley watched as Corporal Grace Armstrong spun the combination on a safe that was bolted to the floor in the back of a bedroom closet. Armstrong opened the safe door, and withdrew a metal attaché case.

The two men then followed her into the kitchen. Armstrong placed the case on the Formica-top table, again entered a combination, and opened it. Inside were five items. A device 12 inches long, 8 inches wide, and about an inch thick was pulled out first. Then came a speaker, a sleek microphone, a small square box and a thin pipe.

As she set things up, Armstrong explained to Cold and Bartley what each device did. The two men obviously understood the microphone and speaker. The small box, which turned out to be rather heavy, was a battery. And the short pipe opened to a four-foot-high antenna with a three-pronged stand.

Cold waited to hear the explanation for the main device into which Armstrong was plugging the other four items. He was struck by how slim the device was. It opened like a book on its side. The part that rested as a base on the table looked similar to the collection of keys on a typewriter, but they laid flat and nothing scrawled on the keys was decipherable to him. And the upright half had a screen that to Cold looked like an advanced television picture. Various symbols appeared on the screen.

Armstrong said, "This is a mobile communications station, or a com-stat." She looked at Bartley and then Cold, as if trying to figure out how to explain it. "In terms of Earth technology, we've managed to, in essence, cram a massive computer, and a radio or telephone communications system into this one device."

"Impressive," declared Bartley.

Armstrong went on to explain what would soon happen to establish a communications link. Weathers then entered the kitchen and asked Armstrong, "Are we set?"

"We are."

"Good. Thank you." He looked at his watch and then turned to Cold and Bartley. "If you two could take your seats?"

Cold and Bartley retreated to two chairs positioned just on the other side of the arched entryway into the kitchen.

Cold watched as Weathers and Armstrong sat next to each other, with their backs now to Cold and Bartley, facing the... *What did they call it? The com-stat.*

Three beeps came from the small speaker, and Cold could see that something new had popped up on the device's screen. Weathers proceeded through the steps that Armstrong had just explained, with the last step being that each placed a finger on the com-stat.

That was followed by three more beeps, and a voice coming from the speaker. "Colonel Weathers and Corporal Armstrong?"

Cold noted the female voice.

Weathers answered, "We are both here, Commander Three. The front door is locked and the windows closed."

Armstrong had informed them earlier that the sentence about the door and windows was the "all secure" code.

"Excellent," declared Commander Three. "Commander One will now take charge of this communication."

Weathers and Armstrong looked at each other in surprise. Weathers said, "We are honored."

Cold listened as Commander One – an authoritative male voice – said, "Commander Three has kept me current with your work, and it seems that you've done reliable work. That is, of course, expected, but also appreciated."

Weathers and Armstrong each thanked him.

Commander One continued, "We're going to need you to be particularly alert for any communications or information you might come across in any way unusual among the Americans regarding the Soviet Union. I know this sounds unremarkable given that this is your primary assignment, but we need another level of intensity. Anything suspicious should be passed on to Commander Three via emergency protocol."

"Of course, sir," replied Weathers.

Commander One said, "You need to be read in so that you fully understand what's happening."

At the edge of the room, Cold listened in horror and anger as Commander One detailed the plan for upgraded and new technology for the Russians being implemented at the secret facility in Khabarovsk Krai, and how the attacks on the U.S. Navy and Seoul would happen. It all lined up with what Eisenhower and Dulles had told him in the White House. But now, Cold had actual dates – the first being the day when the MiG-Xs were scheduled to leave Khabarovsk and the second being the date for the attacks against the Navy and Seoul.

After the communication ended and the equipment was packed back into the attaché, Cold looked at Bartley, Armstrong and Weathers. "This scares the shit out of me."

"Me, too," echoed Bartley.

"I understand," replied Weathers. "It unsettles us as well."

Cold watched as Weathers and Armstrong took each other's hands.

Cold continued, "We need to stop this in a month, at the latest. We start to move tomorrow."

The four sat in silence. Bartley finally said, "I say a drink in the calm before the storm."

Cold replied, "Hell, I could use a drink." He turned his head. "Robert? Grace?"

They agreed, with Grace adding, "No alcohol for me, however, with the baby."

Bartley asked, "Is that a concern?"

"It is, or it should be."

"Fair enough," declared Bartley. "No booze for you."

# Chapter 57

While approaching the front steps of 1734 Q Street, Dean Cold heard music coming from next door. He stopped on the sidewalk, with John Bartley, Robert Weathers and Grace Armstrong standing next to him.

Bartley said, "I think the party might have started."

"Sounds like it," noted Cold.

As they entered, though, it wasn't exactly a party. Instead, Mike Strickland was at his drums, and Cam Jefferson had Papa in his hands. They were playing some slow jazz, with Strickland following Jefferson's lead on the trumpet. Maxine Marshall was in an armchair with a book open on her lap, while Lawrence Silver sat on the couch, jotting in a small notebook. Daria Popov rested in another chair, seemingly just taking in the atmosphere. Everyone was waiting to hear what had occurred in the apartment across the street regarding the Weathers and Armstrong communications with their commander.

As Cold and the others entered the room, the music faded, and all eyes went in their direction.

Cold was about to start relaying what had occurred when he was distracted by a piano that was behind Jefferson and next to Strickland's drums. He pointed at the piano, and asked, "Where did that come from?"

Jefferson half shrugged. "Delivery truck pulled up about 45 minutes ago. The guy hands me an envelope. I opened it, read it, and was satisfied. Three delivery men set it up — even checked that it was tuned — and they were gone."

Cold raised an eyebrow and responded, "You were 'satisfied'?"

Jefferson smiled. "Yeah. Check out the note inside the envelope." He pointed to a manila envelope resting on top of the piano.

Cold pulled out the note, and read it – first to himself and then out loud to the group:

*Dean:*

*You and your team are doing a great service for the nation. I appreciate it, and please let them know that.*

*I understand that you must have your own piano, but I thought this might serve the entire team, perhaps at a gathering place in your HQ. I hope it will provide occasional moments of relaxation for you and your people. Those moments will be needed.*

*Ike*

Bartley commented, "I'm glad I voted for the guy."

That drew chuckles around the room.

Cold announced, "John suggested drinks, and given that things are going to get rolling tomorrow, Ike's timing and suggestion are on the mark."

Marshall asked, "So, what did we learn on the call?"

Cold turned to Weathers and Armstrong to provide a rundown, and answers to questions from the group.

Strickland had sat at his drums listening and twirling his drumsticks. When the room fell quiet, he declared, "This is scary shit."

"Yeah," acknowledged Cold, "I thought the same thing while listening."

While Weathers and Armstrong had been presenting the details of the communication, Bartley quietly readied a small bar that was in the corner of the living room. He said, "I think it's time for drinks."

Lawrence Silver rose from the couch and declared, "I very much agree." He strolled over to Bartley and his bar.

"What can I get you?" asked Bartley.

Marshall looked at Cold, and suggested, "Some music would be nice, too." She paused, smiled and added, "Keys."

Strickland laughed, "Yeah, come on, Keys, join us."

Cold looked at Jefferson with reluctance.

"Hey, you're in demand," said Jefferson.

Bartley handed Silver a bourbon on the rocks, and said, "I would normally do ladies first, but let's get the band primed."

Bartley poured drinks for Cold, Jefferson and Strickland, and as the three took to their instruments, he then provided the others with their beverage selections.

Jefferson looked at Cold and Strickland. "How about we ease into it with something smooth?" The two nodded in response. "Okay, then, Keys, you're going to take us in with 'Sophisticated Lady.'"

Cold and Jefferson always enjoyed playing this piece together. Cold appreciated the piano being central, and when it was just a tiny group like this, Jefferson enjoyed trying to cover the parts meant for clarinet, alto sax and trombone. As Cold began to strike the keys, the rest of the room settled in to watch and listen.

A round of applause came as the three ended the song, with Strickland then asking, "How about 'West End Blues,' Cam?"

Cold laughed, "Twist his arm."

And Jefferson clearly savored the trumpet lead, and again, the small audience was enthralled. That included a smile and a couple of tears, quickly wiped away by Popov.

At the close of the composition by Joe "King" Oliver, Jefferson turned and smiled at Strickland. Jefferson asked, "And what might our drummer enjoy playing?"

While twirling a drumstick, Strickland answered, "If only we had a singer, I'd love to give 'Drum Boogie' a whirl." He looked at Daria Popov.

The smile that she was wearing suddenly disappeared. But she took a deep breath, and a look of resolve crossed her face. Popov stood up, and said, "Why not?"

She was urged on by Bartley, Weathers, Armstrong, and Marshall, and welcomed by the three musicians.

Cold, Jefferson, and Strickland started the number, and after the "Boogie!" call out, Popov came in with "You hear the rhythm rompin'." The four were off on a high-energy roll.

At the close, the rest of the room applauded, but this time with additional enthusiasm. Bartley even offered a couple of hoots. Popov smiled broadly.

Jefferson said, "Wow, Daria, your mother was right. Your voice is angelic."

Cold again was surprised by Popov's reaction of embarrassment. He asked, "What would the lady like to sing?"

"My choice?"

"Absolutely," replied Cold.

Popov paused, and then asked, "Do you know '11:60 P.M.'?"

*Again, a surprise. Miss Popov has a sense of humor, too.*

Cold answered, "Cam and I do."

Jefferson looked at Strickland, "How about you, Scientist?"

Strickland assured, "A fun tune."

As he listened to Popov, Cold finally felt the lightness that usually came over him while playing.

Popov sang...

Eleven sixty pm,
Eleven sixty pm,
The clock was strikin'
One-two-three-four-five-six-seven-eight-nine-ten-eleven sixty pm!

The moon was high in the sky,
You had that look in your eye;
I tried to kiss you

One-two-three-four-five-six-seven-eight-nine-
ten-eleven-twelve hundred times!...

As Popov sang, Cold caught an expression of captivation
on Bartley's face, and he chuckled to himself.

The evening went on with conversation, laughter and just
a few more drinks given what was starting the next day.
Interspersed came a few more songs as well.

As things were about to end, Cold thought about a
particular song. At the end of the war, Doris Day singing
"Sentimental Journey" came to mean a lot to him and so
many other soldiers and their girls. It had become one of
those homecoming songs. He thought about his mission with
Cam, John and Daria that would start tomorrow, and his
desire for a homecoming from that assignment – especially,
he admitted to himself, a welcome home from Max. He
finally looked at Popov, and asked, "Daria, how about
'Sentimental Journey'?"

Popov smiled with a hint of sadness, and said, "Of course,
Dean."

Cam and Strickland responded similarly, and the room
once again settled down, as it had when the music first
started.

Popov closed her eyes and sang...

> Gonna take a sentimental journey
> Gonna set my heart at ease
> Gonna take a sentimental journey
> To renew old memories
> Got my bag, got my reservation
> Spent each dime I could afford
> Like a child in wild anticipation
> Long to hear that, "All aboard"
> Seven, that's the time we leave, at seven
> I'll be waitin' up for Heaven
> Countin' every mile of railroad track
> That takes me back
> Never thought my heart could be so yearny
> Why did I decide to roam?

Gotta take that sentimental journey
Sentimental journey home
Sentimental journey

Not long after the song began, Lawrence Silver stood up, walked over to Marshall, extended his hand, and asked, "Would you care to dance, Maxine?"

She smiled, and replied, "Of course, Lawrence."

As the two moved slowly in the middle of the room, they were joined by Weathers and Armstrong.

At the same time, John Bartley's gaze was fixed on Daria Popov.

# Chapter 58

"Sentimental Journey" ended the music for the night, but the group lingered.

Jefferson was the first person to make an exit. After returning Papa to its case, he looked at Cold and whispered, "A telephone in each of our rooms is appreciated. I think I'm going to give Millie a ring before calling it a night."

"Understand, Cam. Sleep well."

"You, too, Keys." Cam slapped his friend on the shoulder, and then announced to all, "This was great. Good night, people."

General "good nights" were returned, with Strickland adding, "Cam, you and Papa are great."

"Back at ya, Scientist." He looked at Popov, adding, "And Daria, well, you have a beautiful voice."

Popov smiled somewhat sheepishly.

Jefferson walked next door, and went up to his apartment. He took the armchair next to the telephone, looked at his wristwatch, and uttered a small grunt.

He placed a call to Millie Foster's Brooklyn apartment, resulting in no answer. Jefferson hung up the receiver, and said to himself. "Figures."

Jefferson sat for a couple of more minutes staring at the phone. He finally picked up the receiver, and put through a call to a club called "Sweet Betty's."

Betty Crawford answered the telephone, "This is Sweet Betty's."

"Betty, it's Cam. Is Millie available to come to the phone?"

"Well, Cam Jefferson. The man who bailed on my weekend nights."

"Yeah, I explained, Betty. I'm in D.C. for a while."

"Right, right, new job. Good for you, but how am I going to replace Papa?"

"I have no doubt that you've already found a new trumpet."

Betty laughed. "That's true, Cam. I'm just giving you shit."

"Yeah, I know. So, is Millie around?"

"Hmmm. She's about to go back on stage. You aren't going to try to lure her away to whatever the hell you're doing in D.C., are ya?"

"No, Betty. You don't have to worry about that."

"I better not. Cause while you and Papa can be replaced, Millie can't."

"Believe me, I know."

"Fine. Hold on."

About a half-minute later, Millie Foster was on the other end of Jefferson's call. There was an edge of annoyance in her voice. "I assume that you're still in D.C."

"Hey, Millie. I am. I just wanted to hear your voice. I'm going to be out of contact for a while."

Foster seemed to pick up on something in Jefferson's tone. Her voice softened. "What does that mean? Where are you going?"

"Like I said before I left, I can't really get into that."

"Government crap."

"Yeah, I suppose."

An awkward silence was broken by Foster. "I have to get on stage."

"I know. Like I said, I just wanted to hear your voice. Go do what you do so well. And ... I love you, Millie."

That was met by a sharp silence this time. "Cam ... please take care of yourself." She paused and added, "I hope we can talk when you come back to New York. I really have to go."

Foster ended the call. Jefferson placed the receiver down, leaving his hand resting on the telephone with his eyes closed.

# Chapter 59

As Jefferson was heading to his room, the others wandered into smaller groups.

While John Bartley was pouring final drinks for Daria Popov and himself, he asked her, "How is it going to feel going back to Russia?"

She thanked him for the drink, and the two took seats at the kitchen table. Popov then asked, "What do you mean?"

He took a sip from his glass, and said, "Going back there, with everything that happened to your family, to you, and your work for the CIA? Your mission to work against the monsters running your country, and then, well…" He shook his head. "…aliens?"

"When the CIA got me out of Russia, I thought I would never return. I was alright with that as I assumed that I could still work to undermine the Soviet bastards. And when Agent Cold approached me, it seemed obvious that this would be my avenue for doing so. That turned out to be the case, but with this added threat that still seems ridiculous."

Bartley nodded, and they each took another drink.

She continued, "Even after what I saw with my own eyes regarding Stalin, I struggled to figure out exactly what it was. But the notion that it literally was other worldly…" She shook her head.

"I get it. I'm a fan of science fiction – books and movies – and now – what? – I'm living it. This is happening, at least I'm pretty sure it is." Bartley smiled, and Popov did as well.

She commented, "Yes, it's real. And the fact that my country is now under the control of these aliens from another world who seem to fit in too well with the communists…" Her voice trailed. She took another drink. "It scares the shit out of me. So, I'm good with going back to Russia to help stop this."

She raised her glass. Bartley did the same, and they clinked them. And they each finished what was left in their drinks.

Popov got up from her chair, with Bartley following suit.

She said, "It is time for me to get some rest before we set out on our mission."

"Before I let you go, I have to say that Cam and your mother were absolutely right. You have a beautiful voice. And I'm glad you're going to be with us on this mission."

Popov smiled, "I'm glad as well, John." She tilted her head, looked him in the eyes, and said, "Good night, John."

"Pleasant dreams."

She smiled at that, and said, "Thank you."

# Chapter 60

When Bartley and Popov wandered into the kitchen, Lawrence Silver took the chair next to the couch where Robert Weathers and Grace Armstrong were seated.

Silver leaned forward, resting his elbows on his knees and clasping his hands. "I'm bewildered, and hoping that you two can help me."

"Yes?" asked Weathers.

"As you know by now, I had a different reaction to your people – the Nykarians – visiting Earth." Weathers and Armstrong continued to look at him in silence. "I was rather – for lack of a better word – excited. The possibility of intelligent extraterrestrial life has been at the center of my work, and your arrival was the culmination or affirmation of that work." He paused. "Not just my work, but much of my life, my worldview, you might say. And my expectations were that..."

As he paused, Weathers finished his statement, "We understand that you expected arrivals from another world would be friendly, peaceful, better than humans."

"Yes, and I can't help but think that there's something that we're ... missing. Some kind of miscommunication. Sometimes, things are missed or misunderstood that can help explain the real reasons for conflict, perhaps conflict that turns out to be unnecessary."

Armstrong asked, "Do you doubt what we have told you as to why our people journeyed here, and their intentions?"

Lawrence paused before responding. He eventually said, "No, of course not. I don't doubt your interpretation."

Weathers and Armstrong exchanged glances.

Lawrence continued, "Sometimes, though, deeper analysis is needed to get a complete picture."

Weathers said, "Your point of deeply analyzing situations and motivations naturally is correct, and such ongoing work can provide a deeper grasp on what's occurred, and why."

Silver leaned back in his chair with a look of satisfaction. "Yes, that's my point."

"At the same time," Weathers added, "we have to guard against wishful thinking distorting such inquiries. Grace and I can speak firsthand to this. We have been wrestling with the unfortunate reality that many on Nykar accepted the lies, even when they were able to see that these were lies. It was easier, or far less dangerous to do so. It eased consciences. After all, we told ourselves, what else could be done? We lied to ourselves that we had true freedom, and these other notions of freedom were nothing more than evil infections being spread by dangerous carriers. Stopping those carriers was rewarded, made us feel safe, and comfortable. Many were more than willing – whether naïvely or due to self-deception – to accept assertions about the intentions of various individuals and groups, and that ended up in our planet-wide tragedy."

Silver's expression of satisfaction disappeared. The three sat in silence for nearly a minute.

Armstrong added, "And given our position in the American government, we can see how the same thing happened in Russia, with assorted people and groups in the United States either being manipulated into presenting or choosing to present lies to the American people as to what is ongoing in the Soviet Union."

Weathers noted, "Before your last world war, such voices were heard not only in Germany, but in this country about Hitler and his intentions."

Silver bit his lip and took a deep breath.

Weathers looked him directly in the eyes. "Believe me, Lawrence, I wish I could tell you something very different as to why our people have come to Earth. You know, that they have good intentions, desiring peace and to help mankind. However, that's simply not the case."

"But the two of you…"

Armstrong said, "We learned some very different things than what we were immersed in for our entire lives. This isn't about Nykarians being any better or worse than humans. In fact, in the end, we're very much the same. When given the choice of freedom and respecting each life, that's what most would choose. But what happens when you have no understanding of such matters, or live in fear of even talking about such ideas? What happens when such notions have been wiped away from your history, from your understanding of life? What happens when all aspects of life are controlled by those in power, and their intention is all about maintaining control over everyone in order to expand their power? What happens when it's someone else, or another group, that suffers while you remain quite comfortable?"

"Your people," interjected Weathers, "call it totalitarianism. Picture totalitarianism on a planetary scale, and existing for hundreds of years."

Silver slowly rose from his chair. His shoulders sagged. "Thank you, Grace, Robert. I hope you rest well tonight."

Armstrong said, "You as well, Lawrence."

Weathers got up from the couch and extended his right hand. "I'm sorry, Lawrence. I truly am."

Silver shook his hand, and said, "Yes. Good night, Robert."

# Chapter 61

Dean Cold loitered at the piano, just tinkling the keys, when Max Marshall said, "Slide over."

Cold looked up into her eyes, and moved to the left. Marshall sat down. She had two glasses in her hand, and handed one to Cold. "Just water. Two gin and tonics were enough for me. Want something stronger?"

"No, I've had enough, too, given what tomorrow brings."

They each took drinks of the cold water, and placed their glasses on top of the piano.

Cold returned to the keys, and Marshall joined him.

He asked, "Still remember a little piano?"

"Some of what you taught me."

He stopped playing, and watched her hands move as she tried to peck out a few notes of "Holy, Holy, Holy." "You know I always loved your playing, Dean, and you managed to make hymns come alive, especially with the choir at your church." A few more notes, and she added, "Whenever I think about you, I do this. I sit at my piano, and touch a few keys, trying to generate something that sounds like the tune in my head."

Cold was surprised by her comment. He replied, "To be honest, whenever I've thought of you, it's been accompanied by feelings of regret and absence."

*There's that word again, Cold – "regret."*

Marshall smiled – Cold thought with a hint of sadness – as she continued to work on "Holy, Holy, Holy." "At least feelings of absence should go away. Though of course, there's you, Cam, John and Daria heading off to Russia."

During his time with the OSS, Cold made a point of not letting thoughts of not coming back alive creep into his head. But now, here was Max planting that seed. He shook it off.

Cold said, "Max."

She stopped playing with the keys and looked at Cold.

He said, "I told myself when you agreed to join me on this, no more regrets."

Marshall said, "Okay."

"And there's no talk of absence in any ... permanent sense."

She replied, "I understand. It's not helpful."

"Thanks."

"Okay, I'm off to bed."

"Me, too."

Before they got up from the piano, Marshall gently took hold of his arm in a way that no one else still in the room might see. While they already had been whispering, she leaned close to his ear and lowered her voice still further. "Come back safe."

*      *      *

A few minutes later, Cold was in his basement apartment, listening for the voice of the person he was calling.

"Hello."

"Hi, Dad, how are you? I didn't call too late, did I?"

"Not at all, Dean. I'm fine. You?" responded Pastor Gary Cold.

"I'm okay. I just finished up a nice night with the people I'm working with. Played some music, and it turns out that one person, Daria, has an incredible voice." He filled his father in on a bit more of the evening.

His father asked, "Did you move your piano out of the apartment?"

"No, I ... we received a gift."

"A gift? Who gave you a piano?"

"President Eisenhower."

Gary chuckled, "That's impressive. The president of the United States gave my son and his colleagues a piano. And I can't brag to anyone about it."

Dean laughed, and said, "You most certainly cannot."

After a little more chatting about the music, Gary asked, "But you're worried about something?"

"How do you know that?"

"How? Because I'm your father, and I know you."

*You do.*

"I wouldn't exactly say worried, but I'll be ... traveling for a while. And I..."

*It's strange. It was easier to take on a mission during the war. I desperately wanted the separation from Dad, Mom and Alice to end. But that same separation made it easier to face danger. It wasn't like I was saying good-bye to them, and then heading out the door to fight Nazis. But now, here I am, saying goodbye to Dad before journeying into the unknown to take on Russians and aliens. What the hell?*

Gary filled the silence that Dean couldn't. "Son, I'm going to pray for a safe journey for you, as well as for everyone going with you. And as you know, the Lord will be with you every step of the way, no matter what happens. That's our strength, comfort and assurance, right?"

Dean had to clear his throat. "Thanks, Dad. I'll have you in my prayers as well. It might be a few weeks before I can touch base, but try not to worry."

Gary laughed. "No matter what you or even Scripture says, I don't think not worrying is an option for a parent this side of heaven. But I'll try."

"I know, Dad. I love you."

"You, too, Dean. Get some sleep."

The call ended. Dean quickly did his bedtime rituals. But once he laid down, Cold discovered that the ability mastered during the war to grab some shuteye whenever the opportunity presented itself, now proved elusive. He knew this had to do with the lack of separation from his father. But as he laid staring up at the ceiling, Cold also knew that was only part of the story. It had to do with Max, and her being involved in this effort. Before finally drifting off to sleep, Cold acknowledged that he would have to find a way to deal with this when it came to his father and the woman for whom he still cared.

# Chapter 62

The next day at Andrews Air Force Base, an Air Force Convair XC-99 waited, with its five-man crew, and six 3,500 hp Pratt & Whitney R-4360-41 pusher-type engines idling. Three 19-foot reversible-pitch propellers spun slowly on each wing.

A young Air Force lieutenant finished checking each person's ID. He smirked. "Okay, you're the Secret Service officers being flown to Edwards, and then to somewhere else, but we weren't told where?"

"That's right. Thank you, Lieutenant."

The Air Force officer replied, "You know, there's nothing else on that big ass plane except the four of you."

Cold stared back in silence.

"Yeah, okay, I understand. Don't keep the crew waiting." He almost turned away without thinking, but stopped himself to salute the Army officer with the group. Then the apparently annoyed Air Force officer turned and walked back toward his office.

Cold looked at Cam Jefferson, John Bartley and Daria Popov. "Ready?" Each person answered affirmatively.

The four then turned to Colonel Robert Weathers and Dr. Maxine Marshall, who had driven them the relatively short distance from D.C.

Weathers provided an additional layer of assurance in terms of getting onto and moving about the base. Cold knew that this shouldn't have been necessary given where the orders for air transportation came from, but as he put it, "You never know if the right orders get to the right people, so better safe than sorry."

Marshall had merely volunteered to take the ride.

Bartley, Jefferson and Popov came forward, shook hands with and said their good-byes to Weathers and Marshall. Jefferson and Marshall also shared a quick hug.

Marshall whispered, "Be careful, Cam. Oh, and by the way, I don't think I mentioned that the goatee looks great."

He replied, "Thanks, and I'll make sure that he comes back okay. You take care."

She raised an eyebrow at first, and then smiled in response.

As Bartley, Jefferson and Popov moved out the door, with duffel bags over their shoulders, Cold said to Weathers, "Colonel, the information you've provided has been invaluable. But if anything else comes to mind for you or Corporal Armstrong that we could use, don't hesitate in getting us that information before we, effectively, go dark."

"Understood." The two shook hands.

Cold then stepped over to Marshall, while Weathers retreated toward the exit.

Cold said, "Be careful, Max."

"Me? I think I'm supposed to say that to you."

"But there's danger lurking here as well."

Marshall took a step closer, and Cold followed her lead. They exchanged a gentle kiss.

As she leaned her head back and looked into his eyes, she said, "Like I said last night, come back safe."

"I will," Cold managed.

He stood in place, as Marshall turned and walked toward Weathers. Cold then picked up his own bag, exited the building and strode toward the airplane.

The uneasy concerns he had the previous night diminished with each step, replaced by a growing determination to accomplish the mission and return to Max.

# Chapter 63

After driving off the Air Force base, Robert Weathers glanced sideways at Maxine Marshall. The two had said nothing while Weathers steered the maroon Oldsmobile 88 Club Sedan toward the Andrews' exit.

Weathers inquired, "Mind if I ask a question?"

Marshall said, "Fire away." But her gaze turned out the passenger side window.

"How long have you and Dean been in a relationship?"

"That's become a more complicated question than you might realize." She turned and looked at Weathers. "We dated while at Harvard. But with me going to medical school and Dean heading to D.C., it just kind of ended."

"I see."

She briefly laughed. "At this point, I don't. Life has changed in unimaginable ways, thanks to your visit."

He spotted her good-natured smile, and returned it.

Marshall continued, "That change is on a global level, but in terms of our individual lives as well. That includes relationships, whether rekindled or just altered." She paused and looked out the passenger side window, once more. "I'll let you know when I really figure it all out."

"Fair enough. I wasn't trying to pry. It's just that Grace and I are still trying to, as you said, 'figure out' a great deal."

"Oh, come on. Let's see. You've found a new home, on an entirely new planet. Your minds have been placed into new bodies. You're having a baby. You're working with strangers – wondering if they trust you and if you can trust them – to stop forces of oppression that, until recently, you were part of and thought you were doing the right thing. Anything else?"

"That about sums it up."

"Well, Robert, I don't know what the big deal is. Geez. Toughen up, man."

They both laughed.

Marshall advised, "We're all in a strange new world. Heck, I'm now a doctor and a spy, I guess? But the two of you are making great sacrifices, and understand that those are appreciated. I do know Dean well, and once you're part of his team, if that's the right word, he'll do anything for you."

"Thanks. He seems like a good man."

Marshall paused, and then said, "He is."

"And you're a good woman, Max. Thank you for all that you're doing for Grace and for the baby."

"Whatever you two – you three – need, I'm here. I not only took an oath to help treat everyone, but we've all been thrown together into this ... thing ... and I consider you both to be friends."

Weathers nodded, "The same goes for us with you, with the entire group."

# Chapter 64

The conversation between Weathers and Marshall came to an end as he parked the Olds 88 in front of the Q Street townhouses.

As the two stepped onto the sidewalk, a Chevy DeLuxe pulled up behind their car.

Wearing his dark overcoat and fedora, Roy O'Keefe got out of the car with a briefcase in his left hand. He walked up, and said, "Hello. Colonel Weathers and Dr. Marshall, I presume?"

"That's right," replied Weathers warily. "And you are?"

"I trust that Dean Cold mentioned me and that we'd be working together. My name is Roy O'Keefe." He pulled his CIA ID from an inside jacket pocket.

After Weathers examined the ID, he nodded.

Marshall declared, "Yes, Dean mentioned that." She shook his hand, and then Weathers did the same.

"I have information that concerns our..." – he looked around – "mission."

Weathers said, "Let's go inside."

After introducing himself to each person, O'Keefe explained his task of digging through the office and home of Ken Roberts. He observed, "You'd be surprised how loose with national security matters political types can be."

Mike Strickland chimed in, "No, actually, I wouldn't be surprised at all."

"Me, neither," added Weathers.

Grace Armstrong said, "Nor I."

Marshall smiled, while Lawrence Silver watched and listened without much expression.

O'Keefe smirked. "Anyway, he did keep basic scheduling journals, and they date back several years, essentially to the point when he arrived in Washington. I found them locked in a safe in his home. I got the impression that it was a ritual on most nights to jot down a few thoughts about his day, and some upcoming meetings. They do offer some personal observations about assorted colleagues and politicians. There wasn't much I found of interest on that front for our purposes. But what I did find interesting was the fact that there are only two names that crop up regularly in his scheduling throughout these journals – that is, other than his periodic complaints about his ex-wife. And those two are a Clay Walsh and a Jerry Debrowski."

Silver perked up. "Did you say 'Clay Walsh'?"

"I did."

"He works for Senator Kennedy now, correct?"

O'Keefe nodded.

Silver continued, "Walsh is an intelligent fellow, though a bit standoffish."

Marshall started to roll her eyes, but caught herself and looked around to make sure no one noticed.

Silver went on, "He would drop by Harvard for assorted lectures. I chatted with him a good number of times. I got the feeling that he would have enjoyed academia, but he liked to be close to power, and for him, that avenue was the Kennedy family."

Marshall added, "I also met him once or twice at some fundraising events for the hospital, though I'm sure he wouldn't remember."

O'Keefe said, "This is invaluable. Over the years, Roberts, Walsh and Debrowski had a regular bull session together. They'd wind up in one of their offices on the Hill, usually Walsh's, drinking and talking about politics, politicians, and so on. Roberts occasionally would note what they spoke about if it related to what he was doing at the time. But those bull sessions suddenly got more frequent recently, and any references to what they spoke about disappeared."

"Interesting," commented Weathers.

"Yeah, and this seems to line up with when..." O'Keefe hesitated and looked around the room. He continued, "The frequency stepped up, it seems, once Director Dulles started reading Roberts in on what's going on in Russia and the attacks here."

Armstrong said, "Sounds like this man was a loner, but plugged in politically."

"That's right," responded O'Keefe.

"So, I'm a novice at this stuff, obviously, but the same reason why Director Dulles would use Roberts would be the same reason that the Russians or the Nykarians would be attracted to using him?" inquired Marshall.

"Exactly," agreed O'Keefe, with Armstrong and Weathers nodding.

"And what about this Walsh?" queried Strickland.

O'Keefe said, "First run through points to him liking himself a great deal, to the exclusion of most others."

The group looked at Silver. "Yes, I can see that. He was always alone when I'd see him at events, and he clearly had little tolerance for those who were ... not up to snuff intellectually."

Marshall raised an eyebrow to that reply.

"And this ... Debrowski? Is that his name?" persisted Strickland.

"It is," answered O'Keefe. "He works for Senator McCarthy."

Both Strickland and Silver served up audible groans.

"And your take on him?" asked Marshall.

O'Keefe answered, "A political creature – completely consumed by elections and political strategies. He also doesn't seem close to anyone in particular. But I can't say that for sure at this point."

Weathers observed, "These two – Walsh and Debrowski – would make perfect targets to be taken over by Defenders."

O'Keefe sighed. "Unfortunately, that's what I thought you'd say."

"What's the plan, then?" asked Marshall.

O'Keefe started walking around the room, and scratched the back of his scalp, and said, "Right, what's the plan? I wasn't really sure on the way here, other than getting the CIA caught sniffing around a couple of Senate staffers wouldn't be ideal."

Silver surprised the room by saying, "It's obvious what should happen regarding Clay Walsh. I know the man, and I should approach him about ... well, whatever ... and I can get an idea if he's a Nykarian."

Everyone looked at him in silence.

Marshall finally said, "I can join you, Lawrence. Two Massachusetts constituents looking to talk to a friendly face in Senator Kennedy's office about ... funding for medical education."

O'Keefe smiled. "I like that, Dr. Marshall."

"Call me Max."

Silver appeared a bit annoyed that Marshall inserted herself, but he quickly agreed. "That would work well."

Strickland declared, "I can take a run at Debrowski."

"How so?" queried O'Keefe.

"Commies."

"Excuse me?"

"I'll tell him that I'm worried about commies running rampant in the Pentagon. That's why I had to get out of the building. I can be quite earnest, and I'll push him that his boss, Senator McCarthy, needs to do even more."

Weathers said, "He's right. That will get him in the door with McCarthy's people, and he can push to talk with Debrowski."

O'Keefe said, "Well, you people are really coming through. I'm going to like working with this group."

"Thanks, Officer O'Keefe," responded Marshall.

"It's Roy, and if I can press my luck, we need to move fast on this."

# Chapter 65

The back room at O'Malley's Pub quickly went from lively conversation to silence. After the gathering broke up, Father Edward Duffy was alone, seated at one of the tables. His shoulders were slumped over, and he stared at his nearly empty glass of Rheingold Beer.

The quiet was interrupted by the waitress who had been serving drinks to the dozen UFO believers for the past two-plus hours. She had black hair and green eyes. "Can I get you another, Father?"

"What?" Duffy looked up. "Oh, no, thank you, Mary. I need to be getting home."

As she began to wipe down the table, Mary Maloney said, "Father, do you mind if I ask you a question?"

"Of course not."

She stopped what she was doing, put a hand grasping the cleaning rag on her hip, and asked, "What are you doing with this group?"

He looked at her quizzically.

Mary continued, "I mean they come here every month or so to talk about little green men from Mars. And then you started showing up, and as I come in and out with drinks, you just kind of sit and watch. I can't figure it, Father."

Duffy stared at her.

Maloney straightened up and dropped her hands to her sides. "I meant no disrespect, Father. Sometimes I let my mouth run ahead of my brain. My parents warned me over and over again. Please forgive me."

Duffy responded, "You have nothing to be sorry for, Mary. I understand. This isn't the setting where you'd expect to see your priest. I understand." He finished the beer, and got up

from his chair. Duffy took a few steps and stopped in front
of Maloney. "Everyone needs the Lord. Remember, the
Pharisees couldn't figure out why Jesus ate and drank with
those he did. But you're right that I'm just sitting and
watching."

Just above a whisper, Maloney said, "Yes, Father."

Duffy smiled at her reassuringly. "Thank you, Mary, and
get some rest tonight." He walked to the door.

"Thanks. You, too, Father."

After the door closed, Maloney berated herself as she
went back to cleaning tables. "You just can't keep your
mouth shut, can you, Mary? Questioning a priest. What's
wrong with you?" She stopped wiping once again, and looked
to the ceiling. "Jesus, Mary and St. Joseph, forgive me."

Mary Maloney blessed herself and went back to her work.

After exiting O'Malley's, Duffy turned up the collar on his
overcoat, and undertook the 15-minute walk to St. Peter's
Catholic Church. Before heading to the rectory, he entered
the Baroque-style church. Duffy dipped two fingers into the
holy water stoup just outside the doors to the nave, and
blessed himself. He then walked up the center aisle, stopped
at the front pew, genuflected and blessed himself once more.
He slid into the seat. Rather than kneeling, Duffy simply sat
in the pew, looking up at the altar.

The priest bowed his head, and rested his clasped hands
on his lap. He whispered, "Dear Lord, I know that I wound
up here for a purpose. I think I know what I'm supposed to
do. I need your strength to do it, no matter ... no matter ...
the consequences." He looked up at a hanging crucifix above
the altar. "Mary was right. I know I need to be with those
people, but I haven't found the courage to speak up. Help me
to find that courage." He lowered his head and closed his
eyes. "I need help. I thought I might find someone among
the UFO people, but I don't think that will be the case." He
paused and took deep breaths. "I've been wondering if
Pastor Cold might be the person to reach out to, but how?
And how do I know if that is the right thing to do?" Duffy
then chuckled and shook his head. "Please give me strength,
wisdom and that courage to do the right thing."

Duffy rose from the pew, and stepped into the aisle. He genuflected, blessed himself, turned and left the nave, and then the building.

# Chapter 66

Few would have predicted that MGB Officer Sofia Belov and Dr. Maksut Golikova would turn out to be the ideal partnership for running a secret operation at a remote base in Khabarovsk Krai, or anywhere else for that matter. After all, Golikova was a scientist, while Belov seemed not to think about much else than supporting the State via the most severe means possible.

But the two immediately understood their mutually beneficial relationship.

After all, Golikova knew that this mission, and its security, allowed him to immerse himself, along with his team of scientists, in the challenging and fascinating tasks at hand. Golikova was aware of the full story of how the gradual integration of Nykarian technology into the Soviet Union's arsenal would eventually lead to a takeover of the entire planet.

A knock came on his office door, which opened absent an announced invitation. Golikova stood up from his desk, and said, "Please, Officer Belov, come in. Take a seat."

Belov took a chair on the other side of his desk. Golikova sat back down.

He asked, "Would you like something? A drink perhaps?"

"No," was her short response.

"Then, how can I help you?"

"I am checking to make sure that you haven't heard any more rumblings or complaints about anyone wanting to leave the camp, or about what we're doing here."

Golikova offered a mild chuckle. "None whatsoever. Indeed, I haven't expected any since the executions you carried out."

She asked, "Do you disagree with my methods?"

"Not at all. I appreciate them."

"Is that right? I have found that scientists in the Soviet Union understand the need for but only reluctantly accept, let us say, strict security methods. It has long seemed to me that they view such measures as necessary evils – a price, if you will, for the privilege of being able to do as they please with their science. In fact, I believe they would work with anyone allowing them to do their science."

"Yes. I would say that has been my experience as well."

Belov leaned back in the chair, and crossed her arms. "And why would you be any different?"

"Because, Officer Belov, I became a scientist, first and foremost, to serve the State, to serve the people."

The two stared at each other.

Belov finally said, "I hope that is the truth, comrade." She rose from the chair, and as she turned toward the door, ordered, "You will keep me informed if you hear of any complaints, or worse."

Golikova responded, "Most certainly."

"We are, after all, when it comes to this place, ultimately partners in death."

"I would not think of it that way. You and I are doing what needs to be done in service to the State, which is the people. That is about life, Officer Belov."

Belov offered a brief, disturbing smile. "I suppose you could look at it that way, if it helps. I will take you up on that drink, but not now. And perhaps, we can meet other needs that each of us might have in this cold place?"

Golikova smiled broadly. "Of course, anytime, comrade."

Belov's disturbing smile returned, and she left.

# Chapter 67

Pillows propped up Dr. Maxine Marshall as she read in bed. She yawned, removed her glasses, and rubbed her eyes. The telephone on her nightstand rang. She put the glasses back on, and looked at the alarm clock, with its hands pointed at 11:45 pm. She picked up the receiver. "Hello."

"Hi, Max, it's me, Dean."

She sat up. "Dean, it's good to hear your voice. How was the flight? You're in California?"

"Yeah. The flight was fine. Everything okay?"

"Have you spoken with anyone else here yet?"

"No, we haven't been on the ground long, and we're only staying for another couple of hours, and then it's the next leg of the journey. After this, we'll be out of contact until we complete the mission. So, I figured I'd call you to get the latest from D.C., and ... well ... to just talk."

Marshall smiled at that, and then tossed her book aside. "Roy O'Keefe arrived here just as Robert and I returned from the airport." She proceeded to fill Cold in on the details of what O'Keefe had said and their plan to assess both Clay Walsh and Jerry Debrowski.

Cold listened, and then commented, "That's good work by Roy." He hesitated, and then added, "Are you comfortable with this?"

"You knew that each of us would be involved with various aspects of this entire effort. After all, there's only going to be so much for me to do as a doctor, hopefully."

"I know, I know. Thanks for being open to all of the possibilities, including this."

"No need for that. It's what we're doing now."

Marshall and Cold went over further details about her and Lawrence Silver going to meet with Walsh, and Mike Strickland's meeting with Debrowski. Cold mused, "I like Mike's angle on that."

When Cold was satisfied with all he had heard, he said, "Max, please be careful."

"We did this before, so I'll repeat what I said: Come back safe. And please call us when you're able. Let us know that you're okay."

"Will do."

When the call ended, a knock came on the door of the small office that Cold was using at Edwards Air Force Base. "Come in."

Cameron Jefferson stuck his head in the door. "Time to go."

Cold looked at his watch. "Shit. We're early."

"Hey, don't complain about any kind of efficiency in government."

"True." He leaned back in his chair. "You ever make it to Alaska, Cam?"

"Nah. This'll be my first time. Hell, I had no clue what the hell the Aleutian Islands were until the Japs – I mean, the Japanese – took them in the war."

"Me, neither."

Jefferson added, "And neither of us has been in Russia before, either."

Cold smirked as he got up from the tiny, metal desk. "Thank God Daria's with us, and John speaks Russian."

"Geez, didn't realize how parochial we are."

Cold laughed and followed Jefferson out the door.

Meanwhile in D.C., Marshall made the rounds with Mike Strickland and Lawrence Silver, and then across the street to Robert Weathers and Grace Armstrong, filling each in on the details of her call with Cold.

When she returned to her bedroom, it was just after two in the morning, but she wasn't tired. She returned to her propped-up pillows and book.

# Chapter 68

After perfunctory greetings, Lawrence Silver and Dr. Maxine Marshall took seats at the table in Clay Walsh's office. "Thank you for seeing us, Clay," declared Silver.

Walsh took a chair as well, and responded, "It's a pleasure, Lawrence. I have to say that the two of you checked all of the boxes. Like Senator Kennedy, Harvard graduates. You both live in Massachusetts currently, and therefore, are constituents of the Senator. And you're here to talk about something of substance, unlike most of what we deal with in this office each day when it comes to the public." He smiled. "I hope that didn't come out wrong, but quite frankly, I am always pleased to hear from people with some intellectual heft. Despite all of the talk about this being a town of smart people, I find Washington, D.C., to be an intellectual backwater."

While Marshall merely smiled, Silver declared, "I know what you mean."

"Well, what can I – I mean – what can the Senator do for your efforts to further medical education in Massachusetts, and in the rest of the country?"

Marshall then took over the conversation, laying out the need for more doctors in general and in various specialties. Her presentation made clear that this wasn't something she had just thrown together overnight after the group had decided to assess Walsh. This was something she had been thinking about for some time.

As she finished, Walsh responded, "You've made a compelling case, Dr. Marshall. I appreciate that, and I know Senator Kennedy will as well. And while I cannot guarantee anything, I know the Senator would like to hear about this directly."

Silver interjected, "That is good news. I thought you might be interested, given what we had chatted about when meeting back at Harvard."

Without missing a beat, Walsh responded, "Forgive me, Lawrence, but there is so much on my plate, could you refresh my memory on what we had discussed?"

Silver said, "Of course, I understand. We had spoken about the need for the federal government to do much more than the G.I. Bill. I suggested more aggressive direct funding of chairs in top universities in areas of study deemed critical to national security. You were skeptical of the national security angle, but you liked the idea when it came to areas – how did you put it? – 'where we can truly aid all of mankind.' By the end of that discussion, you had won me over."

Walsh smiled. "Yes, yes, as you were talking, the light bulb came on. Forgive me, how could I forget that?"

"I didn't, and that's why I suggested to Dr. Marshall that we reach out to you first."

Walsh commented, "You weren't completely wrong on the national security idea, but in terms of priorities..."

Silver raised his hands as if in surrender. "You were right, Clay. I admit it."

Everyone chuckled, and Silver and Marshall stood up as Walsh did.

Walsh said, "I would love for this conversation to go on, but unfortunately, I have far less interesting meetings to get to this afternoon."

"We completely understand," said Marshall. "Thank you for taking the time to see us."

Walsh shook each person's hand, and pointed them toward the door.

Marshall moved slower than the other two, and looked at the back of Walsh's collar.

Walsh held the door for his two visitors. "As I said, I'll talk with Senator Kennedy, and we will get back to you."

Once outside the office, and walking down the shiny hallway, Marshall whispered, "I couldn't get a look at his neck."

Silver slowed his walk, and leaned in close to Marshall. "If I were the type of person who enjoyed a wager, I would place a large sum on that person not being the Clay Walsh that I had spoken with several times before."

Marshall stopped, and looked at Silver skeptically.

Silver looked around. With no one else in the hallway, and the office doors closed, he whispered, "What I'm about to say is not me being egotistical. But I have a way of making an impression on people."

Marshall folded her arms, and tilted her head.

"I had conversations with Clay Walsh that lasted more than just a few minutes, and do you know what we discussed?"

"You just said it. Federal dollars for university chairs."

"No. We discussed the possibility of intelligent life on other worlds."

Marshall stiffened her back. "You tested him?"

Silver nodded. "And he failed."

"You can't be sure. He might have been appeasing you, to get us out of the office. You know, your talk of aliens has – well, had – a way of chasing people away."

"Alright, but then why take the appointment when I called in the first place?"

"Perhaps he didn't remember you when taking the meeting over the telephone."

"Whether you agreed with me, or you thought I was crazy, I usually make a lasting impression on people when talking about beings from outer space."

Marshall paused, and finally declared, "I can't disagree with that."

# Chapter 69

Mike Strickland had requested a different kind of meeting with Jerry Debrowski. It was in a dark pub across the Potomac River in Alexandria, Virginia, a few blocks off King Street.

Strickland arrived several minutes late. The place was nearly empty, with three people slumped at the bar, and a couple at a table arguing about her mother. Strickland spotted Debrowski in a booth. He grabbed a beer from the bartender, and walked over to the booth.

Debrowski said, "Take a seat, Dr. Strickland."

"Thanks." Strickland slid into the booth across from Debrowski. He took a swig from his glass. Strickland took note of no glass being in front of Debrowski. "Not drinking? Can I grab you a beer or something?"

Debrowski ignored the question, and said, "I was surprised to get your call. I hope this isn't a waste of time."

Strickland stared at Senator McCarthy's aide, and replied, "And I hope you don't waste my time."

"Okay. As you know, my boss has a keen interest in who might be undermining the country, including those within our government."

Strickland went on to relay a fictional tale of what he had overheard at the Pentagon. It was filled with vague tidbits that could be interpreted however one might like in terms of it being nefarious communism or just bitching about life.

As Strickland went on, Debrowski periodically sighed. As usual, he slipped his suit jacket off, loosened his tie, and undid the top button on his shirt.

Strickland took a break from his story. "Hey, I'm getting another beer. You sure you don't want something?"

Debrowski replied, "Yeah, okay. Club soda, and bring over one of those bowls of peanuts."

"Sure." Stickland went over to the bar, and returned with the two drinks. "Oh, crap. The peanuts."

As he returned, Strickland swept the bowl of nuts so that it knocked over the club soda, with the liquid spraying down onto Debrowski's pants.

Debrowski jumped back. "Shit."

"Crap, I'm sorry." Strickland reached down and across the table to grab a napkin and handed it to Debrowski.

Strickland remained standing, as Debrowski turned his legs out of the booth, and leaned down trying to sop up some of the soda on his pant legs. While doing so, Strickland peered down at the back of the man's neck. Thanks to the shirt's top button being undone and it being pulled as Debrowski leaned down to clean his trousers, a relatively clear look was offered at a slight bump and scar on the neck of Senator Joe McCarthy's aide.

Debrowski declared, "This is useless." He grabbed his jacket and stood up. He looked at Strickland, and said, "There might be something there in terms of what you've told me."

Strickland continued the act. "Of course, there's something there." He looked around and lowered his voice. "There are a bunch of Reds there."

Debrowski's impatience now shone through. "Yes, yes. Let me talk to the senator, and we'll get back to you."

Strickland offered a look of suspicion. "You're not just saying that, I hope. I'm not paranoid, you know."

Debrowski took a deep breath. "I know, Dr. Strickland. I take this very seriously, and we will get back to you. What number is best to call you at?"

"How about I check in with you in a couple of days?"

Debrowski slipped the jacket on, and said, "Make it a week. I need time." He shook Strickland's hand, and left the bar.

# Chapter 70

In the main room at 1734 Q Street, as Lawrence Silver was finishing up making his case, Mike Strickland came in the front door of the townhouse.

"There is no way that Clay Walsh would have forgotten what we had spoken about, and on more than one occasion," summed up Silver.

Strickland asked, "Is Walsh a Nykarian as well?"

Robert Weathers, Maxine Marshall, Grace Armstrong, Roy O'Keefe and Silver all looked his way.

Weathers was the one to ask, "'As well'? I assume that means you think Jerry Debrowski is one?"

"I don't think, I know. I saw his neck."

"What? How'd you pull that off?" asked O'Keefe.

After Strickland explained, Weathers said, "Nice work, Mike."

"And sloppy work on the part of Debrowski," added Armstrong.

"What now?" asked Marshall.

O'Keefe answered, "Walsh and Debrowski are scheduled to meet with Roberts in two nights, according to Roberts' journal. We have no choice but to make a move. When Roberts doesn't show up, they're obviously going to know that something is up."

Weathers interjected, "That's right, and they'll likely make an emergency communication with their Commander."

O'Keefe resumed, "There should be no one else around, which is why I assume they chose that time to meet. We'll have the opportunity to stop them."

"Or persuade them," suggested Silver.

Weathers and Armstrong exchanged a quick look.

"What do you mean?" asked Strickland.

"Maybe these two have a different view of humans than what we are assuming." He quickly looked toward Weathers and then averted his eyes.

Strickland half fell into a chair, and didn't hide his incredulity. "Are you kidding?"

Everyone stared at Silver. "No. I mean, I'm not naïve. But maybe there are more like Robert and Grace than any of us might realize."

Armstrong responded, "I hope that would be the case, Lawrence. And I'm certainly not ruling it out ... completely. But Robert and I know our world, and the choice we've made would be unthinkable to most. It's not only considered traitorous, but evil. That's what's drilled into each one of us from the time we're born."

Silver shifted uncomfortably.

"Listen," assured O'Keefe, "we don't go in guns blazing. Yes, we need to quietly apprehend these two. But if these two are in the same place as Robert and Grace, they will have the chance to make their case."

Silver said, "Of course. And that's all I meant."

"Good," said O'Keefe. "Now, let's go over how we're going to get this done."

# Chapter 71

The night offered a bountiful catch in the fishing nets on the Bering Sea. The fish were boxed and covered in ice. But the Russian fishing trawler wasn't ready to return to port just yet. Captain Bogdan Kolchak and his crew of three awaited the emergence of a leviathan from the dark, icy deep.

Kolchak and his men failed to see the metal eye looking their way off the starboard side.

Without warning, the waters broke and up came a metal behemoth – 269 feet long and more than 1,650 tons.

In his years on the sea, Kolchak had seen a great many things, but nothing quite like the sudden appearance of this Tang-class United States submarine. His crew – Kolchak's two sons and a nephew – stood immobile on the deck even as the sea rolled.

On the *U.S.S. Trigger* submarine, Dean Cold, John Bartley, Cameron Jefferson and Daria Popov were about to depart. They were halted by Captain Scott Lee. "Gentlemen, and Miss Popov."

Each person maneuvered their head to look at Lee. Since coming on board the sub in Alaska three days earlier, Cold was struck by how cramped everything was. His OSS service had been on land, not sea, and certainly not under the sea. Despite the danger that loomed ahead, he looked forward to getting topside. He craved fresh air.

Cold replied, "Yes, sir?"

"We'll be ready to come and get you when signaled." Predetermined windows for possible communications had been established. "I just wanted to wish you well, and thank you. I have no idea what you're about to do. I'm not supposed to, but I know that we came to you per direct orders from the president. So, I understand how vital this is. Godspeed."

Each person thanked Lee, and shook his hand.

The four were then led up a ladder, and topside of the *Trigger*. They descended onto a rocking inflatable skiff, and were ferried over to the fishing trawler.

Cold was the last one out of the small inflatable, after thanking the two sailors serving as ferrymen. As his feet hit the deck, Cold looked into the piercing eyes of a large man with thick gray hair and beard.

Kolchak shook Cold's hand vigorously. "Welcome, Mr. Cold. I'm Bogdan Kolchak." He pointed to the other crew members. "This is my oldest son, Ilya, my second son, Lev, and my nephew, Nazar."

Cold, in turn, introduced Jefferson, Bartley and Popov.

Kolchak smiled at Popov. "This is the first time a woman has been on board my boat."

Popov replied, "The captain of that submarine told me the same thing." She tilted her head toward the *Trigger* as the inflatable transport was returning to the ship.

Kolchak laughed. "I'm sure." He turned back to Cold, and said, "Allen Dulles sent us."

"I see," replied Cold.

"I like Mr. Dulles. He pays well, and he hates communists almost as much as I do."

"Almost?" asked Jefferson.

"Yes, trust me on that, Mr. Jefferson. I have reasons to hate the communists more than any of you."

"Perhaps," commented Popov.

Kolchak eyed Popov, and nodded. He continued, "Our home is Ayan. Did you know that this was the last town to fall to the communists during our Civil War?"

Popov answered, "I did."

With his focus on Popov now, Kolchak persisted, "And none of you are aware that my wife is the niece of General Anatoly Nikolayevich Pepelyayev."

"Who?" asked Bartley.

Kolchak turned to his sons and nephew, and said, "It is time to go home." The three then set about their duties.

As Kolchak led his guests to the boat's cabin, Popov answered Bartley's question. "Pepelyayev was the general who led the anti-communist forces in Ayan."

"My wife and her brother are the only ones left alive from his family."

"I see," said Cold.

At the wheel of his boat, now staring out at the darkness and waters, Kolchak declared, "I'm sure there are others who knew General Pepelyayev. But this is spoken of only behind closed doors, and even then, one must be able to trust your own family and friends completely. To you Americans, you might think that, of course, one can speak freely with one's own family and friends. After all, you can speak freely in public. But even what one speaks of in private can have a way of being heard, eventually, by government officials. Say the wrong thing, and you may never say anything again, or you'll only be talking in prison."

Cold, Bartley and Jefferson looked at Popov.

She merely said, "That is the truth."

Cold turned and looked out into the darkness, now listening to the boat's engine and waves hitting the bow.

*And the Nykarians are the same, but with weapons and technology far ahead of us. Dear Lord, help.*

# Chapter 72

Just a few seconds after the doorbell rang, Pastor Gary Cold opened the front door. He smiled, and said, "Hi, Ed. Please come in."

Father Ed Duffy stepped into the house, and replied, "Thanks for allowing me to come over so late." It was just after 11:00 at night.

"You're always welcome here. Just toss your coat on the chair. Would you like something?"

Duffy said, "No. Thanks."

Cold led Duffy into the living room. "Grab a seat."

Cold claimed an armchair, while Duffy sat on the couch. But he didn't sit back. Instead, he perched himself on the edge.

"What's bothering you?" asked Cold.

Duffy half-smiled nervously. He rubbed his hands on his pant legs. "I don't know how to go about this."

Cold offered a reassuring look.

Duffy declared, "After much prayer, I've concluded that I need to reach out to someone whom I can trust for help while also keeping what I'm about to say in the strictest confidence. And you're the only one, Gary."

"Thank you." He assured, "You can trust me. And anything you tell me tonight, I will consider under the seal of confession."

"Yes, part of this ... perhaps all of it ... would fall under the umbrella of a confession." Duffy rose to his feet, and began walking around the room.

Cold watched and waited.

As he paced, Duffy rubbed his hands together. He finally began, "I'm not who you think I am."

"Go on," advised Cold.

"I'm going to tell you something that when you first hear it, you'll think I've lost my mind." He stopped pacing, and looked directly at Cold. "The discussions that we've had about extraterrestrial life aren't a mere intellectual exercise. It's not fantasy."

Cold shifted his hands, and gripped the arms of the chair tightly. His eyes were fixed on Duffy, but his face became expressionless.

Duffy scratched his scalp, and continued, "It's more than that. I'll be able, hopefully, to explain this, make you somehow understand. But I'm not Ed Duffy, or, well, I'm not the original Father Duffy. I'm from another ... planet." He sat back down. "I know how insane this sounds, but..."

Cold interrupted, "The seal of confession goes both ways?"

"What? Ah, yes, but what I'm telling..."

Cold leaned forward. "Does the seal of confession hold with you?"

"Gary..." Duffy took a breath. "Yes. I take the seal seriously, just as you do."

Cold stared at Duffy for nearly half a minute. He finally got up from the chair, and walked over to Duffy. Looking down, Cold said, "Show me your neck."

"What!?"

"You heard me."

Duffy stared up. "How the...?" He cut himself short. "Oh, I think I see. Okay." Duffy proceeded to slip the white strip out of his clergy collar, and undid the top three buttons of his shirt. He turned his body so that Cold could get a clear look, and pulled down the back of his collar.

Cold bent down. He held his breath upon seeing a small scar and a slight bulge. Cold finally breathed and whispered, "Dear God." He leaned in closer, and gazed at Duffy's neck for another minute.

It was Duffy's turn to wait.

Cold returned to his chair. "Did you do this? Were you the one who murdered Father Duffy – the real Father Edward Duffy?"

Duffy shook his head, and then lowered it. "You can't fathom how sorry I am for this. It's evil."

Cold raised an eyebrow at that last word. "Yes, it is."

"All I can say is that I've never been involved in such a thing, or, I mean, directly. But it wasn't long after I ... became Father Duffy that I truly started to learn." He looked up at Cold. "I came to learn how wrong all of this is. I also learned about Christ. I came to believe. I've prayed, studied, and tried to become the best priest I could."

Cold rubbed his chin, and asked, "What the hell am I supposed to do with this, with you?"

Duffy simply stared back with pleading in his eyes.

Cold suddenly leaned forward and said, "Wait. Why was Father Duffy selected to be replaced?"

Duffy responded, "We don't know the mission of the other..."

"Defenders."

The priest was surprised by Cold's use of the word. "Yes. We either work in very small teams or alone. I was chosen to work alone by replacing Father Duffy."

"Why?"

"My assignment was to find out anything worthwhile about the Catholic Church and its operations in the United States. Someone was chosen within the Diocese of New York, given its size and importance within the U.S. While being able to gain access to important information, I would not be vulnerable to discovery. Father Duffy, unfortunately, fit the bill."

"How far does this invasion reach?"

"All I can tell you is that the targets were chosen with great deliberation, and there are hundreds of Defenders."

"My God," whispered Cold as he slumped back in the chair.

Duffy commented, "You know all of this – the injector mark and the word 'Defenders' – because of your son." It was a statement, not a question. "At least some people in Washington know what's happening." He seemed to want to reassure Cold. "My pledge to keep this under the seal remains."

Cold ignored his comments, and asked, "And I am to believe that you've become a traitor?"

Duffy's face twitched slightly at the word "traitor." He responded, "If you choose to put it that way, yes, I suppose."

"Why wouldn't the word fit?"

"Because I don't feel like a traitor to my world or my people. Instead, I want to help them in a way that matters."

"Help how?"

"You know what we talked about at the diner?"

"Meaning?"

Father Duffy declared, "I meant what I said or implied that day. I want to be a missionary for the Church to those here on Earth who believe in UFOs, and to the people of Nykar." He paused and added, "But I need help. I need *your* help, Gary."

Cold sat unmoving. He finally said, "I have no idea about any of this."

"I understand. And while all of this is meant for the two of us, please feel free to discuss it, as you see fit, with your son."

Cold looked directly at Duffy. He repeated, "I don't know what I'm supposed to do with you. I feel like I shouldn't just let you stroll out of here. At the same time, if your immediate intentions were nefarious, I suppose you wouldn't have told me any of this."

Duffy got to his feet, and declared, "You need to think and pray about this. I'm sorry." Extending his hand, Duffy said, "Thank you for listening to me. I'm sure we'll have more to discuss. At least, I hope we do, Gary."

Cold hesitated, but got to his feet and shook Duffy's hand. "One way or another, we will."

Cold closed the door after Duffy left. He then leaned his forehead on the door and closed his eyes, remaining in that position for a couple of minutes. He finally opened the door, once again, and crossed the street. He went into St. Mark's, and took a seat in the last pew.

For a little more than an hour, Cold stared at the altar, and the crucifix hanging from the ceiling...in silence.

# Chapter 73

The evening after Mike Strickland had pegged Jerry Debrowski as a Nykarian substitute, and both Lawrence Silver and Maxine Marshall suspected the same of Clay Walsh, Roy O'Keefe followed Walsh as he left the Senate Office Building. No one else at the Q Street townhouses was aware of his activities.

The pursuit on foot barely got started when Walsh grabbed the first taxi in a line of cabs outside the building. O'Keefe jumped into the next cab, and instructed the driver to "stay close" to the cab ahead of him.

The journey took O'Keefe across the Memorial Bridge into Arlington. The driver followed Walsh's taxi as it turned down King Street, and then made a right. When Walsh's taxi stopped, O'Keefe instructed, "Pull over here."

The driver did so. O'Keefe watched Walsh get out of his cab, and enter a small pub.

"What do I owe you?" O'Keefe gave the driver the fare and a nice tip.

The driver said, "Thanks, buddy!"

O'Keefe got out, and crossed the street. He sat on a bench away from any streetlights, pulled the brim of his fedora down lower than normal, and watched.

Ten minutes later, a car turned onto the street, passed in front of him, and parked to his left, beyond the pub where Clay Walsh was at the moment. As that car was pulling over to the curb, another made the same turn onto the street, but claimed a spot to O'Keefe's right.

While his body didn't move, his eyes widened when looking back to the left and seeing who was exiting the vehicle. It was Lawrence Silver.

O'Keefe whispered, "Shit."

After closing the car door, Silver pulled the collar up on his coat, and lowered his head. He quickly strode to the pub, opened the door and disappeared inside.

As the door to the bar closed behind Silver, two people got out of the newly arrived vehicle to O'Keefe's right.

He whispered to himself, once more. "What the hell?" O'Keefe rose from the bench and stepped into the street. He reached inside his coat and pulled his Colt Commander from its shoulder holster. Crossing the road, he kept his eyes on the two individuals now walking toward the bar. He hung his hand with the gun down at his side.

The two individuals stopped on the sidewalk when they saw his movements.

O'Keefe stepped in their path, and asked, "What the hell are you doing?" O'Keefe moved the gun slightly so that the two could see the weapon.

Grace Armstrong said, "Roy? We could ask the same thing."

O'Keefe was unmoved.

Robert Weathers looked at the gun and then at O'Keefe's face. "Let's be careful. This isn't how it might look."

"Convince me," ordered O'Keefe.

Armstrong replied with annoyance in her voice. "We were following Lawrence Silver."

"Why?"

Weathers answered, "Something's not right about ... his view of this entire situation."

O'Keefe remained silent.

Weathers continued, "Grace and I get the feeling that he doesn't trust what we've relayed about our people and why they're here."

Armstrong added, "He wants to think that they're here for good reasons, and this is all some kind of big misunderstanding."

"Well," added Weathers, "that's what we think is the case with Lawrence."

O'Keefe eased his grip on the pistol, and then re-holstered the weapon. "Come on."

He stepped back into the street, and after exchanging a look, Armstrong and Weathers followed him.

As he returned to the bench, O'Keefe said, "You two take the seat. Sit close."

Weathers and Armstrong did so, while O'Keefe stepped behind them into further darkness.

Armstrong asked, "What are you doing? What are we doing?"

O'Keefe said, "You two are a nice couple enjoying the evening. I was following Clay Walsh."

Weathers asked, "Walsh is in that pub?"

"He is," responded O'Keefe. "And I believe that a third person will be joining them, if he already isn't in there."

Several seconds later, a man came walking from the other direction, and on the opposite side of the street from the three now watching.

O'Keefe observed, "And there he is. That would be Jerry Debrowski."

# Chapter 74

After five minutes, O'Keefe said, "Let's sit in your car." As they crossed the road, he asked, "Who was driving?"

"I was," answered Weathers.

"Give me the keys. Someone's in the back seat."

"Me," volunteered Armstrong.

Less than a minute after getting in the Oldsmobile 88, a car a couple of spaces closer to the pub drove off. O'Keefe moved the Olds up into that spot. The new position offered a clearer view of the front door of the drinking establishment.

After shutting off the engine, O'Keefe said, "So, what did you two pick up on?"

They relayed the questions and points raised to them by Silver, along with his looks and body language.

When they finished, O'Keefe said, "Pretty vague, but I understand your unease. And apparently, your concerns were on the mark."

"Perhaps," commented Weathers.

"Why 'perhaps'?" replied O'Keefe.

"Because he could be doing the same thing that the three of us arc tonight, but taking more direct action."

O'Keefe actually chuckled. "I suppose, theoretically, that's possible. But you know better."

Armstrong chimed in, "Yes, we do." She added, "And if Lawrence is spilling the beans in there to Walsh and Debrowski, they'll head to their communications set to make emergency contact with a Commander. And they will take Lawrence with them."

O'Keefe nodded. "Yeah, I wouldn't let Silver out of my sight now. I assume the communications equipment would be in the home of either Walsh or Debrowski?"

Weathers answered, "Yes."

O'Keefe breathed in deeply. "Are you two armed?"

"We are," informed Armstrong.

Weathers revealed the shoulder holster under his coat.

"Good." A few seconds later, O'Keefe added, "We've got action."

First out the door of the pub was Jerry Debrowski, followed by Lawrence Silver and then Clay Walsh. The three passed Silver's car and continued up the street to another vehicle. Debrowski took the wheel, with Silver next to him in the front passenger seat, and Walsh in the back.

When Debrowski pulled the car away from the curb, O'Keefe followed.

No one said anything at first, as each person's eyes were trained on the car ahead.

"I checked on where Walsh and Debrowski lived, and it looks like we're headed to Walsh's place."

Armstrong observed, "Once there, we can't give them any time."

"Yeah," replied O'Keefe. "Let them get inside, and then we come in fast."

"Keep in mind," advised Weathers, "while these two studied and immersed themselves into who Walsh and Debrowski were, it's not them. They've become Walsh and Debrowski, but they're highly trained Defenders. When we move in, they're not going to react like a couple of bumbling Senate aides. They're going to react like the highly trained soldiers they are."

O'Keefe kept his eyes on Debrowski's car, and replied, "Right. That's just great." He paused, and then continued, "Okay, we don't know the lay of the land at this place. All I know is that it's a pretty standard home in a college town, just a couple of streets from Maryland State College. It should be quiet and, hopefully, pretty dark. We have to assume they'll lock up after they enter."

"Absolutely," confirmed Weathers.

"There's no doing this quietly," O'Keefe observed. "We hit the front door and whatever back or side entrance there is at about the same time. That'll split their attention, and give us some kind of advantage."

"Hopefully," added Armstrong.

Some 20 minutes later, Debrowski pulled the car into the driveway of a brick home on a wide street. As Walsh led Silver and Debrowski to the front steps, O'Keefe shut off the lights of the Olds 88, and pulled over two houses away.

Weathers, Armstrong and O'Keefe checked their weapons. And when the last of the threesome they were following stepped inside, O'Keefe led the other two toward the house.

Weathers and Armstrong moved down the side of the home, while O'Keefe went for the front steps.

O'Keefe paused, giving Weathers and Armstrong time to get around back. After five seconds, he reached out for the front doorknob, and quietly tried to turn it. But it was locked. He took a step back, raised his right leg, and drove his foot at the door.

The timing was near perfect. As the front door crashed open, so did the other door. Everything played out in just a few seconds.

Silver was in a spacious living room to O'Keefe's right. Beyond that was a dining room and then the kitchen. Walsh and Debrowski were in the kitchen, as Weathers and Armstrong came in via the kitchen door opening on the side yard.

Silver gave O'Keefe a shocked look. But quickly started pleading, "No, no, don't do this. You don't understand."

As the last word came out of Silver's mouth, the shooting began in the kitchen. O'Keefe shoved Silver to the side, and he fell to the floor. "Get the hell out of the way, you idiot."

O'Keefe halted his advance, as Debrowski and Walsh were retreating from the kitchen.

Walsh turned, and he and O'Keefe exchanged shots. As O'Keefe dove behind an armchair, Walsh pushed the dining room table onto its side for cover.

In the kitchen, Debrowski's retreat ended with a shot to the chest from Weathers' gun.

Armstrong moved ahead of Weathers in reaching the archway leading into the dining room. She wasted no time, and deposited two slugs into Walsh's back as he started exchanging gunfire with O'Keefe.

The flurry of shots ended. The lone noise that stood out was Silver, now sitting up on the floor, pleading, "No, no. That shouldn't have happened. Why did you do that?" He was rubbing his hair with both hands.

The others ignored him. While Armstrong and O'Keefe stood in place with their weapons drawn, Weathers moved to check the bodies. He initially went back into the kitchen. He announced, "Debrowski is dead."

As Weathers returned from the kitchen, Walsh coughed weakly. O'Keefe and Armstrong trained their guns on the aide to Senator Kennedy. Weathers kicked Walsh's gun away from his reach, squatted down and gently rolled the man over.

Walsh coughed again, with blood expelling from his mouth and nose.

As Weathers, Armstrong and O'Keefe were looking down at Walsh, Silver slowly got to his feet and moved across the room. He had a wild look on his face.

Walsh offered up another discharge of blood, and then ceased breathing.

In a low voice, Weathers declared, "He's gone."

Silver bent down and picked up Walsh's gun. "You didn't understand, and you killed them."

He raised the pistol at Armstrong, and just as he pulled the trigger, Weathers launched himself up. "Don't!"

The shot went off, and the projectile entered Weathers' upper left chest.

O'Keefe fired off two shots – the final two bullets he had in his M1911. One struck Silver in the side of the head. As he hit the floor, his eyes went lifeless.

As O'Keefe turned in the direction of Weathers, Armstrong already was at his side. "No, no, no. Don't do this, Robert."

Weathers grimaced in pain.

O'Keefe now sprang into action in a different way. He looked at where Weathers was hit. He said, "Grace. Grace!"

She looked up at him.

O'Keefe said, "It missed his heart, but he's losing blood quickly."

Weathers groaned again.

O'Keefe continued, "We're going to get him in the car and you're going to get him to a hospital…"

Weathers interrupted, "No!"

"What? You have to," replied O'Keefe.

Weathers looked up at Armstrong. "Grace, we can't go to a hospital. They'll find out. You and the baby."

O'Keefe said, "Shit. Okay. We get him to the car, and you" – he looked at Armstrong – "will get him to the lab. I'll call Max and Mike. They'll hopefully be waiting for you."

"Okay," answered Armstrong, as she and O'Keefe lifted and started to drag Weathers. The colonel bit his lip and tried to help. Armstrong asked, "And you, Roy?"

"Once one of Dulles's clean-up team arrives, I'll be right over."

Armstrong and O'Keefe laid Weathers in the back seat of the car, with the vehicle then speeding off with Armstrong at the wheel.

O'Keefe ran back into the house, and called Q Street.

Maxine Marshall answered. O'Keefe briefly explained, and Marshall and Strickland were on their way to the lab by the time O'Keefe was on to his next call with CIA Director Allen Dulles.

# Chapter 75

Mike Strickland was waiting next to a gurney inside the front door of the small two-story brick building on U Street NW. As Grace Armstrong whipped the car into the parking lot, Strickland emerged.

Armstrong jumped out of the front seat, and Strickland opened the passenger side back door. Weathers made no noise, having passed out during the drive.

Strickland said, "Max is setting up everything inside."

All Armstrong could do was nod.

The two maneuvered Weathers out of the car and onto the gurney.

As they rolled Weathers into the building, Strickland said, "Ike fully stocked this place."

Armstrong simply stared down at Weathers as they moved.

When reaching the back of the first floor, they busted through the swinging doors and into the small hospital-like part of the building. Marshall was ready, and when she started to cut and tear away Weathers' clothes, she asked, "Grace, do you know his blood type?"

"A positive."

"Either of you A positive?"

Armstrong said, "No."

"Me, neither," added Strickland.

Marshall said, "Okay. I need the two of you to wash up and help."

Twenty minutes later, Marshall pulled the slug from Weathers' chest. As she began to further clean and sew up the wound, O'Keefe arrived. He stuck his head in between the doors, and asked, "How is he doing?"

Marshall responded, "What blood type are you?"

"A positive," O'Keefe answered.

Marshall ordered, "Good. We'll be taking some of your blood." As she continued working on Weathers, she said, "Mike, I need you to get Roy ready for a transfusion."

"I'm on it," replied Strickland. "Let's go, Roy."

Looking down at her work on Weathers, Marshall said to Armstrong, "Grace, can you clean up that blood?"

Armstrong did as instructed without saying a word.

Marshall said, "Thanks."

A few minutes later, as they prepared Weathers and O'Keefe for the transfusion, Armstrong asked, "Max?"

"I'm hoping, praying and doing all I can."

# Chapter 76

Pastor Gary Cold called his son several times, but there was no answer.

He then proceeded to call the other numbers Dean had given him, including one for Cameron Jefferson and one for Maxine Marshall.

Again, no one answered.

He sat next to his phone, sighed and rubbed his forehead. Cold said out loud to himself, "Dean, I need to talk to you about this, for your sake and what you're doing, and to figure out what I'm supposed to do."

In his prayer life and sometimes when reading his Bible, Cold would speak aloud when by himself in the church.

Since his wife died, Cold found himself doing so whenever he was alone in the house or at the church, and it was no longer limited to praying and reading Holy Scripture. Doing so, for some reason, gave him comfort. He felt less alone. At the same time, he worried that if someone overheard him, they'd conclude he had lost his mind.

He rose from his chair, and took another walk across the street and into St. Mark's. He slipped into a pew toward the front of the nave.

Cold pulled down the kneeler, and bent his knees. He blessed himself, clasped his hands, and lowered his head.

"Dear Lord, what am I supposed to do with this?" He actually chuckled. "I mean, visitors from space? And the one I know has ... what? ... taken over a Catholic priest? And now this alien-priest wants to become a missionary to his fellow aliens? And he wants my help?" He looked up toward the altar. "Given what Dean told me, and what I saw and heard with Ed, my feeble mind is assuming that this is all true." He shook his head. "You certainly have a sense of humor, don't you? Well, I hope you're finding this amusing." He shifted on his knees, and then added, "Sorry. That wasn't called for, I know. There's nothing funny about any of this."

He shifted the focus of his chat with the Lord. "What would Theresa think and tell me if she were here? Whatever it would have been, she would have given me..." His voice broke, and he went silent.

He lowered his head, once more, and said, "I need your strength, Lord, and some wisdom." He began to repeat the Kyrie: "Lord, have mercy upon us. Christ, have mercy upon us. Lord, have mercy upon us."

Cold sat back in the pew and reached for the copy of *The Lutheran Hymnal* in front of him. He paged to the section offering prayers for specific instances and needs. While scanning the short prayers under various titles, Cold smiled and said, "Okay, Lord, which one of these applies to space aliens?"

His finger stopped at "For Divine Grace and Help." He read and prayed, "Direct us, O Lord, in all our doings with Thy most gracious favor and further us with Thy continual help, that in all our works begun, continued, and ended in Thee we may glorify Thy holy name and finally, by Thy mercy, obtain everlasting life; through Jesus Christ, our Lord."

Cold closed his eyes and breathed deeply. He then returned to the open hymnal on his lap. His eyes stopped next on "For Charity." Once more, he read and prayed: "O Lord, who hast taught us that all our doings without charity are worth nothing, send Thy Holy Spirit and pour into our hearts that most excellent gift of charity, the very bond of peace, and all virtues, without which whosoever liveth is counted dead before Thee, Grant this for Thine only Son Jesus Christ's sake."

He closed and returned the hymnal to the rack in front of him. Cold then closed his eyes, and sat, once again, in silence in the church.

# Chapter 77

Once the trawler was secured to the dock in Ayan, Captain Bogdan Kolchak's sons and nephew went about unloading their night's catch. It was still dark and frigid enough that unless one had an essential reason to venture out into the early morning, no one did. So, Kolchak leading his four guests off the trawler and into the village didn't seem to draw any interest.

When they stepped into Kolchak's house, a woman, nearly as large as Bogdan, and a short, rail-thin man greeted them with stares.

Bogdan introduced Dean Cold, John Bartley, Cameron Jefferson and Daria Popov, and then announced, "This is my wife, Anna, and my brother-in-law, Matvey. He is Nazar's father. As I said, the last direct family members of General Pepelyayev."

While the four guests said "Hello," "Good to meet you," or "Thank you," Anna and Matvey remained silent.

Bogdan sighed and declared, "Welcome our visitors. They come here to do something that the communists will hate." He chuckled, and turned and looked at Cold. "Right?"

Cold replied, "That's the hope."

"Good. Good." Bogdan looked back at his wife and brother-in-law.

Anna rose from her seat and said, "Yes, yes, welcome. I'm sorry if my brother and I seem … wary. We must be careful."

Popov replied, "Of course, we understand. I most certainly do."

Anna was surprised by Popov's Russian accent. She smiled, and then seemed to take each guest off guard, by hugging each one of them. Matvey's face remained stoic, but he rose and shook each person's hand. He then looked at Cold, "You are in charge?"

"Yes, I am."

"I have the weapons that your leader arranged for stored on my farm just outside of the village."

"Thank you," replied Cold.

Matvey added, "It is a ... powerful collection. I wonder why you might need so much."

Cold didn't answer, nor did Bartley, Jefferson or Popov.

Bogdan broke in, "You can wonder all you want, Matvey. I do as well. But they most certainly will not tell you, or me."

"Yes," declared Matvey.

Bartley spoke up. "Trust us. If we are successful, Chairman Stalin will not be pleased."

Matvey's stone face finally cracked. He sneered. "That is good enough for me."

Bogdan looked at Cold's group. "Anna will make one of her magnificent meals, and then you can rest. When darkness falls, once again, you will go with Matvey to his farm. You can take stock of the weapons, and if their schedule remains, the supply truck will leave the village early tomorrow morning, and drive right by the front door of Matvey's farm. That will be your chance."

"Thank you – all of you – for your help," said Cold.

Anna looked at Popov and asked, "Daria, perhaps you would like to help me with the food?" No demand could be heard in her voice. It wasn't an expectation. Instead, it had the ring of kindness, a certain warmth.

Popov smiled with a hint of sadness, and nodded. As she looked at the food spread across a worn, wooden kitchen countertop, she commented, "I haven't done something like this since I was a child, helping my mother." She looked Anna in the eyes. "This reminds me of that."

Anna smiled.

Bogdan offered chairs at a long table that not only served as a dining table, but also as the central point of activity in the small home.

Matvey took a chair next to Jefferson. "So, Mr. Jefferson, I have never met a black man before."

Jefferson responded, "And I've never met a Russian farmer before."

Matvey actually laughed at that.

Jefferson continued, "Well, at least, I don't think I have."

"What does that mean?" asked Matvey.

"I met a few Russians in Berlin at the end of the war, so – who knows? – maybe some were farmers before the war."

"Ah, you fought the filthy Germans."

Jefferson nodded. "Yeah, like most Americans my age, I suppose."

"Of course, just like most Russians. I was at Stalingrad." He looked around the table at Cold, Bartley and Jefferson. "You all fought?"

Cold nodded, and Bartley said, "That's right."

Matvey leaned back in his seat. He reflected, "It had to be done, of course. And Stalin suddenly had the ability to make us all love *his* Russia, or so he thought. But it wasn't *his*. It was an invasion, a war against *our* Russia, against our homeland, against Mother Russia. We all fought, and most bravely. And so many died at the hands of those Nazi pigs, but also at the hands of Stalin's indifference and incompetence."

Cold, Bartley and Jefferson sat enraptured, with Popov stopping and listening from behind them.

Matvey continued, "Stalin and his generals hurled men at the Nazis because they didn't have much more. And like Napoleon, Hitler discovered what Russians and our weather were capable of inflicting. But then…" He sighed. "When the war ended, after defeating this great evil, we were reminded of the evil that reigns over us. The reach of that evil has moved beyond Russia. That expansion of power has seduced many more Russians to support this government. What is it being called, this war that you four are here to fight in some way, the Cold War?" He shook his head. "All of our wars are cold."

Cold could find nothing to argue with in what Matvey was saying.

*And if you knew what else was now happening, Matvey, what would you say and do? Another invasion of your Russia already has taken place, and your Motherland is an ally of something even more powerful.*

His thoughts then went to what Weathers and Armstrong relayed about Nykar. Matvey noted how many Russians came to support a government expanding Russia's reach. Robert and Grace basically pointed out the same thing about Nykarians rallying in support of expansion to the other planets.

After Bogdan and Matvey offered information about day-to-day life in Russia, Ilya, Lev and Nazar arrived. Anna and Popov then brought the food to the table.

As Popov placed a bowl down near Bogdan, the big Russian looked up at her, and said, "So, you, too, Daria, are going on this mission? Is this going to be safe for a woman?" He chuckled and looked around the table, apparently seeking some kind of approval. None was forthcoming.

Cold, Jefferson and Bartley froze, with only their eyes shifting to look up at Popov.

Looking down and then smiling in a way that made Bogdan lean back ever so slightly from her, Popov said, "It's not safe for any of us. But if you are truly worried, I could demonstrate that I am able to take care of myself."

Bogdan swallowed hard while still staring up at Popov.

She said, "Look at that knife."

Pulling his stare away from Popov, he looked down at the table.

"Do you see how dull it is?" Bogdan didn't answer. Popov continued, "I imagine it takes a good deal of effort to cut into any kind of meat with it. Nonetheless, I could still use that knife to slit your throat, and it would all happen so quickly, that you wouldn't have time to realize what was happening, never mind stop me."

Anna came over to the table with the final additions to the meal. "Does that answer your question, Bogdan?"

He cleared his throat, and just above a whisper, said, "Yes, it does."

"Good," said Anna. "Now, shut up and eat." She offered a slight smile to Popov, and then said to everyone, "Please, eat."

# Chapter 78

In a rundown barn on Matvey's farm, Dean Cold, Cameron Jefferson, Daria Popov and John Bartley spent the night taking inventory. They marveled at what Allen Dulles managed to put at their disposal for this mission.

At one point, Cameron Jefferson asked, "What the hell was offered as bribes to make this happen?"

Daria Popov answered, "As an American, you might be surprised at how little it might take."

"I guess," replied Jefferson, with a shake of the head.

Popov smirked, "Ah, you rich Americans."

Bartley laughed at that, as did the other two.

A few seconds passed, and Bartley commented, "I think you scared the crap out of Bogdan with the talk about slitting his neck with a dull knife."

"Hell, scared the shit out of me," added Jefferson with a smile and raised eyebrow.

Popov said, "I meant no disrespect. I know the risks that Bogdan and his family are taking, and why they are doing it. But at the same time, what he said, you know, it annoyed me."

"I get it," observed Jefferson, "and I'm going to be damn sure that I don't annoy you."

"Me, too," commented Bartley.

Cold said, "Yeah, I'm glad you're on our side."

*The voice of an angel, and a lethal warrior bent on ... what? Justice? Revenge? both?*

A few hours later, Matvey, who had ordered Nazar to remain at the house, guided a horse and cart into the narrow, snow-covered road at the end of the path down from the farmhouse. Cold, Jefferson, Bartley and Popov got out of

Matvey's small truck, in which they had followed the horse and cart. Matvey detached the horse, and tied it to the back of the truck. At the same time, Bartley, Jefferson and Cold dumped over the contents of the cart.

Matvey stayed by the cart, while the other three retreated behind the truck.

"Now, we wait," declared Cold.

It didn't take long. The lights of the vehicle they were waiting for came around the curve in the road. As the supply truck slowed, its headlights illuminated Matvey waving his arms.

The driver stopped the truck and lowered his window as Matvey approached. "What the hell happened, Matvey?"

"What hasn't happened this morning, Benedikt? The horse bucked. I had to get the truck, and tie him up. And now I have to clean up this mess. I'm sorry for delaying you."

"I understand. Ari and I will help you." Benedikt and his brother, Ari, got out of the vehicle.

Matvey started to say, "Thank you. That will get you on your..."

He was interrupted by a man who jumped out of the back of the supply truck with a rifle in his hands. "No." He approached the other three men now standing in the light cast by the truck's headlamps. He pointed to Benedikt, "You will get back in the truck, while you" – he pointed his rifle at Ari – "will help this fool clean up."

"Who are you?" asked Matvey.

Benedikt and Ari looked increasingly nervous.

"It's none of your business." He paused, looked around, and then shook his head. "Get over there." He indicated that Matvey should move to the side of the road.

"What?"

He raised his rifle at Matvey. "Put your hands up, and move." As he continued looking at Matvey, the man called out, "Now, you two get this garbage out of the way."

Benedikt weakly responded, "What are you going to do?"

The anger rose in the man's voice. "I will do what needs to be done, and if you ask any more questions, I'll do the same to you."

Benedikt and Ari warily moved toward the cart.

Crouching with Jefferson, Popov and Bartley next to the truck, Cold whispered, "Shit." He looked at the others and said, "Be ready."

The M1911 was already in his hand.

*God, forgive me.*

He rose and took several steps forward as quietly as he could. His weapon was trained on the Russian holding the rifle.

Cold said, "Drop it."

The Russian spun himself and the rifle around.

Cold squeezed off two shots. Each hit the Russian, who fell to the road of snow and ice. The rifle slid away, and he took his last breath.

Cold turned his weapon on Benedikt and Ari, who slowly raised their hands into the air. The brothers' eyes grew wider at the sight of three more people emerging from the side of the road with guns also pointed at them.

During the standoff, Matvey said, "Thank you."

Cold turned quickly, and saw that Matvey was looking at him. Cold nodded. He then looked over at Bartley, Jefferson and Popov, and said, "Watch them." He then walked over to the dead Russian, bent over, pulled back the dead man's collar, and looked at the back of his neck.

As he walked back, Bartley asked, "Well?"

Cold shook his head.

Matvey then walked over to Benedikt and Ari. He said, "We've known each other our entire lives. These people are here to do something important. You can be part of that for a brief moment, and get paid very well for doing so, or, well…"

He glanced over at the body of the dead Russian.

Popov added, in Russian, "We can hurt Stalin and his men. I think you might be interested in that. And if we succeed, you'll get none of the blame, and you'll be paid far better than what you've been getting for shuttling supplies to that facility."

Benedikt continued to wear a bewildered look, with his hands still in the air.

Ari, however, slowly lowered his hands. "Americans?"

Popov nodded. "They are."

Ari's eyes stopped on Jefferson for a moment, and then he looked at Popov. "You went over?"

"To do what I could for Russia."

Ari grinned and asked, "How much?"

Bartley answered, "What do you need? We have food, vodka, rubles and, if interested, we might even be able to get you out of Russia."

Ari looked over at his brother. Benedikt finally lowered his hands, and nodded at Ari.

Ari turned and declared, "Yes."

"Yes to what?" asked Matvey.

Benedikt said, "Food would be good, but vodka and rubles would be better."

# Chapter 79

The lights in the narthex of St. Mark Lutheran Church were on, along with a desk lamp in Pastor Gary Cold's office. The rest of the church, though, was dark.

Cold was using the lamp to read Matthew's Gospel. His eyes glanced up briefly with the noise of the front door to the church opening and closing. His eyes went back to the pages open on the desk in front of him, even as the clicking of shoes on the marble floor grew louder until they stopped at the entrance to his office.

"Gary," said Father Edward Duffy.

Cold looked up. "Come in, Ed. Grab a seat."

Duffy took his coat off, set it down on the office couch, and took the chair offered by Cold. "I appreciate you calling and inviting me over."

"I've been thinking and praying about what you revealed to me. That's a gross understatement. It's pretty much been all I can think about."

"I understand."

"And I have more questions."

"Of course."

"First, before you, well, became Father Duffy, you had to have some knowledge of what it meant to be a priest in order to pull this off?"

Duffy took a deep breath. "Yes, that's right. I studied for nearly three years."

"Three years? Up there?" He pointed skyward. "I mean you studied while circling the Earth in a spaceship."

"I did. That's what each Defender has to do, with the time and intensity varying by the assignment. Before leaving our planet and on the journey, we learn your languages and about humanity in general."

"Dear Lord," Cold whispered. He paused, and then asked, "So, when and how did you 'come to believe,' as you put it the other day?"

"Not easy to explain."

"It's not for many of us," agreed Cold. "It's often a process."

"Looking back, I've come to realize that even before I replaced Father Duffy, what I was studying interested me. It started working on me." He paused and added, "The Holy Spirit was working on me."

Cold said nothing.

Duffy went on, "It was being in the parish, though, where I began learning about how the faith of those in the pews affected their lives. I couldn't treat this as a Defender was supposed to – as an assignment meant to be part of the larger effort. A subversive invasion. There was a moral code that further clarified things for me. At the same time, it intensified my guilt. I didn't want to be the one responsible for driving people away from their faith, away from God. The guilt pushed me to try to serve as the best priest I could to these people, and it intensified my need for answers. I had to reject the justifications that I was clinging to about this invasion. It was evil."

Duffy closed his eyes, and lowered his head. He remained in that position and said, "Anger at my people, coupled with self-loathing, paralyzed me for a time. The small staff and parishioners at St. Peter's became worried about me, which only made me feel worse. The diocese sent over a priest to cover the Sunday masses for a few weeks." He paused for a few seconds, and then continued, "Father Duffy was murdered to implant me into this man. I was the one who deserved death. I seriously considered killing myself." He used his right hand to rub his forehead. "And then I realized that if I did that, everyone would think that it was Father Duffy who killed himself. I couldn't bear that, either. I came to realize that trying to somehow fulfill Father Duffy's mission was my cross to bear, my penance, my responsibility. But I realized that it wasn't just his mission; it had become mine."

Duffy looked up at Cold with tears in his eyes.

Cold opened his mouth, but no words came out.

Duffy continued, "And then the full message of Christianity finally became clear, why it was different than other religions or philosophies about doing good. It was about that, of course, but so much more. It was about God actually becoming man. And because He so loved us, He took on our sins and died for them, and then He conquered death, the ultimate consequence of sin, one might say, and offered forgiveness, redemption and salvation for all. All is grace, and all we need is faith, to believe, to receive these unwarranted gifts." He paused and breathed deeply. "And then I struggled with a question: Was this just meant for humans? I looked at what so many had written and reflected on over the centuries – as you and I have discussed – about what you humans refer to as alien life. My doubts eventually melted away. God created everything, all life, whether here on Earth, on Nykar, or elsewhere. And I understood quite clearly that Nykarians, like humans, are fallen creatures – sinners in need of saving. Jesus came to save us all. Right?"

Cold found his voice, and simply answered, "How could He not?"

"Exactly!" Duffy smiled. "And then I realized I had a mission by being placed in this place. I was part of the Church's mission to spread this Good News, to evangelize, and that didn't stop with bringing Christ to those who enter the doors of St. Peter's. I realized that if Christ could save me, then He could save my Nykarian brothers and sisters. And the enormity of that hit me. Am I the only one in position to start that task, to...?" His voice broke.

Cold looked down at the open Bible. "You highlighted this before." He cleared his throat and read the Great Commission at the end of Matthew, "Go ye therefore, and teach all nations, baptizing them in the name of the Father, and of the Son, and of the Holy Ghost: Teaching them to observe all things whatsoever I have commanded you: and, lo, I am with you always, even unto the end of the world. Amen."

He moved his eyes back to Duffy.

The priest said, "Yes. That's right. I know the Lord will be at my side. I know the Holy Spirit will be there, is there. But ... I know my ... weaknesses." He then repeated the request that he had previously made to Cold. "I can't do this completely alone. I need someone to at least be ready to listen, to advise, to just be there. I need help."

Now, Cold didn't hesitate. "He 'sent them two and two before his face into every city and place...'"

"Luke, Chapter 10," confirmed Duffy.

"I'll help in whatever way I can, Ed."

The look of relief on Duffy's face was palpable. More tears came from his eyes, but now he smiled as they flowed. He said, "Thank you. Thank you, Gary. You also need to know that if the Commanders on our ships learn about what I'm doing, they can simply terminate my life."

"What?"

"Yes, without getting too far into this, my original body is kept functioning on board a ship. If the Nykarians learn of what I am doing, they can simply shut down my body, and that will end this life."

Tears now formed in Cold's eyes as well. "You're willing to make the ultimate sacrifice."

"I discovered that I had no choice."

After a minute or so, Cold said, "I do need you to do something for me, Ed."

"Yes, what is it?"

"I need you to sit down with my son, and tell him everything."

It was Duffy's turn not to hesitate. "Of course, I will."

# Chapter 80

The drive from Matvey's farm to the MGB facility was along an uneven, narrow, snow-and-ice-covered road. After waiting for several hours before getting underway, the journey took four hours. In addition to the food supplies being delivered, the truck carried cans of gasoline for the drive there and back. On this trip, though, there was additional cargo.

Dean Cold, John Bartley, Cameron Jefferson and Daria Popov followed the delivery truck in Matvey's smaller vehicle.

Within a half-mile of the facility, Benedikt stopped the delivery truck amidst a heavy group of trees and brush. Jefferson turned the smaller truck around, and parked it on the side of the road. Cold, Popov, Bartley and Jefferson left that truck behind, which hopefully would be their ride back later.

The four climbed into the back of the delivery truck. Their additional equipment awaited them – two bazookas, grenades and machine guns – stored next to the boxes and bags of food.

Cold's group had two plans.

According to Plan A, which was what Cold and the others were hoping for, the delivery truck would be let in as usual. When Benedikt and Ari parked for the delivery, Cold and Popov would move into the facility and, as quietly as possible given the time of night, make their way to the director's office. That would be the place, it was assumed, where the controls would be located for detonating the network of explosives that would destroy the facility. Meanwhile, Jefferson and Bartley would be ready at the truck with a cadre of weapons for whatever came their way. If all went well, the group would still have some fighting to do to get out of the facility while destruction rained down around them.

If matters went awry rather quickly, including the controls for the network of explosives not being found, Plan B would be a messier path. In fact, deep inside, there was a recognition by Cold that Plan B was the more likely scenario, and that meant their ability to escape would be a long shot. Their objective would be to destroy as much of what had been created at the facility as possible. The two tanks or the half-track reportedly on site would have to be used, along with the bazookas and grenades they brought along. Jefferson and Bartley would systematically use the tanks, taking out target by target. Much would be the same for Cold and Popov inside the building. And they all would hope that most of their goals could be achieved before personnel arrived from the barracks building.

Either way, Cold appreciated that Dulles had acquired a detailed layout of the facility, while also praying that the information was accurate.

As he pulled up to the gate of the facility, Benedikt rolled down the driver's side window. A small man enclosed in a massive coat with a hood came out of the small booth. All one could see under the hood were two brown eyes and a small nose. "You're late."

Benedikt replied, "I'm well aware, comrade. You would not believe the trouble that we've had. It started when..."

The guard interrupted, "I don't care. It's too cold to give a shit. Where's Mikhail?" He was referring to the now-dead man who started the journey with Benedikt and Ari.

Benedikt replied, "I think he's been asleep in the back for the past couple of hours. He had a few blankets with him when he got in."

"Fine, fine. Again, I don't care. Pull the truck into the usual spot and unload. There's not going to be anyone to help you at this hour. You two will have to do it all yourselves."

Benedikt shrugged. "We'll get it done. I just want to get this over with and head back home."

The hooded man replied, "Home? Must be nice. I understand that." He walked in front of the truck, unlatched the gate, and dragged it open. He then waved the truck through, and as it drove toward the buildings, the guard quickly closed the gate and scurried back into his shack.

Having heard most of the conversation, Cold whispered to the others. "Step one."

The truck pulled around to the back of Building A and Benedikt backed it up to a loading bay. Once the engine was shut off, Benedikt and Ari got out, and climbed the few steps onto the loading area. Ari opened the back of the truck, and the four passengers stood ready, each with an M1911 in hand, a machine gun slung over a shoulder, and a small satchel filled with grenades strapped to a belt.

Cold nodded at the loading dock door. Jefferson stepped forward. He bent down and grabbed the bottom of the roller bay door. Cold, Popov and Bartley stood ready with weapons in hand, depending upon what, or who, was on the other side.

The door came up, and they were met by a dark, quiet stillness.

Cold whispered, "Step two."

Cold and Popov moved into the darkness.

As they disappeared, Bartley and Jefferson pulled out the two bazookas.

Bartley looked at the two Russians, and asked, "You remember what we taught you earlier today about helping to load the shells?"

Each of the two brothers nodded nervously.

\*      \*      \*

Cold led the way with Popov close behind. He was working from memory as to how to get to the office of Dr. Maksut Golikova, the camp director and lead scientist.

As the two approached what Cold thought was Golikova's office, he spotted a light streaming out from underneath the closed door. He tested the door quietly. It was locked. Cold stepped back, and thrust his leg at the door, which crashed open.

Golikova, who was leaning back in his office chair, nearly fell backwards. He managed to ask with dread in his voice, "What is this? Who are you?" As Cold and Popov moved closer with their guns trained on him, he raised his hands shakily into the air.

Popov asked, "You are Dr. Golikova?"

The man nodded.

Cold grabbed Golikova's shirt at the back of the collar, pulled the man forward, and slammed his face into the desk. He then looked down, and saw the bulge and scar.

Cold and Popov exchanged looks.

Cold then tossed Golikova back into his chair, and asked, "I assume you learned English?"

Golikova nodded.

Cold said, "We're giving you two options. Cooperate with us, and perhaps get out of this alive. Or resist, and be assured of your death. Which will it be?"

Golikova clearly was trying to work out what was going on, but an instinct to live kicked in. "What do you need me to do?"

Cold began looking more closely around the room.

Golikova apparently worked on clearing his mind. He said, "You are an American."

"Your point?"

"You've learned about who we are and this place. And you've come to destroy it. I knew not to underestimate you."

Cold said, "Ah, trying to get in good with the people who hold your life in their hands."

Golikova merely replied, "Well, yes. You want me to set off the network of explosives to level this place."

Cold noted that it wasn't a question. "That's the idea."

"Fine," replied Golikova now rather coolly. "But there's more you can do."

"What the hell does that mean?"

"One of our MiG-Xs is supposed to be tested in the morning. It's ready to take off, sitting in Building C. If you have someone who can fly it, you can take it. And if you take me with you, I will be able to let you in on all of its technology and more."

"Aren't you being cooperative? Why would a Nykarian working with the Soviets help us?"

"I want to live, and I'd prefer continuing my work if I do live."

Popov broke in, "But once they get a whiff of what's happened, wouldn't your Commanders simply terminate you, as they would with any Defender?"

Golikova smiled. "You have been informed by Defenders who either have confessed to you or have defected, for lack of a better word. How interesting." He paused, and said, "No, my dear, that is a story. It's a lie to keep our people in line. How many would turn against us if they knew that they would die once their bodies on one of our ships could simply be shut off? But it is not true. That's not how it works. We don't have the ability to do that to our Defenders. They actually act autonomously, but they are not meant to know that."

"Dear God, you people are evil," commented Cold.

Golikova shrugged. "From what I have seen, no more evil than you humans."

Cold said, "Maybe. How do the explosives work?"

While Cold and Popov kept their guns on Golikova, the scientist walked over to a table up against a wall, and pulled out a drawer. Cold looked down at what was a control panel.

Golikova asked, "How much time will you … will we need to get out?"

*       *       *

Five minutes later, Bartley and Jefferson saw Popov emerge from the darkness.

Bartley asked, "What's happening?"

"We've got less than 10 minutes. Cam, you need to head down there" – she pointed – "to the last building. Travel light. Just your handgun. You're flying a jet out of here."

"I'm doing what?"

"We've got a chance to take some serious shit with us."

"Okay. What about you guys?"

Popov turned to Bartley. "John, you and I are going to take our new friends here with us, and grab the half-track." She pointed at the vehicle in the opposite direction from where Jefferson would be headed. "We'll swing over and pick up Dean, along with Dr. Golikova."

"The director?" asked Bartley.

"Yes. No time to explain much more."

Everyone moved in the directions dictated by Popov.

\*　　\*　　\*

Jefferson finished his sprint at an open hangar-sized door, and he saw Cold and Golikova standing by a black MiG-X.

Cold asked, "Are you up for this, Cam?"

Jefferson whistled while looking up at the aircraft – clearly admiring it. He replied, "Shit, yeah."

"Good. I thought you'd say that."

Jefferson merely glanced at Golikova as he moved to a ladder leading to the cockpit.

As he climbed the stairs, Golikova said, "I understand you are a versatile pilot."

Slipping himself into the seat and putting on the waiting helmet, Jefferson was taking everything in, and didn't reply to Golikova.

"If so, you should catch on to what you're seeing. You just need to understand that this plane will take longer to take off than anything you have flown before, and needs more runway to land. And you must understand that this can hit speeds three times faster than anything you Americans might have."

Jefferson looked down at Cold, still seemingly ignoring Golikova.

Cold pulled the stairs away and asked, "Do you know where you're going to take her?"

Jefferson glanced at Golikova and then looked back at Cold. "That place you and I visited for the first time."

Cold gave him a thumbs up.

Jefferson glanced at Golikova and back to Cold. "What about him? Just a Russian?"

Cold shook his head. "Nykarian."

Jefferson said, "I hope he comes in handy." As the half-track approached in the distance, he added, "Time to go."

Cold said, "Godspeed."

"You, too."

Cold led Golikova toward the half-track, and Jefferson pulled the MiG-X's cockpit cover closed.

Popov was at the wheel of the half-track, with Benedikt and Ari in the cab with her. When the vehicle came to a stop, Cold and Golikova climbed into the back.

Bartley was at the mounted machine gun. He said, "Good to see you, Dean."

"Thanks."

Bartley called out, "Let's move."

Popov kicked the truck back into gear, and turned in the direction of the gate.

Bartley said, "I'm pretty sure this is an American-made M3 half-track. Lend-lease. Ironic, I guess."

Cold commented, "I guess."

A response began to emerge to their activities, as two guards were approaching in a GAZ-69 4x4 vehicle.

Behind them, Jefferson had moved the MiG-X out of the building, and started to turn it onto one of the facility's runways.

Bartley asked, "How long before the fireworks start?"

Golikova held up his watch for Cold to see.

Cold announced, "Ten seconds."

Bartley nodded and started to pivot the machine gun. In the distance, the network of explosions began. The barracks building suddenly seemed to heave up at the center, and then the five-story structure began to fall in on itself.

Cold fought off thoughts about how many people who were dying in that building would be deemed combatants. His theological background kicked in briefly.

*What would St. Augustine say? Lord, forgive us.*

He could not know that one person had made it out of the barracks, and drifted into the darkness.

Cold's Augustinian thoughts disappeared as shots from the approaching 4x4 hit the side of the half-track. Bartley fired the machine gun and quickly finished off the small vehicle.

Building A started to get consumed by a series of explosions that turned into massive fireballs reaching up into the dark sky. Due to the light thrown off from the fiery plume, for the first time since arriving, Cold had an ever-so-brief look around at the totality of the facility. But that quickly was erased by subsequent explosions and fire destroying the other two main buildings.

The glowing jet engine nozzles illuminated the MiG-X accelerating down the runway, and lifting off into the sky.

*God be with you, Cam.* He turned back and saw a few armed men emerging from the two remaining small buildings. *And with us.*

Bartley leveled the gun at those shooting, and dispatched them. And the same had to be done to the guard at the shack at the front gate, who had decided to come out into the cold to face what must have seemed like certain death. He drew his pistol and started shooting in apparent futility. But before dying, one of the guard's shots struck Ari. His head slammed sideways, landing on the shoulder of Benedikt.

The two small buildings were the last to explode.

After smashing the half-track through the front gate, Popov looked over to see Benedikt crying and cradling his brother's bloody head.

# Chapter 81

Once clear of the Soviet base and reaching a comfortable altitude, Cameron Jefferson started enjoying himself.

He had clear skies as he flew the MiG-X northeast, and began to test the aircraft cautiously. But as his confidence grew at the controls, so did the trials he decided to put the jet through.

His flight took a mere 90 minutes.

*     *     *

Shemya Air Force Base in the Aleutian Islands was in general disrepair due to neglect and the brutal Alaska weather. Hangars had been battered by snow, ice and wind. But one small building, next to an enormous runway, was usable. The CIA periodically took up temporary residence there.

Days earlier, two CIA officers waited for a plane to arrive transporting Dean Cold and his team. After landing and a layover of less than three hours, the two – who simply introduced themselves as Paul and Harry – took Cold, Bartley, Jefferson and Popov on board a boat and out into the Bering Sea to meet a submarine.

Since then, Paul and Harry had to fill time, waiting for the Cold team to return. If some or all of the team came back, they weren't expected for at least another three days.

Chess, checkers, reading and occasionally being able to tune in a show on the radio filled the time. They treated it as a triumph when they were able to listen to Bob Hope or Bing Crosby. During the war, Paul had been fortunate to attend a USO show featuring Crosby, and Harry had even gotten on stage with Hope.

Currently, the two were listening to Hope creating some laughs with special guest Jimmy Stewart. While Stewart fake stuttered his way through a bit with Hope, the two CIA officers jumped as, seemingly out of nowhere, engines roared. They grabbed their handguns, and plunged into the frigid night.

At the far end of the runway, all that could be seen now were two glowing circles and a few blinking lights. The rest of the aircraft blended into the darkness.

The aircraft turned and taxied in their direction, as they ran toward it. They stopped and raised their weapons in the path of the plane. Each man stood motionless as the jet came to a stop a mere 20 feet away.

Jefferson slid back the cockpit cover, and called out, "I don't think you'd be able to do much against this baby."

Harry and Paul glanced at each other, and then in the direction of the voice. "Agent Jefferson?" asked Harry.

"That's right. We stole this beauty, and now we need to park it in a hangar. Which one is in the best shape?"

Paul and Harry now smiled at each other, with Paul calling out, "Follow us."

They began trotting toward one of the hangars, with Jefferson closing the cockpit lid and guiding his prize not far behind the two CIA officers. He said to himself, "Gotta hide this from … what? Flying saucers? Unbelievable."

Jefferson didn't have to be concerned very long if the MiG-X was sufficiently covered. His layover at Shemya Air Force Base would last barely two hours.

After leaving the hangar and entering the small building where Harry and Paul were holed up, the two CIA officers made contact with their boss, Director Allen Dulles. Over a special telephone line, Dulles ordered Harry and Paul to leave the building while he spoke directly with Jefferson.

Once the two officers put their coats back on and walked out, Jefferson said, "Director Dulles, they're outside."

"Good. Alright, I need a complete rundown on what happened."

Jefferson proceeded to provide the details of what had occurred from when he, Cold, Popov and Bartley left the *U.S.S. Trigger* through his landing the MiG-X at Shemya just moments ago.

"Thank you, Agent Jefferson. The success of this mission, and your taking and flying that jet, will make a major difference in this fight. Good work."

"Thank you, sir."

"As you can imagine, I don't want you lingering at an abandoned runway in the Aleutian Islands."

"I understand, sir."

"Good. Get some coffee and food in you, fuel up, and then you're returning to the skies with that prize."

"Yes, sir. Where am I headed?"

"First, from this point forward and until you get other orders, you're under complete radio silence. No one – including the officers with you – is to know where you're going. Second, when you get there, I have three people that will be waiting, and they will direct you to where we're going to park that jet. Your job then is to get comfortable with that plane. Consider it yours. Guard it. Don't leave it, unless you need to take a shit, and in that case, leave the door open so you can see and hear everything. Got it?"

Jefferson replied, "I've got it, sir. Shit with the door open."

Dulles actually chuckled. "Good." He then gave Jefferson the location where he would be flying the MiG-X.

# Chapter 82

Dean Cold, Daria Popov and John Bartley, with Dr. Maksut Golikova in tow, returned to Ayan early in the morning. They stopped at Benedikt's home. Cold and Popov helped him get his brother's body inside, while Bartley kept watch over Golikova.

Cold felt awkward at having to express his sympathies through Popov, given that Benedikt didn't speak English.

Popov asked Benedikt, "How can we help?"

Staring down at his dead brother now lying on a couch, Benedikt responded in a distant voice, "There's nothing, nothing that anyone can do now." He looked at Cold, and added, "You have done enough. I must tell his wife, and their small child."

Cold saw Popov's distress at what Benedikt had just said. He leaned toward Popov and said, "Ask him."

Popov took a deep breath and said, "We can get you out of Russia."

Benedikt stared at Popov for a few seconds. His gaze moved to Cold. He then turned and looked back down at his brother's body.

Cold thought the man was considering the offer, but that he would reject it.

"I cannot," declared Benedikt, still looking at Ari's body. "His family..." His voice broke. "My family needs me."

Popov shook her head at Cold.

As they went to leave, Cold nodded at Popov, who said to Benedikt, "I know that it can never make up for your loss, but we can make sure that you get some resources to help."

Benedikt didn't respond. He stood motionless as the two left.

It was a short drive to the Kolchak home. Bogdan, Anna, Matvey, Ilya, Lev and Nazar were all there, apparently waiting to find out what had happened.

Bogdan let them in the back door, and everyone was crowded around the table. Tilting his head toward Golikova, Cold asked, "Where can we put him, with one of us watching him, of course?"

Bogdan told him which of the two bedrooms would work best.

Bartley volunteered, "I've got him."

Cold replied, "Thanks."

After Bartley closed the bedroom door, Bogdan asked, "Did you succeed?"

Cold answered, "We did."

Bogdan, Anna and Matvey smiled, with Bogdan nodding at his sons and nephew, who knew no English.

Popov then relayed, in Russian, what happened to Ari.

Bogdan hung his head. "I know his family. I knew him for his entire life."

"We're so sorry," declared Cold.

As Popov relayed what Benedikt said, Cold looked at his watch. When the group went silent, Cold said, "Bogdan, I don't mean to be crass, but our first window for radioing the sub comes in about a half-hour."

"I understand. Whenever you are ready, we will get you out to sea."

Cold said, "Thank you. But..." He looked at the others. "Can we speak alone?"

Bogdan nodded, and led Cold into the other bedroom and closed the door. "What is it, my friend?"

Cold rubbed his chin. "Without the details, you understood the danger involved in helping us."

"I have long known this, since I first started helping my Russia by working with your CIA."

"This could be different. I don't know what the fallout might be."

Bogdan seemed sympathetic. "Anything we do in opposition to the communists will have two possible results:

Either we get shipped off to some prison camp, or we die. Most likely, we would be sent to prison and then killed."

Cold nodded. "I have an offer. You and your family could come with us. We could get you out of Russia, set you up for new lives in the United States." Bogdan started to reply, but Cold continued, "Before you answer, I think all of you would have to come. Anyone left behind would stick out, and suffer at the hands of the government."

Bogdan sat on the edge of the bed. "Who do you mean by 'all of you'?"

"Do Ilya, Lev and Nazar have families?"

Bogdan shook his head. "No, not yet."

"I see. Unless I'm missing someone in your family, it would be best if you, Anna, Matvey, Ilya, Lev and Nazar all came."

Bogdan stared up at Cold. "As I told you before, Agent Cold, we are the last direct link to the last resistance to the communist revolution in Russia. If we leave... I just don't know what Anna or Matvey will say. I..." His voice trailed off, and he looked down at the floor.

"You've continued to fight – you and your family – in the shadows, and that's to your great credit. But there are other ways to continue to fight the Soviets, to help your fellow Russians, from a place outside the country where it is safe for you and your family, if that's what you want."

Bogdan was silent.

"I know this is hard, and I'm sorry. Unfortunately, at best, you'll have an hour, perhaps two, to decide, before we'll need to set out for the rendezvous."

# Chapter 83

Once more, Captain Bogdan Kolchak looked amazed as the *U.S.S. Trigger* emerged from the waters off the port side of his trawler.

When the skiff arrived from the submarine, Cold looked down at the two sailors. "Thanks for coming. Fortunately, we have guests."

One of the sailors said, "Excuse me, sir?"

"We have guests, and I'm not sure we'll all fit safely on one trip. Besides, we have a little work to do here. So, if you can ferry them over, and then come back for us, that would be greatly appreciated."

"Um, sir?" said the other bewildered sailor.

Cold asked, "You're both armed, right?"

"Well, yes, sir," answered one of the sailors.

"Good. One of our guests is a prisoner." He pulled Dr. Maksut Golikova over.

Golikova smiled, and said, "Hello, gentlemen."

While directing Golikova to climb down, Cold said to the sailors, "I don't think Dr. Golikova here is stupid enough to try anything..."

Golikova interrupted, "To what end, Agent Cold?"

Cold ignored that and continued, "But keep an eye on him and assume nothing."

The two members of the *Trigger's* crew had no choice but to help Golikova down into their small boat. And one replied, "Aye, aye, sir."

Next came Ilya and Lev. Anna Kolchak grabbed hold of her husband and pulled him close. She whispered, "I wish Matvey and Nazar came with us."

Nazar had decided he couldn't leave behind Ayan and the farm where his family members were buried, including his mother. And Matvey agreed.

He replied, "They will be fine. They are survivors."

Cold listened, and could tell that there was little confidence in Bogdan's voice.

Anna kissed her husband and then got into the inflatable as well.

Cold asked the sailors, "Okay?"

"I guess. Uh, sir, does Captain Lee know that you have ... guests?" asked a sailor.

Cold reassured, "I'm sure he'll be fine with it. I know I don't have to say this, but I will anyway: Make sure the doctor gets tossed in the brig."

Golikova looked up and responded, "Agent Cold, is that really necessary?"

Cold again ignored the comment and said to the two sailors, "Now, while you ferry our friends over to the *Trigger*, we'll set the explosives."

"Explosives, sir?"

"Of course, we just can't leave this vessel floating around to be found by the Soviets, right?"

"I guess so, sir."

After the skiff headed back toward the submarine, Bartley said, "You enjoyed screwing with them, didn't you?"

Cold laughed. "I confess that I did." He turned to Bogdan. "Are you ready to do this, Captain?"

Bogdan looked at his family being ferried to the American submarine, and replied with a tinge of sadness, "I am, Agent Cold."

The explosives were set, and as the skiff returned, Cold said, "You three get in. I'll set the timer and follow you."

Bogdan declared, "No. You three will get in, and I will set the timer to sink my own boat."

Popov and Bartley watched the exchange between Cold and Kolchak.

Cold saw that there would be no arguing the point. "Of course, Captain."

After Cold, Popov and Bartley were in the inflatable with the two sailors, Kolchak sighed deeply, leaned down and flipped the switch on the timer. He wiped away a small tear forming in an eye, and then turned and descended into the skiff.

When the crossing was complete, and the sailors were breaking down the inflatable, Cold stood next to Kolchak on the deck of the submarine.

When the sailors completed their job, one asked, "Gentlemen, it's time to go below."

Kolchak stood unmoving with his eyes fixed on his now-empty trawler. Cold looked at the sailor and shook his head ever so slightly.

Captain Scott Lee emerged onto the deck and dismissed the sailor. Lee moved next to Cold and Kolchak. He said nothing. Instead, he looked out at the trawler as well.

The explosion was large enough that it cut the boat into shards. The little that remained sank below the waters.

Kolchak wiped away a couple of tears, and then turned to Lee.

The captain of the *Trigger* saluted Kolchak, who returned the gesture. Lee said, "I'm deeply sorry that your boat had to be scuttled, Captain."

"Thank you, Captain," replied Kolchak.

Lee extended a hand, and said, "I'm Captain Scott Lee, welcome aboard the *U.S.S. Trigger*, and I thank you for the sacrifice made by you and your family."

"I appreciate that, Captain, and thank you for taking us in."

"It's our pleasure. It's a tight fit on a sub, as you can imagine, but I've ordered that accommodations be made that should provide your family some comfort for our journey."

Kolchak nodded additional thanks.

Lee turned to Cold. "Congratulations on your success, Agent Cold, on whatever it was that you did. I'm glad that your team came back safely. Your prisoner is in the brig."

"That's appreciated, Captain, and thanks, once again, for the lift."

After the three descended into the submarine, an officer accompanied Kolchak to his family.

With Popov and Bartley standing nearby, Lee said to Cold with a smile, "Agent Cold, next time, please let me know that you're bringing people home from the office for dinner."

"I'll try, sir," said Cold, returning the smile.

Lee looked at Cold, Bartley and Popov. "Whatever your mission was, you received a message from the top. You'll find the teletype in an envelope in the quarters where you two" – he looked at Bartley and Cold – "bunked on the way here. I understand that Agent Jefferson found another way home." He didn't wait for any kind of acknowledgement, and turned to Popov, "Once more, Agent Popov, you will have my quarters."

"Captain, please, no. That's not necessary."

"You said the same thing last time, and I'll respond the same way: Yes, it is."

Popov sheepishly replied, "Thank you, Captain."

Lee went on, "Now, why don't you read your message and get some much-needed rest? By the way, we'll be running silent, so you won't have an opportunity to send a response."

"Yes, sir," responded Cold.

"Much appreciated, Cap," said Bartley.

"Cap?" asked Lee.

Bartley smiled, shrugged his shoulders, and then followed Cold and Popov.

When the three entered the area where Cold, Jefferson and Bartley had bunked before, a sealed envelope rested on one of the bunks. "For Agent Dean Cold's eyes only" was written on it.

Cold grabbed the envelope and sat on the edge of the bunk. He invited Bartley and Popov to sit as well.

Popov asked, "Should we leave while you read that?"

"What?" responded Cold. "No. Of course not. This is meant for all of us, or it should be. Please, grab a seat."

Popov did so.

Cold opened the envelope and read, "Excellent work. Beyond my expectations. CJ reported with the prize. Again,

well done. I look forward to seeing you soon. We have much
to discuss. Thank you and your team for their service. DDE."

Cold looked up and smiled.

Bartley said, "Thanks from Ike. Not bad."

Popov beamed.

# Chapter 84

MGB Director Arkadi Sokolov knocked on the door to Joseph Stalin's office at the Kuntsevo Dacha. Sokolov normally would start opening the door even before Stalin offered a response. But that wasn't the case this time.

Stalin said, "Come in."

Sokolov hesitated. He drew in a deep breath before slowly opening the door.

Stalin smiled. "Arkadi."

Stalin was behind his desk, with General Arseni Demyan and Dr. Oleg Abramov occupying two chairs at the nearby table.

At the sight of Sokolov's slumped shoulders and anguished look, the three others tensed.

Stalin slowly rose from his chair, and demanded, "What is it? What's wrong?"

Sokolov fell into a chair, and while rubbing his forehead, confessed, "The entire operation has been wiped out."

Demyan leaned forward. "What the hell are you talking about?"

Sokolov went from rubbing his forehead to running a hand through his hair. His eyes suddenly darted around wildly between Stalin, Demyan and Abramov.

Stalin commanded, "Out with it!"

"The plant in Khabarovsk Krai – there's nothing left of it. It's been leveled, destroyed. There's no one left."

Stalin dropped back into his chair.

Abramov said, "How can that be? That's impossible." The fear in his voice was palpable.

Sokolov seemed to try to calm himself. "We might have thought that it was impossible. But it's happened. It's destroyed."

Each man went silent.

Abramov said, "You know what this means? We are dead."

"Shut up," ordered Demyan. He looked at Sokolov. "Was this an attack? A mishap with the self-destruct mechanism? Did one of our own go mad, and set it off?"

Sokolov replied, "How the hell do I know?"

In a cold voice, Stalin said, "You had better find out. Put your spies and snitches in high gear. You're going to find out so we can make sure that we limit the blowback on us. Do you understand?"

Sokolov buried his face in his hands.

Stalin slammed his fist down on the desk. "Do you understand what's at stake here? Oleg is right. If we want to survive this, we need to find out all of the details so we can..." He looked at the others. "So we can get our story straight."

Sokolov opened his eyes, and straightened up. He reported, "There was one survivor, as far as I know. Officer Sofia Belov contacted me. I am providing her with a group of MGB men. They will find out what exactly happened, and once they have all the information, they will terminate everyone involved. In the meantime, we can start working on our story, and adjust it accordingly with what Belov relays."

# Chapter 85

Dr. Wanda Maxine Marshall said, "You're lucky, Robert. You're going to be fine. Your body heals well. You're ahead of where you should be."

Grace Armstrong, who was standing next to Weathers, wiped away a tear and then retook his hand.

Weathers, lying on a bed in Marshall's mini-hospital, smiled. "I don't think luck had much to do with this, Max. You saved my life."

Armstrong interjected, "Robert is right. Thank you, Max. If not for you, our baby wouldn't know its father."

Marshall smiled, and said, "A baby needs his daddy."

Weathers declared, "And mother, too. Max, would you mind giving us a few minutes?"

"Of course not."

After Marshall left, Armstrong looked down at Weathers, and asked, "What's going on? Is everything alright?"

"It is," replied Weathers. "But I have to tell you something that I should have a long time ago. And I don't know why I haven't."

"Yes?"

"I knew my mother."

"What? How is it possible that you knew the Breeder who...?" She paused. "I mean..."

"I know," said Weathers.

Armstrong gathered herself. "How could you have known your mother? That wasn't allowed. In fact, any Breeder that even attempted to find out who her child was would be terminated, never mind one who somehow found out and then reached out to her ... son."

"Believe me, I know. And I have no idea how she ever found out. I don't know her name. We never met in person."

Armstrong soothingly said, "Please, tell me."

"It began when I officially started my Defender training. Once or twice a year, I would receive what seemed to be a standard network message, but when I opened it, there she was. Her message would be only a minute or two long, and then it would disappear.. I mean from the entire system, without a trace. In the first message, she confessed who she was. She apologized for what she was doing, but she just wanted to tell me that I was..." His voice broke. Armstrong squeezed his hand. "My mother told me I was loved."

"Oh, my, Robert."

Weathers forged ahead and told her of other messages from his mother.

Armstrong hung her head, and repeated, "Robert."

"Are you alright? Are you ashamed of me?"

She looked up with tears in her eyes. "How could you think that? That's so wonderful. I wish I could have heard from my ... mother. But I knew that it would never happen."

"I told no one, until you just now."

"I understand why you didn't, but I'm very happy that you did."

Weathers said, "So, when you said that you were pregnant, I told you that I felt overjoyed, and that is still the case. But I also knew how important it was for our child to know us, or at least one of us."

"The baby will, now," reassured Armstrong.

Weathers nodded. "But as we've talked about before, we not only need to be here for our child, but we have to make sure that he or she is protected from our people. We know what will happen if they ever find out."

\*     \*     \*

On the other side of the closed door, Mike Strickland and Roy O'Keefe were seated at a couple of desks. Each was drinking coffee.

When Marshall came out, she poured herself a cup and rolled over a chair.

O'Keefe asked, "How is he doing, Max?"

"Excellent. He's recovering better than I could have hoped." She proceeded to give a quick rundown on Weathers' status, answering a couple of questions from the others.

Strickland said, "That's good to hear. It would be nice if we heard something on what's going on with Dean, John, Cam and Daria."

"It sure would," replied Marshall.

As Strickland raised a mug to his mouth, the telephone a couple of desks away started ringing.

O'Keefe raised an eyebrow and put his coffee down. "Are we dealing with clairvoyance now, too?" He got up and answered the telephone. "Hello." He then listened for a few minutes, and finally said, "Thank you, sir." Another couple of minutes passed with O'Keefe listening. Marshall and Strickland watched.

O'Keefe said, "Yes, sir. I understand. We'll stand pat. Thank you." And then he hung up the receiver. He looked at Strickland and declared, "Your wish was fulfilled."

"Well?" asked Marshall.

"Should we bring Robert and Grace in on this?"

Without hesitation, Marshall answered, "Absolutely." She got up and led the other two to her mini-hospital. Marshall knocked and stuck her head in. "Is it okay if we come in?"

"Yes," answered Weathers.

Armstrong nodded.

"President Eisenhower just called," announced O'Keefe.

Marshall shook her head, and commented, "I don't know if I'll ever get used to the president of the United States calling us."

O'Keefe replied, "Trust me, you don't."

Armstrong asked, "And why did the president call? News about our friends?"

"That's right. It not only went well, but they came back with a jet fighter."

"A what?" asked Marshall.

Weathers said, "That is very good news."

"Give us the details," requested Armstrong.

O'Keefe began, "It turned out that Dean, John, Daria and Cameron..."

# Chapter 86

A knock came at the front door of Benedikt Wolkoff's small house. He was sitting at a kitchen table with Ari's wife and five-year-old son. Ari's body was lying inside the cheap coffin against the wall in the main living space of the home.

Benedikt said, "I am sorry, Mila. Someone apparently has come early to pay respects."

The woman merely nodded.

Benedikt pushed himself up from the table, left the kitchen, passed his brother's body and opened the door. Taken off guard, at first, he stood up a bit straighter. "Yes?"

Sophia Belov stood in front of him with four men looming behind her. "Comrade Wolkoff?"

"That's right."

"I am Officer Sophia Belov. I have some questions."

"Officer?"

"Correct. I am with the MGB, as are my associates." She indicated the four men behind her.

Benedikt's rigid posture quickly fell away to rounded shoulders. "Questions? About what?"

Belov merely raised an eyebrow,

Benedikt slouched still more.

She said, "Do you mind if we come in?" It wasn't really a question.

Benedikt stepped aside. Belov strode past him.

The first male MGB officer waited for Benedikt to follow Belov, and then the other three stepped into the home.

Belov paused at the casket and looked down at the body. "Your brother, Ari. Such a waste. You need to tell me who is responsible. Let's go sit with your sister-in-law and nephew, shall we?" She waved her hand, and Benedikt entered the kitchen to see Mila clutching her son in fear.

Belov instructed, "Sit down, Benedikt."

He did as ordered, sitting close to Mila.

Belov's colleagues spread out against the walls of the kitchen, as she took the last chair, sitting across the table from the three Wolkoffs.

"I don't have much time, so I hope you will not make this difficult. Quite simply, you, Benedikt, must tell me everything about the attack that you and your brother were part of the other night" – Mila shot a quizzical look at Benedikt – "and in return, I can make sure that the three of you..." She smiled at the five-year-old, and continued, "...will not have to worry about how you will be able to go on without your dear Ari." She again looked at the five-year-old, and added, "Without your father."

Benedikt licked his lips, and his eyes moved back and forth between Mila and her son to Belov.

After a few seconds, Belov said, "Remember what I said about not having much time, Benedikt."

He replied, "You promise that we will be safe."

Belov sighed. "Do you people believe in God?"

Benedikt and Mila looked surprised by the question.

Belov went on, "Yes, yes, I know. We officially are an atheist place. But as we saw during the war, there is room for God even in the Soviet Union. Do not be afraid to answer the question."

Both Benedikt and Mila nodded ever so slightly.

"Then you will be safe." She pulled her chair closer to the table, and her eyes narrowed. "Now, I want all of the details as to what happened."

As Benedikt confessed all, his rate of speech increased. Belov listened stoically, while Mila wore an expression of disbelief.

Less than a half-hour later, Belov glanced at the coffin as she went to leave the house. When the last of her four colleagues closed the door, the flow of blood from the sliced necks of the three Wolkoff family members spread and intermingled on the kitchen tabletop.

\* \* \*

After finding the home of Bogdan Kolchak empty, Sophia Belov proceeded to her next target. She sat in the front passenger seat of an olive-colored Moskvitsh-400. One of her men turned the vehicle onto the dirt road leading to the home of Matvey Rytov. After coming through a patch of trees, the remaining 100 yards to the house were clear.

Sophia Belov declared, "I do not like this. Park over there."

The driver followed the order, and then all five got out of the vehicle roughly 30 yards from the rickety front porch.

Belov looked around. Nothing moved. She said, "Secure the house."

The four men withdrew their weapons from inside their coats. They spread out, and slowly approached the house. At the same time, Belov moved to put the car between her and the house.

The four men froze at the sound of breaking glass.

The nozzle of a rifle now protruded from a window, and the first shot hit one of the MGB officers in the chest. As he fell to the dirt and snow, the other three returned fire, and another window was broken from the inside, with shots coming from another rifle.

The remaining three officers were caught in a no man's land – halfway between the car they arrived in and the targeted house. While returning fire, they moved forward.

One went toward the right side of the house, the other the left, and the third ran and dove at the foot of the porch.

The two people – Matvey and his son, Nazar – firing from inside now had no targets. Nazar scrambled to a window looking out from the side and broke a pane. But before he could get another shot off, two shots from an MGB pistol sent him to the floor.

Matvey whirled to see his son. He called out, "No!" And with that, another MGB officer came crashing through the back door, firing as he did. Two shots hit Matvey. The second entered his skull and ended his life.

When the gunfire ceased, Belov walked toward the house and by the fallen MGB officer. She entered the room and looked around. Belov walked over and stared down at Matvey's unmoving body. She turned and went over to Nazar. The man was struggling to breathe, with blood coming from his nose and mouth. She announced to her men, "We're not going to get any more information. I have all I need, nonetheless." She withdrew her holstered Makarov. She pointed the gun at Nazar's head. But she didn't fire as his breathing ceased.

After re-holstering her weapon, Belov turned, and strode toward the door. "Let's go. It's time to call in the order."

# Chapter 87

Unlike when Cameron Jefferson had appeared, Harry and Paul knew when Dean Cold and the rest of his team would be arriving. After all, they had to take a boat out to meet them at sea. However, the CIA officers were surprised to find a prisoner among the guests.

When arriving back at the near-barren Shemya Air Force Base, Dr. Golikova was held in the now-empty hangar where Jefferson had parked the MiG-X. Golikova was handcuffed to a pipe, with an armed Harry nearby.

In the small, fully operational building, Paul served up some hot coffee and food to the Kolchaks, John Bartley, Daria Popov and Dean Cold. They ate and drank quickly, and then Bartley and Popov led the Kolchaks over to the hangar as well.

That left Cold waiting as Paul put a call through. Once more, CIA Director Allen Dulles ordered Paul to leave the hut so he could speak with Cold alone.

Cold provided his own rundown on what had occurred, covering some of the same ground as Jefferson had. But he added details about first meeting Golikova and what had happened after Jefferson taxied and flew off with the MiG-X.

While he had sprinkled in some questions along the way, when Cold was essentially finished, Dulles declared, "My God, Cold, that is fantastic work."

"Thank you, sir."

"But what about this Golikova? Given that he's a Nykarian, given that they think he died with everyone else at the facility, won't they just pull the plug on his body up on their ship, and he'll die anyway?"

"Actually, no, sir. Dr. Golikova told us that the idea that the bodies of these Defenders are being kept alive on their ship is a lie. It's a tactic for keeping their people in line."

Dulles said, "I see. In case anyone thinks about not following orders or even going over to the other side, there's this false threat. Smart and evil."

"Yes, sir."

Dulles added, "Wait a second. Colonel Weathers and Corporal Armstrong don't know that."

"Correct."

Dulles took in a breath. "Well, then, that says a great deal about them."

"Definitely, sir."

"Alright, Agent Cold, you, your team and our guests will be flown to Andrews Air Force Base. Stay completely silent on all of this, including with my two men there. Someone will meet you at Andrews, and we'll go from there."

"Yes, sir."

"Once again, good work by you and your team."

"Thank you, sir."

# Chapter 88

MGB Director Arkadi Sokolov finished relaying all of the information he had received from Officer Sophia Belov. He added, "And our men have found nothing left of value at the Khabarovsk facility."

The room then fell silent.

Dr. Oleg Abramov finally asked, "Do we give the order?"

Joseph Stalin said, "Do I give the order?"

Sokolov, General Arseni Demyan and Abramov exchanged glances.

Stalin looked at the group. "Unless any of us disagree?"

No one replied.

Stalin then looked directly at Demyan. "Make it happen, General."

Demyan nodded, got up from his chair, and quickly walked across the vast office and out the door.

\* \* \*

The three Ilyushin Il-28 bombers approached Ayan from the west.

The pilot of one of the aircraft commented to his co-pilot, "This does not feel right. Our own people?"

"Orders are orders. And according to our briefing, this place remains as it was before the Revolution. It was the last holdout of the Tsarists, and it turns out that it has remained a base of operations to fight the people."

"Everyone in Ayan? Hard to believe."

The co-pilot sighed. "Do you really want to raise these questions?"

The pilot shook his head. "No, I don't."

In formation, each of the three aircraft dropped half their load on the first run over Ayan. The carpet bombing wiped out much of the town, and, after a gentle turn in the sky, the second run came.

The crews of the three bombers obviously couldn't hear the cries of horror and death on the ground, nor see the people crushed, torn apart and bleeding.

The second made sure that no one was left alive and little was left standing in the port town of Ayan.

\*     \*     \*

After Stalin received news from Demyan, he looked at Sokolov. "Let the news leak out. Make sure that people know that Ayan was a haven for those who opposed the State, the Party, and me, and that they understand what happens if anyone else considers such actions."

Sokolov said, "The lesson could not be clearer."

Demyan added, "Now, we just have to convince the Commanders of what happened."

# Chapter 89

In orbit above the Earth, Commander One listened to the grim news presented by his Defenders who had claimed the bodies of Chairman Joseph Stalin, dictator of the Soviet Union; Arkadi Sokolov, head of the MGB; Minister of War Arseni Demyan; and Dr. Oleg Abramov.

Indeed, Commander One said nothing when, along the way, Stalin paused and clearly was expecting some kind of question or feedback.

Stalin finally completed his report. The four men were in the chairman's personal study at Kuntsevo Dacha, sitting in an arc around the com-stat device. Now, they waited. Abramov's eyes darted between the others and the speaker.

Commander One finally said, "I'm not pleased."

"Of course not, Commander," replied Stalin. "To say the least, none of us are."

"Yes, I am sure." There was another notable pause. "The leveling of Ayan?"

Sokolov answered, "It was the best decision. My top aide, Officer Belov…"

"She survived?" interrupted One.

"She did. Apparently, the only one."

One said nothing in response to that.

Sokolov continued, "Officer Belov gathered all of the information we could have hoped for. Word about the destruction of the town will spread, and serve as a warning that these are the consequences for those who oppose the regime."

One responded, "I see." He added, "With the Americans involved, you could be right that one or more of our Defenders in the United States might have been compromised or even turned. Although I would find the latter possibility to be the most unlikely, given the obvious consequences. At the same time, nothing can be assumed. Everyone will have to be evaluated. And that goes for each of you as well."

Stalin said, "Yes, we understand, sir."

Commander One said, "Do you? Ultimately, this had to come from one of you or from the humans in your inner circles."

Demyan jumped in, "I have to point out that for the security measures put in place at the Khabarovsk facility, there were still some who came and went – transporting assorted goods, for example. And then there's the task of making sure that everyone at that facility never slipped out physically or communicated something beyond those fences that reached the wrong ears. The most likely leak, for lack of a better word, came on that front. After all, consider the report from Officer Belov to Director Sokolov about the two men transporting food being involved."

Sokolov added, "Officer Belov did have to take severe actions when first arriving there to beef up security and discipline."

"Yes, that's all noted. Rest assured, this investigation will not be, as the humans say, a witch hunt. But we have to be sure."

Demyan responded, "Naturally, sir."

Stalin interjected, "There is something that has been gnawing at me regarding this. Are we assuming that the American attack was prompted by word of a secret Soviet facility creating cutting-edge weapons? Or does the possibility exist that they somehow could have found out about ... well ... us being involved?"

Commander One answered, "We are looking into everything, and you will know more when I deem it appropriate. For now, examine the people close to each of you, and proceed with the work on the other facility. Over the coming day or so, each of you will be interviewed separately."

The communication was then ended by Commander One.

The four men looked at each other in silence, until Abramov declared, "That could have gone worse, I suppose."

# Chapter 90

Commanders Two and Six from the supply ship were the last to arrive. They claimed the two empty seats at the metal table. Their shuttle arrived just a few minutes behind the one that transported Commanders Three and Four from the troop ship.

Once Two and Six were seated, Commander One began, "I have grave news. The facility in Khabarovsk Krai has been lost."

Among the subsequent barrage of questions, Commander Six's voice stood out. "What exactly does that mean, Commander One?"

One raised his voice, "Please, settle down. I will explain."

He went on to lay out what had occurred. When he was finished, the group sat in stunned silence.

Six finally said, "Perhaps wiping out the town wasn't the wisest course? After all, more information might have been acquired."

"I understand, but I trust what Sokolov relayed and there is no downside in issuing such an unmistakable warning."

Commander Two chimed in, "Even the hint of traitorous actions will be met by death. Fear is an essential tool. This has been a central tenet in the way Nykar has been governed for as long as anyone can remember. It naturally should be the way with our subjugation of Earth. Indeed, it is more imperative here and now."

"Well said," commended One. "At the same time, we will look into all of this to make sure that it was, as I suspect, the result of a weakness in the security at the Khabarovsk facility." Commander One paused, and then added, "This is the right time to have our senator step up his work."

Everyone at the table nodded in agreement.

One looked at Five and declared, "We will make sure that this will be impossible at the new facility. Won't we, Commander Five?"

"Yes. Of course, Commander."

One then turned to Commander Three. "We're supposed to be prepared for any possibility, and ready to replace all of those lost. I trust we are, Commander Three?"

"We are, Commander," she answered. "Of course, it took us eight Earth years to get where we are." While Commander One started to open his mouth, before he could say anything, Three continued, "We've come so far since we arrived. And as you say, we're prepared for this unfortunate possibility. Still, it will take some time to insert this many Defenders."

"Get me a timeline quickly."

"Yes, Commander."

One added, "Five and I are going to do an overall reassessment of the situation, and see what's called for. When I report to the Ruler, we will have to have answers to all questions and scenarios that he puts forward."

Agreement, again, was heard from around the table.

Commander One concluded, "I know this looms in each of our minds, but I will say it. If our assurances are not accepted by the Ruler, we will be recalled and replaced. And we will be the ones used as examples for others."

The other five remained silent and unmoving, as Commander One rose from the table and left the room. Five looked at the other faces, and then followed One out of the room.

Commander Six stood up, looked down at the others, and cryptically declared, "You have to wonder, now and then, don't you?" He left the room with Commander Two in tow.

Three and Four stared at each other, communicating without talking.

After their shuttle exited the control ship, Three and Four finally were able to speak freely. With exhaustion in his voice, Four observed, "They wiped out an entire town."

"Are you really surprised?" retorted Three.

"I suppose not."

After a stretch of silence, Four said, "The destruction of the Khabarovsk facility might give us time."

"To do what?" asked Three.

Four sighed. "I'm not sure. Maybe we can figure out something. Perhaps there were Defenders on Earth who had turned, and they were the reason why this happened."

"If it happened to us, maybe some Defenders, too." For the first time, the slightest trace of hope could be heard in Commander Three's voice. After another stretch of silence, Three asked, "What do you think that Commander Six meant by that last comment?"

"I wish I knew," replied Four.

# Chapter 91

The off-the-books flight touched down at Andrews Air Force Airbase at 9:40 pm. As the plane taxied to the most remote hangar on the base, Agent Dean Cold looked out one of the windows. He said, "Let's see who's here to greet us."

While comfort hadn't been an option during the flight, Cold, Daria Popov and John Bartley nonetheless were able to grab some shut-eye.

That wasn't the case for the Kolchak family – Bogdan, Anna, Lev and Ilya – due to some apparent combination of excitement and worry for each.

Throughout the journey, Dr. Maksut Golikova was handcuffed and watched by a member of the crew. But he seemed to sleep quite soundly.

Bartley answered, "Maybe they'll have some cold beer waiting for us."

Cold smirked, but Popov declared, "That would be nice. I could use a beer."

Bartley smiled at Popov.

As the plane moved into the hangar, Cold saw that six men in trench coats and three vehicles were waiting for them. He was glad to see that one of those men was Roy O'Keefe. "Roy's here," he relayed to Bartley and Popov.

Cold led the way off the plane.

O'Keefe stepped forward, and extended his hand. "Dean, it's good to see you" – he looked at Bartley and Popov as well – "to see each of you. Successful and safe – that's a great combination."

"Thanks, Roy. It's good to see you, as well. How's everyone else?"

"Not sure what you've heard."

"Heard? Nothing."

"Well…" He looked around and then into the concerned faces of Cold, Bartley and Popov. "Let's get this taken care of, and I'll go over everything in the car." He paused, and then asked, "Dr. Golikova? The Kolchaks?"

Cold responded, "In the plane. One of the crew is guarding Golikova."

"Alright. The Kolchaks will be taken to a safehouse by those two men." He pointed. "The director made sure it's our best in the area."

Cold nodded. He was trying to stay completely focused, and not let his mind go in wild directions about the other members of the team. *Max?*

"Those three will take Golikova."

Bartley asked, "Where?"

"No one has shared that information with me," answered O'Keefe. "And I'm supposed to drop you two" – he looked at Bartley and Popov – "at Q Street, and then you and I" – he turned to Cold – "are due at the White House."

After they watched the Kolchaks and Golikova be driven off, O'Keefe got behind the wheel of the Chevy, with Cold in the front passenger spot, and Bartley and Popov in the back seat.

As O'Keefe started up the engine, Cold immediately asked, "What the hell happened?"

O'Keefe began, "Lawrence Silver is dead."

Cold reacted, "What?"

Bartley asked, "How?"

Popov declared, "Shit."

O'Keefe gave the details on what Silver had done, including his shooting of Robert Weathers, and Max later saving Weathers. When O'Keefe finished his report, it was met with silence.

Cold finally spoke, "Thank God Robert is going to be alright." His voice went lower, "But Larry, I can't…"

When Cold's voice trailed off, Bartley interjected, "The others are okay?"

"They are," said O'Keefe.

"What about the baby?" inquired Popov.

Cold snapped back from thinking about Silver as his college roommate and his attempt to kill Weathers, and started to blame himself for getting Silver involved at all.

*A baby. Right.*

"Max says the baby is doing fine." He turned the car onto Q Street. "Have you guys heard anything about Cam?"

Cold didn't answer immediately, so Bartley filled O'Keefe in on what Cold had relayed from the brief conversation with Dulles.

"That's basically what we were told as well," confirmed O'Keefe. He stopped in front of the two townhouses.

Cold advised Bartley and Popov, "Get some rest. Hopefully, we won't be that long at the White House." The news about Silver and Weathers made him feel a kind of exhaustion that this entire mission hadn't inflicted up to this point.

Bartley and Popov thanked O'Keefe, and got out of the car.

For a few minutes, Cold and O'Keefe were quiet as O'Keefe wound the car through the streets of Washington, D.C.

O'Keefe finally said, "Don't blame yourself about Silver. He made his choices."

"Yeah, I get it. At the same time, if I hadn't dragged him into this, then he'd still be alive, spouting off and writing his book about aliens in blissful ignorance. And Robert would be fine."

O'Keefe didn't respond for a few seconds. And then he said, "First off, from what I heard, Silver wasn't dragged into anything. He was the only one who dove into this enthusiastically, apparently without the doubts that the rest of us sanely had. It's not your fault that he fooled himself about who these invaders are. That's on him. The guy went so far around the bend that he became a traitor and tried to kill one of us."

Cold said nothing.

O'Keefe went on, "You ever lose anyone under your command during the war?"

"I did."

"Was it your fault?"

"No, but that was different."

"I get why you might say that, but this isn't all that different. Let's be straight about this. We're on the front lines of what is another war for our world. Situations and, yeah, people, are going to be FUBAR. Silver chose his path, his own traitorous, murderous path. And it cost him. I know he was an old friend of yours from college, but, quite frankly, he got what he deserved."

"I know, Roy. I know."

A short time later, Cold and O'Keefe were seated in the Oval Office across from President Eisenhower and CIA Director Allen Dulles. Cold was still trying to process what had happened to Silver and Weathers. He tried to focus on Ike and Dulles. It didn't take long for the president to seize Cold's attention.

Eisenhower said, "What you and your team accomplished was essential, and you have my gratitude."

"Thank you, sir," replied Cold.

Cold noted the glance that Ike exchanged with Dulles.

"But there's still more bad news as to what the Soviets have done since you got out of the country."

"Sir?"

Eisenhower gritted his teeth. "The bastards leveled Ayan."

"What?" asked Cold in disbelief.

Dulles weighed in. "From what we have heard and can figure out, they carpet bombed the entire town."

"Dear Lord, no," whispered Cold.

O'Keefe muttered, "Crap."

Cold's thoughts went to Matvey, Nazar and Benedikt. He felt like a massive weight had crashed down on him.

Eisenhower said, "The enemy will react when delivered a severe blow. These enemies completely disregard the value of life."

Cold actually slumped back on the couch.

Ike leaned forward. "No matter what, this will eat at you, Dean, just as it will eat at your team. You must remember that in the end, this isn't on you in any way."

"You're the second person to tell me that in the last hour, Mr. President."

Ike looked at O'Keefe, and then back at Cold. "Lawrence Silver?"

Cold merely rubbed his forehead.

"Dean," said Eisenhower.

Dulles and O'Keefe seemed to be spectators.

"Yes, Mr. President. I understand what you're saying. If I could think clearly at the moment, I'm sure that I'd agree with both you and Roy. But right now..."

Eisenhower's gaze moved to O'Keefe, and then to Dulles. He finally turned back to Cold. "Trust me. I understand. You two need to get back to Q Street. Get some much-needed rest – a short vacation. We'll talk about what's next in about a week."

Cold summoned the strength to say, "Mr. President, I should be the one who tells Bogdan and his family about what's happened to Ayan, to their family and friends."

Eisenhower again looked over to Dulles, and then replied, "I don't think so, Dean. We'll have someone else take care of that, and..."

"Sir, please," interrupted Cold.

Ike shut it down. "Not going to happen. It will be done properly, and we'll provide them whatever is needed."

Cold wanted to say more, but didn't.

*He's having me move on from the Kolchaks. I get it. But it doesn't feel right.*

Cold reluctantly nodded. "Yes, sir. Might I ask what's the status with Cam?"

Eisenhower stood up, and the others got to their feet. He answered, "Rest assured that Agent Jefferson is doing well, and he is with ... his plane." Ike smiled slightly at his own comment. "When we get together, Allen and I will take you through what we're thinking. We have a few things to sort out still, but we obviously can't take too much time."

"Can I ask where Cam and his plane are?" queried Cold.

Dulles responded, "That's part of what we'll cover in the next meeting."

Cold again nodded.

Ike then said, "The work that both of you and the entire team are doing is much appreciated, gentlemen."

Each man thanked the president, while shaking his hand.

Dulles added, "I'm damn impressed."

# Chapter 92

When Dean Cold and Roy O'Keefe entered the living room of 1734 Q Street NW, or as it also was known, the women's dorm, John Bartley and Daria Popov smiled as the rest of the group reacted.

Mike Strickland and Grace Armstrong welcomed him warmly, as did Robert Weathers from his seat on the couch. But it was Max Marshall who hugged Cold in such a way that neither wanted the embrace to end anytime soon. That was clear to everyone else in the room. When the embrace finally ended, the two remained shoulder to shoulder.

Cold said, "Thanks, everyone, for all you've done." The sentiment was reflected back to Cold.

Cold turned to the seated Weathers. "How are you, Robert?"

"Healing well, according to my doctor," he smiled and looked over at Marshall.

Cold then asked Armstrong, "And you and the baby?"

Armstrong patted her belly, and replied, "We're good, Dean."

Cold looked over to Bartley and Popov, and asked, "Did you say anything?"

They both shook their heads. Bartley said, "I figured that should come from you."

Cold looked back at the couple, as Armstrong sat on the couch next to Weathers. She asked, "What is it?"

"It's good news. We captured the doctor, Golikova, who ran the facility..."

"Yes?" asked Weathers.

"He's a Nykarian, and... I'll just say it: He told us that your people actually don't have the ability, the technology, to end your lives."

Armstrong's mouth dropped open, while Weathers inquired, "What?"

"Shutting down your bodies on the ship, that doesn't kill you. It was a lie to keep you, to keep Defenders, and anyone else, I guess, in line. To make sure that you didn't do anything you weren't supposed to do. You know, like fight for each other, for your child, or for, well, freedom."

His words hung in the air.

Strickland, Marshall, Weathers and Armstrong didn't move.

When Weathers and Armstrong finally reacted, their faces transformed from bewilderment to joy. They embraced each other, and everyone else in the room smiled.

Some tears followed amidst the congratulatory conversation.

As what amounted to a celebration went on, Cold quietly slipped out the back door and went into the neighboring townhouse. He hesitated at the door of what had been Lawrence Silver's apartment.

*Why? How could he have done it? Fooled himself in such a way? And to the degree that he became so ... angry ... that he tried to kill Grace?*

Cold proceeded to poke around Silver's room. He opened the closet, and looked down at a file box. He picked it up and dropped it on the bed. He opened the lid and there it was.

*His book.*

Cold sat down and proceeded to flip through the pages randomly. After a few minutes, he decided to jump to the bottom of the stack, and found his former roommate's concluding thoughts on aliens. A particular paragraph stood out to him:

> It's clear that any civilization possessing the knowledge and technology to journey through space and visit Earth must be more advanced than mankind in all ways. That would include

either moving beyond or never being infected in the first place with the petty greed, racism and hunger for power that so dominates humanity. It seems obvious to me that the widespread reports of their ships hovering above us means that they are observing humanity to see if they are able to help us rise above our sad state. Also, even if a fraction of abductions turn out to be true – and as I have argued, I do believe that many are – the visitors' efforts must rest in trying to assess if mankind is worth the effort. They are here to help us. I see no other viable conclusion. I hope that we prove worthy, and that we do not react in a hostile manner if or when visitors reach out to us.

Cold read a bit more when a gentle knock came at the door. He turned to see Marshall standing in the doorway.

"Hey, are you okay?" She said, "Slide over," and sat next to him on the edge of the bed.

Cold replied, "Not sure."

"Come across anything of interest?"

He pulled out the sheet with Silver's assumption about visitors to Earth, and handed it over to her. "What Lawrence … Larry … wrote... Read that and then think about how he reacted before dying."

Marshall read it, while Cold scanned a few more pages. When she finished, Marshall said nothing, and just handed the page back to Cold.

Cold observed, "This was more than him just snapping due to fear or guns going off around him." A trace of anger leaked into his tone. "He chose to side with the invaders." He dropped the manuscript back into the box, and closed it. "I don't see how it's any different than people who should have known better joining the Nazis or the Soviets."

Marshall placed a hand on his shoulder, and said, "Come on, we can go through this stuff later. I think they need a piano player next door, especially with Cam off at a mysterious location."

Ten minutes later, Cold sat down at the piano, and Bartley handed him a cold beer. "Thanks, John."

As Cold took a drink, Strickland looked over from his spot at the drums and asked, "You alright?"

"I think so."

"Sure you want to play?"

"Yeah," Cold answered tentatively. He took in a deep breath, sat up straighter, and declared with greater confidence, "Let's play something with some energy."

Strickland smiled, "I like that idea, Keys." He twirled his drumsticks, and said, "How about 'Caravan'?"

"Perfect," replied Cold.

Strickland opened, and then Dean jumped in.

Popov moved over to stand next to Bartley, just like the last time music was played at Q Street. Armstrong and Weathers watched and listened from the couch, and Marshall took things in while leaning against a wall.

After a couple more songs, Strickland looked at Popov. "How about it, Daria?"

She smiled and walked over. The two musicians looked at her, and she asked, "I love singing 'Day In Day Out.' Can we do it without Cam and his 'Papa'?"

Dean assured, "We'll manage, I think."

When she joined the tune, Weathers, Armstrong, and Marshall listened intently, with Bartley clearly captured.

Popov sang another, and then asked about singing "At Last."

Strickland replied, "Might be a sin without any brass, but I won't tell Cam if you don't."

As she sang the romantic standard, Popov focused on Bartley.

At the end of that song, the three "on stage" decided to stop and join the others.

Marshall strolled over to Cold, and he made room for her on the bench. He smiled, "We've done this before. I like it."

"Me, too." She added, "My God, Daria does sing like an angel."

"She surely does."

Marshall asked, "Are you going to visit your dad during our break?"

He nodded. "I was thinking about it."

"I think it would be good for you."

"Want to come?"

"Love to, but I'd like to keep an eye on Robert."

Cold said, "Makes sense." He paused, and then added, "How about dinner when I get back?"

"Are you asking me out on a date, Keys?"

"I am."

"That sounds great."

The smiles they exchanged transformed into a gentle kiss.

# Chapter 93

Later that night, Cold was back in his apartment. He eyed the clock. It was just after one in the morning.

*He'd want me to call.*

After several rings, Gary Cold answered, "Hello?"

Dean could hear the grogginess, and felt bad. "Dad, I'm sorry for waking you up."

"It's fine, son. I'm glad you did."

Dean was amazed at how quickly his father could come to life.

Dean asked, "Are you sure? I can call back in the morning."

"Come on, Dean. It's not like I've never gotten calls in the middle of the night as a pastor."

"True."

"How are you?"

Dean said, "I'm fine. I got back to D.C. earlier today."

"I'm glad you're safe. How did your journey go?"

"Overall, I guess it went well."

"You 'guess'?"

"Well, a lot has happened."

Gary inquired, "Can I help? Do you want to talk about it?"

"I'd like to do that. I've got a few days off. Would you mind if I came up for a visit, and I could fill you in on what happened?"

"Would I mind? You know you never have to ask if it's alright to come home for whatever amount of time."

"I know, Dad. Thanks."

"Good. Do you know when you're arriving?"

Dean thought for a moment. "I think I'll drive up tomorrow. Probably leave mid-morning."

"That's great." Gary then added, "Something has happened here as well that we need to discuss."

"Is everything okay?"

Gary actually chuckled. "I'm alright, so is your sister and the family, if that's what you mean. As for what we need to discuss, I think you'll have to tell me if it's okay."

"That's pretty mysterious."

"I know. Sorry, son. When we talk, I think you'll agree with my ... caution. But please don't dwell on this. I think it's good news."

*He "thinks" it's good?*

"You don't want to discuss this now, or at least let me in on it?"

Gary answered, "You don't want to talk over the telephone about what happened to you, right?"

"Right."

"Same here then. This should be face-to-face. And it can wait until tomorrow."

"Fair enough, Dad."

After they finished the conversation and Dean hung up the receiver, he rubbed his forehead.

*Lord, I could use a good night's sleep.*

# Chapter 94

The bottles on the bar in his Capitol Hill home hadn't been opened in months. And the few beers in the refrigerator also went untouched and seemingly unnoticed.

For good measure, since breaking off his engagement, his life had become quite solitary, especially for a U.S. senator.

But it wasn't necessarily out of the ordinary. Whether by choice or by temperament, Senator Joe McCarthy was a loner.

That fact, and his position in the Senate, made him an ideal target for the Nykarians. He had been replaced six months earlier.

McCarthy entered his bedroom, pulled the case from the back of the closet, and opened up the com-stat device on a small desk.

He was looking at his watch when the signal went off.

The voice of Commander Three came through. "Senator McCarthy?"

"Yes, Commander."

Three immediately declared, "You called for this contact, what's happened?"

"I just got news that Jerry Debrowski and Clay Walsh are both dead."

"What? How?"

"There are the news reports and what I've been told."

"Explain."

"The news is telling a story of the two purchasing sexual favors from a few prostitutes, and for unexplained reasons, the night went awry. Each man was shot dead, and the murderers are being pursued."

"And what were you told?"

"I had a visit from CIA Director Allen Dulles, and he told me that Debrowski and Walsh were discovered to be part of a Soviet spy ring in Congress. And when confronted together, the two men attempted to fight their way out and were shot dead."

"I see."

McCarthy added, "Dulles and the CIA have been irritated by some of Senator McCarthy's many accusations falling on the CIA. So, he made it very clear that I should back off from, as he put it, 'this damn ridiculousness,' and if not, the truth would be revealed."

"And that would be?"

"The country would be told that one of my aides was a spy."

"Smart."

"I suppose." McCarthy waited for his superior to say something more. When she didn't, he added, "No matter what's happened, they're dead, and that means that…"

Three cut him off. "I'm well aware of what this means. Manage the public story, and continue tracking down more information."

Before McCarthy could say anything else, Three ended the communication. He leaned back in his chair, and pulled a pack of cigarettes and a lighter out of his pocket. He lit a cigarette, took a long drag, and sat back in his chair. He said out loud to himself, "Does anyone on Earth or on our ships have a clue as to what they're doing?"

McCarthy took another drag on his cigarette, shook his head, and smiled.

On the troop ship orbiting the planet, Commander Three was alone with Commander Four ten minutes after speaking with McCarthy.

She explained what was relayed to her.

Four responded, "Do we report this? Part of it? None of it?"

"None? That's not an option. As much as I command the Defenders on planet, any other Commander could step in to speak with any Defender."

Four agreed, "Yes, of course. That rules out telling only part of the story."

The two sat quietly for a few minutes. Three finally said, "I have to relay all of this to One."

"I know, I know. But this still offers a bit of hope."

"How?" asked Three in a tone carrying more hope than pessimism.

"So much has happened. The two Defenders killed in the White House. Now these two, and of course, the Khabarovsk facility being destroyed. The Americans know something."

"True, but how much?"

"That is the question."

"How will the others react?"

"At this point, at least, they can only do so much."

"For now."

"Yes, for now." Four added, "It's up to us to figure this out and find a way to pass along information that might make a real difference."

Three stared at him, and then said, "If we do this, you know that..."

"I know, Three. Which is worse – doing something, or standing by and letting this happen?"

# Chapter 95

Arriving at his family home in Brooklyn, Dean Cold, as was always the case, felt more at ease seeing his father.

The two men sat in the living room, and over bottled beers with low music coming over the radio, Dean gave Gary a detailed rundown on what had occurred over the past few weeks.

While his father said little, Dean could see the range of emotions that he was experiencing. As each man was about halfway through a second Rheingold, Dean completed his tale.

Gary initially managed to declare, "Holy crap."

Knowing that even such a relatively mild comment was usually out of bounds for his father, Dean responded, "Yeah, I know."

As his son's experiences seemed to fully sink in, Gary asked more questions. There was a part of Dean tugging at him, serving as a reminder that he technically shouldn't have shared any of this with his father. But Dean's trust in his father was complete. It also felt like a relief to be able to talk to someone about what he was doing, someone who wasn't involved in this dangerous and now-strange work.

Gary returned from the kitchen with a third beer for each of them.

*Three's the limit for Dad. He's not relaxed with all I'm telling him. He's worried, but there's more.*

Dean asked, "Okay, Dad, what was it that you wanted to talk about but not on the telephone?"

Gary downed a swig from the bottle, and then answered, "You're not going to believe this, and I'm not sure you're going to be pleased about it. Father Ed Duffy..."

"Yes?"

"It turns out that he's one of the visitors. He's a Nykarian."

"What!?"

It was Gary's turn to detail what had happened, and he left nothing out, including the details of the conversations that he had with Duffy.

"He wants you to help him," declared Dean when his father was finished. It could have been phrased as a question, but for Dean, it was simply a statement mixed with concern, annoyance and beleaguerment.

"He does."

"And you think he's legitimate?"

Gary smiled with a tinge of melancholy. "My years as a pastor help in such matters, but in the end, I can't read what's in a man's heart and head. Besides, that always was your specialty – you and your gut."

"You and Mom always hated that."

"'Hate' might be too strong, but we did disapprove. At the same time, you had an undeniable knack for being right. Perhaps it's time to put that gut to the test once more."

"I trust your take, Dad, but I will need to talk with Father Duffy myself. Is he willing to talk to me?"

"He wants to, and I arranged for him to come over for breakfast tomorrow morning. I knew you'd want to talk to him as soon as possible."

"You're right about that."

*So much for Dad not being involved directly in all of this. And so much for feeling relaxed at home.*

\*     \*     \*

Gary Cold had prepared a full breakfast of scrambled eggs, bacon, fried potatoes, toast and coffee. It was ready when Father Edward Duffy arrived. Both Dean Cold and Duffy said little when Gary introduced them.

Dean was anxious, while he saw serenity on the face of Duffy.

Gary led a prayer.

And while Duffy took his first bite of toast, Dean demanded, "I need to know everything."

For more than two hours, Duffy spoke and answered Dean's many questions. While Gary ate a full breakfast listening, and Duffy managed to consume most of his meal, Dean only drank coffee. About a third of the way through the part-conversation, part-interrogation, Gary cleared away the food and dishes, and refreshed each coffee.

It had taken less than 30 minutes for Dean to be convinced about the sincerity of this Father Duffy's faith and intentions. But he couldn't let Duffy see that, and he had a responsibility to banish any trace of doubt from his own mind. His inquiries were unrelenting, direct and at times, confrontational.

Toward the end of the discussion, Dean knew that even though he was convinced about Father Duffy's conversion and commitment, he should have taken Duffy with him back to D.C., and handed him over to Dulles. But his gut not only said to trust what Father Duffy was telling him, but it also said that removing this priest from his mission simply would be wrong.

As the meeting came to an end, Gary watched closely as Dean and Duffy rose to their feet. It was Dean who offered an outstretched hand first.

Father Duffy warmly thanked the father and son. Gary returned the sentiment, while Dean purposefully projected a certain detachment.

That professional aloofness held until Duffy reached the front door, turned and said, "Dean, may God bless you and your work."

Dean replied without hesitation, "And you, too, Father."

After Duffy left, Gary commented to his son, "You see it. You believe him like I do."

"How would you know that?"

Gary smiled. "A father knows."

"You're right. But this presents all kinds of potential problems. I have to report this to the president."

"Yes, obviously."

Dean shook his head. "You seem far more at ease with what might result than I am."

"Maybe, but I think deep down in you know what will happen."

Dean laughed. "Please, tell me."

His father replied, "From all you've said, President Eisenhower knows to trust you."

"You know, Dad, that optimism of a pastor that you emanate at times can be annoying."

Gary now laughed. "I don't think you find it annoying at all, Dean."

Dean acknowledged, "Of course not."

"Maybe Father Duffy's efforts will be the first good to come out of this entire thing, Dean," observed Gary.

"There's that pastor optimism thing at work."

# Chapter 96

After the drive back from New York, Agent Dean Cold parked his Studebaker on Q Street. But before he was able to take the first step down from the sidewalk toward his apartment, the front door of the adjacent townhouse opened. John Bartley stepped out.

"How was the drive, Dean?" asked Bartley.

"Fine. You doing okay?"

"I am. But don't settle in, we have an appointment."

Dean sighed slightly. "When?"

"As soon as you're ready."

"Give me a few minutes. Just you and me?"

"No. Daria as well, and we're meeting Roy."

After dropping his luggage, splashing cold water on his face, and getting a quick drink of water, Cold re-emerged onto Q Street. He grabbed the passenger seat next to Bartley in his Ford Custom V8. Daria was in the back seat, and after pleasantries, Cold asked, "Where?"

"CIA."

Cold inquired, "What's this all about?"

Bartley shrugged. "All we know is that we have a meeting."

An hour later, Cold was in the basement of CIA headquarters on E Street, NW. From his days with the OSS, he knew this hallway.

*Seems like the same ceiling lights are still flickering.*

Roy O'Keefe led Cold, Bartley and Popov to a locked door on the right. O'Keefe unlocked the door, letting Cold, Bartley and Popov enter the room before him.

Sitting on a narrow bed, with his back against the wall, was Dr. Maksut Golikova. He was casually smoking a cigarette, and actually smiled when the four looked at him. He focused on Cold and Popov. "Ah, the two who captured me. Welcome."

Cold looked around. In addition to the bed, the room had a desk and chair, and a toilet. Four chairs stretched across the center of the room, facing the bed. They clearly had been added for this meeting.

Golikova spotted Cold scanning the room, and declared, "It's not much, I know. Ironically, though, this cell is not all that much worse than the barracks in Khabarovsk. And we were helping the Russians." He chuckled. "By the way, I refuse to use that toilet. I insisted on using a bathroom with at least some degree of privacy."

Bartley smirked. "How civilized. Are the other murdering and invading Nykarians as civilized?"

Golikova actually smiled. He took another drag on his cigarette, and then stubbed it out on an ashtray. "I think I'm going to like working with you."

Cold raised an eyebrow.

*There it is.*

"We'll judge whether you're going to work *for* us or not, Doctor," declared Cold.

"Yes, yes, I've been told. But clearly, your Mr. Dulles wants this to happen, and so do I."

Cold moved to a chair. The three others followed his lead. "And why do you want this to happen?" asked Cold.

"The most obvious reason, like I told you before, is that I would like to live, and I would prefer not to live in a prison."

Bartley pressed, "That's it?"

"I think that's probably enough, but no, there is more. I'm not interested in the things that you humans, or at least most of you, value. Freedom, democracy, blah, blah. Not that I necessarily have anything against such lofty ideals. But, to be honest, I just don't care all that much."

The four stared at him in silence.

Golikova continued, "I had a similar conversation with a Russian, and she said that she found that scientists were willing to tolerate almost anything as long as they could just do their work."

Popov interrupted, "I know more than a few scientists who would disagree with that."

"Yes, I'm sure you do," said Golikova dismissively. "Nonetheless, there are a good number of human scientists who think this way. Just look at the men who worked for the Nazis, and now work for you, for the United States."

Cold shifted uncomfortably in his chair at that remark.

Golikova went on, "So, yes, I'd like to live and be able to do my work."

Cold leaned forward. "And you would have no qualms that your work would now contribute to stopping your own people? That your work could lead to the deaths of some Nykarians?"

Golikova looked at Cold and replied, "I have no such qualms, Agent Cold. As I said, I'm interested in staying alive, even among you humans. But let me say something that you" – he pointed at Cold – "should think about." He narrowed his eyes. "If we are to succeed, there will be far more than 'some' Nykarian deaths. Just as there will be far more human deaths than I think you can imagine at this point in time. The leaders of my people are desperate to remain in power, and they will do whatever is necessary to stay there."

Golikova put one of Cold's greatest fears into words. Cold glanced sideways, and could see that Bartley, Popov and O'Keefe shared his discomfort.

*There's not a trace of doubt in his voice.*

Cold got up from the chair, and moved toward the door. The other three followed him.

As Cold reached for the doorknob, Golikova broke what had become a somber silence. "I look forward to working with you to stop the enslavement of your people."

The light was still flickering in the hallway. O'Keefe locked the door.

Bartley commented, "That was fucking cheery."

Popov observed, "I don't think he was exaggerating. Do any of you?"

Cold answered, "No, I don't. We need to get back to Q Street, think through what we've just heard, and then..."

O'Keefe interrupted, "That will have to wait, at least for you and me, Dean. We're supposed to go see the president."

# Chapter 97

President Eisenhower and CIA Director Allen Dulles were waiting for Agent Dean Cold and Officer Roy O'Keefe.

Ike rose from the Roosevelt desk and invited both Cold and O'Keefe to take seats on one of the couches, with Eisenhower and Dulles, as usual, across on the other couch.

Eisenhower said, "I unfortunately don't have much time, but we need to go over a couple of matters. First, how did your meeting with Golikova go?"

Cold answered, "I think he was being honest with us." He glanced at O'Keefe, who nodded in agreement. "In fact, it could be said that he was painfully honest. He wants to continue doing his science, for lack of a better way to put it, and doesn't seem to care who lets him do so."

"It's not like we don't know the type," commented Dulles.

Ike merely added, "A necessary evil, at times, I suppose."

*He doesn't sound fully convinced of that, and neither am I.*

Eisenhower cut to the chase, "His knowledge will be invaluable for however this plays out. Can you work with him?"

"Can we? Yes, I think we can, but I would want someone at his side the entire time – a person we can trust."

"Dr. Strickland?" inquired Dulles.

Cold wasn't comfortable moving this fast, but understood why. "Yes. He would be the right person, if he's willing to do so."

"Good," declared Ike. "Find out if Dr. Strickland is alright with this."

"Yes, sir." Cold went on, "I know time is tight. But there's something I need to tell you, and it can't wait."

"Go ahead."

On the way to the White House, Cold had rehearsed this in his head, and he proceeded to report the situation with Father Edward Duffy and his father, including Duffy's intentions and his own reactions and those of his father. As he spoke, O'Keefe's eyes widened.

Cold concluded, "After we met with Father Duffy, I did some checking over the following days around the St. Peter's parish and neighborhood, and all I can say is that Father Duffy seems to be working hard at doing the things one would hope a priest would do."

Dulles said, "Shit, these guys are everywhere. And you just let him stay in New York? What the hell were…?"

Ike cut him off. "Allen."

Dulles stopped talking, but his irritation now seemed magnified.

Eisenhower looked at Cold. "Dean, you and your father are sure about this … conversion and the mission of this Father Duffy being legitimate?"

Cold thought about his father's response, and said, "As far as one can be sure about the hearts and minds of others, yes, he was sincere. And besides, if that weren't the case, why would he expose himself to my father?"

Dulles said, "There could be all sorts of reasons."

The president gave him a stare. Dulles leaned back on the couch. Ike turned back to Cold. "I see your point, and if what you say about this…" – Cold saw him working to find the right word – "…this priest is true, then I certainly don't want us to get in the way of what he wants to do." Ike smiled ever so slightly. "It's not all that different than what various Christians have been working to do in the Soviet Union. Assuming that you and your father are right – good for the soul and for freedom."

Dulles, Cold and O'Keefe kept their eyes trained on the president, who was now staring down at the carpet.

Eisenhower looked up, and said to Cold, "Your father helping Duffy in his efforts I think would be a good thing. These are, to say the least, extraordinary circumstances. So, what I am going to suggest is not meant as a request for your father to compromise his principles or requirements of his job as a pastor, but he would need to keep you up to date on Duffy's work. In turn, you would need to determine if this priest might require additional help at times, but also be aware to identify anything that would be problematic."

Cold didn't hesitate in responding, "That's what my father and I expect to do, and I think Father Duffy expects the same."

Eisenhower sat up straighter and looked at Cold. "This Father Duffy doesn't know that the Nykarians have lied about being able to pull the plug on Defenders, correct?"

"Yes, sir – at least as far as I know. I didn't let him or my father, for that matter, in on that."

Ike nodded, and looked at each man gathered. "Like Colonel Weathers and Corporal Armstrong, that says a great deal."

Cold agreed. "It does."

"All right, then, let's get to the final item for today." Ike looked at Dulles. "Allen."

Dulles pushed forward on the couch, and said, "It's time to expand this Q Street operation in terms of both personnel and location. We have a place out west that fits key requirements. Also, if you agree, we're going to acquire the two townhouses across from the two we already have on Q Street." Cold wasn't given a chance to respond yet. Dulles went on, "And while the president and I have some ideas, your Q Street team is going to expand. Based on this" – he handed Cold an envelope – "you and your people have to digest this, add and subtract as you see fit, and then come up with a list of potential candidates."

Dulles summarized what he and the president came up with, and Cold was able to sprinkle in a question here and there. Dulles concluded, "It's all laid out in greater detail in there." He pointed at the envelope. O'Keefe listened throughout. It was only 45 minutes after sitting down that Cold and O'Keefe left the Oval Office with an expanded agenda and a long set of tasks.

# Chapter 98

Gary Cold answered the telephone call from his son.

"Dad, I have important news relating to Father Duffy," announced Dean.

"Yes?"

"President Eisenhower agrees with your assessment, and as we expected, he says that we should give help where we can while also making sure that we keep the president up to date."

"That's excellent."

"The president made a point of saying that keeping him up to date is not meant to compromise your work in any way."

"I understand. I guess I'll be reporting to you, Dean." He chuckled.

Dean laughed as well, adding, "I don't know if I'd put it that way." He paused, and then said, "There's more."

"What else?"

"Father Duffy's people have been lying. They don't have the power to simply end the lives of their people. It's a fiction meant to keep everyone in line."

"My God, Dean, that's outstanding. It will be life-changing for Father Duffy."

"You should be the one who tells him."

"Are you sure?"

"Of course."

Gary went quiet for several seconds. Dean asked, "Are you alright with this, Dad?"

"Yes, yes, I am. It's just sinking in what this would mean to Father Duffy. He's been willing to risk it all – to work for

Christ – in the face of death, and now he will have this threat removed."

"It'll still be dangerous, but yes, I understand what you're saying."

*       *       *

Father Ed Duffy answered the knock at the front door of the St. Peter's rectory. Seeing Gary Cold, he smiled and invited his friend inside.

When Duffy shut the door, Cold asked, "Is anyone else here?"

"No. We're alone. What's the news that you couldn't tell me over the telephone?"

"I'm just going to say it. The Nykarians have been lying to you."

"What does that mean?"

Cold took a deep breath. "Dean's people have found out that they can't actually end your life, or any of your Defenders' lives. It's been a lie to keep you all in line, to keep you afraid to stray from what they want you to do."

Duffy stood immobile in front of Cold. He managed to whisper, "Gary, are you sure?"

Cold nodded. "Dean and the people he works with are sure."

Tears started to fill Duffy's eyes. "Oh, God. Dear Lord. Thank you. Thank you, Gary."

Duffy reached out and hugged Gary Cold in joy.

# Chapter 99

As the CIA aircraft made its descent in the darkness, Dean Cold liked what he saw out the window, namely, very little. Other than those on the runway, no lights could be seen nearby. He estimated that a dim cluster of lights in the distance was probably 15 or 20 miles away.

The plane touched down smoothly on the runway, and taxied toward three buildings and two hangars.

Maxine Marshall, John Bartley, and Mike Strickland followed Cold off the plane – each with a duffel bag over the shoulder. A figure stood under one of the few dome-covered, low lights that led the way to the hangars. Cameron Jefferson whistled and said, "It's about time you people got here. What took you so long?"

"My God, Cam, it's good to see you," declared Cold.

"You, too," said Jefferson as the two hugged and slapped each other's back.

Jefferson turned to Marshall. As they embraced, Marshall asked, "How are you, Cam?"

"I'm good. You?"

She nodded. Jefferson then shook hands and greeted Strickland and Bartley.

Jefferson said, "It's late, but you obviously have to take a look at what I flew out of Russia."

As the group started to walk over to the hangar, Jefferson asked, "So, what the hell has been going on while I'm here babysitting my plane?"

Cold asked, "'My plane'?"

"Hey, that's what Dulles said."

"Ike, too," added Cold.

After a brief laugh, the group did their best to quickly bring Jefferson up to date on the key developments. When they reached the side door to one of the hangars, Jefferson banged on the door three times, paused, and then knocked twice.

Bartley said, "That's the signal?"

Jefferson shrugged.

Cold and Bartley recognized the person opening the door. It was Paul from Shemya Air Force Base in Alaska. Seated at a table several yards beyond him was his partner, Harry. The two CIA officers jokingly thanked Cold and the others for getting them out of Alaska. "It's a hell of a lot warmer in Arizona."

Jefferson said, "These gentlemen have become our security team." He led the group over to a massive canvas curtain hanging down in a circle from the ceiling in the middle of the hangar. "Time for a peek behind the curtain." They stepped through a partition.

Cold, Marshall, Bartley and Strickland stood looking in amazement at the black, sleek MiG-X jet fighter that the curtain surrounded.

Cold commented, "It's more than I remember."

"It's amazing. I've been over it and over it, but there are still some things that I don't fully grasp in terms of the materials, technology and capabilities. But let me walk you through what I do know."

Cold smiled, and said, "We can go through your comprehensive notes later as well."

"Damn right. Part of my job."

For more than an hour, Jefferson offered the others a detailed look at the aircraft, and answered questions. He concluded with an admiring gaze at the jet, saying, "I can't wait to get this thing in the sky again." When back outside the curtain, Jefferson asked, "You guys tired or do you want to grab some drinks and a bite to eat?"

No one was tired, and all four said they could eat. They climbed into a van and Jefferson drove to the small town roughly 15 miles away. He parked in front of an adobe-style building with a neon sign letting everyone know it was "Sue's Saloon."

Jefferson led the group into the establishment that at best could be described as well-worn. Two men sitting at the bar didn't turn to see who had come in, but the bartender looked up from cleaning glasses. "Hey, Cam, good to see you. Brought some friends, I see." The woman was in her late thirties with brunette hair pulled back in a ponytail. Her eyes were dark, and she had the look of someone who had a life that felt longer than her age.

"Hi, Sue. Yeah, I work with these guys. Can we get a couple of pitchers of your best on tap and some glasses?"

"Sure. I'll bring it right over."

Round tables populated the floor, with three large booths along a wall. Along another was what passed for a stage, with a covered drum set, a piano, and a microphone stand pushed against the wall. A jukebox was playing some R&B.

Jefferson picked the table farthest from the bar. "No one can hear us from back here."

When Sue arrived with the pitchers and glasses, Jefferson introduced everyone, and then asked, "Any chance you might be able to fire up the grill for some of those delicious burgers of yours? These folks haven't eaten in a while."

"Sure, Honey." She looked around the table and asked, "How do you want 'em?"

As Sue left to start the order, Jefferson commented, "Sue offers hamburgers, fried chicken, and pie. Not much on the menu, but it's all good."

Marshall said, "Seems like you're making yourself at home here."

Jefferson said, "Not sure if that's the case, but I guess it might be?" It was a question tossed Cold's way.

"It will be for some of us — either full-time or splitting time between here and D.C. The CIA is handing over its Elias Ranch to us…"

Strickland interrupted, "Why is it called the Elias Ranch?"

Cold answered, "They just kept the name of the place when they purchased it from the Elias family. Kept a low profile."

Strickland said, "Look at that – a government decision that makes sense." He took a swig of beer.

Jefferson said, "So, they're giving us a ranch?"

Cold nodded. He looked at Jefferson, and said, "And a hell of a lot more. We've been discussing this, and now it's time to bring you into the loop." He looked around the room, and was sure that the two guys at the bar couldn't hear them, with a combination of the music playing and their argument over horses. "We'll dig into this over the coming days, but essentially, Ike, with Dulles in agreement, wants to expand this operation. To start, that means identifying what we need and who we need. Max will be leading a small medical team that will be taking care of our people while also figuring out more about the Nykarians themselves, including their biology. John will be in charge of everything on the security front. Daria is going to be the go-to person on all things Russian. And you and Mike are going to divvy up as you guys best see fit, the weapons and technology matters."

"Wow. Okay," replied Jefferson. "And, I suppose, you're our fearless leader?"

Before Cold could answer, Bartley chimed in, "Yeah, he gets to meet with all of the important people in D.C."

Cold laughed along with the others. "If that was it, you could shoot me now."

"What is it, then?" persisted Jefferson in a good-natured way.

Marshall jumped in, "The president has put him in charge of the whole thing."

Cold detected a touch of pride in her voice, and that made him feel good.

"He has, so not only do you people report to me..." he sarcastically declared, and received mocking grunts in response. "I'll also be working to figure out how everything ties together. We all will work to counter and eventually end this Nykarian threat."

"Oh, is that all?" asked Jefferson.

"Easy peasy," added Bartley.

Cold said, "That's our task. Robert and Grace are essential, obviously. I'll be reporting directly to the president on all of this. Oh, and Roy will continue to be part of our security effort while being our liaison, for lack of a better word, with Dulles and the CIA." No one said anything, so Cold continued, "Over the coming days, we're going to map out more of how this will all work, decide who and what we require, and figure out where each of us will be spending our time between the Elias Ranch and Q Street. It sounds like our entire effort is going to be known as Q Street from now on."

Marshall declared, "Maybe a bit on the nose, but it works."

Strickland asked, "And our budget?"

"At this point, I haven't been given one. We should think freely about what's needed, and then we'll see what Ike says."

Strickland declared, "Very government."

Cold spotted Sue getting ready to bring over their food. He sat back in the chair, and said, "At least for the rest of tonight, let's relax. We'll get started in the morning."

The conversation stopped as Sue approached, who was skillfully balancing six plates of cheeseburgers and hamburgers on two arms. She distributed the plates with the confidence of a card dealer, and said, "Let me know when you need refills."

Each person thanked her, and then started on their burgers.

As he swallowed the first bite of his burger, Strickland looked over at the drums and piano. "What's the deal, Cam, with music acts?"

"The few times I've been here, absolutely nothing. I don't think Derringer, Arizona, is overflowing with musicians."

Sue returned with a couple of plates of French fries. "I thought you might like some fries." She again was thanked. Strickland asked, "Sue, does anyone play?" He tilted his head toward the instruments.

"Not in a long time."

"I was wondering because a few of us play."

The owner of Sue's Saloon brightened. "Hey, if you guys ever want to jam, that's fine with me."

"Thanks. Who knows? Maybe."

Bartley asked, "What if they're no good?"

Sue shrugged. "How bad could you guys be? Take a look around. Like I said, feel free. And if it turns out that you're not too bad, it might put a few more asses in seats." She folded her arms, and offered, "And you'd get free beer and grub."

"Just so you know, Cam plays the trumpet, Dean the piano, and I'm a drummer. And one of our other co-workers has the voice of an angel."

"I'm game. Let me know," declared Sue, who then returned to the bar.

Cold looked at Jefferson, "From the clubs of New York to Derringer."

Jefferson grinned and declared, "Hey, it's about the music."

Laughs around the table were followed by more eating.

Marshall swallowed, dabbed her mouth with a napkin, and then asked, "So, Cam, is this the only place to eat in this town? It turns out that Dean asked me to dinner, and then forgot about it."

Cold stopped chewing with food still in his mouth, and the barrage of barbs came from around the table.

"Not surprising," jabbed Bartley.

Strickland added, "Geez, I thought you were smarter than that, Dean."

And Jefferson commented, "You know the deal, Max. Dean's always been a clod when it comes to women, never mind romance."

Cold swallowed and said, "Hey, wait a minute..."

Jefferson ignored the protest and continued, "It's here, and a small diner down the street."

Cold tried to recover. He looked at Max and said, "I know..."

Marshall interjected, "No, Dean, you had your chance. So, for our long-overdue date, I will make us a nice dinner after work tomorrow night. How does that sound?"

Cold smiled, and said, "That sounds great. Thanks."

"And then you owe me," added Marshall.

"You sure do, Dean," commented Bartley.

Amidst further conversation, Dean Cold let his mind take a step back to become an observer.

*Lord, we'll need each other and times like this to get through what lies ahead. And I need to be there for all of them, especially Max.*

He looked around the table at each face, and his mind returned to his friend, Andrew Stanton.

*Stant would have enjoyed this.*

# Chapter 100

The next morning, President Eisenhower was speaking with Agent Dean Cold on the telephone.

Ike wrapped up, "We've got a hell of a lot of work ahead, Dean, and it's going to be hard to balance secrecy with urgency. But I have confidence in you and your team, and it sounds like things are off to a good start at the Ranch. Thanks for your efforts, and we'll talk again in a few days."

After the call ended, Eisenhower looked across his desk at Allen Dulles and his current scowl. "What's wrong, Allen? I thought you were on board with Cold and his people?"

"I am, Mr. President. Truly, I am. But I still don't like the fact that Agent Cold not only left that alien priest in New York, but also that it took him days to let us know about him."

"I understand, Allen. And I need you to keep raising your concerns."

"Yes, sir."

Eisenhower walked over and looked out the window. He added, "I trust Dean Cold. I put him in this position for a reason, and he's proving himself to be up to the job. He's smart, versatile and has the right instincts. And given what we're dealing with, and what might be coming, he's also grounded. The war taught me the importance of having grounded people."

"I agree, sir," declared Dulles.

Eisenhower continued, "As for his father and the priest, I wouldn't feel very comfortable stepping in to stop what each of them sees as a legitimate effort to spread the faith – and in the face of death. I don't think I need to remind you of what happens when the government tries to squash or control what people believe." He turned and looked at Dulles with a wry smile. "Besides, do you want to have to answer to God if He asks why you put a stop to the work of a priest and a pastor? I don't."

The mission of the Q Street team will continue in the next Agent Dean Cold novel...
*The Race*

# Author Afterword: Why Science Fiction?

After writing thrillers and mysteries in my Pastor Stephen Grant series, I ventured into historical fiction with the Alliance of Saint Michael novels. But I wanted to take another journey. Science fiction has fascinated me since I was a kid. *Menace: An Agent Dean Cold Novel* – something I had a character mention in *Heroes and Villains: A Pastor Stephen Grant Short Story* – was born. I hope readers enjoy this book and that it will be the first entry in another continuing series.

I've enjoyed all kinds of science fiction over the years, but writing a blend of science fiction and historical fiction, while incorporating some spy thriller elements, has truly captured my imagination.

And then there are the Christian aspects of this story – not all that typical in sci-fi (especially in recent times). There were a few key influences on this front.

First, I've been a big *Star Trek* fan since I watched reruns on WPIX growing up on Long Island. If I remember correctly, the original *Star Trek* ran weeknights at 6 pm on Channel 11. And while I love so many episodes – including classics like *The City on the Edge of Forever, Balance of Terror, The Doomsday Machine, Amok Time, Mirror, Mirror* and *The Trouble with Tribbles* – as I grew older, one episode fascinated me more and more. And that was *Bread and Circuses*.

At first glance, this episode is one of those entertaining, but perhaps a bit out-there episodes with the crew of the *Enterprise* visiting a planet where the Roman Empire survived into the 20th century. So, Kirk, Spock and McCoy are confronted by being thrown into televised gladiator games, including talk of ratings and valuable time slots. But the story is, in fact, quite good, including the interplay between Spock and McCoy. But the closing dialogue on the bridge really grabbed and has kept my attention.

> KIRK: Gentlemen.
> MCCOY: Captain, I see on your report Flavius was killed. I am sorry. I liked that huge sun worshiper.
> SPOCK: I wish we could have examined that belief of his more closely. It seems illogical for a sun worshiper to develop a philosophy of total brotherhood. Sun worship is usually a primitive superstition religion.
> UHURA: I'm afraid you have it all wrong, Mister Spock, all of you. I've been monitoring some of their old-style radio waves, the empire spokesman trying to ridicule their religion. But he couldn't. Don't you understand? It's not the sun up in the sky. It's the Son of God.
> KIRK: Caesar and Christ. They had them both. And the word is spreading only now.
> MCCOY: A philosophy of total love and total brotherhood.
> SPOCK: It will replace their imperial Rome, but it will happen in their twentieth century.
> KIRK: Wouldn't it be something to watch, to be a part of? To see it happen all over again?

This was my foray into thinking about life on other planets and what it might mean in terms of Christianity.

Second, amid a conversation on the topic of life elsewhere in the universe, a pastor I once knew said that if such life were ever discovered, it would seem to undermine the Incarnation. I didn't pursue that with him, but I was surprised by his observation, to say the least. After all, the guy was a pastor. Since then, it has come to my attention that assorted Christians seem to think that intelligent alien life would shake the Christian faith.

Whether one believes in intelligent life elsewhere or not, for some, apparently, even mere speculation about alien life provides problems or obstacles on the faith front. Since I love fun discussions about these kinds of topics, it distresses me to think that pondering such matters – whether seriously or just having a fun conversation over some food and drink – might somehow work against the Christian faith.

Interestingly, there has been, as alluded to in this book, a long history of speculation about intelligent life elsewhere within Christian circles. I didn't expect to discover such dialogue going back centuries. That's intriguing.

I did a fair amount of reading on this topic while preparing to write and while writing this book. In particular, I found great value in a variety of sources, including the following:

- "The Seeing Eye" by C.S. Lewis in *Christian Reflections*
- "Religion and Rocketry" by C.S. Lewis in *The World's Last Night and Other Essays*
- *Extraterrestrial Intelligence and the Catholic Faith: Are We Alone in the Universe with God and the Angels?* by Paul Thigpen
- *Off the Edge: Faith, Science, and the Future*, Adam Francisco, author, and Jesse Yow, consultant, Concordia Publishing House

You can see the influences of the above in the theological discussions in *Menace*.

In the end, while I'm personally undecided about intelligent alien life elsewhere in the universe, and have deep doubts about their ability to journey to Earth, I immensely enjoy kicking such ideas around, and watching movies and television and reading science fiction about humans engaging on Earth or in space with alien species. I agree with those Christian thinkers and writers who not only don't see this possibility as some kind of contradiction with Christianity, but instead view such discoveries, if they ever materialize, as further examples of God's creative love and, yes, if necessary, perhaps an opportunity to further spread the Good News.

As Captain Kirk observed, "Wouldn't it be something to watch, to be a part of?"

I hope that *Menace* entertains and intrigues the reader, while perhaps contributing in some small way to assuring people that intelligent life elsewhere in the universe in no way undermines the Christian faith.

Ray Keating
June 2025

If You Enjoyed this Book, Consider Ray Keating's
Pastor Stephen Grant Thrillers & Mysteries, and His
Alliance of Saint Michael Historical Fiction

Following is the first chapter from
*Cathedral: An Alliance of Saint Michael Novel...*

# Chapter 1

**Moscow, Early 1928**

Pastor Gabriel Fischer's hands trembled. Yet, his knuckles were white from squeezing the handles of the box. Sweat dripped from his brow, despite it being frigid in Moscow and inside St. Michael's Lutheran Church.

When it was agreed earlier in the morning that Fischer would do the final inspection of the basement, it never would have crossed his mind what awaited discovery.

Time had run out. The order had come down that the church would be handed over to the military and torn down, so that the area where it stood could be integrated into a factory. Pastor Fischer, Eckhart Konig, St. Michael's senior pastor, and the Moscow bishop had contacted everyone they could think of who might help to stop the process.

After all, St. Michael's possessed the deepest Lutheran roots in all of Russia. It was the oldest Lutheran congregation in the country, dating back to 1576 and the reign of Ivan the Terrible. And the current building was the oldest Lutheran church in Moscow, built in 1764. However, the communists had made clear that religion and the Church were enemies of the State, and destined for annihilation. And despite being able to have a service of celebration at St. Michael's in 1926 to mark the 350th-anniversary of the congregation, the inevitable, barring a miracle or some other intervention, crept ever closer. Indeed, now, it was at hand. St. Michael's was to be officially taken at the end of this day.

This ongoing tragedy – with the enemy literally at the church door – made Fischer's discovery even more incredible.

Pastor Konig was kneeling at the Communion rail. His head hung down, shoulders slumped, elbows resting on the wood. It appeared that if the railing were removed, he would simply crumble to the floor. He seemed to have to work to raise his head when Pastor Fischer called out his name from the back of the nave.

"Eckhart! Eckhart, dear Lord, you must see this." Fischer rushed up the center aisle, still trembling and sweating.

Konig turned and rose to his feet. He watched as Fischer nearly stumbled, but then regained his equilibrium. Fischer suddenly stopped a few feet in front of Konig. The younger pastor took a deep breath, and then slowly and gently placed the box on the floor in front of his gray-haired colleague.

Konig appeared more interested in looking at Fischer's face awash in sweat and emotion. Konig asked, "What is it, Gabriel?"

Fischer seemed unsure as to how to answer the question. His eyes searched – looking up at the altar, down at the box, and then at Konig. "A miracle?"

"What do you mean?" He finally glanced down at the box.

While staring down at the container, Fischer explained, "I was finishing my final inspection of the basement, when my eyes were drawn to a gap between two stones in the wall. I had never noticed it before, but then again, given what was stored down there, I had never seen the wall itself before." He looked up at Konig, whose expression of weariness was now one of anticipation. Fischer went on, "I dropped down on the floor, and could see that there was some space behind the stone. I spent nearly an hour with the help of a metal bar freeing the first stone. I reached into the space and could feel this." He looked back down at the box. "The other stone moved more easily, and I was able to drag this out." The excitement in his voice rose. He now spoke more quickly. "I picked it up and moved under one of the torches to get a better look."

Fischer paused and looked at Konig.

Konig asked, "Yes, and what did you find?"

Fischer kneeled down in front of the box, and indicated that Konig should do the same.

The two pastors were on their knees with the altar just a few feet away.

Fischer explained, "It actually was wrapped in two blankets. I left those in the basement. I unwrapped it and then opened these." He proceeded to repeat his steps, flipping up three black metal latches across the front of the dark wood chest. He opened the top, and the two men peered inside.

Fischer said, "These also were wrapped in cloth. I returned each to the way they were, well, as best I could." There were five separately wrapped items. "I confess that when I discovered what this was, I opened each and turned many pages." He added, "Of course, I did so carefully."

Konig's eyes were now wide open and there was a life in them that had been absent for many months.

Fischer reached in and pulled out one of the wrapped items. He unfolded the cloth to reveal a collection of pages of parchment. Fischer and Konig looked at each other, and then Fischer handed the volume over to Konig.

Fischer smiled and pointed to a name at the bottom of the page. It said, "Ernst Glück."

"What? Could it be?" The questions came in a whispering tone from Konig.

"It is," confirmed Fischer. "This clearly is Pastor Ernst Glück's translations of the Bible – from what I can tell, the New Testament and parts of the Old Testament – into Russian."

As he began to gently look through various pages, Konig said, more to the air around him than to Fischer, "This was undertaken at the behest of Peter the Great, or perhaps these were done, at least in part, while he was in Livonia."

Both men were familiar with Ernst Glück, a Lutheran pastor who died in Russia in 1705. He had translated the Bible into Latvian, and undertook the task of translating Holy Scripture into vernacular Russian.

Konig commented, "This work was all lost, or presumed so."

The two men spent the next 45 minutes going through many of the pages, and suddenly Konig snapped out of his reverie. He looked at Fischer in sudden panic. "If what we think is true, then this would be the first translation of Scripture into the day-to-day Russian language."

Apparently missing the shift in Konig's tone, Fischer smiled, continued reading, and simply replied, "Yes."

"We need to hide this." He looked around, and then added, "We need to get this out of here, to get it somewhere safe."

"What?" asked Fischer, appearing somewhat bewildered.

"Gabriel. The radicals are taking our church later today. What do you think they would do with this if they found it?"

Understanding dawned on Fischer's expression. "Dear God. Of course. What should we do?"

As Konig started to wrap the volumes back in the cloth, he said, "Let me think."

The two men proceeded to pack the historic work of Pastor Ernst Glück back into the chest. The top was shut and re-latched.

Konig asked, "Do you trust your Orthodox friend?"

"My 'Orthodox friend'?"

"The one in hiding..."

"Yes. I do trust him. He saw what these people were capable of early and firsthand."

Konig nodded. "He does work at the Cathedral of Christ the Saviour, correct?"

"After he left the communists and returned to the Church, he went to the academy in hopes of finishing his studies at the seminary. But since the seminary was closed, he has been working and studying in secret."

"The priests have been protecting him?"

"For nearly a decade now, that has been the case."

"They sound like the right people to get this to" – he placed his hand on the chest – "for hiding."

Several minutes later, Fischer and Konig quickly filled up a horse cart, stacking mundane items around and on top of the chest. Pastor Fischer hopped up on the cart's seat, took the horse reins in his hand, and looked down at Pastor Konig.

Konig said, "God be with you, Gabriel."

"And with you, Eckhart." He paused, and added, "I know this will work." He turned his gaze skyward to the steeple of the white church. "Those demons might tear down St. Michael's, but they do not have the nerve, or the stupidity, to do something like that to the cathedral." He looked back down at Konig. "I will be back by late this afternoon."

It was nearly six in the evening when Fischer returned. As he approached St. Michael's with a now empty cart, he was greeted by a group of nearly 50 people holding candles and singing. They were members of St. Michael's, and they knew that the building was being handed over to the government. Fischer tied up the horse, and walked toward the front doors of St. Michael's. Pastor Konig was standing there, looking out at the gathered parishioners and leading the singing.

Konig glanced over at Fischer with a raised eyebrow. Fischer nodded in response, and then standing next to his fellow pastor, turned to the gathered and joined in singing. Konig placed his right hand on Fischer's shoulder, and Fischer saw the tears forming in the corners of Konig's eyes. The same started to happen to Fischer.

But as the gathered faithful began the next stanza of this particular hymn, thundering horse hooves cut through the air. Three figures with long coats flowing and high hats upon their heads approached on the galloping beasts. The riders pulled up just on the outside of the singing crowd.

The members of St. Michael's turned to see who had arrived, but their singing continued.

On the heels of the riders came a small group of soldiers. They trotted in unison, and halted several feet behind the horses.

The singing continued.

An order was given, and the soldiers moved to encircle the gathering.

Konig tightened his grip on Fischer's shoulder.

The captain of the squad moved his horse forward. The animal's teeth and nostrils now hung inches behind a woman at the outer edge of the congregants.

The captain looked over his shoulder at one of his men on horseback. He ordered, "Get their attention."

The soldier replied, "Yes, sir." He pulled out a revolver, pointed it in the air, and fired a shot. People jumped, the singing stopped and a few people yelled out in fear.

The captain guided his horse forward, cutting through the crowd. He stopped in front of the steps leading to the church door. Konig and Fischer were at the same eye level as the captain. The two pastors stared at the man with their backs stiffened.

Konig began to open his mouth, but the captain immediately raised a hand in the air, making clear that Konig should say nothing. The captain's look intensified. His hatred was unmistakable. "Silence," he demanded.

Konig remained quiet.

The man turned the horse so that he could address the crowd. "I am very disappointed to see this. This should be a joyous moment as this relic of the past" – he swept his hand around theatrically pointing to the church – "is swept away to make way for the factory that will serve something real – the people, all of you, and the State."

His comments were met with silence.

The captain shook his head. "Yes, I am disappointed, but not surprised. It takes some of us longer to learn than others. All religion is a superstition. It must be overcome and uprooted. Churches like this one must be smashed and destroyed. I know of the pleas that many of you have made to our leaders to save this house of superstition. In fact, hundreds of people signed a petition to stop progress by maintaining this and another such building." Once more, he dramatically shook his head. "When I heard of this, I initially was angry. How could our fellow countrymen fail to see what the party and the State were doing for all of us? However, my anger soon gave way to sadness and pity. Again, though, I wondered: How could they be so blind?"

The captain then waved forward the other riders. They pushed their horses through the crowd. People struggled to move out of the way. The men halted their horses in front of the church, one on each side of the captain. The two riders faced Konig and Fischer, while the captain faced the crowd with his back to the two pastors.

The captain continued his speech, "I have come to realize, though, how it is that people such as yourselves could be led astray."

Konig whispered, "Are you prepared, my friend?"

Fischer swallowed hard, also whispering, "I pray that I am."

"It is because of men like these." With his back still to the pastors, the captain raised his hands in the air, turned his head a bit from side to side, making clear that he was referencing the two clergy members atop the stairs behind him. "They are perpetrators of lies. They stand as true threats to the party, to the State, and therefore, to each of you."

Fischer whispered, "Christ be with you, Eckhart."

"And you, Gabriel," replied Konig.

"The lesson must be made as clear as possible." He turned his head to look at the rider to his right and then turned to the one on his left. The captain declared, "Men such as these must be dealt with; they must be stopped for the good of us all."

With that, the other two riders pulled out their revolvers.

Konig further tightened his grip on Fischer's shoulder.

Each rider fired off a shot. Konig and Fischer were each struck in the chest, and they fell to the stone floor.

Screams and cries erupted from the crowd.

The two assassins drove their horses up the church steps. Looking down at the bleeding pastors, more shots were fired, making sure that the earthly lives of these martyrs came to an end.

**Get your copy of *Cathedral*, and Ray Keating's other novels, at Amazon.com and at RayKeatingBooksandMore.com.**

# Acknowledgments

Thank you to the members of the Pastor Stephen Grant Fellowship for their support:

## Silver Readers
*Gregory Brown*
*Timothy Brown*
*Rick Charlton*
*Chris Comerford*
*Christopher Hazzard*
*Tony Hunt*
*Sue Kreft*
*Sue Lutz*
*Mary Makuta*
*Robert Moeller*
*Steven Muther*
*Daniel Provost*
*Leila Rish*
*Robert Rosenberg*
*Karen Stubelt*
*Gary Walbert*
*Mark Wildermuth*
*Gary Wright*

## Bronze Readers
*Michelle Behl*
*Carol Ann Brogan*
*James Fryckman*
*Marda Kirkwood*
*John Manweiler*
*Peter Meier*
*Beth Nagy*
*Jared Tucher*

Thanks for the feedback from Pastor Christopher Hazzard on a few points in this book.

I'm always grateful for my family's support and love. Thanks to my wife, Beth, and son, David, for their editing contributions to this book. And thanks to my son, Jonathan, for the spectacular book cover.

Any shortcomings in my books are all about me, and no one else. I thank readers for the interest, and as long as someone keeps reading, I'll keep writing. God bless.

Ray Keating
June 2025

# About the Author

Ray Keating is a novelist, an economist, a nonfiction author, a podcaster, a columnist, and an entrepreneur.

Prior to this book, Keating had penned 19 Pastor Stephen Grant thrillers and mysteries – *Warrior Monk*, followed by *Root of All Evil?*, *An Advent for Religious Liberty*, *The River*, *Murderer's Row*, *Wine Into Water*, *Lionhearts*, *Reagan Country*, *Heroes and Villains*, *Shifting Sands*, *Deep Rough*, *The Traitor*, *Vatican Shadows*, *Past Lives*, *What's Lost?*, *Persecution*, *Under the Golden Dome*, *For Better, For Worse*, and *Christmas Bells at St. Mary's*.

Keating also writes the Alliance of Saint Michael historical fiction series. The first two books in that series are *Cathedral* and *Subversion*.

In addition, Keating is a leading economist on entrepreneurship and small business. Among recent nonfiction books are *10 Points on Entrepreneurship from Walt Disney*, *The Weekly Economist III: Another 52 Quick Reads to Help You Think Like an Economist*, *The Weekly Economist II: 52 More Quick Reads to Help You Think Like an Economist*, *The Weekly Economist: 52 Quick Reads to Help You Think Like an Economist*, *Behind Enemy Lines: Conservative Communiques from Left-Wing New York* and *Free Trade Rocks! 10 Points on International Trade Everyone Should Know*. Keating also hosts three podcasts – Free Enterprise in Three Minutes, the PRESS CLUB C Podcast and the Dose of Disney.

Keating is the editor/publisher/columnist for DisneyBizJournal.substack.com. He was a columnist with

RealClearMarkets.com, and for more than two decades was a weekly newspaper columnist with *Newsday, Long Island Business News*, and the *New York City Tribune*. His work has appeared in many periodicals, including *The New York Times, The Wall Street Journal, The Washington Post, New York Post, The Boston Globe, National Review, The Washington Times, Investor's Business Daily*, New York *Daily News, Detroit Free Press, Chicago Tribune, Providence Journal Bulletin, TheHill.com, Touchstone* magazine, and *Cincinnati Enquirer.*

# Never Miss a Book by Ray Keating – Join the Pastor Stephen Grant Fellowship!

Never miss a book by Ray Keating by joining the Pastor Stephen Grant Fellowship. Become part of a community of fellow readers, and open additional communications with Ray. By joining the Pastor Stephen Grant Fellowship, you also help make sure that more books are coming!

Check it all out at **www.patreon.com/pastorstephengrantfellowship.**

There are a variety of levels to join, including...

**Bronze Reader**

1) You immediately receive three signed books by Ray Keating and a special 20% off coupon covering purchases of additional books at RayKeatingBooksandMore.com.

2) Going forward, you receive all new novels and short stories FREE and earlier than the rest of the world, while also receiving books not available to the wider reading public.

3) Your name is included in a special "Thank You" section in forthcoming novels.

4) You have access to the private Pastor Stephen Grant Fellowship Facebook page and private Patreon messages, which include author reflection on books, regular author

updates, excerpts from forthcoming books, Pastor Stephen Grant journal entries, recipes from various characters, periodic videos and more!

## Silver Reader

All of the benefits from the Bronze level, plus you receive two special gift boxes throughout the year with fun and exclusive merchandise.

## Book of the Month Club

1) 12 Books a Year! Receive a FREE book EVERY MONTH written and signed by Ray Keating. Included are Pastor Stephen Grant thrillers and mysteries (new books in the month of release), Alliance of Saint Michael, other fiction books, and Ray's nonfiction books. If you request, Ray will personalize his signing to a person of your choosing.

2) Two special gift boxes throughout the year with fun and exclusive Pastor Stephen Grant merchandise.

3) Your name included in a special "Thank You" section in forthcoming novels.

4) You have access to the private Pastor Stephen Grant Fellowship Facebook page and private Patreon messages, which include author reflections on books, regular author updates, excerpts from forthcoming books, Pastor Stephen Grant journal entries, recipes from Grillin' with the Monks and other characters, periodic videos and more!

## Gold Reader

All the benefits of the Book of the Month Club level, plus your name or the name of someone you choose to be used for a character in **one** upcoming novel.

# *Enjoy All of Ray Keating's Pastor Stephen Grant Adventures!*

## *Paperbacks and Kindle versions at Amazon.com*

## *Signed books at RayKeatingBooksandMore.com*

• *Christmas Bells at St. Mary's: A Pastor Stephen Grant Short Story*

If you appreciate the spirit captured by many classic Christmas films, then you're just like Pastor Stephen Grant ... and you'll enjoy this latest adventure. From the pages of his own journal, Pastor Grant paints a picture of Christmas at St. Mary's Lutheran Church, emphasizing gratitude for family; for a new clergy friend; for a special handbell concert; and yes, for movies of the season. But danger also lurks, and sin, justice, forgiveness, suffering, sacrifice, and salvation mix together in a rare way.

• *For Better, For Worse: A Pastor Stephen Grant Short Story*

From Finland to California, the tension builds and the action never falters. Pastor Stephen Grant arrives on the West Coast to officiate at the wedding of two friends. But the past reaches out to disrupt the festivities. Can Grant and his former CIA colleagues stop an attack by a team of killers sent by a powerful figure bent on revenge?

• *Under the Golden Dome: A Pastor Stephen Grant Novel*

Pastor Stephen Grant and his wife, economist Jennifer Grant, are invited to a conference at the University of Notre Dame. While they look forward to speaking at the same gathering, unexpected dangers materialize, fueled by distorted, political impulses among some in the Church. Defending religious freedom isn't limited to a conflict of ideas, as the struggle turns deadly.

• *Persecution: A Pastor Stephen Grant Novel*

While the charge of "persecution" gets tossed about rather casually, Pastor Stephen Grant and some of his closest friends and associates get a close-up, bloody view of what it truly means to be a modern-day martyr. From the White House to the Vatican, and from Russia to the Middle East, the action is unrelenting and the suspense is palpable. Can Grant and his former CIA colleagues act in time to save innocent lives?

• *What's Lost? A Pastor Stephen Grant Short Story*

From the pages of his own journal, Pastor Stephen Grant tells a riveting mystery involving deception, betrayal, sacrifice and friendship, along with plenty of action and questions about what we truly can know about others. Grant takes us on a personal journey across decades and around the world, from Long Island to Vietnam. This is the second Pastor Stephen Grant story told from Grant's own viewpoint, unfolding each day in the pages of his journal.

## • *Past Lives: A Pastor Stephen Grant Short Story*

Torn from pages of his own journal, Pastor Stephen Grant tells about threats, murder and puzzling people from his past. It's a compelling mystery involving action, unexpected turns, lost innocence, sought-after perspective, and twisted revenge. This is the first Pastor Stephen Grant story told from Grant's own viewpoint, unfolding each day in the pages of his journal.

## • *Vatican Shadows: A Pastor Stephen Grant Novel*

More than 500 years ago, two men – Jan Hus and Martin Luther – tried to bring about change in the Catholic Church. They suffered, with one burned at the stake. Could a modern-day pope transform these reformers from heretics to heroes in the eyes of the Catholic Church? Shadowy figures inside and outside the Vatican oppose Pope Paul VII's efforts, and stand willing to do anything to stop him. For help, the pope turns to Stephen Grant, a Lutheran pastor, former Navy SEAL and onetime CIA operative.

## • *The Traitor: A Pastor Stephen Grant Novel*

Stephen Grant – former Navy SEAL, onetime CIA operative and current pastor – looks forward to a time of prayer and reflection during a retreat at a monastery in Europe. But when he stumbles upon an infamous CIA traitor in a small village, Grant's plans change dramatically. While a debate rages over government secrets and the intelligence community, a deadly race for survival is underway. From a pro-democracy demonstration in Hong Kong to the CIA's headquarters in Langley to a monastery in France, the action and intrigue never let up.

### • *Deep Rough: A Pastor Stephen Grant Novel*

One man faces challenges as a pastor in China. His son has become a breakout phenom in the world of professional golf. The Chinese government is displeased with both, and their lives are in danger. Stephen Grant – a onetime Navy SEAL, former CIA operative and current pastor – has a history with the communist Chinese, while also claiming a pretty solid golf game. His unique experience and skills unexpectedly put him alongside old friends; at some of golf's biggest tournaments as a caddy and bodyguard; and in the middle of an international struggle over Christian persecution, a mission of revenge, and a battle between good and evil.

### • *Shifting Sands: A Pastor Stephen Grant Short Story*

Beach volleyball is about fun, sun and sand. But when a big-time tournament arrives on a pier in New York City, danger and international intrigue are added to the mix. Stephen Grant, a former Navy SEAL, onetime CIA operative, and current pastor, is on the scene with his wife, friends and former CIA colleagues. While battles on the volleyball court play out, deadly struggles between good and evil are engaged on and off the sand.

### • *Heroes and Villains: A Pastor Stephen Grant Short Story*

As a onetime Navy SEAL, a former CIA operative and a pastor, many people call Stephen Grant a hero. At various times defending the Christian Church and the United States over the years, he has journeyed across the nation and around the world. But now Grant finds himself in an entirely unfamiliar setting – a comic book, science fiction and fantasy convention. But he still joins forces with a unique set of heroes in an attempt to foil a villainous plot against one of the all-time great comic book writers and artists.

### • Reagan Country: A Pastor Stephen Grant Novel

Could President Ronald Reagan's influence reach into the former "evil empire"? The media refers to a businessman on the rise as "Russia's Reagan." Unfortunately, others seek a return to the old ways, longing for Russia's former "greatness." The dispute becomes deadly. Conflict stretches from the Reagan Presidential Library in California to the White House to a Russian Orthodox monastery to the Kremlin. Stephen Grant, pastor at St. Mary's Lutheran Church on Long Island, a former Navy SEAL and onetime CIA operative, stands at the center of the tumult.

### • Lionhearts: A Pastor Stephen Grant Novel

War has arrived on American soil, with Islamic terrorists using new tactics. Few are safe, including Christians, politicians, and the media. Pastor Stephen Grant taps into his past with the Navy SEALS and the CIA to help wage a war of flesh and blood, ideas, history, and beliefs. This is about defending both the U.S. and Christianity.

### • Wine Into Water: A Pastor Stephen Grant Novel

Blood, wine, sin, justice and forgiveness... Who knew the wine business could be so sordid and violent? That's what happens when it's infiltrated by counterfeiters. A pastor, once a Navy SEAL and CIA operative, is pulled into action to help unravel a mystery involving fake wine, murder and revenge. Stephen Grant is called to take on evil, while staying rooted in his life as a pastor.

### • *Murderer's Row: A Pastor Stephen Grant Novel*

How do rescuing a Christian family from the clutches of Islamic terrorists, minor league baseball in New York, a string of grisly murders, sordid politics, and a pastor, who once was a Navy SEAL and CIA operative, tie together? *Murderer's Row* is the fifth Pastor Stephen Grant novel, and Keating serves up fascinating characters, gripping adventure, and a tangled murder mystery, along with faith, politics, humor, and, yes, baseball.

### • *The River: A Pastor Stephen Grant Novel*

Some refer to Las Vegas as Sin City. But the sins being committed in *The River* are not what one might typically expect. Rather, it's about murder. Stephen Grant once used lethal skills for the Navy SEALs and the CIA. Now, years later, he's a pastor. How does this man of action and faith react when his wife is kidnapped, a deep mystery must be untangled, and both allies and suspects from his CIA days arrive on the scene? How far can Grant go – or will he go – to save the woman he loves? Will he seek justice or revenge, and can he tell the difference any longer?

### • *An Advent for Religious Liberty: A Pastor Stephen Grant Novel*

Advent and Christmas approach. It's supposed to be a special season for Christians. But it's different this time in New York City. Religious liberty is under assault. The Catholic Church has been called a "hate group." And it's the newly elected mayor of New York City who has set off this religious and political firestorm. Some people react with prayer – others with violence and murder. Stephen Grant, former CIA operative turned pastor, faces deadly challenges during what becomes known as "An Advent for Religious Liberty." Grant works with the cardinal who leads the

Archdiocese of New York, the FBI, current friends, and former CIA colleagues to fight for religious liberty, and against dangers both spiritual and physical.

- *Root of All Evil? A Pastor Stephen Grant Novel*

Do God, politics and money mix? In *Root of All Evil?*, the combination can turn out quite deadly. Keating introduced readers to Stephen Grant, a former CIA operative and current parish pastor, in the fun and highly praised *Warrior Monk*. Now, Grant is back in *Root of All Evil?* It's a breathtaking thriller involving drug traffickers, politicians, the CIA and FBI, a shadowy foreign regime, the Church, and money. Charity, envy and greed are on display. Throughout, action runs high.

- *Warrior Monk: A Pastor Stephen Grant Novel*

*Warrior Monk* revolves around a former CIA assassin, Stephen Grant, who has lived a far different, relatively quiet life as a parish pastor in recent years. However, a shooting at his church, a historic papal proposal, and threats to the pope's life mean that Grant's former and current lives collide. Grant must tap the varied skills learned as a government agent, a theologian and a pastor not only to protect the pope, but also to feel his way through a minefield of personal challenges. The second edition of *Warrior Monk* includes a new Introduction by Ray Keating, as well as a new Epilogue that points to an upcoming Pastor Stephen Grant novel.

# Alliance of Saint Michael Historical Fiction Series

## *Cathedral* and *Subversion* from Ray Keating

### Paperbacks and Kindle versions at Amazon.com

### Signed books at *RayKeatingBooksandMore.com*

The Alliance of Saint Michael brings together men and women with varied backgrounds and talents to work covertly against the two most significant threats to Christianity and civilization at the dawn of the 1930s - communism and fascism.

• *Cathedral: An Alliance of Saint Michael Novel*

In Moscow, the Cathedral of Christ the Saviour is going to be obliterated to make way for the Palace of the Soviets. The Alliance of St. Michael readies itself for its first mission – find and salvage a rare item of great significance from the cathedral before the building is lost.

• *Subversion: An Alliance of Saint Michael Novel*

It's the early 1930s, and a priest is murdered on Long Island. Meanwhile, in Germany, a Jewish businessman and his wife are targeted for violence by members of the Nazi Party. What do these two events possibly have in common? Members of the Alliance of Saint Michael find themselves at the center of each situation, as they work to aid those in danger while countering Nazi lies within the Church.

*The Weekly Economist:*
*52 Quick Reads to Help You Think Like*
*an Economist*

*The Weekly Economist II:*
*52 More Quick Reads to Help You Think*
*Like an Economist*

*The Weekly Economist III:*
*Another 52 Quick Reads to Help You*
*Think Like an Economist*

**All Books by Ray Keating**

**Paperbacks and for the Kindle at Amazon.com
and Signed books at
RayKeatingBooksandMore.com**

If you don't have a degree in economics, how do you figure out what actually makes economic sense and what doesn't? Ray Keating, a leading economist on small business and entrepreneurship, offers help with *The Weekly Economist* books series.

Whether via CNBC, CNN, FOX, websites, or other outlets, observations about the economy are presented that leave people wondering what's accurate. That's especially the case when declarations by one talking head are conflicted by the next one. *The Weekly Economist* series offers quick reads on topics essential to thinking clearly on economics, and applying sound economic principles to hot topics.

# Free Trade Rocks!
# 10 Points on International Trade Everyone Should Know

## by Ray Keating

### Paperback and for the Kindle at Amazon.com

### Signed books at RayKeatingBooksandMore.com

While free trade has come under attack, Ray Keating lays out in clear, simple fashion the benefits of free trade and the ills of protectionism in *Free Trade Rocks! 10 Points on International Trade Everyone Should Know.*

Tapping into his experiences as an economist, policy analyst, newspaper and online columnist, entrepreneur, and college professor, who taught MBA courses on international business and entrepreneurship, Keating explores and explains in straightforward fashion 10 key points or areas that everyone - from entrepreneurs and executives to students and employees to politicians and taxpayers - needs to understand about how trade works and how free trade generates benefits for people throughout the nation, around the world, and across income levels.

# *Behind Enemy Lines: Conservative Communiques from Left-Wing New York*

## by Ray Keating

### Paperback and for the Kindle at Amazon.com

### Signed books at RayKeatingBooksandMore.com

Enjoy this wide-ranging collection of columns and essays from Ray Keating covering faith, economics, politics, history, trade, New York, foreign affairs, immigration, pop culture, business, sports, books, and more. Keating is a longtime newspaper and online columnist, economist, policy analyst, and novelist. In these often confusing and contradictory times, Keating describes his brand of conservatism as traditional, American and Reagan-esque, firmly rooted in Judeo-Christian values, Western Civilization, the Declaration of Independence, the U.S. Constitution, and essential ideas and institutions such as the Christian Church, the intrinsic value of each individual, the role of the family, freedom and individual responsibility, limited government, and free enterprise and free markets. There's a great deal to enjoy, learn from, agree with, get annoyed by, appreciate, reflect on, roll your eyes over, and argue with in this book that offers perspectives on where we are today, where we've been, and where we might be headed.

# 10 Points from Walt Disney on Entrepreneurship

## by Ray Keating

Who better to learn from regarding entrepreneurship than Walt Disney?

Walt Disney ranked as one of the great entrepreneurs of the 20th century. In *10 Points from Walt Disney on Entrepreneurship*, Ray Keating, editor and columnist for DisneyBizJournal.substack.com and a leading economist on entrepreneurship and small business, turns to Walt for inspiration and insights on what it means to be an entrepreneur, on embracing entrepreneurship, and on learning lessons for the entrepreneurial journey.

Walt Disney, with his brother, Roy, founded what today is The Walt Disney Company. And throughout the voyage of starting up and building what became one of the leading entertainment businesses in the world, Walt Disney learned from positive and negative experiences, and provided advice that can help current and future entrepreneurs.

For good measure, the pages overflow with motivation from Walt Disney that Disney fans – entrepreneurs or not – will enjoy.

**Available at RayKeatingBooksandMore.com.**

# *Visit DisneyBizJournal and Listen to the Dose of Disney with Ray Keating Podcast*

## News, Analysis and Reviews of the Disney Entertainment Business!

DisneyBizJournal.substack.com is a media site providing news, information, reviews, and analysis for anyone who has an interest in the Walt Disney Company, and its assorted ventures, operations, and history. Fans (Disney, Pixar, Marvel, Star Wars, Indiana Jones, and more), investors, entrepreneurs, executives, teachers, professors and students will find valuable information, analysis, and commentary in its pages.

DisneyBizJournal.substack.com is run by Ray Keating, who has experience as a newspaper and online columnist, economist, business teacher and speaker, novelist, movie and book reviewer, podcaster, and more.

In addition, listen to the *Dose of Disney with Ray Keating* podcast to hear some Disney-related quotes and insights.

**Check everything out at
DisneyBizJournal.substack.com.**

# *The Disney Planner:*
# *The TO DO List Solution*

If you love all things Disney, then get a touch of Disney each day of the year with *The Disney Planner: The TO DO List Solution.*

Gain inspiration, get organized and set goals using Ray Keating's "TO DO List Solution," while enjoying quotes from Walt Disney, other Disney leaders, experts, and hundreds of characters, along with facts about theme parks, movies and much more.

*The Disney Planner: The TO DO List Solution* combines a simple, powerful system for getting things done with encouragement and fun for Disney fans, including those who love Mickey, Marvel, Star Wars, Indiana Jones, Pixar, princesses and more. Special features...

• Spiral binding so that the planner lays flat for easy use.

• Since this is an undated planner, it allows you to fill in months and dates, and get started whenever you like, whether that's on January 1 or June 15, for example.

• Break down your TO DO List in three key ways. First, set the big goals for the year, and update that each month throughout the year. Second, make a one-page list for each week. Third, fill in a daily list that makes sure each day is organized.

**Available at RayKeatingBooksandMore.com.**

# *The Lutheran Planner:*
# *The TO DO List Solution*

We all need to get things done each day, while also planning our coming week, month and year. However, it's crucial to maintain the right perspective on such matters. *The Lutheran Planner: The TO DO List Solution* is a tool for each of us in this ongoing endeavor. And you don't have to be a Lutheran to use and enjoy it.

Get organized and set goals using Ray Keating's TO DO List Solution, while enjoying and reflecting upon quotes from Holy Scripture, the Church fathers and other Christian thinkers. In addition, since *you* fill in the dates, it's easy to get started in any month, and to use the planner during any year.

*The Lutheran Planner: The TO DO List Solution* combines a simple, powerful system for getting things done with encouragement, inspiration and consolation from our Christian faith.

**Available at RayKeatingBooksandMore.com.**

Made in the USA
Columbia, SC
23 August 2025